DISCARD

PRAISE FOR BRIAN FREEMAN

"Freeman's latest psychological thriller is sure to seize readers and not let go . . . Gripping, intense, and thoughtful, *The Night Bird* is a must-read."
—*Romantic Times* on *The Night Bird* (Top Pick)

"This one will keep you guessing, but read it with the lights on."
—*Publishers Weekly* on *The Night Bird*

"Once you start you will sprint through the pages . . . *Marathon* is a fascinating, captivating, and involving thriller."
—Great Mysteries and Thrillers on *Marathon*

"If there is a way to say 'higher' than 'highly recommended,' I wish I knew it. Because this is one of those thrillers that go above and beyond."
—*Suspense Magazine* on *Goodbye to the Dead*

"Writing and storytelling don't get much stronger . . . and thriller fiction doesn't get much better than *The Cold Nowhere*."
—Bookreporter on *The Cold Nowhere*

"My discovery this year has been the Edgar-nominated crime writer Brian Freeman. . . . Fleshed-out characters, high tension and terrifying twists put Freeman up there with Harlan Coben in the psychological crime stratosphere."
—*London Daily Mail* on *The Burying Place*

"*Spilled Blood* is everything a great suspense novel should be: gripping, shocking, and moving. Brian Freeman proves once again he's a master of psychological suspense."
—Lisa Gardner, #1 *New York Times* bestselling author, on *Spilled Blood*

THE
VOICE
INSIDE

THE
VOICE
INSIDE

BRIAN
FREEMAN

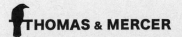THOMAS & MERCER

Published by Thomas & Mercer, Seattle

www.apub.com

Amazon, the Amazon logo, and Thomas & Mercer are trademarks of Amazon.com, Inc., or its affiliates.

ISBN-13: 9781542049047 (hardcover)
ISBN-10: 1542049040 (hardcover)
ISBN-13: 9781477809075 (paperback)
ISBN-10: 1477809074 (paperback)

Cover design by Rex Bonomelli

Printed in the United States of America

First edition

For Marcia

"One of the most striking differences between a cat and a lie is that a cat only has nine lives."

—*Mark Twain*

1

Frost Easton felt a shiver in the house, which jolted him from a deep sleep. He assumed it was the beginning of an earthquake.

His eyes shot open, blue and wide. In an instant, he was off the sofa, where he typically slept, and on his feet in the chill of his Russian Hill home. His black-and-white cat, Shack, sensed the disturbance, too. Frost saw Shack frozen on the coffee table, with his back arched and his tail puffed like the bloom of a bottlebrush tree. He waited for the ground beneath them to shudder like a fun-house ride.

This was San Francisco. Tremors routinely shook the city with a rumble of subterranean thunder. Most came and went without doing damage, but he'd lived through the deadly Loma Prieta quake when he was only eight years old. You never knew when the next Big One was coming. However, Frost saw none of the telltale signs of a temblor this time. His sister's blue angel figurine, which was hung from a hook above the bay window, didn't sway. The empty Sierra Nevada beer bottle he'd left on the coffee table hadn't walked itself to the edge and tipped over onto the carpet.

This wasn't an earthquake. This was something else.

He realized that the disturbance was man-made. A bitter breath of cigarette smoke lingered in the house, the way it did when a smoker passed you on the street. Shack, who was normally an oasis of calm, tensed his entire feline body and emitted a throaty growl, as if to say an intruder had been here. When Frost glanced at the glass door leading to the patio, he noticed that it was six inches open, letting in the night air.

He hadn't left it that way. Someone had been inside the house.

He crossed to the patio door and stepped outside. It was the middle of Saturday night, it was Halloween, and the coastal air was cold and damp. The city fell off sharply below the railing, leading down over flat rooftops toward the blackness of the bay. Frost wore sweats and a T-shirt with a caricature of Mark Twain on the front. His feet were bare; his slicked-back brown hair was messy. He grabbed the patio railing and listened, but he heard no evidence of someone escaping nearby. No car engine on the street. No movement in the dense foliage on the hillside below him.

It felt like a dream, but it wasn't.

Shack scampered outside to join him. Using his claws, the tiny cat did his best King Kong imitation by wrapping his paws around Frost's leg and climbing up to his shoulder, as if it were the summit of the Empire State Building.

"I've mentioned that those claws of yours hurt, right?" Frost said, grimacing at the pinpricks in his skin. Shack purred and ignored him, as if all were right with the world again. The cat's tail swished against Frost's beard, and his paws batted at the bed-head tufts sticking up from Frost's hair.

The two of them went back inside. Frost closed the door, and Shack made a graceful leap to the sofa. In the darkness, Frost crossed through the living room past the kitchen to the formal dining room, which doubled as his office, and looked out through the tall windows. Below him, Green Street was deserted. No one loitered in the doorways of the apartment building on the other side of the dead end.

He dug inside the pocket of his black sport coat, which was draped over one of the chairs. His badge was untouched. His pistol was still in its holster. Frost retrieved it, and with the gun in his hand, he checked the upstairs rooms one by one. He was alone in the house. And yet something wasn't right. The smell of smoke told the story. Someone had broken in, but whoever it was had taken nothing and left nothing behind.

Why?

"What about you, Shack?" Frost murmured as he came back downstairs, where the cat waited for him. "Did you see who it was?"

Shack simply turned and made a beeline for his empty food bowl. Frost followed him into the kitchen and filled it. He opened the refrigerator and grabbed a plastic bottle of orange juice. The juice bottle was lonely on the shelf. There wasn't much else inside. Unless his brother, who was a chef, rescued him with a care package, he typically ate his meals out.

The Russian Hill house was lit only by the glow of the city. In the living room, he pushed aside the fleece blanket and sat down on the tweed sofa near the bay window. He took a swig of orange juice and resealed the bottle. He was wide awake now. He thought about reading—he was halfway through a Stephen Ambrose book about the Lewis and Clark expedition—but he didn't think he'd be able to concentrate.

Then a shrill alarm filled the room, startling him.

It came from the bar near the kitchen, where his phone was charging. He recognized the wake-up buzzer, which was as harsh and loud as the shout of a drill sergeant. He always set an alarm for six o'clock in the morning, but it wasn't even close to that time yet.

Before he could get up to turn it off, a second alarm blared from upstairs. The clock in the master bedroom wailed like a fire signal, demanding attention. There was no reason for that alarm to go off. He never slept up there, and he'd never set that alarm as long as he'd been living in the house.

And then another clock. Another alarm, in one of the guest bedrooms upstairs.

And another alarm, in the third bedroom.

Then the radio in the kitchen turned on, broadcasting KSFO talk radio at top volume.

Frost sprang to his feet. "What the hell?"

Finally, one more alarm clanged, like the warning bells of a railroad crossing. This one came from the dining room. Frost didn't even *own* a clock that made a noise like that. He stood there, surrounded by a deafening chorus of bells, buzzers, radios, and alarms, and he watched Shack stampede like a madman up and down the stairs in confusion.

Frost went to shut down the alarms one by one, but when he picked up his phone, he noticed the time staring back at him in bright digital numbers.

3:42 a.m.

The sight of those numbers stopped him cold. He was paralyzed by his memories. Another minute passed before he broke out of his trance long enough to switch off the alarm. Then he ran upstairs and yanked out the plugs for the clocks in the bedrooms, and he turned off the radio in the kitchen. Finally, he went to find the strange clock in the dining room.

A double-bell Halloween clock sat on the table.

He hadn't even noticed it in the darkness. The clock didn't belong to him. Its face was orange and black, like a grinning jack-o'-lantern, and black bat wings jutted from the sides, waving up and down with the noise of the alarm. The intruder had left the clock for him.

Trick or treat.

The clapper hammered back and forth between two bells, making a noise louder than any of the others. He didn't know how to stop it. He shook it; he pushed buttons; he twisted knobs. Nothing worked. Finally, with his head pounding, he took the clock to the sink and smashed it with a hammer from the utility drawer. The bells finally went silent, but his ears rang with the echo of the alarms.

3:42 a.m.

This wasn't an accident or a Halloween prank.

It was a reminder. A taunt.

Someone knew exactly what that time meant to Frost and knew that he would understand its importance. It didn't matter how much time had gone by. Five years had passed since the last victim was discovered. Four years since Rudy Cutter was found guilty of murder and sent away for life. Even so, Frost never forgot.

3:42 a.m.

That was the time set on the broken watches that had been left on the wrist of every victim. The watches—each one different, each one belonging to the previous victim—were a bloody chain tying together the seven women who had died during Rudy Cutter's killing spree.

Including Frost's sister, Katie.

This wasn't just a sick game. Something else was going on.

Frost realized he was still cold. He felt a draft, and when he listened, he heard the wind whistling like a ghost. The glass patio door was closed, and so were the windows, but when he made his way to the house's white-tiled foyer, he saw that the front door was ajar. It opened and closed, opened and closed, as currents of air dragged it back and forth an inch at a time.

He crossed the foyer and ripped open the door.

One of Frost's long-bladed kitchen knives—exactly like the knives Rudy Cutter had used in all his murders—had been impaled deep in the chambered walnut of the door. Metal chopping wood. Was that what he'd heard? Was that the heavy thump that had awakened him?

The knife held a small postcard in place. It was something you'd buy at one of the dozens of souvenir shops at Fisherman's Wharf. On the front of the postcard was a black-and-white '20s-era photograph, which showed the famous Cliff House restaurant overlooking the Pacific surf. Frost didn't miss the significance of the location.

Cliff House rose above the sand and rocks of Ocean Beach. He'd found Katie there in the back seat of her blue Chevy Malibu.

Frost retrieved a latex glove from inside the house so that he could carefully remove the knife from the door. He didn't want to disturb any fingerprints, although he doubted that he'd find any. He took hold of a corner of the postcard with his gloved hand and turned it over. His name was scribbled on the address block of the postcard, but the street address written below his name wasn't for the house on Russian Hill. Instead, it was for a location somewhere in the Mission District.

Somebody wanted him to take a drive.

The postcard had a message for him, too. One sentence.

Can you live with a lie?

Less than an hour later, at four thirty in the morning, Frost parked his SFPD Chevy Suburban under the Highway 101 overpass. He had Duboce Avenue mostly to himself. Even in a city that never slept, this was a dead time. The night was over, but the day hadn't begun yet.

Frost got out of the Suburban. His eyes scoured the neighborhood under the streetlights. Painted murals adorned the massive columns of the freeway overpass. A gust of wind tumbled an empty paper cup down the street. Behind a metal fence, he saw the concrete ramps of a skateboard park, but in the overnight hours, there was no rattle and bang of kids doing acrobatics with their boards.

He knew this area well. His older brother, Duane, ran a food truck in the SoMa market only a few blocks away.

The address on the postcard was located on Mission Street behind him, but Frost walked the other way, toward a cobblestoned alley that led past a deserted parking lot under the freeway. Just like the time on the alarm clocks in his house, the choice of location was no accident. He'd been here before, when he was one of dozens of police officers canvassing the neighborhood, searching for any sign of a young woman named Melanie Valou.

Victim number seven.

Melanie was twenty-six years old, half-French, half-Algerian. Her parents had money, but Melanie, who was a San Francisco native like Frost, lived a Bohemian life, singing for tips in clubs and experimenting with bath salts and other new-age drugs. She had long, mussed black hair against ivory-white skin. Her lips were pale, and her eyes were dark and sunken. When she'd disappeared on November 17 five years earlier, she wore a wrinkled beige blouse and a knee-length garage-sale jean skirt. She'd been spotted on an ATM camera near Market and Van Ness, but that was the last time anyone saw her alive.

Everyone assumed Melanie had gone south from the bank to head home to her Mission District apartment. Police officers, including Frost, had fanned out across the area with her photo, knocking on doors, asking questions at homeless camps, and peering into the parked cars. Back then, Frost had gone up and down this alley a dozen times, trying to find a witness, but no one had seen Melanie.

No one except Rudy Cutter.

They'd finally found her body on Thanksgiving Day, in the trunk of a Honda Accord near Garfield Square.

Frost remembered the panic that had choked the city back then. Seven victims in four years. Seven women wearing macabre blood necklaces, where their throats had been slashed. They were all twenty-something in age, but beyond that, the victims had nothing in common. That was what made the killing spree so difficult to solve and why the fear had reached into every neighborhood. They were white, black, Hispanic, Chinese. They were tall and short. Heavy and thin. Rich and poor. They lived in different parts of the city, from Stonestown to South Beach to the Presidio. They had names like Nina. Natasha. Shu.

Katie.

When his sister had been killed—the fifth victim—Frost wasn't a cop. He was a lawyer who'd never practiced law. A former taxi driver. A former captain of a charter fishing boat on the bay. An Alcatraz tour guide. He was restless, tall, good-looking, unattached. To the frustration of his parents, he had no idea where his life was going, but Katie had changed all that. Her death had given him a purpose. Now, six years after finding her body at Ocean Beach, Frost was a homicide inspector.

He left the alley and headed for Mission Street, where the postcard on his door had led him. In his dark imagination, he knew what he expected to find at the address that had been scrawled under his name. Another body. An eighth victim. And yet he knew that was impossible. The killings were over. Rudy Cutter was in San Quentin, and he was never getting out.

Power wires for the MUNI bus line made a web over his head. There were plenty of places to hide in the nighttime shadows of Mission Street. Frost wondered if his overnight intruder had come here, expecting him to follow, and was spying on his progress. He checked doorways as he hurried down the street and kept an eye on the homeless men, asleep under ratty blankets. The handful of cars parked at the meters looked empty. The building windows around him were dark. He didn't feel watched, but that didn't mean someone wasn't following him.

The address from the postcard was three blocks down. It wasn't what he expected.

He found a one-story building that looked as if it belonged in the Haight-Ashbury neighborhood. The front wall was covered in swirls of psychedelic paint, dominated by two huge, staring blue eyes above the door. The chambered glass-block windows didn't allow him to look inside. A sign over the painted eyes advertised palm readings, incense, herbal medicines, and erotic gifts.

The neon sign above the windows glowed with the word *open*. Frost knew there was no way this store would be open in the middle of the night. Someone was waiting for him.

He pushed open the black front door, went inside, and closed it behind him. Dozens of flickering candles lit the dim interior. The shop smelled of vanilla. An odd assortment of merchandise shelves filled nearly every square foot, forcing him to squeeze past ceramic Buddhas, strings of lights shaped like red peppers, Mardi Gras plastic beads, origami-style paper fans, and lifelike mannequins dressed in peekaboo lingerie. He saw a narrow desk for the cash register, and behind it, a tiger-striped curtain led to a back room.

Frost called out, "Hello?"

He waited. No one answered.

He tried again, louder. "Hello? Is anyone here?"

Finally, the curtain swished, but he didn't see anyone walk into the shop. Then a voice at the level of his knees surprised him. "You must be the cop."

Frost looked down. A little man stood beside the register desk, barely four feet tall and at least seventy years old. He was completely bald, with a head as brown as saddle leather and gray muttonchops worthy of a nineteenth-century politician. He wore a royal-blue silk kimono, embroidered with a gold dragon, and red slippers with a beaded floral design.

This was San Francisco. Absolutely nothing surprised Frost anymore.

"He said you'd come," the man announced. He ducked behind the desk and scrambled onto a high stool and leaned forward with his elbows on the top of the cash register. They were eye to eye now.

"Who said that?" Frost asked.

"The guy who paid me two hundred dollars to open up tonight."

"And who are you?" Frost asked.

"My name's Copernicus," the man replied.

"Like the astronomer?"

"I *am* the astronomer. That was me in a past life." As Frost's lips bent into a smile, the man added, "I realize there are plenty of nonbelievers."

"Oh, I don't know," Frost replied. "Who were you after Copernicus? Shakespeare?"

"Actually, I was a Chinese concubine in the city of Dadu during the Ming dynasty."

"No kidding? You'd think the whole earth-revolves-around-the-sun thing would have gotten you a better gig the next time around."

"Don't mock what you don't understand," the man said.

"Fair enough. You're Copernicus. So who paid you two hundred dollars to be open in the middle of the night?"

"I didn't ask his name," Copernicus replied. "He paid cash. That was good enough for me."

"What did he look like?"

"Tall. And yes, don't joke, I know everyone is tall to me. He wore a Giants cap and big sunglasses, so I didn't see much of his face. He wore a bulky coat. I don't know if he was heavy or skinny or what."

"And what exactly did he want you to do?" Frost asked.

"He said I should open up the store at four in the morning and wait for a detective who looked like Justin Timberlake to show up," Copernicus said.

"Funny."

"Honestly, I don't know who the hell that is, but I assume he meant you."

"Well, I'm here," Frost said. "Now what?"

"Now I'm supposed to give you this."

Copernicus opened a cherrywood music box on the desk, which started playing a plink-plink version of the waltz from *Carousel*. Hidden inside was a woman's watch, which the man grabbed and dangled by its clasp from his tiny hand. He held it out to Frost at the end of his arm. Before taking it, Frost slid on a pair of gloves, and then he pinched the edge of the band and examined it.

The watch was expensive and very distinctive. The face was teardrop shaped, surrounded by diamonds, and the silver band was encrusted with ruby and topaz stones. Frost recognized the design. Like everything else about this night, it was meant to evoke a memory of events that had happened five years earlier.

This was an exact replica of the watch owned by Melanie Valou. She'd been wearing it on the day she disappeared; it had been visible on her wrist, shiny and dazzling, on the ATM camera from Market and Van Ness. But the watch hadn't been on her wrist when Melanie's body was found. Instead, everyone knew that the watch would eventually be found on the wrist of the next victim. Just like all the others.

His lieutenant, Jess Salceda, had made it her mission in life to find where Rudy Cutter had hidden Melanie's watch. After several searches of Cutter's home that turned up nothing, she'd finally outsmarted him. His hiding place was ingenious, just a utility hole in the ceiling above a hardwired smoke detector, but Jess had spotted a small flake of plaster dust in the carpet that roused her suspicions. When she'd rooted about inside the hole with her finger, she'd discovered Melanie's watch.

Finding it was the break that had finally put Rudy Cutter in jail for life. It was the break that had brought the murder spree to an end.

"Am I supposed to be impressed?" Frost asked. "I get it. This is a copy of Melanie Valou's watch. Why should I care?"

Copernicus laughed. His muttonchops danced, and his teeth were tea stained.

"This isn't funny," Frost told him.

"No, it's not that. Look, I don't know whose watch this is or what the hell it means. The guy said give it to you, so I gave it to you. But he told me what you'd say, and he was right. That's why I'm laughing. He said you'd call it a copy of this girl's watch."

"So what?" Frost asked.

"So he said I should tell you it's *not* a copy. He says the other watch—the one you guys found—was the fake. The cops planted it."

2

Frost didn't go home.

He drove through mostly quiet streets to the far corner of the city. Dawn was still a long, dark hour away. He parked his police Suburban in the empty lot where buses normally unloaded tourists to walk across the Golden Gate Bridge. Ocean gusts buffeted the vehicle. Above the waters of the bay, gauzy lights outlined the bridge deck, and fog shrouded the tops of the red towers. He watched the headlights of crazy-early commuters head south toward the city.

For tourists, this was the symbol of San Francisco. For the locals, it was just a bridge. It meant tolls and traffic jams. Frost had lived here his whole life, and he knew it was easy to become jaded about the beauty of this place. Sometimes, he forced himself to stop and stare and see his home through the eyes of strangers. He had to remind himself that he was lucky to be here, because there were days when he couldn't see past the darkness of being a cop. Today was one of those days.

Melanie's watch was in his gloved hand.

It had the heaviness of real silver and the shine of real jewels. It felt authentic, exactly the kind of watch that a rich woman like Camille Valou would have bought for her daughter in a boutique jewelry shop in Switzerland. But even if it was real, even if it was an exact match for the watch Melanie had worn, it had to be a replica. Jess Salceda had found

Melanie's watch in Rudy Cutter's ceiling. Melanie's mother, Camille, had identified it in court. There was no mistake.

He turned the watch over in his hand. Squinting, he made out a tiny inscription in French etched into the metal. *La rêveuse.*

The dreamer.

The original watch, which Jess had discovered, had no such inscription on the back. That was something Camille would certainly have noticed when Jess showed it to her. And yet the coincidence of an inscription in French—Camille had been born in Lyon—bothered Frost.

The watch was stopped. The mechanism had wound down, and the time was frozen in place.

3:42 a.m.

He told himself that someone was manipulating him. Playing with his head. He knew who it was. From inside the walls of San Quentin, Rudy Cutter had found a way to make all of this happen. Cutter was a smart, methodical man, who'd patiently stalked and killed seven women, who'd outsmarted Jess and the rest of the San Francisco Police for years. This mystery had his fingerprints all over it.

Rudy Cutter.

Jess and Cutter had played a game of cat and mouse before Melanie's death. He was her prime suspect in what the press had dubbed the Golden Gate Murders. They'd called it that because the first victim, Nina Flores, had been found right here where Frost was parked, in the shadow of the Golden Gate Bridge.

The clue that had helped Jess pinpoint Cutter came from a combination of luck and shoe leather. After one of the victims had been found in a hotel parking lot near the Cannery, a tourist had sent the police a series of videos taken in that area during her weekend vacation, which overlapped with the victim's disappearance. Jess studied the videos and ran the license plates of every vehicle she saw parked near the Cannery. One car, one name, raised a red flag with her. The owner of the car—a forty-eight-year-old data entry clerk named Rudy Cutter—had come up in her investigation before. He'd used a credit card at the coffee shop where Nina Flores had worked. Jess had talked to him three years earlier, but back then, she'd had no reason to consider Cutter a suspect. He was just one of dozens of coffee shop customers she'd interviewed after Nina's murder.

But the same man parking his car near the site where another victim had been abducted and killed? Jess didn't believe in coincidences.

For a year, she'd hunted for evidence tying Cutter to the murders. For a year, she'd followed him, hoping to catch him stalking his next victim. And still Melanie Valou died. Even with the police breathing down his neck, Cutter had managed to kill again and leave no physical evidence behind to connect him to the crime.

Not until Jess found Melanie's watch hidden in Cutter's ceiling.

Frost dangled the watch in front of his eyes the way a hypnotist would. He thought about the message Copernicus had given him.

This is Melanie Valou's watch.

Frost didn't want to believe it. He didn't want to think about what it would mean if that was true. This was only a ruse. A game. The Golden Gate Murders had been put to bed four years earlier with Cutter's conviction. The victims and their families had justice. Katie had justice. No one would thank him for raising questions now. All he would do was bring back the pain for everyone.

And yet.

It was the watch that had put Cutter behind bars. Without Jess finding the watch, Cutter would never have been arrested, never been found guilty.

The other watch—the one you guys found—was the fake.

The cops planted it.

If that was true, then Jess was the one who had planted it.

Frost climbed out of the Suburban and slipped the watch inside his pocket. He felt mist on his face. His black jacket offered little protection against the roaring wind. He crossed an empty plaza past the welcome center and followed a ramp that led him toward the bridge deck. He walked quickly, with long strides. Traffic streamed from the Marin Headlands, emerging like ghosts out of the fog. As he reached the bridge itself, the bay water opened into a dark expanse two hundred feet below him. The gusts intensified, blown through the narrow passage from the Pacific. Pinpoint lights swept the city skyline and the East Bay, and the brighter lights over the railings threw his shadow at his feet.

He was alone on the crossing. He wondered if the drivers who spotted him thought, *Jumper.* Dozens of unhappy souls went over the edge to their deaths every year. The bridge was a magnet for the lonely and the desperate.

Beside him, the mammoth main suspender cable rose toward the first tower. He continued until he was over deep water and stopped midway between the lights, where he was mostly invisible. He leaned on the railing and looked down. His brown hair, which was normally slicked back over his head, blew into his face. His skin felt raw.

He dug inside his pocket and cupped the watch in the palm of his hand.

All he had to do was let the watch slide down between his open fingers. No one would see. No one would know. Seconds later, the watch would strike the bay. It would sink slowly, like a dead leaf in the wind, settling toward the bottom. The deepest area of the bay was here, more than three hundred feet from surface to sand. The watch would never be found, never raise ugly doubts about the evidence in Rudy Cutter's trial. The mystery would drown with it.

Frost wasn't the only one who knew about the duplicate watch. Obviously, someone else had already found it and led him to it. Whoever that was might raise questions about how the second watch had gone missing, and he'd have to offer excuses. He'd lost it. It was stolen. Someone might suspect there was more to the story, but without the watch itself, no one would ever be able to prove that the watch Jess had found in Cutter's house was a fake. The story of the Golden Gate Murders would end here, atop the Golden Gate Bridge. There was a satisfying irony in that.

He felt the watch in his hand. In the darkness, he could barely see it. It was featherlight, weighing almost nothing. Let it go. Let it fall. One meaningless speck in the sea. A minute passed, and he still held it, his hand outstretched, nothing but water below him. Then two minutes. Then ten. Over the eastern hills, the sky flushed as dawn inched closer. He was running out of time.

Frost shook his head. Jess had always called him a Boy Scout. The cop who played by the rules. It wasn't a compliment. On his first day, she'd told him about "the line." The line between going by the book and taking shortcuts. It was a line that every cop faced sooner or later, when he had to decide if the end justified the means. Sometimes doing the right thing meant a criminal going free. Sometimes doing the wrong thing saved lives.

He remembered how Jess had described it to him: *The line's not one color, not easy to see, no way to know which side of it you're on. If a lawyer or politician thinks you're wrong, you might end up out of a job, and there's nothing you can do about it. But that doesn't mean you shouldn't cross it when you have to. If all you want is your fricking pension, go be a bus driver or something.*

For Frost, this was the line.

The easy thing, the smart thing, was to drop Melanie Valou's watch into the deep water. Standing there, numb with cold, hearing Jess's voice in his memory, he realized that he couldn't do it.

Can you live with a lie?

That was the question, and the answer was no.

He closed his fingers around the watch and returned it to his pocket. Like a jumper who'd thought better of it, he walked back off the bridge.

3

"Ms. Valou?" Frost asked.

The raven-haired woman at the restaurant Zazie looked up from her organic granola and her copy of the *New York Times*. The morning was cold enough to see your breath, but she sat outside with only a lightweight jacket and an espresso to warm her. Her legs were bare below her knee-length skirt.

"Yes?" she replied, her accent thick and French. "May I help you?"

"My name is Frost Easton. I'm a homicide inspector with the San Francisco Police. The doorman at your building said I could probably find you here. I was hoping we could talk for a couple minutes. It's about Melanie."

Camille Valou's face showed a hint of anxiety. Five years had passed since her daughter's murder, but five years was nothing. Her dark eyes had a permanent sadness. Her pale-pink lips made a thin, emotionless line. "Sit," she told him.

Frost took a chair opposite her as Camille neatly folded her newspaper. She nodded at a waitress through the window, who appeared in a flash to take Frost's order. He shook his head, but Camille was having none of that.

"You must have something," she said. "Please, it's my treat."

"Coffee," Frost said.

"Oh, that is not breakfast. You're a busy, important man. You need to eat. Bring him the Avignon scrambled eggs, Suzy."

"That's really not necessary," Frost said.

Camille shrugged. "Life is about more than what's necessary. And more espresso for me, Suzy, please."

The waitress smiled and disappeared.

Camille still had espresso left in her cup, and she took the last sip and dabbed at her mouth with a napkin. She was intelligent. He could see it in her stare as she watched him, making calculations about his intentions. He'd seen many photographs of Melanie Valou, and he could see the resemblance between mother and daughter. Camille was in her midfifties, matchstick thin, with sharp, bony lines outlining her white face. She was pretty and elegant. Well dressed. Manicured nails. Her black hair, a little too black for her age, was cut short in a deliberately messy style. Her appearance didn't scream of money, but people with money didn't need to advertise it.

"So," she said. "You look familiar to me, Inspector. Do we know each other? Did you work on Melanie's case?"

"I did, but that's not where we met," Frost replied. "Some of the families of the victims got together a few years ago. It was sort of a support group to help each other. I went with my parents. We met there."

"Many of us still meet," Camille told him. She pursed her lips. "Easton. Your parents are Ned and Janice?"

"Yes."

"So that means—" she began, and he could see empathy in her stare as she put the pieces together. "Your sister? She was one of the victims, too, yes?"

"Katie," Frost said.

"I am very sorry."

"Thank you."

"Your parents have not been to one of our meetings in a couple of years," Camille said. "I hope that means they are okay."

"They moved to Arizona," Frost explained. "They split up for a while, but then they got back together. Katie's death put a lot of stress on their relationship."

Camille held up her left hand, which had no ring. "I understand. My own marriage did not survive the grief."

The waitress returned with coffee and put a plate of scrambled eggs in front of him. He realized he was hungry, and he ate quickly, in large bites. Camille sipped her next cup of espresso and left behind most of her granola.

"Those were dark days," she said. "I wish I could say it's over, but it's never really over, is it?"

"No."

"After all, here you are, and you say this has something to do with Melanie."

"Yes, it does. I'm sorry."

"Well, what can I do for you, Inspector?"

Frost put down his fork. He felt reluctant to say the things he needed to say. He slid a hand into the inner pocket of his sport coat and extracted the watch, which he'd now secured in a plastic evidence bag. He put the bag on the table between them and watched Camille's eyes as she studied it. She was cool, but she couldn't hide a stiffening in how she held herself. She saw the watch, recognized it, and looked away without a word. Maybe it was just the pain of what this watch meant to her. Or maybe it was something more.

"What is this?" she asked.

"Someone led me to this watch overnight," Frost told her. "They wanted me to find it."

"Why would they do that?"

"To make me believe that *this* is Melanie's watch," he said. "Not the one that Jess Salceda found in Rudy Cutter's house."

"Obviously, that's not true."

"I'm sure you're right, but that's why I'm here. You'd know the truth better than anyone. You bought the original watch for your daughter. I was hoping you could look at it."

Camille picked up the bag with obvious reluctance. He waited to see what she would do next. Her face had the strain of profound grief. Her slim, birdlike fingers trembled. Her eyes pored over the watch face, the band, and the jewels, as if caressing it.

And then she did the one thing he didn't want her to do. The one gesture that told him everything.

She turned the watch around.

She studied the back. Where the inscription was. *La rêveuse.* Looking at it, her eyes went dead. The life went out of them. She put the bag down on the table as if it were hot to the touch. "It's a copy. It's not Melanie's. Just as you would imagine."

"Okay."

"Throw it away," she said lightly, dragging the words out of her throat. "It means nothing."

"Thank you for confirming it," he said, although she'd unintentionally confirmed the opposite of what she was telling him. She expected there to be an inscription on that watch as she picked it up. Just looking at it, she already knew its history. Now he needed to figure out how and why.

"Are we finished here, Inspector?" she asked.

"I have a couple more questions," he said.

Frost took the bag and slipped it inside his pocket again, and Camille's mouth twitched as it disappeared from her view. He thought she might reach across the table and grab it from him.

"This is a very distinctive watch," he said. "Someone must have gone to a lot of trouble to find an exact duplicate."

"It's distinctive, but apparently not unique."

"I recall from the trial that the watch was designed and sold by a small jeweler in Switzerland," Frost said.

"Yes, my ex-husband's family owns a chalet in Wengen. The jeweler was related to my in-laws, a cousin of a cousin or something like that."

"So an exact match of Melanie's watch would probably have come from the same jeweler?"

Camille shrugged. "I assume so."

"Was it expensive? It looks expensive."

"Expensive depends on your means."

"Did you notice the inscription on the back of the watch?" Frost asked. "That puzzles me."

"Why?"

"Well, why go through the trouble of obtaining an exact duplicate of Melanie's watch when it has an inscription that clearly indicates that it's not hers? I mean, Melanie's watch *didn't* have any inscription on the back, right?"

Her eyes drilled through him as if she could see to the back of his head. "That's right."

"Because obviously you would have noticed if the inscription was missing," he went on. "I was in court when you testified. I saw you identify the watch that was found in Rudy Cutter's ceiling. You were very convincing. You were very certain."

"Yes, I was."

"That's not something you're likely to make a mistake about."

"No, it's not."

"Was Melanie's watch returned to you after the trial?" Frost asked.

"Yes."

"Do you still have it?"

Camille bristled. She'd begun to see him as an enemy. "No, I don't."

"Really? What happened to it?"

"I destroyed it, Inspector. I took a hammer, and I reduced it to pieces. It no longer exists. To me, it was a source of pain and misery, a reminder of what I'd lost, and I wanted to be rid of it."

"I understand."

"Do you?" she demanded, her voice trembling. "Then for the life of me, I cannot understand why you are here asking me these questions all these years later. Particularly when your own sister was another of Rudy Cutter's victims. What on earth do you think you're doing? Why are you bringing this up now?"

Frost had been asking himself the same thing for hours. He wasn't surprised by Camille's reaction. Any mother who had gone through what she had would be outraged. However, Camille's outrage also felt calculated. It masked something else. She knew more than she was telling him.

"I'll be honest with you, Ms. Valou," Frost told her. "My first instinct when I found this watch in my hand was to do what you did. Destroy it."

"That's what you should have done. That's what you should do right now. I already told you. Throw it away."

"I wish I could, but we're beyond that now."

"Why?"

"Because you're lying to me," Frost said sadly.

Camille didn't say anything to deny the accusation. Her body relaxed, and she went back to her espresso. "Let me ask you something, Inspector."

"All right."

"Do you have the slightest doubt that Rudy Cutter was the man who murdered all those women? Including my daughter. Including your sister."

"None at all," Frost said.

"Then justice has been served."

"That's true, but justice demands a fair trial that plays by the rules."

"Cutter got that."

"I hope so. I'd like nothing more than to believe that this watch is nothing but a copy and that the original was found in Cutter's ceiling."

"It was," Camille snapped. "There's no mystery here. Melanie was wearing the watch I bought for her when that beast abducted and murdered her. Rudy Cutter kept it. He hid it. His plan was to put it on the wrist of the next woman he killed. Just as he'd done six times before. He would have succeeded, if your fellow detective Ms. Salceda hadn't discovered it at his house. She found *Melanie's* watch, Inspector. I confirmed it when she showed it to me. I testified to it under oath at that man's trial. That's the only truth that matters."

He suspected that she'd said those words to herself many times over the years, as she tried to convince herself that she'd done the right thing.

"If you're right, then someone is playing a sick game with me," Frost said.

"No doubt someone working with Rudy Cutter," Camille replied.

"Most likely. I'd like to know how they managed to locate this watch. What would a person have to do to put their hands on an exact duplicate like this?"

"Fly to Switzerland," Camille said impatiently.

"The jeweler doesn't have a website?"

"It's a one-man business in a small village. Not every corner of the world is online, Inspector."

"And do you think the owner would keep records of his customers and what they purchased?" Frost asked. Because he knew what those records would show, and so did she.

A shadow crossed Camille's face. "I have no idea."

"What was the name of the jeweler?"

"I really don't remember. For all I know, he's dead by now. He was very old even then, and this was a decade ago."

"What about your ex-husband? Would he remember? You said the jeweler had some kind of family connection."

"You'd have to ask him," Camille said, her voice growing exasperated. "Honestly, Inspector, I really don't understand the relevance of any of this. I already told you, *it's not Melanie's watch.*"

"I'm just trying to understand how hard it would have been to obtain an exact copy," Frost replied. "It sounds like it would have been pretty hard. Almost impossible, in fact. A very expensive watch from a jeweler in a remote town overseas? I can't imagine how Cutter would have pulled it off."

"I'm sorry. I don't have any answers for you, Inspector."

Frost stood up. He picked up the mug and finished his coffee. "Well, I appreciate your time, Ms. Valou. Thank you for breakfast."

"You're welcome."

He made sure they were alone. There were no morning pedestrians on Cole Street. The door to the restaurant was closed. He leaned across the table toward Camille and whispered just loud enough for her to hear. "There were two watches, weren't there?"

Her nostrils flared with annoyance. Her eyes were hard black sapphires. "What?"

"You bought two watches back then, didn't you? One for you, one for your daughter."

"I have nothing more to say."

"Was it *your* watch that Jess found in Cutter's ceiling? And if so, how did it get there?"

"I think you should leave, Inspector," Camille said.

Frost straightened up. "If you'd like."

He turned away from the restaurant, but Camille called after him in a loud voice. "Inspector, before you go. There's an old French proverb you may know. *Il ne faut pas réveiller le chat qui dort.* It means, when the cat is asleep, you don't wake it up."

"Let sleeping dogs lie?" Frost replied.

"That is exactly right. Let sleeping dogs lie. You should remember that."

4

Rudy Cutter listened for the boots of the prison guard. He'd been waiting for him for hours. Waiting for news.

It was late afternoon. Shadows stretched across the lower bunk of his cell at San Quentin. People said the nights were worst in prison, but really, it was the long, dull, dead afternoons. He heard the noises of the south block around him. Smack talk bounced from cell to cell. Someone sang. Someone prayed. Above him, his cellmate, Leon, played the same rap by Lil Wayne over and over. "Hustler Musik." When Leon played the song more than ten times in a stretch, Rudy would kick the mattress to shut him up, but he didn't like to anger Leon. If you wanted to stay alive in here, you learned to get along.

Lying in his bunk, Rudy stretched out his arms. He could touch both stone walls on either side of the cell. He did that sometimes, to remind himself where he was, to confirm that this wasn't a dream.

It wasn't. This was life. Fifty-four square feet. A sink. A toilet. Two men.

The chaplain had told him to make the most of his time inside. Read. Take classes. Find God. The first step was to accept your fate. Instead, Rudy had spent the last four years making plans. The people of the State of California had said that he would never be a free man again, but the people were wrong.

The day was almost here, and he was ready.

Rudy stared into nothingness. His blue eyes were sunken into his face, surrounded by deep wrinkles and dark bags. Haunted eyes, some people said. Or predator eyes, others said. They were focused and unblinking, like alligator jaws that clamped around you without letting go. His skin was pale and freckled, his blond hair short and dirty. When he rubbed his chin, he felt the roughness of half-gray stubble. He was fifty-three years old, but one advantage of prison was that he was in the best shape of his life. In here, it paid to be muscled and strong and to develop a sixth sense for what was happening behind your back.

Over his head, Lil Wayne rapped about not being a killer. The lyrics always annoyed Rudy when he heard them. If you weren't a killer, you couldn't understand what it felt like, so don't sing about it, don't talk about it, don't write about it. The only way to really know was to do it. That was the fraternity of murderers.

He thought about his late wife, Hope, who was part of that fraternity. She was always with him. She never went away. When he closed his eyes, she was in his dreams. When he stared outside the cell, he could see her taunting him on the other side of the bars. Her smile. Her blood. Her grotesque pride in what she'd done.

Thirty years in between had changed nothing.

Looking back, he wondered why he'd ever married Hope. They were both only twenty years old then. He was still in college, and she was in nursing school. What did he see in her? It wasn't her looks. She was slightly heavy, and it showed in her face. She had puffy cheeks and a rounded chin. Her mousy hair was short and practical. Her face was forgettable. Ten minutes after meeting Hope, you'd struggle to describe her.

What was it?

Maybe he'd thought he could fix her. Hope was bipolar, and when she had her episodes, she would scream, she would explode in jealous rage, she would throw things, she would cut him, she would hit him. When he talked about leaving, she would tell him how much she needed him, how much she loved him, and how she would kill herself if he left her. So he stayed.

It wasn't all bad. For a while, after college, things got better. He got a job as an underwriter at a savings and loan; it was a boring job, but boring worked for him. He didn't have to deal with people. He could focus on numbers and formulas. He could plan, analyze, and make risk assessments, and he discovered that he was good at it. Like a chess player, he could anticipate options and alternatives ten moves away. The company promoted him quickly.

Hope became an ER nurse. She got on meds, which smoothed out her moods. She started seeing a therapist, who advised her to turn to her artistic side and paint or sketch when she felt the stress of life overwhelming her. Her violent outbursts faded. He began to think that they were happy.

And then came Wren. Their daughter.

Until Wren, Rudy had never had a clue what love really was. That little girl, in his arms, became his reason to live. She was beautiful. She was innocent. She was perfect. He found it nearly unbearable to leave for work in the morning. On the bus coming home, he would grow agitated, because he was so anxious to see his daughter again. Seeing her face made every bad thing in the world vanish.

He was so enraptured with Wren that he hardly noticed Hope beginning to disintegrate again.

Her moods swooped up and down; her meds seemed to have no effect. The art she used to escape wasn't nearly enough. She began to lash out at him, the way she had in college, and she spent less and less time with their daughter. When she held the girl, her face grew empty and pained. Eventually, the doctors would tell him it was postpartum depression, magnified by her existing mental illness, but by then, it was too late. The baby sucked up all of Rudy's time and love, and Hope herself seemed incapable of giving any love to either of them.

He thought it would pass with time. He didn't realize how volatile the situation had become. And how dangerous.

Not until the November night that changed everything.

Hope had come home late from an exhausting shift at the ER. She found Rudy holding Wren in the nursery, and she flew into a rage, screaming obscenities, telling him that he loved his daughter more than he loved her—and it was a difficult accusation to deny, because it was true. He tried to calm Hope without success. Wren began crying and was inconsolable. Eventually, he put their daughter in his wife's arms to give the two of them time to be together. He'd always believed that Wren had magical healing powers. If the little girl could make him happy, then she could do anything at all.

Rudy slept. He slept until the middle of the night. He didn't know what awakened him, but maybe it was the sudden silence. Wren was crying, and then she was not. Hope wasn't in bed. He got up and called his wife's name, several times, louder and louder, and she didn't answer. A feeling crept over him, like a foreboding of evil, strong enough to make it hard to breathe.

He went to the nursery and crossed the river into hell.

His girl, his angel, his perfect daughter, was blue. In that instant, he could physically feel God reach into his chest, remove his heart, rip it to pieces, and tread on it. He wailed. He bellowed. He went to Wren to revive her, but she was gone, her life suffocated by nothing more than a bunny pillow that lay next to her. He held her, sobbing, pacing back and forth.

Wren was dead. Rudy felt as if he had died with her.

Only then did he notice the blood on the floor, trickling in little ribbons downhill from under the crib.

He went around to the other side and found Hope on her back, arms and legs spread wide. She had a terrible, wicked grin fixed on her face. Her eyes were open, lifeless but still staring at him. She had a kitchen knife clutched in one hand that she'd used to slice open her own throat in a grotesque U from below one ear to the other.

Thirty years had passed since that moment, and yet he could still recite every detail of that scene from memory, like a photograph. His dead daughter in his arms. His dead, murdering wife on the floor.

And on the nightstand next to the crib, a digital clock showing him the time.

3:42 a.m.

The strange thing was, the tears stopped when he saw Hope on the floor, and they had never come back. Every emotion drained out of him, like Hope's blood. He couldn't feel pain. He couldn't feel anger. He wanted to cry for his daughter; he wanted to feel rage at his wife. Instead, he felt nothing, and nothingness was far worse than grief. From that moment forward, he'd lived his life in a kind of void, and when the void became unbearable, he'd tried to kill himself. Four times he'd tried, but each time he had failed, as if God didn't want him.

Day became day, month became month, year became year, melting away like spring snow.

Twenty years passed that way.

Twenty years of numb, interminable, empty time.

Until the numbness finally stopped.

It stopped nine years ago, on April 1, in a coffee shop in the Ferry Building. It was luck or fate or destiny or whatever else people believed in. He'd never been to that coffee shop before or since, but his brother, Phil, had been late to pick him up for the Giants game, so he'd ordered an iced latte from a chatty barista named Nina Flores. It was Nina's birthday. She was a sweet kid. Hispanic. Cheerful. Fluffy pile of brown hair. So perky it was annoying. She talked and talked, about her job, about school, about her parents and siblings, about her best friend, about her birthday. She showed him childhood photos made into buttons on her T-shirt. She sang "Happy Birthday" to herself.

Nina was an ordinary girl, but for Rudy, she was also a thunderbolt. Nina woke up the monster in him. Seeing her brought Hope back to life, like an evil ghost in Rudy's head, and he knew that ghost had to be destroyed.

By the time Rudy finished his coffee, everything had changed for him. He'd found his path to revenge because of that girl in the Ferry Building. He became nothing but cold, implacable anger. After twenty years of emptiness, he finally had a purpose and a plan.

Rudy had smiled at Nina as he left, but he was already considering the next steps in his strategy. He'd paid by credit card; he wouldn't make that mistake again. He had to be careful; he had to choose, observe, think, and anticipate, but those were his best skills. Even then, he'd known Nina would be the first, but she wouldn't be the last. There were many others, and he knew exactly where to find them.

Nina Flores, Rae Hart, Natasha Lubin, Hazel Dixon, Shu Chan, Melanie Valou. Dying one by one in the years that followed.

Do you remember them, Hope?

And he wasn't done. Oh no.

The time in San Quentin was only a temporary delay, caused by a detective who refused to play by the rules. Jess Salceda hadn't beaten him; she'd cheated. Now Rudy would show her what happened to those who got in his way.

He put his hands behind his head and waited. His senses were hyperalert, although he knew he was being impatient. Maybe it wouldn't be today. Maybe it would be tomorrow. Or the next day. But finally, finally, he heard the sound he'd been anticipating. Footsteps. Boots on the concrete walkway, coming closer. Coming for him.

He saw the bulky prison guard stop directly outside the bars. The guard called to him in a growly voice. "Cutter?"

"Yeah, what is it?"

"You have a visitor."

5

Frost had hoped never to see Rudy Cutter again, but there he was. The guard shackled him to the metal table in the small interview room. Cutter, who was wearing jeans and a loose blue smock, studied Frost on the other side of the table the way a tiger sizes up prey. There had been a moment during the murder trial when Cutter looked back at the gallery with the same stare. Frost had never forgotten those eyes, so empty and brutal. It had taken everything in Frost's power not to jump across the railing in the courthouse and strangle Cutter with his bare hands.

He felt the same way now.

"Rudy Cutter," Frost said.

"Hello, Inspector." Cutter didn't say, *I was expecting you.* He didn't need to gloat. The message was clear in the way he held himself. This man knew exactly why Frost was here.

Frost slid the evidence bag with the watch out of his pocket and put it on the table between them.

"This came from you, I assume," Frost said.

Cutter didn't say anything for a long time. He leaned forward to study the watch. The contrast of the expensive, sparkling jewelry with the drab, oppressive surroundings of the prison room was striking. Even under a dusty fluorescent bulb, the diamonds and rubies shined.

"It's beautiful," Cutter said finally. "The Swiss are very talented. How much do you think a watch like that is worth? Ten thousand dollars? More?"

"I have no idea."

"Well, it's so unusual you'd think it would be one of a kind," Cutter said. He paused, and his eyes narrowed. "But we both know it's not."

"I'm not sure what you think you're doing, Cutter," Frost said.

The man gave him a look of surprise, as if the truth was obvious. "I'm getting out of prison. And you're going to help me."

"Why would I do that?"

"Because no matter what you think I did, you can't live with a lie," Cutter said. "Isn't that why you're here?"

Frost picked up the evidence bag and twisted it between his fingers. "You're clever. It's a clever game, but it won't work."

"No?"

"No. A judge will never let you out over this. A duplicate watch isn't enough evidence to free you. It doesn't prove a thing."

"Except it's not an *exact* duplicate, is it?" Cutter asked.

Frost shrugged. "The inscription on the back won't help you. I already talked to Camille Valou. She said Melanie's watch had no inscription. This watch didn't belong to her daughter."

"She's lying," Cutter said.

"And just how do you expect to prove that? It's your word against hers. Who do you think a judge is likely to believe? A convicted serial killer or a mother whose child was murdered?"

"I don't have to convince a judge," Cutter replied calmly. "I just have to convince *you*. The fact is, I already have. You're sitting here. You came to talk to me. That means you know the truth. You know the watch in your pocket belonged to Melanie Valou. You know that your colleague, Jess Salceda, planted a fake watch in my house in order to frame me. You know that I'm in prison because of a lie."

Frost shook his head. "Is that what this is about? You think you can take Jess down? You want to put a cloud over her career and make everyone think she's a corrupt cop?"

"She *is* corrupt."

"And like I said, you'll never prove it. You want me to take this watch to a judge? Fine. I'll do it. Nothing will come of it. There'll be a hearing, and Camille will testify that the watch I found didn't belong to Melanie, and Jess will testify that she found Melanie's real watch in your ceiling. The judge will throw out your motion, and you'll be right where you are now. It's a waste of time. You see, you're forgetting one thing, Cutter. Even if anyone secretly believes that *this* is Melanie's watch, they'll still know you're guilty."

"Really? Why is that?"

"Because the only way you could have found Melanie's real watch is if you'd had it hidden all along."

Cutter actually smiled. Frost had never seen him smile before. Cutter leaned across the table and whispered, "That's a good point, Inspector. *Except I never had that watch.*"

Frost hesitated. "What are you talking about?"

"I didn't challenge the authenticity of the watch that Jess found at my trial," Cutter said, "because I assumed that Jess had found Melanie's *real* watch and planted it. Not that I had any way to prove that at the time. But I knew *I* didn't have it."

"Then who did?" Frost asked.

"That's a good question. I thought about that for a long time as I sat here in prison. I always thought the whole thing was strange. Melanie Valou was *wearing* her watch in the video footage from the ATM. So where on earth did Jess find it? I had no explanation. Not until very recently."

"What happened?" Frost asked.

"I was listening to a Giants game on the radio this spring," Cutter said. "They did an interview with one of the starting pitchers. Hector

Veracruz. He mentioned a little incident from a few years ago. When I heard it, I knew exactly what had happened to Melanie's watch. It was sort of like a bunch of alarm clocks going off at the same time. Know what I mean?"

Frost got the joke, which was like a sick boast that Cutter had been behind the whole overnight game.

"Go on," he said.

"Hector got mugged," Cutter told him. "It was a week after their last World Series victory. Some kid pulled a gun on him and took his cash and his last series ring, too. That was five years ago. *November* five years ago. Does that ring a bell with you, Inspector?"

It did. Frost understood the timing. Melanie Valou had disappeared five years ago. In November.

"Go on," Frost said.

"I had someone on the outside do some research for me. Guess where Hector got mugged? It was near a skateboard park under 101. I bet that rings a bell, too. It's only a few blocks from the ATM where Melanie Valou took out cash. Do you see where I'm going with this, Inspector?"

"You think Melanie got mugged," Frost said. "The mugger took her watch."

"Right."

"Before she met *you*," Frost said.

"Before she met whoever killed her," Cutter replied.

"That's quite a story. Do you expect me to believe it?"

Cutter shrugged. "You already do believe it, Inspector. I can see it in your face. You know it won't be hard to confirm everything I've told you."

"The mugger. Do you know who he is?"

"His name was Lamar Rhodes."

"Was?" Frost asked.

"He broke his neck in a skateboarding accident six months after Melanie was killed. Police found a gun and a lot of cash in his pocket. Hector pegged him as the kid who heisted his series ring."

Frost took out the evidence bag from his pocket again. "If Rhodes is dead, how did this watch get in my hands? Where has it been for five years?"

"That took a while to figure out. Remember, I still thought that Jess planted the real watch. I assumed she must have found Lamar Rhodes and taken the watch from him. Or maybe he fenced it and she tracked it down on the street. Either way, I was simply trying to prove what Jess had done. I had someone digging into Lamar's background, talking to people who knew him, trying to figure out what had happened to the watch. One of the people was Lamar's sister, Yolanda. She sprang quite a surprise on us."

"How so?"

"She was wearing the watch," Cutter said.

Frost didn't say anything, but he was thunderstruck.

"Yeah, it surprised me, too," Cutter said. "That's when I realized there must have been *two* watches. A mother-and-daughter set. And Camille Valou gave her own watch to Jess to plant in my ceiling. They figured it was safe because they assumed *I* had Melanie's watch and couldn't produce it without incriminating myself. Instead, a teenager in the Mission District had it the whole time. She thought the jewels were plastic. Imagine this kid walking around with a few thousand dollars on her wrist and not even knowing it.

"Yolanda Rhodes," Frost murmured.

"That's right. Go talk to her. She'll tell you all about it. And just in case you think I paid her off to feed you a crap story, there's proof, too. She's got a picture of herself and Lamar from five years ago where she's wearing the watch."

Frost wanted to believe that Cutter had concocted an elaborate lie, but he didn't think so. The story was crazy, but it had the ring of crazy, simple truth. He knew who'd really been lying all along. Camille Valou. And Jess.

He stared at the watch and shook his head.

"Why me, Cutter? Why the game?"

"I could have had my attorney talk to the district attorney, but do you think anyone would listen to him? I don't think so. They'd cover it up to protect their own. But a cop on the inside? A cop with a personal stake? If you're the messenger, they have to take it seriously."

"Why were you so sure I wouldn't destroy the watch?" Frost asked. "I thought about it."

"Because I hear you're a Boy Scout," Cutter said. "Don't worry, we got an affidavit from Yolanda, along with photos. Even if you'd gotten rid of the watch, it wouldn't have made a difference. But I didn't think you would. The word is, you're a cop who does what you have to do."

Cutter was right. Frost knew what he had to do.

He was going to make bad things happen. He was going to confirm Cutter's story. He was going to destroy Jess. He was going to set his sister's killer free.

6

Frost sat in total darkness in the window seat of his Russian Hill house, where he'd spent the last two hours. He nursed a pale ale, but the beer had grown warm as he held the bottle. Outside, rain slapped like gunfire against the glass. Thanks to the fog and the storm, the hillside and the city below him were mostly invisible.

The house smelled of reheated Peruvian saltado, which his brother, Duane, had delivered to his refrigerator sometime during the day. Everything Duane prepared was delicious, but Frost didn't have much of an appetite. He'd given up after a couple of bites, and Shack had eaten more of the dish than Frost had.

Now Shack slept on Frost's knee, his legs splayed as if he didn't have a bone in his little body. The black-and-white cat was as tiny as a kitten, but he was full grown. They'd been roommates for two years. The ornate, old-fashioned house didn't belong to Frost, and he'd never felt at home here, but living in this place was a requirement for staying with Shack. The cat's original owner was an old woman who had been murdered in the upstairs master bedroom, and Frost and Shack had adopted each other when he investigated the case. What Frost hadn't realized was that the woman's will included a provision requiring anyone who adopted Shack to stay in the house for the rest of the cat's life at a rental price of one dollar per year.

So Frost had given up his apartment near the baseball stadium, and now he lived with Shack in one of the most exclusive addresses in the city. The only furniture he'd brought with him was his old tweed sofa, which he kept in the living room and doubled as his bed.

It was nearly midnight. It had been a long day and evening. From San Quentin, he'd returned to police headquarters to look up the Mission District muggings, and he'd confirmed the details Cutter had given him about Lamar Rhodes. An hour later, he'd found Lamar's sister, Yolanda, who identified the watch. She'd had it on her wrist for five years, and she had the photos to prove it. It was all true.

He needed to think about what came next, but he wasn't ready to do that yet. Instead, he thought about his sister.

Katie, with the blond hair that made you think of a summer day. Katie, four years younger than Frost, although strangers had sometimes thought they were twins. They'd been as different as a brother and sister could be, but they'd also been best friends. Frost was an introvert, content to sit in silence and read history books. He'd never had a serious attachment to a woman in his life; his relationship with Shack was more of a commitment than he'd made to anyone else. Katie was the opposite. She'd lived for people. Strangers became friends. Boys fell at her feet.

Katie, with handwriting so bad she couldn't read it herself.

Katie, who could play Schubert on the piano like Horowitz and follow it up with "The Vatican Rag."

Katie, who should have been thirty-one years old now, but who had died in the back seat of her Malibu at the hands of Rudy Cutter.

Thinking of it, thinking of finding her body, thinking of the blood, made Frost squeeze his eyes shut with pain. Six years in between hadn't softened his grief. The memory burned like a fire that made it impossible to breathe.

He got up from the window seat, dislodging Shack. The cat blinked blearily, but then climbed up his shoulder and hung on for the ride as Frost went upstairs. He made his way into the master bedroom—across the white carpet, which still bore the faded bloodstain where Shack's original owner had died—and into the huge walk-in closet that stored almost everything Frost owned.

His "Katie box" was on the top shelf at the back. He slid it into his arms and sat down cross-legged in the closet with the box in front of him. He put aside the lid, which Shack hopped down to explore. Inside the box was everything he had from his relationship with his sister. Silly things. Theater programs. Paper fortunes from the cookies at Chinese restaurants. Photographs from a family camping trip to Yosemite when he, Katie, and Duane were all young. Postcards and letters. Frost had only crossed the California border twice in his life, but Katie had traveled a lot. She'd gone to Europe twice, to Hawaii, to Mexico, and to Alaska. He grabbed a postcard she'd mailed from Barcelona and tried to read it, but as usual, her handwriting was all but indecipherable. Even so, seeing her writing helped him hear her voice in his head.

He thought about the last time he'd heard that voice, two hours before she disappeared from the restaurant where she worked.

Haight Pizza, she'd answered the phone, unmistakably Katie.

Really? he'd said. *How can anyone hate pizza?*

Really? How many times can one brother make the same joke?

I'll let you know. How late are you delivering tonight?

Ten. Want me to bring you a pie when I go?

Definitely. Sausage and pineapple.

Got it. Sausage, absolutely no pineapple.

But she never showed up.

At eight forty-five, Katie had left for a delivery run in her Malibu. An hour later, a man named Todd Clary had called to complain that he'd never received his pizza. The pizza place tried to reach her, but Katie wasn't answering her phone. They'd called Frost, and Frost had called Duane, his parents, and Katie's friends. No one had seen her. He'd driven to Haight Pizza and traced out the route between the restaurant and Todd Clary's house, in case Katie's unreliable Malibu had died somewhere along the way. There was no sign of her anywhere.

And then the phone call came. The phone call that had sent him to Ocean Beach.

The man's voice had been distorted, like the hiss of a snake. He'd only learned much later that the voice belonged to Rudy Cutter.

Frost picked through the box on the floor, taking out keepsakes and memories one by one. It took him a while to find what he was looking for. Then, behind a true-crime memoir—Katie was a voracious reader, like him, and they always traded copies of books they liked—he spotted the jewelry case that held the flower tiara.

He'd given it to her on her last birthday as a joke. She was always complaining that she lived in San Francisco, but she'd never seen any-one with flowers in their hair. So he'd bought her a cheap silver tiara studded with rhinestone flowers and fake pearls. Looking at it now, he realized that it was pretty hideous, but Katie had worn it everywhere. She hardly ever took it off.

She'd been wearing it when he found her at Ocean Beach. Her skin was gray, her eyes closed. Blood was everywhere, on her neck, on her clothes, pooling obscenely on the seat and the floor of the Malibu. And there was the flower tiara, nestled in her hair, as if any second her fingers would come to life and trill across the piano keys and she would break into the Scott McKenzie song. Finding her that way, he'd peeled the tiara from her head and slipped it into the pocket of his coat without even thinking about it.

He knew now, as a cop, that he'd made a mistake. He'd removed evidence from a crime scene. He never showed the tiara to Jess. He never showed it to anyone, not Duane, not his parents. It was some-thing between him and Katie alone. When he'd joined the SFPD, he'd quietly had a test run in the crime lab to make sure there was no DNA other than Katie's on the tiara that might prove useful to the case. There wasn't. So Frost saw no need to correct his innocent mistake. He'd kept the tiara here in the box ever since.

When he held the tiara in his hand, he didn't just see Katie's face now. He saw Rudy Cutter, too, smiling at him in San Quentin. It infuriated him, having Cutter there in the middle of his memories. Everything was about to come crashing down. Friends, family, strangers, would hate him. All because of Melanie Valou's watch. All because he was a Boy Scout who couldn't live with a lie.

On the lower level of the house, he heard the chime of the doorbell. He checked his watch in surprise. It was late. He went downstairs, with Shack hopping beside him. He opened the front door, where the rain beat down, loud and strong.

The woman on the step was soaked to the skin, but she still had a cigarette smoldering in her mouth.

"Hey, Frost."

It was Jess Salceda.

7

"I got a phone call today," Jess told him as she crushed out her cigarette and marched into the house without an invitation. "It was Camille Valou. She was freaked out. She said you ambushed her at a restaurant and started asking some very odd questions."

"I guess I did," Frost agreed.

"You want to tell me what's going on?"

"Funny, that's what I was going to ask you, Jess."

That elicited a sour laugh. Jess peeled off her khaki trench coat and shook rain out of the chocolate-colored bangs that hung down below her forehead. She stepped out of her wet boots and wandered into the living room, shivering at the cold. Shack, who knew Jess well, followed beside her. She put her hands on her hips and watched Frost with angry eyes, which didn't surprise him. Anger was Jess's calling card. She'd grown up in a cop's world—cop father, cop ex-husband—and she was typically tough, hard, and serious.

"Want a drink?" Frost asked.

"Yeah."

He went to the bar and poured a shot of Trago Reposado. He didn't drink tequila himself; he kept it in the house for Jess. She downed the shot and handed him the glass, and they stood there for a moment, looking at each other. The house was silent, except for rain thundering on the roof. They stood very close to each other, and he could see, not far behind the wall in her eyes, that she was scared to death.

He felt a fleeting desire to kiss her. He could see her debating whether to slap him or rip off his clothes. It was always that way between them. They'd slept together twice last year when she was breaking up with her husband, but then they'd cut it off because they both knew it was stupid. Neither of them was looking for love or a relationship, but that didn't lessen the electricity when they were alone and together.

She was heavy and didn't waste time with diets. Her nose was hooked like the beak on a bird of prey, and she had copper skin. She was in her forties and didn't try to hide it. She had a rose tattoo high on her forearm, which was the only hint of softness in her armor. Being in bed with her was like taming a tiger.

"Where is it?" Jess asked.

"The watch? It's safe."

"Give it to me."

"So you can get rid of it?"

"Yeah."

Frost shook his head. "Sorry, Jess. It's too late for that."

They were still only inches apart, like lovers, like prizefighters. Finally, she spun away with a low growl of frustration and marched to the patio door and slid it open. Shack followed, but when the rain spattered his fur, he shook himself and retreated. Jess lit another cigarette and blew smoke outside, but Frost could smell it wafting toward him.

"So what happened?" she asked.

He told her everything. The overnight break-in. The alarm clocks. Copernicus and the watch and the inscription. Meeting with Camille Valou and Rudy Cutter, and then confirming Cutter's story. Jess stood by the patio door, smoking, listening, but not looking back at him. When he was done, they were both quiet.

"All these years," she murmured, as if there were a statute of limitations on ghosts coming back to haunt you. Then, after another minute of silence passed, she added, "We can still beat this."

"By lying?"

"Yeah. What does Cutter really have? The sister of some punk mugger? She won't hold up on the stand. We can say Cutter had a duplicate watch made and paid this girl to say she got it from her brother. Lamar's not around to say yes or no."

"There are photos, too," Frost said.

"Then we'll say the photos are fake. Camille will stick to her story, and so will I. We'll win. No judge *wants* to turn this guy loose, Frost. That's not how you get reelected."

Frost shook his head. "I won't do that."

"Are you kidding? You're really going through with this?"

"I have no choice."

"And you don't care about Cutter getting out?"

"I care, but that doesn't change anything, does it?"

Jess threw the cigarette onto the patio, where it sizzled as it burned out. "I can't believe you, Frost. This guy murdered Katie."

"You don't need to remind me," he replied icily.

She folded her arms across her chest. He watched her breathing. The room got cold. She closed the door, but she stayed there, staring into the darkness and the rain. He could feel her trying to contain an explosion. She was ready to scream. To lash out. To throw things. They both knew what this meant for her. She'd lose her job. She'd probably go to jail. In the shadows, her eyes were like black holes. Her lips were pushed together, her mouth turned downward.

"Do I need a lawyer?" she asked.

"Yes."

"I hate lawyers."

"I know." He caught the irony, because he was a lawyer himself. He added, "Why did you do it, Jess?"

She shrugged. She left the patio door and came around and sat on the sofa. It was obvious that she wanted to talk. To confess. Maybe to brag about what she'd done. He knew how she felt about "the line." You crossed it when you had to. You took the consequences when they came.

"Melanie's father came to me," she said. "It was his idea."

Frost said nothing.

"Melanie was killed in November," Jess went on, as if he didn't remember. "I knew it was Cutter, but for the life of me, I couldn't find any hard evidence. Nothing we could use in court. And I was running out of time. You know that. By the next November, I knew it wouldn't be long before he struck again. He had a pattern. If I didn't put him away soon, we'd find another body in a car."

"I know," Frost said.

"And then Melanie's father called me. Sam Valou. He asked me to meet him in Golden Gate Park. Somewhere no one would see us. That was when he showed me the watch. He said Melanie's mother, Camille, bought *two* watches, one for Melanie, one for herself. Sam said Camille never wore hers, because he got her a kick-ass diamond watch around the same time. They kept the other watch—the match for Melanie's watch—in a safe-deposit box. No one knew about it. Just him, Camille, and some ninety-year-old jeweler six thousand miles away in the Alps. He said the watches were *identical*. So if his wife's watch were to show up in Cutter's house, who would know the difference?"

"He convinced you to plant it," Frost said.

"Convinced me? Hell, I jumped at the chance. I didn't think twice about it. Not for a second. When we got the next search warrant for Cutter's place, I made sure I had Camille's watch in my pocket. It was easy to pretend I'd discovered it in the ceiling."

"But the two watches *weren't* identical."

"No, Sam didn't know that Camille had added an inscription before she gave the watch to Melanie. Camille always called her daughter 'the dreamer,' and so she had the words engraved on Melanie's watch in

French. It was a little thing for the two of them. I didn't find out about that until it was too late. I showed Camille the watch to identify it, and she looked at the back, and she was speechless. She knew what we'd done. Sam persuaded her to go along with the ruse at Cutter's trial, but when she was on the stand, I really didn't know whether she'd back us up. I was holding my breath the whole time."

Frost shook his head. He didn't even know what to say. "Jess."

"What, are you judging me? Don't give me that shit, Frost. I did what I did to save lives. I'd do it again. Cutter needed to go down, and I couldn't get him the straight way. So I got him the crooked way instead."

"I know the pressure you were under."

"You don't know the half of it. The whole damn city was crucifying me because I couldn't catch the guy who did this. And I couldn't even stand up in public and say, 'I know who the son of a bitch is, I just can't prove it.' Yeah, the pressure sucked, but I didn't do it to get myself out from under the heat. I did it because Rudy Cutter was a murderer, and my job is to put murderers away. Sometimes you have to cut corners to do what's right."

"Is that what you call it? Cutting corners? I call it a felony."

"Gee, it must be nice to be the only noble cop in San Francisco. You think anyone is going to thank you for exposing what I did?"

"No."

"If this guy gets out and kills again, you'll be the one who gets hung out to dry."

"Maybe so."

"I told you, we can still make this go away, Frost," Jess insisted. "I'm not saying that for myself. I don't care what happens to me. Think about all those women. Think about Katie."

"Do you really believe I've been thinking about anything else tonight? I don't need a lecture from you, Jess. I didn't ask for any of this. You're the one who put me here."

Jess stood up again. "Okay. Whatever. Do what you have to do."

"I wish you'd come to me about this back then," he told her.

"What would you have said?"

"Don't plant the watch," Frost replied.

"That's why I didn't ask."

He went to the bar and poured her another shot of tequila. A larger one this time. He brought it to her, and she took it without a word and gulped it down. She wiped her mouth, and then she went to the bar herself and poured the next shot and drank that one, too. She kept talking.

"I remember the look on Cutter's face," she told him. "The bastard was actually impressed. I mean, he knew it was a setup. But he didn't say a word. It was like he was giving me credit for figuring out a way to win the game. And besides, what was he going to say? 'Hey, that can't be the real watch, because I've got the real one stashed in a safe-deposit box somewhere'?"

"Except Cutter didn't have it stashed," Frost pointed out. "He never did. Lamar Rhodes had the watch, and he gave it to his sister."

"Well, I didn't know that little fact, did I? Damn, what are the odds? Cutter grabs a watch off every other victim, but Melanie's watch gets stolen before he took her. Unbelievable."

"Yeah."

Jess came and stood in front of him. She was uncomfortably close again. He smelled the tequila on her breath. He thought she might reach for him and kiss him. Sex him into a coma and, while he was sleeping, search the house until she found the watch and could destroy it.

"Tell me you don't think he's innocent," Jess said. Her voice was loud and slurred.

"No, I don't think that."

"I did *not* put an innocent man behind bars."

"I'm not saying you did."

"Rudy Cutter is a serial killer."

"Yes, he is."

Jess walked unsteadily toward the foyer, where she grabbed her trench coat. She slipped it on and opened the door to confront the rain. Frost followed her to the threshold. She stepped into the downpour, and then she turned around, with her hands shoved in her pockets.

"We both had to make a tough choice on this one, Frost," she called over the noise of the storm. "I can live with mine. Can you live with yours?"

8

The worst part was telling Duane.

Frost opened the door, expecting his brother to be alone, but instead Duane had his latest girlfriend with him. His brother hoisted two bags of groceries from Bristol Farms in the air. He whipped inside the Russian Hill house like a hurricane, leaving a pert redhead on the porch in his wake.

"Bison burgers!" he called to Frost over his shoulder. "On my famous garlic-rosemary focaccia buns, with melted Flagship cheddar. Plus sweet potato matchstick fries, edamame salad, and red-velvet truffles."

Duane was already out of sight, heading toward the kitchen, but Frost heard him call, "Shack, Shack, Bo-Back, how are you, buddy?"

The girl on the porch, who was left alone, grinned at him. "I'm Tabitha, by the way, but everyone calls me Tabby. Tabby Blaine."

Frost heard a belated shout from inside as his brother introduced them. "Frost, meet Tabby. Tabby, this is my bro!"

"Come on in," he told her.

"Thanks." She strolled into the foyer and then the living room, and she headed immediately to the panoramic view over the bay. "What a place."

"It's my cat's," Frost said.

Tabby glanced at him over her shoulder, and her green eyes sparkled with amusement. She had very long eyelashes. "Yeah, Duane told me about Shack. I bet that line works pretty well with the girls. 'Hi, I'm Frost, I rent a mansion from my cat.'"

"It does, actually," Frost admitted. "And here's the little land baron himself."

Shack hopped onto the back of the sofa, and from there, he jumped immediately into Tabby's arms. She caught him with a startled giggle, but she knew exactly how to hold him, and Shack settled against her shoulder and began to purr and swipe at her long red hair.

"I hope you're not allergic," Frost said.

"Wildly, actually, but that's okay. I love cats. You can't have the nickname Tabby and not love cats, right? I popped a Benadryl before coming over here, so I should be good for a while."

"Aw, Tabs, you made these matchsticks too thick," Duane called in a crabby voice from the kitchen.

"They're perfect," Tabby called back. "Quit complaining."

To Frost's astonishment, Duane let it go. He'd never seen anyone challenge Duane about ingredients and live to tell the tale.

"So you're a chef, too?" Frost asked her.

Tabby's head bobbed. Shack continued to tickle her hair. "Yeah, I work over at Boulevard on the Embarcadero."

"Impressive. They've got a Beard Award, don't they? I figured you worked with Duane in SoMa."

"Work with Duane? Oh please, do I look like a masochist? I helped him get ready for tonight, but that's as far as I go. Did you know his nickname in the chef community is the Beast? Duane Beaston, that's what they call your brother."

"I did know that, actually."

"So are you a beast, too?" Tabby asked, teasing him. "You don't look like a beast."

"Only during a full moon," Frost replied.

"Well, well. I'd like to see that."

Tabby held Shack and wandered comfortably around the house as if she owned the place. She had a firecracker personality, unabashed and unafraid. That made her different from most of the girls that Duane dated, who usually looked scared to say a word in front of him. Tabby didn't look older than thirty, and she was only a few inches taller than five feet. She wore tight jeans and an untucked men's yellow dress shirt that she'd probably borrowed from Duane. Her freckled cheeks had a permanent rosy flush, and her smile went easily from innocent to wicked to smart.

"What a beautiful figurine," Tabby said, reaching up to caress the blue glass carving over the bay window. Her touch was delicate, as if she sensed that it was special.

"It belonged to our sister, Katie," Frost replied.

Tabby's green eyes became two little sympathetic emeralds. "Oh, of course."

From the kitchen, Frost heard the sizzle of meat and smelled an intoxicating mix of seasonings. The house always smelled good when Duane came to visit. "I'm going to get a beer," he told Tabby. "Do you want a drink? Chardonnay or something?"

"Beer sounds good."

"Glass or bottle?" he asked.

"Oh, bottle, please. I may look like a girly girl, but I'm a tomboy at heart. Although I guess Tabby should be a tomcat, right? My mom was Catherine, and she was Kitty. So naturally her daughter became Tabitha and Tabby."

Frost chuckled. He liked her a lot.

Leaving Tabby to cuddle and coo with Shack, he went into the kitchen, where Duane seemed to be in five places at once. He was a whirlwind of motion. Meat grilled, buns baked, edamame shelled, olives chopped, and through it all, he sang a bad karaoke version of "Heathens" by Twenty One Pilots.

"Listen, I want to talk to you about something," Frost told him. "Can we grab a few minutes alone after dinner?"

Duane eyed him curiously. "Man of mystery. What's going on?"

"It can wait. I'll tell you later."

"Sure, whatever." His brother didn't waste time on anything else when he was cooking.

"Tabby's great," Frost added.

"Yeah, she is." Duane raised his voice. "Hey, Tabs, Frost thinks you're great."

"He's great, too," she replied from the living room.

"You want to help me with the cooking in here?" Duane called to her.

"Nah, you're good," Tabby replied.

Frost laughed. He enjoyed seeing another chef stand up to Duane. "How long have you two been going out?"

"Six months," Duane said, with a hint of a smile.

Frost's mouth fell open in surprise. To Duane Easton, six months was a lifetime. His brother usually went through sous chefs as lovers like a kid grabbing chocolates from a box. Duane's life was his career, and the girls he dated were mostly about burning off sexual energy at the end of a fourteen-hour day.

"And I'm only finding out about her now?" Frost asked.

"I wanted to see if it was real first. Actually, we're practically living together. She stays at my place most of the time."

Frost had nothing to say, but he liked hearing it. He was almost willing to believe that a miracle had happened and that his brother was in love.

Duane was older than Frost by five years, but he'd always acted younger. Frost and Katie had looked like twins, but Frost didn't see much resemblance to himself in his brother's face. Duane was shorter than Frost by nearly half a foot and as skinny as pencil asparagus. His hair was straight and shoulder length, and tonight he had it tied behind his head. He had a narrow nose that was so long that it seemed to droop at the end by its own weight.

"Have you told Mom and Dad about her?" Frost asked.

"They introduced us."

"Seriously? How did that happen?"

"It's a long story," Duane said.

Their parents lived in Arizona and didn't come back to San Francisco very often. The city was mostly about bad memories for them. Frost waited for an explanation of how his parents had brought Duane and Tabby together, but Duane was back in the middle of his bison burgers, and he didn't have anything more to say about the origins of his new relationship.

Frost grabbed two Sierra Nevada beers and returned to the living room.

He drank with Tabby on the sofa near the window. Shack licked beer from her finger, which made her giggle. She told him about her job in the restaurant, her time in culinary school, her favorite foods, and her cousin who played for the 49ers, but when he tried to maneuver her to the topic of how she and Duane had met, she smoothly changed the subject.

Before he could try again, his brother interrupted. Dinner was ready, and Duane's food waited for no one.

They laughed their way through the meal for the next hour. Duane told dirty jokes, but his were like Ivory soap compared to the ones Tabby told. Frost was in no rush to finish, because he was preoccupied with a sense of dread about the after-dinner conversation. Duane wasn't going to like what he had to say, so Frost put off telling him.

In the midst of dessert, however, the phone rang. Frost let the machine take it, which was a mistake. Everyone heard the message.

"Inspector, this is Khristeen Smith at the *San Francisco Chronicle*. I'd like to talk to you about the court hearing for Rudy Cutter next week. There are a lot of rumors flying, and the one name that keeps coming up is yours. Please call me back."

The reporter left her number, and then the house was silent. He watched a concerned glance shoot back and forth between Duane and Tabby. His brother put down the truffle that was in his hand, and he shot Frost a laser-like stare. The two of them had eyes that didn't let go.

"Rudy Cutter?" Duane asked.

"That's what I wanted to talk to you about," Frost said.

"So talk."

Frost glanced at Tabby, but Duane quickly intervened. "She can hear anything you have to say."

"Okay. Cutter's attorney filed a motion to have his conviction thrown out."

"What the hell for?" Duane asked.

"Jess manufactured evidence against him. The watch she found in Cutter's house was planted. A fake. It didn't really belong to the last victim."

Duane stood up in the dining room. He went to the front windows and peered through the curtains. He was silent for a long time. On the other side of the table, Tabby stared at her plate with a kind of quiet shock fixed on her face.

"Is Cutter going to get out?" Duane asked.

"That depends on the judge, but it looks that way."

"Are you kidding me?"

"I wish I was."

"This is bullshit. That son of a bitch killed Katie and all those other women. What judge is going to put him back on the street?"

"I know that. The thing is, what Jess did—"

"I don't care what she did," Duane interrupted him. "I wish we'd fried him in the electric chair. That piece of shit doesn't deserve to be breathing."

"I hear you. You're right."

Duane turned back from the window and jabbed a finger at him. "Why does this reporter want to talk to you? She said your name keeps coming up. Why are you involved in this?"

Frost rubbed a hand across his beard. He tried to come up with words. Tabby still didn't look up.

"I'm the one who blew the whistle on Jess."

"What?"

"I found out that she planted fake evidence. I took it to the captain and the district attorney."

Duane shook his head. "Why would you do that?"

54

"What do you mean, why? I had an obligation. It's my job."

"Your job? Your job is to let murderers out of prison?"

"Jess committed a crime, Duane. She rigged the whole system. Don't you get it? Cops can't do that. If I let that slide—"

"He murdered Katie!" Duane shouted, his voice filling the room.

Frost stopped talking. There was nothing to say.

"I can't believe you," Duane snapped. "I can't believe you would do this. You're going to have to tell Mom and Dad, you know that? You realize what this is going to do to them?"

Frost didn't have an answer. He knew Duane didn't really want one.

"We're out of here," Duane went on. "Come on, Tabs."

His girlfriend finally looked up. Her bubbly, ever-present smile was gone, and her face had clouded with sorrow. "Actually, Duane, could you wait in the car for a minute? I want to talk to Frost."

Duane nodded and then said something that Frost didn't understand. "Yeah, that's right. You can tell him what he's done."

His brother stalked out of the dining room, and Frost heard the thunder of the front door slamming.

The two of them were alone. Tabby stared at him. The sparkle had left her green eyes, but he saw something he hadn't seen in his brother's face. Empathy. She brushed away a strand of red hair.

"I know how hard this is for you," Tabby said. "Duane knows, too. He's just angry."

"I'm angry at myself," Frost admitted.

"You didn't have a choice, did you?" Tabby got up and came around to the other side of the table and sat in the chair next to him. She took his hand; her skin was warm. "Listen, Frost, I didn't realize that Duane hadn't told you about me, which pisses me off a little. I guess that means you don't know how we met."

"He said my parents introduced you."

"Sort of. I've known your parents for several years. When they found out I was a chef, they told me about Duane. Of course, I already knew who he was. Everybody in the culinary community knows Duane. Your mom said I should meet him, but I wasn't really interested. He has a reputation for playing the field. But earlier this year, Duane called me. I guess your mom was pressuring him, too."

"My mom usually gets what she wants," Frost said.

"Apparently."

"How do you know my parents?" he asked.

"Through the victim support group meetings."

He closed his eyes. Suddenly, it made sense. "Who are you connected to?"

"Nina Flores. Cutter's first victim. Nina was my best friend. We grew up two blocks apart. Actually, Nina and I knew each other before we could walk. She was more like a sister to me than my own sister was. The families were kind enough to include me in the support group."

"I was never really into that sort of thing," Frost said. Grief wasn't something he shared with strangers. It was personal and private. He had to feel close to someone to invite them into that part of his life.

"That's okay. It's not for everyone. Anyway, believe me when I say, I really do understand what this is doing to you."

"Thanks."

"I should go," Tabby said. "Duane is waiting for me."

"Sure."

She let go of his hand, and she stood up. "I don't blame you for any of this. Duane won't, either, when he settles down. It's not your fault."

She bent down very near his face, and he realized how pretty she was in close-up. A hint of perfume drifted across the space between them. He was jealous of his brother, having this woman in his life.

"What happens next?" she asked. "I mean, if they let Cutter out of prison."

"I put him back inside," Frost said without hesitation.

"Good," Tabby replied with a casual confidence that he was a man who kept his promises. "That's what I was hoping you'd say."

9

Frost sat in the last row of the courtroom.

He'd already testified for two hours that morning, questioned by Rudy Cutter's attorney and then cross-examined by Hang Li, the San Francisco district attorney. He related the whole story, including his temptation to destroy the watch that first night on the Golden Gate Bridge. He stuck to the facts of what he'd found, but facts didn't matter to the stone faces of victims' families packing the courtroom.

To them, he was the enemy. He was the man who'd brought the monster back to life.

The media filled the courtroom, too. Print. TV. Radio. Bloggers. To them, he was a study in contradictions. Brother of a victim. Cop. Whistle-blower. They'd made the story front-page news for days, and they all wanted interviews with him. He'd turned them down. The last thing he wanted was publicity.

Yolanda Rhodes followed him on the stand. She testified about her brother, Lamar, giving her the watch with the funny inscription on the back. When the attorney showed her the watch, she identified it right away and confirmed that she'd been wearing it since long before the other watch was found in Rudy Cutter's ceiling.

"That's it. That's mine. I wish I could get it back, too."

And then Jess came.

Frost didn't know what Jess would say. That was the mystery of the day that made everyone hold their breath. He wondered if she'd lie and try to hide behind the blue wall. She could say that Frost was mistaken, that Yolanda was lying, and that the watch Jess had found was the one and only watch belonging to Melanie Valou. Melanie's mother, Camille, would probably back her up.

Instead, she told the truth.

Her testimony caused a gasp of disbelief among the spectators. She admitted the entire conspiracy. The watch never belonged to Melanie. She planted it in Rudy Cutter's house. She perjured herself during his trial. She never flinched once as she laid out what she'd done, and the entire time, she stared at Frost in the back row. When her testimony was over, she marched out of the courtroom with her back straight, ignoring the shouts and taunts that followed her as the judge swung his gavel hard for silence.

Now it was almost done. The final arguments. And then the ruling.

District Attorney Hang Li stood in front of Judge Elwood Elgin.

Li was small, slim, forty years old. He had a shock of black hair, wire-rimmed glasses, and an expensive brown suit.

"Your Honor, I'm not going to defend Lieutenant Salceda," Li told the judge. "She falsified evidence. She lied to the court. The police have already dismissed her from her job, and I assure you, she will face legal consequences for her actions, too. The watch that she planted in the defendant's house no longer has any evidentiary weight against Mr. Cutter. However, I would argue that the other evidence that was presented at trial would be sufficient to sustain a guilty verdict against him. Simply put, the jury *did not need* the watch to reach their decision. As such, the fraudulent behavior by Lieutenant Salceda—while illegal and inexcusable—shouldn't prejudice the rest of the case against Mr. Cutter."

Cutter's attorney rose to his feet with outrage turning his face red, but Judge Elgin calmly waved him back to his chair. "Save your breath, Counselor," the judge told him in an unflappable voice. "I've got this."

Frost knew what was coming. Everyone did.

Judge Elgin was a long-time member of the San Francisco Democratic political establishment, an environmental lawyer with roots in Nancy Pelosi's congressional office. He was fifty years old, a white-bread liberal who spoke softly but wielded a big stick from the bench. He'd railed against the excesses of police misbehavior in the city for twenty years, and Hang Li had just handed him a cut-and-dried case of a rogue police officer rigging the justice system.

"Mr. Li, do you know what you get when you add rat poison to a steak?" Judge Elgin asked.

"Your Honor, I don't really understand—"

"You get *poisoned steak*," the judge continued, emphasizing each word. "It doesn't matter whether it's a perfect prime-cut ribeye. Once you put poison on it, you have no choice but to throw it out. And that's what we have here. Lieutenant Salceda's actions have compromised the case against Mr. Cutter in its entirety. Your argument about the other evidence would be insufficient on its face, because the watch was the linchpin of your case, and we both know it. But even if you had other compelling evidence against Mr. Cutter, the police misconduct would void it. It's distasteful to both of us, but I have no choice but to vacate the guilty verdict against him."

The crowd erupted. The judge pounded his gavel.

"Your Honor, we ask that you keep Mr. Cutter in custody while we prepare to refile charges against him," Li pleaded. He was grasping for legal straws.

"Denied. If you're able to build evidence for a new criminal case, I'll examine the question of bail at that time."

"In that case, Your Honor, I'd like to raise the issue of electronic monitoring," Li went on.

Judge Elgin leaned forward on the bench. "Also denied. Mr. Li, you seem to be under the impression that you still have some sort of case against Mr. Cutter, and let me be clear. You don't. This is not a question of pasting together prior evidence without the watch that was planted in Mr. Cutter's house. I'm throwing it *all* out. If you refile charges based on evidence gathered or supervised by Lieutenant Salceda, then I will be forced to dismiss the case, and at that point, I'll do so with prejudice. Her behavior has poisoned the entire investigation."

"Your Honor!" Li protested.

"Enough. We're done here. Everyone who has touched this case should be ashamed of themselves. If you think Mr. Cutter is guilty, and you want to put him back in San Quentin, then you and the police have one job. *Start over.*"

And that was that.

Katie's killer was free.

Frost found himself unable to move. He wanted to get up and leave the courtroom immediately, but the awful reality of what he'd done pinned his feet to the floor. He sat in the back row, in the aisle near the walnut door, as spectators filed past him. The media shouted questions that he ignored. Family members of the victims swore at him. One man, a father, spat in his hair. The guards tried to create a bubble around Frost, but he didn't care what they did or said.

He blamed himself, just like they did.

Slowly, the courtroom emptied. Rudy Cutter, surrounded by police protection, was the last to leave. Frost wondered if someone from the families would be waiting outside the courthouse with a gun. Or a knife. He had to dig inside himself to ask whether there would be anything wrong with vigilante justice right now.

It didn't matter what the judge said or what Jess had done. Cutter was guilty. Nothing changed that.

Frost realized that Cutter had stopped right next to him. He stared back at the man, eye to eye, cop to killer. Cutter had cleaned up for his court appearance; his face was smoothly shaved, his blond hair neat, his suit and tie pressed. He could have been Daniel Craig, a suave and sexy spy, not a serial killer. Cutter was whistling under his breath, but loud enough for Frost to hear it. The tune was familiar. The police tried to herd the man away, but he lingered in the aisle, not moving, and then he bent down so close to Frost that no one else could hear what he said. Frost felt the heat of the man's breath.

"Tick tock, Inspector," Cutter whispered.

Then he was gone, still whistling. The doors closed on him. The courtroom was empty and silent. Frost was alone.

It took him a moment to identify the tune that had been on Cutter's lips, and when he did, the chill of it made him clench his fists. Cutter was taunting him, daring him to notice what he was doing. It was a confession that no one else would understand or believe.

Cutter had been whistling the Scott McKenzie song, "San Francisco."

Be sure to wear some flowers in your hair.

That was the song Frost and Katie had joked about—the song that had led him to buy the tiara with the pretty rhinestone flowers that was now hidden away in a box in Frost's upstairs closet. The tiara had been nestled in Katie's hair when he found her body at Ocean Beach, but he was the only person in the world who knew that.

Other than her killer.

10

The waves at Ocean Beach lapped to Frost's feet with a whooshing rhythm that was like a heartbeat. Other than a few sundown joggers, he didn't have much company on the drab stretch of sand. The November wind had driven most people away.

Something about being here brought Katie a little closer to him. Memories of her life came and went as he stood near the water. He pictured the two of them, as kids, flying a kite in Golden Gate Park. Katie playing the *Nutcracker Suite* on the piano at a high school Christmas play. Katie scowling playfully at the camera like Al Capone as he took her on a tour of Alcatraz. Those were good times.

With each in-and-out rumble of the surf, he also heard Rudy Cutter's voice in his head: *Tick tock.* It was like Cutter was throwing down a challenge at him to stop what came next. The time on the clock was already counting down to another murder. This was personal for Frost now. He'd been the one to set Cutter free. He had to be the one to put him away again. He owed it to Katie.

Frost felt a presence near him and realized he wasn't alone on the beach anymore. His head turned, and he saw a black woman no more than twenty yards away. She was looking at him, and she even raised her hand in a little wave. Her face was familiar. He knew her, and yet he didn't know her.

She took a few tentative steps in his direction. She was as tall as he was and skinny to the point of being gaunt. They were probably close to the same age, halfway between thirty and forty. She had bushy black hair with tight corkscrew curls. Her thick eyebrows got lost in her hair. Her eyes were black marbles, intense and smart, analyzing the world with suspicion. Her face was narrow and long, her nose flat, her mouth a straight, emotionless line.

Her mocha skin was interrupted on her neck by a reddish discolored scar that sliced across her windpipe. She'd had her throat cut.

"Inspector Easton?"

"That's right."

"I'm sorry to intrude. My name is—"

She didn't have to finish the sentence. Her face landed in his memory. They'd never met, but he recognized her from the photo on her book jacket and her appearances on television. It was the scar that distinguished her. She was both a writer and a survivor of a terrible crime.

"Eden Shay," he said.

She was surprised and looked uncomfortable that he knew who she was. "That's right."

"I read your book, Ms. Shay."

"I'm honored," she said.

He heard a hint of her Australian roots in her voice, although her time in the US had tamed her accent. He remembered from her memoir that she'd grown up in Melbourne.

"I usually read history, but my sister enjoyed your book," Frost said. "She made sure I read it, too."

"Your sister. So that would be—"

"Katie," he said.

Eden nodded. She didn't pretend not to know what had happened to Katie. Similarly, he didn't pretend not to notice the scar, which told Eden's own horrific story. Ten years earlier, in her twenties, she'd attended the writer's program at the University of Iowa to get her MFA.

During her first term, she'd been kidnapped and held by two sadistic brothers in the basement of their Iowa City house. Imprisoned like a slave. Starved. Tortured. The brothers would kill small animals in front of her and tell her she was next. Eventually, they cut her throat and left her to bleed out, but instead, she escaped in the middle of a February night. She was rescued on a frozen rural highway on the brink of death.

The experience put her on the cover of *People* magazine. Her memoir about it became a number-one bestseller and a hit movie. Looking at her now, he somehow knew that all the fame and money hadn't erased a minute of the time she'd spent in that basement.

"How did you find me, Ms. Shay?"

"I'm Eden, please."

"Okay," he said. "Eden."

"Please don't think I'm stalking you," she said. "I was coming to see you at your house, and I saw you driving away. I followed you here."

"That was an hour ago," Frost pointed out.

"I know. I waited in my car. It seemed to me that you needed your privacy."

The noise of the surf made it hard to hear her. A wicked gust roared from the water, and he watched her body absorb the blow. She wrapped her arms around herself. She wore a red blouse that was too light for the season and jeans that clung to her long legs. Her black curls quivered.

"Are you cold? Do you want to talk somewhere else?"

"I'm fine. The cold keeps me alert."

"So what can I do for you, Eden? If you're writing an article, or if you're looking for an interview, I'm not interested. Sorry."

She didn't say anything immediately. Then she told him, "I was in court today."

"I didn't see you there."

"No, I kept a low profile. I didn't want to be recognized. I understand the hurt of the families, but they were unfair to you. The only thing you could have done is come forward with what you found out."

"Why do you say that?"

"Because based on what I know about you, you're not the kind of man who looks away."

"From what?"

"From anything," she said.

"How is it that you know me at all?" he asked. He was wary because she was a journalist, but he also found it flattering that this woman had sought him out.

"I've been doing my homework on you," Eden said.

"This sounds like an interview," Frost replied.

"It's not. Not really."

"Then how can I help you?"

"Well, mostly, I want to help you."

"I'm sorry, I don't understand," he said.

There was almost no one else on the beach, but she made sure they were alone. "Can I ask you one question first? It's off the record and unofficial. I just want to know if I'm in the right place, talking to the right person. Although I'm pretty sure I am."

"What's the question?" Frost asked.

"Do you plan to reinvestigate the Golden Gate Murders?"

He stiffened. "That's a question for my captain, Ms. Shay. I don't have anything to say about it. My sister was one of the victims. Obviously, I can't take the lead on any new investigation."

She closed some of the distance between them, physically and emotionally. "I'm still Eden, not Ms. Shay. And I hope you won't be offended if I call you Frost. This won't work if we're formal with each other."

"What won't work?"

"I wasn't asking if the police are going to open the case again. Of course they are. I want to know if *you* plan to investigate the case yourself. Behind the scenes."

"I have nothing to say about that."

"Frost, once I walk away, this conversation never happened. No matter what you tell me, if you ask me to go, I go, and your secret is safe. I know you'd never put any new legal proceedings against Cutter in jeopardy."

For some reason, Frost didn't want her to walk away. Not yet. "Assume you're right about me and my plans. Then what?"

"I told you. I want to help."

"How? And why?"

Eden grabbed his hand. Her fingers were ice-cold. She knew she had him hooked and that he wouldn't let her go until he'd heard what she had to say. "Look, I pretend to be a superwoman, but I'm freezing my ass off out here. Take me to dinner, and I'll explain everything."

By the second glass of wine, he'd finally seen Eden smile, but it was a sad smile. They were at Sutro's at the Cliff House, a hundred yards up the highway from the beach. Their window table overlooked the ocean, but that was her doing, not his. The maître d' and the waiter both knew who she was.

"Is it strange?" he asked. "Being recognized wherever you go?"

She sipped her pinot grigio and stared at the dark waves below them. "Don't be too impressed. Since I moved back to the city, this has been one of my favorite haunts. That's the only reason they know me."

"I think you're being modest. I remembered you."

"Well, it doesn't happen much anymore. I still publish in some of the major magazines, but people don't really notice a byline. I've been out of the news for a few years. Most of the time now, people look at me, and they think they know me, but they can't place the face. For a while, though, you're right, I couldn't go anywhere without people knowing who I was. I didn't like it much."

"No?"

She touched her neck, where the scar was. "No. They didn't see me and think, *That's the writer, Eden Shay.* They saw me and thought, *That's the girl who was imprisoned in that basement in Iowa.* I don't want to be famous for that. I want to be famous for what I write in the *Atlantic* or the *New Yorker*. But that's not how life works."

"Sorry," Frost said.

"You don't have to be sorry," she told him with a shade of annoyance. He understood. Everyone who met her was sorry, and it didn't change a thing or make anything better. It had been that way with him after Katie died, too. People never knew what to say.

"You moved back to the city recently?" he said.

"That's right. I moved to San Francisco after the assault. I owned a house over on Baker for a few years. That's where I wrote my book. Then I went home to Australia six years ago to be with my father, and I only came back this year."

"You don't have family ties in the city?"

She shook her head. "No, I just love it here. We moved to the US when I was a teenager, and we spent a couple weeks here before heading to New York. I swore if I ever had the money, I'd move here. Eventually, I did."

"So why did you leave?"

"You sound like you can't imagine anyone leaving San Francisco," she said, and that was when he saw the smile.

"I can't."

"You're a lifer?" she asked.

"Born and raised."

"Well, that must be nice. Honestly, I didn't want to move away, but life intervened. My father found out he was in the early stages of Alzheimer's. He wanted to go back home to Australia for his final years, and I moved there to take care of him. He passed away last year, so I came back to San Francisco. Now I'm like you. I don't think I'll leave again."

"Welcome home," Frost said, raising his glass.

"Thank you."

They drank more wine. They both ordered mussels and Thai bouillabaisse. They talked, and he found himself sharing more than he usually did with a stranger, which meant that she was a savvy journalist. He told her about his parents divorcing after Katie's death and then getting back together again. He told her about his fight with Duane, who hadn't spoken to him in more than a week. She shared things about herself, too. She told him about her older brother, who'd overshadowed her his whole life. He was a CNN war correspondent who'd spent years embedded with the troops, living with them, seeing war through their eyes, and telling their stories. Until an IED killed him in Afghanistan.

He realized they had grief in common. They'd both lost siblings.

They were drinking coffee and eating tiramisu when she finally said, "You've been very patient with me, Frost."

"I'm a patient guy."

"I didn't want to tell you what I'm doing until we knew each other a little better."

"So what are you doing?" he asked.

"I'm writing a book. I've done magazine work ever since my memoir, but never another book. Now I'm ready."

Frost frowned. "Let me guess."

"Yes, it's about the Golden Gate Murders." She rushed on before he could object. "Please, don't say anything yet. This isn't a new project. I've been planning it for years. When I moved to San Francisco the first time, I was caught up in writing my memoir and then the book tour and the movie. I was hardly ever home. I barely had time to breathe. When things finally settled down, I needed to find a new project for myself. There had been so much drama in my life, and suddenly, it was gone. It left me empty. I liked doing magazine work, but I wanted something bigger. That was when the third victim was discovered. Natasha Lubin."

He watched conflicting emotions take over her face. She retreated inside herself briefly, like a turtle inside a shell, but then she pulled herself out and began talking again.

"Being involved in a violent crime changes you," Eden went on. "I struggled for a long time to figure out who I was. A writer? A victim? I didn't know. Then I read about Natasha, and I found out about the two earlier victims, and the whole case had a strange draw for me. Here was a serial killer, still unknown, still in the midst of his crimes. I could be a part of it. I decided to follow the case and learn everything I could about it."

Frost saw more than a journalist's curiosity in her face. This was personal to her.

"Do you mind if I make an observation?" he said.

"Go ahead."

"This doesn't sound like a healthy obsession for someone like you."

"Very few of my obsessions are healthy," she joked. "And I have a lot of them."

"I mean, you had your throat cut, Eden. You nearly died. Not that you need me to remind you of that. Is it really smart to be diving into a case about a serial killer who cuts women's throats?"

"My shrink said the same thing," she told him. "He said I felt guilty that I lived and these women didn't. He told me to quit the project. Go write about happier stuff, like global warming or opioid addictions."

"But that didn't stop you?"

"No. You're right, it was my obsession, healthy or not. I couldn't let go. I began to research the victims. One thing you'll learn about me, Frost—I really, really do my homework. I talked to everybody, and not just the people around here. I flew to Minnesota to meet Natasha's brother. I flew to Texas to find Rae Hart's parents. I knew the women in this case better than the police did."

"So why didn't you finish the book?" he asked.

"Like I said, life got in the way. When my father got sick, I left the country. I still did some magazine work, but I had to put the book project on hold. Then last year, when I moved back, I found out that the crimes had been solved and that the killer, Rudy Cutter, was in prison. So I started working on the book again."

"And what do you want from me?" he asked.

"I want to help you put Rudy Cutter back in jail."

"Why would you do that?"

"I interviewed Cutter in prison several times. I told you, I do my homework. I know what kind of man he is, because I've met men like him before. Up close. He scares me."

"He should," Frost said. "But you're a writer. You're not the police. How do you expect to help?"

"I heard the judge say that the police have to start over and pretend the original investigation never happened. I've done dozens of interviews. I can make all of my research available to you."

"Why give it to me?" he asked. "I told you I won't be leading the investigation."

"Yes, but you're the brother of one of the victims. Cutter manipulated you into helping him. You're not going to let that go. I know you'll be behind the scenes, feeding the case. That's where I want to be. With you. You're the most interesting man in this story right now."

"Ah. The story."

Eden shrugged. "I won't lie to you. I'm a writer working on a book. That's my priority. I thought the book was almost done until this whole new angle came up. Now the case is wide open again and even more shocking than it was before. I want to help you get Cutter, and in return, I hope you'll let me be a part of whatever you do. That's how it works for me, Frost. I learned about being a writer from my brother. You have to embed yourself with the subject to tell a story. You can't be an outsider. So let me go inside with you."

He felt the sensuality of her offer. He didn't think it was an accident that she used sexual language in how she talked to him. She had a frankness about her intentions that made an interview feel like a seduction. She was manipulating him, and if he called her on it, he didn't think she'd apologize. As a writer and a woman, she was used to getting her way.

"Is this really about Cutter?" he asked.

"What do you mean?"

"It feels like a personal crusade. Is this just a way to get revenge for what those boys did to you?"

"That's between me and my shrink. Does it really matter to you?"

"I guess not."

"Then let's work together."

"You first," he said.

Eden smiled again. It was the smile of someone who knew she was winning. "What do you want?"

"Everything. All your notes. Your interviews. Your draft manuscript."

"Do I need to get you to sign a nondisclosure agreement?" she asked with a flirty little smirk.

"I'm not a writer."

"All right. I'll give you everything I have. And that's a big leap of faith for me. What do I get in return?"

"I'll have to think about it."

"That sounds pretty one-sided," Eden said, pouting.

"For now."

"Well, you drive a hard bargain, but I'm in. I'll print off copies of my work tonight, and you can pick them up at my place tomorrow."

"You work fast," Frost said.

"We need to work fast. We don't have much time. I told you, I know Rudy Cutter. You don't think he's done, do you?"

Frost thought to himself, *Tick tock.*

"No, Cutter's not done," he replied. "He's going to kill again. And it's already November."

71

11

Rudy Cutter enjoyed his first beer as a free man, and it went straight to his head. He and his brother, Phil, sat at a corner table squirreled away in a Mission District bar, where he could watch the crowd. It was his old neighborhood, his old hangout. Twenty-somethings filled the floor shoulder to shoulder and spilled out into the street. The music was loud, the drinkers were loud, and the bar glowed under a dozen television screens mounted high on the walls. The Warriors were playing the Bucks.

To the people who didn't know him, Rudy was anonymous. He wanted it that way. He wore a white Warriors cap low on his forehead and sunglasses despite the darkness of the bar. Even so, he knew he was being watched. Two men at a nearby table kept looking over their shoulders at him. Two more near the door filmed him surreptitiously from their phones.

"Cops," he murmured to his brother.

Phil's gaze flicked casually around the bar. "They're itching for any excuse to bust you again."

"Yeah, they'll send somebody over to start a fight soon so they can take me in. Count on it."

He turned his attention back to his beer. Phil was already on his second.

Rudy's brother was only a year younger, but Phil had gone downhill during the time Rudy had spent inside and was so skinny now that his bones showed through his skin. Phil's hair was black but thinning. He drank hard and smoked hard, and it showed in his sallow, sunken face. He had a rumbling voice and raspy cough. He was gruff with everyone, a curmudgeon who'd never married. They'd lived together for a long time. After Hope. After Wren. It had been a bland existence for both of them, two lifetimes whittled away watching sports and drinking in places like this.

"Listen, about the house," Phil said. "Neighbors aren't crazy about all the police and reporters hanging around."

Rudy rubbed his chin. He needed a shave, and he needed a shower. "You want me to stay away?"

"Just keep a low profile when you come by. Wait until dark. Use the back."

"Okay."

His brother lowered his voice. "Are you going to need an alibi for anything?"

"I'll let you know."

"I got some money for you," Phil added. "A couple thousand bucks. That should buy you time."

"Where'd you get it?" Rudy asked.

"A few small jobs." Phil waggled his fingers. He'd always been good with locks. He'd been caught a few times, but the cash-strapped California jails didn't have room for low-level thieves.

Rudy took another casual swig from his beer. "Did you a find a guy for the switch tonight?"

"Yeah, he's sitting at the end of the bar."

Rudy followed Phil's glance and spotted a man nursing a whiskey rocks by himself. He was at least ten years younger than Rudy, but they could make it work. Their build was similar. The man wore sunglasses, a loose 49ers jersey, and tan corduroys. A navy knit cap covered his forehead and ears.

"What did you tell him?" Rudy asked.

"Nothing. For fifty bucks, he didn't ask questions. I text him, we're good to go."

"Okay," Rudy said. "I'll call you as soon as I can. You have the burner phones?"

"You bet. So what are you going to do, Rudy?"

"Don't worry about it."

"Hey, I never interfere, but you're out, man. That's huge. Maybe you should think about getting out of town. San Francisco is too hot right now. Everyone's keeping an eye out for you. You could head to LA or Reno or someplace like that. You could start over. Or at least lay low for a while."

"I've got things to do. Now text your friend, and let's go."

His brother whipped off a quick text on his phone. Out of the corner of his eye, Rudy saw the man at the bar grab his phone and make an awkward, obvious survey of the crowded room. Fortunately, no one saw him; no one cared. The man climbed off the bar stool and pushed through the crowd toward the narrow hallway leading to the men's restroom.

Rudy waited until the man was gone, and then he got out of the chair. A dozen eyes in the bar followed him as he got up. He pretended not to notice. He signaled the bartender with two fingers. *Two more beers over here.*

Then he headed for the restroom.

The door was closed, but he rapped his knuckles on the wood, and the man from the bar opened it a crack and looked outside. Rudy pushed past him into the tiny room and locked the door behind them. There wasn't much space for the two of them inside. A single dim light-bulb overhead cast shadows. The sink was dirty and wet, and the toilet stank.

"Get undressed," Rudy said. "Fast."

"What?"

"You heard me."

Without waiting for the other man, Rudy yanked off his own suit coat and quickly stripped off his tie and unbuttoned his dress shirt. He kicked off his shoes, undid his belt, unzipped his pants, and stood in the bathroom in nothing but his underwear and socks. He shoved the man's shoulder hard.

"Move," he said.

The other man sprang into action. He pulled off his 49ers jersey, and Rudy slipped it on. Same with the man's corduroys. They switched sunglasses, and Rudy took the man's knit cap and handed over his own Warriors hat. The man squeezed into Rudy's suit, and when he struggled with the tie, Rudy reached out and did the knot and shoved it up tightly against the man's throat.

"Go straight back to the table with my brother," Rudy told him. "Sit down, and don't let anyone get a good look at your face. Drink the beer. Talk to him like you're best friends, okay?"

The man looked nervous. "I don't know about this."

"You only need to pull it off for five minutes," Rudy told him. "Phil will give you an extra twenty bucks if this works."

"Yeah, okay."

"Now get out of here," Rudy said.

He unlocked the bathroom door and shoved the man through the narrow opening, then locked the door again and waited. He counted off ninety seconds. Enough time for the man to make it back to their table and for the cops and reporters to notice the suit, the Warriors cap, and the sunglasses. Not enough time to look carefully and realize they were being conned.

Rudy opened the door. No one else was waiting to get into the bathroom. He saw the standing-room-only bar crowd ahead of him at the end of the corridor. Something happened in the basketball game;

a cheer filled the room. Everyone was distracted. He pushed casually through the throng and ignored the faces, and they ignored him. Beyond the tables, he saw the exit door, illuminated by a neon sign. He didn't look at his brother, and he hoped Phil was smart enough not to look his way.

No one saw him. No one recognized him.

He crossed the bar floor and pushed through the door into the cold, drizzly night. Across the street, halfway down the block, cops watched from inside a sedan. He ignored them and walked the other way. At the corner, he turned onto Guerrero and marched uphill with his head down and his hands in his pockets. He was in no hurry. He listened for the noise of cars turning to lay chase behind him.

None did.

At the next intersection, he ran. He sprinted through darkened streets and lost himself in the neighborhood. Back at the bar, they'd probably figured out their mistake by now, but they were too late to find him. He was already gone.

He slowed to a walk and found a deserted park where he could sit and enjoy the San Francisco air. But not for long.

Someone was waiting for him.

She just didn't know it yet.

12

Frost turned into the parking garage across from Pier 39.

It was late, and most of the tourists were back in their hotels, except for a few couples wandering hand in hand past the fairy lights of the Wharf. The garage itself was largely empty of cars. He drove to the third floor and parked near the elevated walkway that led over the Embarcadero to the shops and restaurants. He got out and wandered into the midnight air. From the far side of the pier, he heard the 24/7 barking of the sea lions who made a home there. The smell of fish wafted in the air.

In the shadows, no more than twenty yards away, Jess waited for him. Her spiky bangs looked longer and messier than usual. She wore a heavy jacket against the wind that emphasized her bulky physique. A cigarette hung from her mouth, as it usually did.

He joined her at the railing. "This is sort of like Deep Throat, isn't it? A parking garage at midnight?"

"I've got spies at my place," Jess told him through a cloud of smoke. Her apartment building was only a few blocks away on Kearny Street. "I had to lose somebody when I left."

"You think it's the press?"

"Maybe. Or maybe Hayden is making sure you and I don't talk. I'm radioactive. Nobody is supposed to have any contact with me."

Captain Hayden was the top cop in the major-crimes unit. He was also Jess's ex-husband, and their marriage hadn't ended well. The captain had probably heard the rumors about his wife's short-lived relationship with Frost, but Frost wasn't sure if Hayden thought the affair had begun before or after their separation. Either way, he and the captain were colleagues but not friends.

"I don't care about Hayden," Frost said.

"Well, you should. This isn't your case. You should stay out of it."

"I *am* out of it. Officially, at least. But we're talking about the man who killed Katie. If Hayden doesn't like me getting involved, he can fire me, too."

Jess gave a disgusted little sigh. "Don't be stupid, Frost. You don't need to go down in flames like me. This was my mistake. I was wrong to say any of this is your fault. This is on me, not you. I knew what I was doing. I knew there'd be a hell of a price to pay if it ever came out."

They were silent for a while.

Then Frost said, "They already lost Cutter. The alert came over the radio this evening."

"Are you serious?"

"Yeah. He and his brother were at a bar. Cutter switched clothes with some guy in the men's room. By the time the cops following him figured it out, he was long gone."

"What did Cutter's brother say?"

"That he has no idea where Rudy went. Which is probably true. He says he told him to leave town and start over somewhere else."

"You think that's what Cutter did?" Jess asked.

"No."

"Me neither," she agreed. She lowered her voice, even though no one was around to hear them. "Listen, I need to tell you something. After we talked last time, I printed out everything about the investigation from my computer. I copied as much as I could from the murder boxes, too. I didn't know how long I'd have access to any of it. I know the judge said we have to throw out my research, but if you want it, it's yours. No one has to know."

Frost frowned. It was tempting. Jess had built an encyclopedia of information about the Golden Gate Murders over five years, and without her legwork, they had nothing. Even so, the risk was too great.

"If I find something because of notes you give me, people will ask how I got it, and I'll have to tell them. We'll be right back where we are now. The judge will toss it. I have to start over."

Jess shrugged. "Okay. So how can I help?"

"Point me in a direction. Tell me where to start looking."

"I wish I could," Jess replied. "I worked this case for years and got nowhere. There was almost no hard evidence. No DNA, no fingerprints, no witnesses. Cutter was too smart. Everything other than the watch was circumstantial. We could place him near some of the vics and crime scenes. That's all."

"There must be something else."

"I'm just saying that you won't nail him with forensics. If there was something to find, I would have found it. The only way you'll get Cutter now is if you can tie him directly to the victims."

He waited for her to explain. Jess finished one cigarette and immediately lit another.

"The thing is, Cutter makes plans," she went on. "You should have seen the files he wrote up when he was an underwriter. Unbelievable detail. Page after page of analysis about the pros and cons."

"What am I supposed to take away from that?" Frost asked.

"A methodical guy like Cutter doesn't pick random women off the street. And it wasn't sexual. He's not your typical pervy serial killer. There was no rape, no molestation, on any of them. So why did he pick these particular women as victims? My original theory was that it had something to do with Wren—that he was taking some kind of twisted revenge for his daughter's murder—but I'm not convinced I was right about that."

"He met Nina Flores on her twenty-first birthday," Frost reminded her. "Wren would have turned twenty-one the same year. That seems like more than a coincidence."

"Maybe, but after Nina, age didn't seem to be a factor. The other victims had nothing in common with each other or with Wren. We had seven different women, and none of them knew each other. None of them lived near each other. They didn't share a physical type. I didn't find any overlap in places they'd gone or people they knew. I couldn't find any intersection between their lives and Cutter's life. And yet I knew there had to be a connection that ties these women together. I simply missed what it was."

"I'm not likely to catch something you didn't, Jess."

"Well, you have one advantage," she replied.

"What's that?"

"Katie. You know her life backward and forward. If anyone can figure out why Cutter picked her, you can."

"I didn't figure it out back then," Frost said.

"You weren't a cop back then. And this was my case, not yours."

Frost knew she was right. That was the worst part of what lay ahead. He was going to have to dive back into Katie's life. More than that, he was going to have to dive back into Katie's death, which was something he wished he could forget. He'd been starting to make the tiniest peace with the past, and now it was in his face again.

"I have one more question for you," he said.

"Sure."

"Do you know Eden Shay?"

"The writer? Yeah, I know her."

"She's doing a book about the Golden Gate Murders. She's amassed a lot of research, and she offered to share it with me, in case it helps with the investigation."

"What's the catch?" Jess asked.

"I have to let her shadow me."

"Yeah, she approached me a long time ago with the same proposal," Jess told him. "We had just found Natasha Lubin, the third victim. Shay wanted to 'embed' with me. Be a silent observer of the whole investigation. A fly on the wall. In return, she'd give me copies of her research and interviews."

"What did you say?"

"I said no. I didn't need a writer slowing me down or second-guessing me. Besides, she was a crime victim herself, and victims usually bring baggage and agendas. Of course, in retrospect, maybe I should have agreed. She might have spotted something that I missed."

"Do you think I should do a deal with her?" Frost asked.

"That depends. If you do this, she'll make your whole life an open book. You may not like what she writes."

"I know that."

"Well, if you're prepared for what it means, then go for it. She may be able to help you more than I can."

"Thanks."

A sarcastic smile played across Jess's lips. "By the way, I've seen what Eden Shay looks like. Remember, Frost, the term is 'embed.' Not 'in bed.'"

◆ ◆ ◆

Jess walked alone on Kearny Street from the Embarcadero, leaving the bay and the piers behind her. She kept her head down into the wind and used an impatient stride. Her hands were buried in the pockets of her heavy coat. It was after midnight, and she had the neighborhood to herself. Her building was two blocks away, where the street ended at a sharp wooded cliff below Chestnut Street.

When she reached the park next to her building, she stopped for a last cigarette. The park was a square of green space, with leafy trees quaking in the wind and neatly trimmed hedges crowding the sides of the adjacent buildings. She stood on the sidewalk, not hurrying. Moments of freedom like this were going to disappear for her soon, and she needed to savor them. Everything was about to change in her life. The DA would be coming after her.

She pinched the cigarette between her fingers and exhaled through pursed lips. The smoke vanished into the gloom of the park. It was a strangely dark night. Too dark, in fact. Four lampposts typically glowed in the square, but tonight the park wasn't lit at all, which aroused her suspicions. She ground out her cigarette, put her hands back in her pockets, and wandered toward the nearest park light.

Broken fragments of white glass littered the sidewalk. The dome had been shattered.

She knew what that meant, because she'd been expecting it. He was here. And he was hunting her.

Jess made a slow, cautious circle. She heard something nearby. Breathing. A footstep. Or maybe the wind was playing a game with her brain. She followed the hedgerow beside her building, looking behind her with every step. She traced the entire square and then made her way into the center of the muddy grass. Her eyes adjusted, and she could see into the shadows. The trees loomed in front of her, with wide, empty arms and thick trunks. She could smell the remnants of her own cigarette.

Something rustled in the bushes behind her, and Jess spun around. A small animal streaked across the square, making her jump. It was a rabbit. She laughed at herself and realized that her nerves were frayed. She was alone in the park. The broken lights were the work of kids.

Jess turned around again.

Rudy Cutter stood in front of her.

A gasp of surprise spilled from her lips, but she was ready for him. Her hand slashed from the deep pocket of her coat, and in an instant, she jumped forward with an eight-inch kitchen knife at the end of her arm, the tip of the blade poised near the bulge in Cutter's throat.

"Do you think I didn't figure you'd come for me?" Jess hissed.

Calmly, he put up his hands, palms outward, and took a step backward from her. "Easy," he said.

"You're going to have to do better than that if you want to get at me, Cutter. I'll cut your throat and not think twice about it."

His face was as dead as a zombie's in the darkness. His eyes receded into his skull, and his mouth was a grim line. "No, I don't think you will. That's not who you are."

"Yeah? Don't test me."

"If you wanted to kill me, I'd already be on the ground," Cutter said.

Jess didn't lower the knife. "So what do you want? To gloat about beating me?"

"Actually, I feel bad for you, Jess. You've lost your job. You'll probably be heading to prison. Trust me, you won't like it there. Was it really worth it?"

"Yes, it was," Jess said.

Cutter shrugged. "And yet here I am. Right back where we started. I'm free again."

"We got four years with you nowhere near a woman."

"At the price of your whole life," Cutter said.

"I don't care."

"You must be disappointed in Frost Easton. He could have saved you, and he didn't."

"Frost does what's right, even when he's wrong."

"So I hear. That's why I picked him."

"Watch out for Frost. He's a better cop than me."

"Really?"

"That's right. You're smart, but he's smarter."

"Then this should be interesting. Will he cheat like you did to win?"

"I hope you don't expect me to apologize for not playing by the rules."

"I don't. The question is how far you're willing to go to stop me."

Cutter stepped closer again. His hands were still in the air, and she still had the knife poised at the end of her fingers. He bent down until the point of the blade pushed into the cartilage of his own windpipe. Any harder, and blood would flow. His black eyes locked with hers across the darkness.

"Do it," he whispered. "You said you wouldn't even think twice."

"That's right."

"Well, here I am, Jess. Kill me. This will be your only chance."

She felt sweat on her palm, and she was dizzy. Each of the faces of the seven victims flashed in her brain, echoing what he said: *Do it.* If he stayed free, there would be more bodies. All she had to do was jab the knife, thrust and rip. Sever his throat, watch him slowly succumb to death, exactly as he'd done to so many others. She didn't care about the consequences for herself.

Do it.

Instead, Jess drew back the knife and secured it in her pocket again. She'd finally found one line that she couldn't cross.

Cutter didn't say a word, but she felt his smug satisfaction, as if he knew her better than she knew herself. Even giving her the chance to kill him, he knew she wouldn't take it. Just like he must have known that Frost would never throw that watch off the Golden Gate Bridge.

"Good-bye for now, Jess."

Cutter backed away from her until he was at the fringe of the park. Then he turned without a word and melted into the night.

13

"Talk to me, Katie," Frost murmured aloud.

His sister had all the answers, but she wasn't here to tell him what had really happened to her.

Instead, Shack walked across the dashboard of the Suburban, put his front paws over the steering wheel, and shoved his wet nose against Frost's beard. Shack had never gotten the message that cats weren't supposed to like cars. He put up a fuss to accompany Frost whenever he left the house, and some days, Frost gave in and let the cat ride along with him.

It was nine o'clock in the morning on a cool, sunny day. He was parked in the heart of the flower-power area, near Haight and Clayton. Wild, psychedelic colors adorned the storefronts. He could buy hemp clothes, shop for original Grateful Dead LPs, and get any part of his body pierced and tattooed here. If he wanted a rainbow-colored cat, he could get Shack's fur painted, too.

He was outside the hole-in-the-wall restaurant called Haight Pizza that had been serving up wood-fired pies with outlandish toppings since the Summer of Love. Frost had an artist friend, Herb, who'd grown up in that era and had a gallery a few blocks away. Herb swore he'd been to Haight Pizza on its very first day of operation in 1967. They made edamame pizzas. Sushi pizzas. Twinkie pizzas. If you knew the secret code word, you could get marijuana pizzas, too.

On a Thursday night six years ago, at eight thirty on March 10, Katie had scribbled down an order for a pizza delivery to a man named Todd Clary at 415 Parker. His address was half a mile away near the University of San Francisco campus. She wasn't even supposed to make the delivery herself, but the other driver had been late getting back. It was dark when Katie left. Frost could imagine her bouncing out of the restaurant door in a T-shirt and jeans, long blond hair tied in a ponytail, Todd Clary's olive-and-arugula pizza with garlic cream sauce balanced on her palm. She'd whipped away in her imperial-blue Chevy Malibu. Headlights on. Probably speeding.

And then—what?

It was a mystery.

Todd Clary never got his pizza. No one saw Katie or her Malibu again until Frost found her after midnight at Ocean Beach. Somewhere in that half mile, Rudy Cutter intercepted her and took her.

None of it made sense. The timing of the crime didn't fit. The first of Cutter's victims, Nina Flores, had been murdered in April, but after that, every other victim died in November. Except Katie. The police initially suspected a copycat, but they soon confirmed that the watch found on Katie's wrist belonged to the previous victim, Hazel Dixon. There was no doubt they were dealing with the same killer and the same string of murders. But her death was a break in the pattern.

Why?

Frost scooped up Shack from the dashboard and put him in the passenger seat. He started the engine and headed west on Haight to retrace his sister's steps that night. No one knew the exact route Katie had taken, but the shortest route was to take Haight until it ended at Golden Gate Park and then head north before cutting over to Parker. Katie was a city native like Frost, and she would have known the fastest route.

She had only one delivery to make. She didn't need to stop anywhere between Haight and Parker, but Frost knew Katie's grasshopper mind, and he could imagine her dashing inside a store for a quick errand along the way. The route took her past a coffee shop. A record store. A bicycle shop. Whole Foods. She could have stumbled into Rudy Cutter at any of those places.

But no one remembered her. No one had seen her.

Frost turned where Golden Gate Park bordered the street on his left. He drove past the Panhandle, and three blocks later, turned right. The road ended at a T intersection across from the dome and gold columns of Saint Ignatius Church. This was Parker Avenue, where Todd Clary lived. Frost turned left and drove three more blocks. He found himself across from a two-story green apartment house with a clay-tile roof. On his right was the sharp wooded hillside of Lone Mountain near the USF campus, dotted with thick brush and trees.

That would have been the best place for the killer to take her.

At night, anyone could have hidden on the hillside, unseen. When Katie got out of the Malibu, she would have been an easy target as she reached back into the car to grab the pizza box.

Take her from behind, push her inside, and drive away. That was what Jess thought the killer had done.

As he sat in the Suburban, Frost saw a man emerge from the apartment house and stare defiantly across the street with his hands on his hips. The man was small, in his forties, with a comb-over and wire-rimmed glasses. He wore a suit and tie, although the tie was loose at his neck and the suit had seen better days. It was Todd Clary. They knew each other. Years earlier, Frost had pounded on Clary's door, demanding answers and making wild accusations. That was before he was a cop and after he'd spent a night drinking with Duane, drowning their grief over Katie's death.

Clary hadn't forgotten. He stormed across the street toward Frost.

"You!" the man shouted. "Get the hell out of here!"

Frost rolled down the window. "Mr. Clary—"

"I knew you'd be back here! I saw they released that guy, and I knew you'd be looking at me again. It never ends! Do you know how many people threw crap at my house? Do you know how many neighbors called me a killer? All because I ordered a damn pizza!"

"Mr. Clary," Frost said calmly, "I know you weren't treated fairly by anyone, including me."

"I didn't see anything! I told you people that over and over and over. I was watching TV. I ordered a pizza, and when it wasn't there an hour later, I called the store and asked where it was. That's it. The next day, I've got cops going up and down the block, searching my house, going through my garbage, talking to my boss, making my life hell. Do you think I got an apology from anybody? No!"

"I'm sorry. Really."

Clary acted as if he didn't hear him. "Even after you caught the guy, you people kept saying I had something to do with it! Like this Cutter guy had me order a pizza so he could wait outside and grab the girl. I never met him! I had no idea who he was!"

"Mr. Clary, I know you're innocent," Frost told him. "I can't say it any plainer than that. I apologize for the suspicion that landed on your head. All I can say is, what happened that night was hell for me, too."

The man breathed heavily. His face was red, and his comb-over hung in the wind like the fin of a catamaran. Even so, Frost's words got through to him. He opened his mouth, and then he clamped it shut again. Finally, he said, more quietly, "Look, I know this girl was your sister. I'm sorry for what happened to her. Nobody was happier than me to see that guy behind bars. It makes me sick to have him out on the streets again."

"Me, too. I want to get him back in prison, and that means I need to go back to the crimes he committed and figure out what we missed. That includes the night when Katie disappeared."

Clary shook his head. "I don't know what happened to her."

"I understand." Frost knew that the man was wearing his armor. Clary had been saying no, no, no for years, without even listening to what people were asking him. "This may sound strange, Mr. Clary, but you were probably the last person to talk to my sister alive."

Clary smoothed down his hair. He looked embarrassed. "I get what you're saying, but all I did was order a pizza. It's not like I had a conversation with her."

Frost laughed. "I think you may be the first person in history to say that. Katie had a rubber mouth, always talking. Most people couldn't shut her up. The restaurant guys had to keep telling her to get off the phone, because she'd have half a dozen people on hold while she was still gabbing with the last person placing an order."

Clary cocked his head. "You're right, I told the cops that. She was a chatty one. Kinda scattered, too."

"How so?" Frost asked.

"Oh, I remember she rattled off 'onions' instead of 'olives' when she read the order back to me. I was nervous she was going to get it wrong."

"That sounds like Katie."

"She was nice, though. Bubbly."

"Yeah, she was. Anything else?"

Clary shrugged. "Sorry. It was a long time ago."

"Well, I appreciate your talking to me."

"Hey, I'm not trying to be a jerk, but you're wasting your time. You're not going to find any answers at my place."

Frost nodded without replying. Clary turned around and retreated into his apartment. When the man was gone, Frost got out of the Suburban and studied the street in both directions. The neighborhood was empty. So was the wooded hillside leading up to the college. He tried to imagine Rudy Cutter at night, hiding in the bushes, but he knew that theory didn't make sense. Cutter didn't simply grab random women off the street, and there was no way he could have known in advance that Katie would be making a delivery to this address.

Todd Clary was right. Frost was wasting his time.

Somewhere in his head, he could also hear Katie talking back to him. It was as if she were sitting in his Suburban with Shack on her lap, impatiently waiting for him to drive away. Her chatty, scattered, bubbly voice called through the open window to him.

Katie said, *Get a clue, Frost. I was never here.*

14

Frost had to navigate a gauntlet of security to get to the elevators in Eden Shay's building. Eden owned a condo in the Rincon Hill neighborhood in a tower that was new, modern, and glass. When she answered the door and led him inside, he saw varnished gray wood, floor-to-ceiling windows, and appliances that were so clean he wondered if she ever used them. Her twentieth-floor flat faced east toward the Bay Bridge.

"Pretty nice place," he said, which was an understatement. It was beautiful, but it had a sterile, impersonal feel.

"Says the cop with the house on Russian Hill," Eden replied, smiling.

"That's a long story."

"I know. Your cat."

He stood at the window, but he looked back at her, impressed. She wasn't lying when she said she did her research.

"Do you want a Sierra Nevada?" she asked, as if to emphasize the point. "I bought a six-pack of Torpedo for you."

"No, thanks."

"I'm an afternoon wine gal myself, so I hope you don't mind if I indulge." She toasted him with a wineglass from the counter that was already poured high with pinot grigio. "Wine is just one of my unhealthy obsessions."

"Go ahead," Frost said.

Eden joined him by the window. Her corkscrew curls danced on her face. In her heels, she was as tall as he was. She wore gray slacks that somehow matched the colors of the condo, and her sleeveless pink blouse showed off a lot of smooth skin. Her body had a faint citrus aroma, like grapefruit.

"Why'd you choose to buy here?" he asked, watching her in profile as she drank her wine.

"I had a house when I lived in the city the first time, but a house is more work than I want right now. I was looking to go simpler and smaller when I came back. This building is mostly filled with finance geeks and corporate lawyers. Not exactly my type, but that's okay. I don't hang out with the neighbors."

"Who do you hang out with?" Frost asked.

"An Aussie girl like me? Mostly midgets, priests, and carnival workers."

He realized she was teasing him, and he smiled. He also felt guilty because his gaze kept drifting to the scar on her neck. It made him feel like a cliché, because he was sure that everyone she met did the same thing. She drank more wine, then ran one of her fingers along the zipper-like seam in her skin.

"Do you want to ask me about it?" she said.

"Only if you want to talk about it."

"Well, the kid hesitated when he slashed me," Eden told him. "That's what saved my life. He'd never killed anyone before. He didn't go deep enough, and then he didn't stick around to make sure I bled out. He and his brother just wanted to get the hell away from me after it was done. They were scared to death. More scared than me. Isn't that strange? My brother always told me that a writer had to be aware of every single moment. The whole time in that basement, I was so focused on remembering the experience that I was never scared."

"Was it hard to write about it?"

"It was like living it all over again," she admitted. "It nearly killed me. After I wrote the scene about them cutting me open, do you know what I did? I spent two weeks volunteering at an animal shelter that had to perform euthanasia on cats and dogs."

"Why on earth would you do that to yourself?"

"Because I needed to cry over and over, constantly, for days, without stopping. So that's what I did. And because I felt as unwanted as those animals."

Frost didn't know what to say. It was horrifying to imagine what the brothers had done to her, but almost more horrifying to think about the emotional suffering she was willing to inflict on herself. Eden projected an aura of dormant calm, but he felt as if he were staring into a volcano at a churning, melting river of lava. All these years, because of Katie, he'd thought of himself as a crime victim. But talking to Eden, he realized that he'd never had a clue what being a victim was really like. What she'd gone through was never over; it simply reemerged in her life in different forms like a nightmarish shape-shifter.

"Do you hate the brothers for what they did to you?" he asked.

"No, they're too pathetic to waste an important emotion like hatred on them. And the irony is that they gave me my life. For all the savagery they inflicted on me, I'm where I am today because of those vicious little boys."

"That's true of me and Rudy Cutter, too. He's why I'm a cop."

"And do you hate him for what he did?" Eden asked.

"Yes, I do."

Eden nodded, but she didn't say anything. He wondered if she thought he was wrong to feel that way. Or maybe she was lying to cover up how much hatred she felt herself.

"How did you wind up in the US originally?" Frost asked, changing the subject and trying to pull her away from the worst of her past.

"We moved here when I was a teenager. My mom was American. A teacher from South Carolina. She met my dad on an ecotourism trip in

Costa Rica. They got married and lived in Melbourne for twenty years, but eventually, we moved to New York when Dad got a job offer with one of the global finance partnerships. My brother was already studying journalism at Columbia, so it made sense."

"Is your mom still alive?"

"No, it's just me. Mom died not long after we came to the States. Then we lost my brother in Afghanistan. And now my dad. I'm an orphan."

"Sorry."

Eden turned away from him and pointed at three boxes stacked beside the condo door. He got the message; she didn't want to talk about herself anymore. "Those are copies of my notes. The draft manuscript, too, at least as far as I've taken it. You can bring everything with you. I hope it helps."

"I appreciate your sharing it with me."

"It's not free, you know. I have a price. I want to be part of your investigation."

"Embedded?" Frost said.

"That's right."

"Do you want to move in with me and Shack?" he joked.

"Say yes, and I will." She wasn't joking.

"Jess thinks it's a bad idea to let you get too close to me."

"Maybe she's right. I won't stop until I know everything about you."

"Really?"

"Really. Let's start with Jess. Are you sleeping with her?"

The question came out of nowhere, and it set him on his heels. "No."

"That's not what I hear."

He should have lied, but he was tired of lying about it. "Okay, yes, we had a brief affair. It's been over for a long time."

"Interesting. She's rough-and-tumble. You're polished. She's older, too. And she was married, right?"

"She was separated when it happened."

"You don't have to apologize for it."

"I'm not apologizing," Frost said.

"I know what Jess says about being willing to cross 'the line.' Several cops told me about it. Was she wrong to do what she did with the watch?"

"Cutter's back on the streets now, so yes."

"What if no one had found out? Would it still be wrong?"

"Yes."

"Would you have done the same thing?"

"No."

"Even if it meant more women dying?"

"Yes."

Eden pursed her lips, as if she were impressed with him. "Personally, I think Jess made the right call. We all cross lines. Sometimes you have to be willing to go too far to get the story. That's what my brother always said."

"When cops do it, we break laws."

"So you really are a Boy Scout."

"I guess so," Frost replied.

She grinned with satisfaction, as if they'd gone through a round of foreplay. She had half a glass of wine left, but she finished it in a single swallow. Her curls shook as she tossed her head. "Well, that was fun."

"Is that what that was?"

"It was fun for me. Do you want to talk some more? Or would you like to do something else?"

"I have to go."

"Right. Duty calls. I'll get someone to bring the boxes to your car."

Frost wandered over to the boxes that were stacked by the door. He tipped up the lid of the topmost box. Inside, he saw a stack of neatly printed manuscript pages. This was her story of the Golden Gate Murders. He read the words on the title page.

95

"*The Voice Inside*," he said aloud. He could hear Katie's voice inside his head, saying those same words when she was a child. "Why did you choose that as a title?"

"It's from a poem by Shel Silverstein. But I suspect you already know that, Frost."

"Yes, I do. Katie loved that poem as a kid. She'd recite it all the time. She had it framed over her bed for years."

"I know. I saw it on the bedroom wall when I met your parents. It's the kind of quirky little detail I look for."

"That doesn't answer my question," Frost said. "Why use it in your book?"

"You know the poem. It's about listening to the voice inside to decide what's right and what's wrong. No one else can decide for you. It seems to me that everyone in this case has had to decide at some point in their lives whether to listen to the voice inside. Hope. Cutter. Even Jess."

"And now me?" Frost asked.

"That's right. And now you, too. You had to decide on the bridge whether you were going to destroy that watch. I don't think that will be the last time you have to make a choice like that, Frost. You're not done."

15

Four years in San Quentin had given Rudy Cutter eyes in the back of his head. After a while, you could feel when someone was stalking you, and that was what kept you alive. He relied on that intuition now to make sure that no one was watching him, because the police and media had plastered his face everywhere.

He walked north on Stockton toward the tunnel that carved its way under Bush Street. He wore a dirty black hoodie, wraparound sunglasses, and jeans. He hadn't shaved since he was released, and his beard was filling in like a wire brush. A backpack was slung over one shoulder. The crowded sidewalk made him wary, but no one looked at anyone else here. This was a melting pot where city neighborhoods converged. Upscale shops and hotels bled out of Union Square. Lawyers from the Financial Center squeezed into dim sum restaurants in Chinatown. Vape shops and massage parlors marked the fringe of the Tenderloin.

He stopped at a taqueria for lunch, but he took his order to go and ate it in the shadows of the Bush Street tunnel, where he could watch people come and go from the building across the street. White men in suits visited the Asian sauna. A homeless man with greasy hair limped past the liquor store and stuck his hand out at the customers. Two fifty-something women floated from the nail salon, caught up in their own world as if the people around them didn't exist. Buses came and went, sucking up and belching out a dozen people at a time.

He waited an hour.

No cops. It was safe to go inside.

Rudy crossed the street to an eight-story apartment building. Fire escapes dangled over his head. He buzzed the number of an apartment on the fifth floor and pushed through the entrance door when it clicked open. He took the stairs rather than the elevator to avoid being seen. He found the number he was looking for and drummed his knuckles on the apartment door. As he waited, he listened to the empty hallway, but all he heard was the noise of the television inside.

An eighty-year-old man in a wheelchair opened the door. His gray hair cropped up in tufts, and his skin was pallid and saggy. He had a thick crocheted blanket spread over his lap, and his feet jutted out from under the blanket, in worn brown dress shoes with no socks. He wore blind man's sunglasses, and his face pointed straight ahead, not looking up or down.

"I called a couple hours ago," Rudy said. "You've got a Taser for sale?"

"Yeah, yeah, come in."

The man wheeled backward, and Rudy eyed the studio apartment, which didn't look much bigger than his San Quentin cell. He could see everything with a glance. A twin bed against the wall, sheets tangled. The efficiency kitchen. The bathroom with toilet and shower. A window looking out on the street. The walls had chipped yellow paint and were decorated with an odd mix of movie posters. He saw Sean Connery in *Goldfinger*. Herbie the Love Bug. A porn flick with Marilyn Chambers.

A square twenty-four-inch television, balanced on cinder blocks, blared *Jeopardy!* at a volume that made Rudy want to cover his ears.

"My name's Jimmy Keyes," the man barked. "Who are you?"

"Carl Smith," Rudy lied.

Keyes snorted at the name, as if he didn't believe for a second that it was real. His lips pulled back from brown teeth. "How did you find me?"

"You put up a flier in a bar a couple blocks away."

"And you want to buy my Taser, Carl Smith?"

"That's right."

"Why?"

Rudy shrugged and made up a story. "Somebody's been hassling my wife. I want her to carry some protection."

"Yeah? Why not buy a new one? Why come to me?"

"I had a problem with the law a few years ago. I think traditional sellers might not be too crazy to sell to me."

"You realize these babies have serial numbers, right? You fire this thing, it sprays little ID tags. Easiest thing in the world for the police to trace it back to me. If you use it, I get cops at my door. I don't like that."

"That's why I'm paying you two hundred dollars more than it's worth," Rudy said.

"Fair point," Keyes agreed.

"Why does a blind man have a Taser, anyway?" Rudy asked.

"I wasn't always blind. Damn cataracts."

Rudy wandered to the window over the street. He glanced out at the fire escape. As he did, he slipped a pair of plastic gloves out of his pocket and silently pulled them over his fingers. He turned away from the window and lifted a foam pillow from the twin bed beside the wall. Bending down close to Keyes, he waved a hand in front of the old man's sunglasses, no more than an inch away. Keyes didn't flinch. Rudy grabbed a wooden chair from the small kitchen table and sat on it and put the pillow on the floor next to him.

"So where's the Taser?" he asked.

"Where's the money?" Keyes asked.

Rudy slipped a stack of bills from his pocket and slapped it in the old man's open palm. Keyes closed his fingers over the cash.

"I better not find out you're shorting me," Keyes said.

"It's all there."

"Okay. The Taser's in that case on the floor."

Rudy spotted a small hard-shell case by the wall. He placed the case on his lap and unlatched it. Inside was a black-and-yellow Taser and four cartridges, each packed with probes and fifteen feet of wire. One of the cartridges already had its shipping cover removed. It was ready to go.

"You ever use one of these things?" Keyes asked.

"Yeah, I know how they work."

"Well, I'm not taking any chances with you being an amateur. Let me show you."

Keyes flicked his fingers at him, and Rudy slid the case into the old man's lap. Without tilting his head down, Keyes gracefully removed the Taser and cradled it in his wrinkled hand.

"The battery pack is fully charged and loaded. I always keep it that way. The safety is right here. Down is safe, and you click it up when you want to fire. The cartridge clicks on the front. Easy peasey, like this, see? Just don't stick your fingers in there, got it?"

"Got it," Rudy said.

Keyes flicked up the safety switch. A red laser dot appeared on the apartment wall.

"You can turn on an LED light for better sighting at night," he said, "or you can just use the laser. This thing fires two probes, which is what completes the electrical circuit and turns the person you're shooting at into jelly. It works fine through clothes, but don't be more than ten feet away, or you'll probably miss. Key is to aim the laser high on the chest. One probe goes straight, and the other goes about eight degrees down. You don't want the second probe missing between the guy's legs."

"Right."

"Like this," Keyes told him.

The old man swiveled the gun, and the red laser dot appeared like a shiny bead on Rudy's chest. Rudy shouted in alarm, but before he could leap out of the way, Keyes fired. Instantaneously, Rudy collapsed backward onto the floor, the chair spilling free. His limbs twitched; he was rubber, unable to control any of his muscles. His body was on fire, his blood carrying acid to every nerve end, corroding him from inside.

"See, the thing is, Rudy Cutter," Keyes told him, yanking off his sunglasses and pulling the trigger again and again to add more juice to the probes, "I've only got a cataract in *one* eye, and I know exactly who you are. You're that piece of shit who just got out of prison after killing all those women. Now here you are, looking to buy a Taser from me? I don't think so. And you didn't grab that pillow off my bed so you could take a nap, did you? You're not concerned about the ID tags this thing blows off, because you figure when the cops trace the tags back to me, I'll be dead on the floor with that pillow on my face."

Keyes reached between his legs under the crocheted blanket and came out with a black-handled revolver. He dropped the Taser on the floor and then used his thumb to drag back the hammer and cock the weapon. He pointed it at Rudy, who lay on his back as the jolts of current finally drained from his body.

Rudy felt pummeled, as if a hammer had come down on all his bones. The pain rolled like marbles around his brain. He propped himself up, balancing on his elbows. His breathing came heavily, and his eyes stung as he squinted at the barrel of the gun, pointed at his head, no more than six feet away. His fists clenched and unclenched, in a tic of humiliation and rage. He didn't like being outsmarted. Not by Jess Salceda. Not by Jimmy Keyes. Not by anyone.

"So now what happens?" Rudy gasped, trying to calm his frenzied heartbeat so he could think. "You shoot me?"

"Now I call the cops, and we wait until they get here."

"You assaulted me," Rudy said. "You're the one they're going to arrest."

"Oh, I'll take my chances. The cops are going to think it's pretty interesting that you're here trying to buy a weapon off the books."

"Look, you're right about who I am. I lied. The Taser is for my own defense, that's all. Every vigilante on the street is looking to kill me. They want to be heroes by taking me down."

"Don't tempt me," Keyes told him. "I may do that myself. I've got a granddaughter in her twenties. Same age as the women you cut up. She'd be a lot safer if I put a bullet in your head. It wouldn't be hard to come up with a story, you know. You rushed me, I shot you. No one's going to care what happens to you, Rudy Cutter. So reach back and grab the phone and toss it over here before I change my mind and drill one into your skull, okay?"

Rudy sat up and put his hands in the air. "Take it easy. Whatever you say."

"Slowly. I have an itchy trigger finger."

"I couldn't move fast if I wanted to," Rudy said. "That thing packs a punch."

He got up from the floor with a groan. His body swayed from dizziness, but he exaggerated his movements to make himself look more unsteady than he really was. The effects of the Taser were short-lived. Below him, Keyes sat in the wheelchair, looking small. Behind the old man's cockiness, Rudy could see a nervous tremble of fear. Keyes tried to hold the revolver steady, but his hand shook, and he squinted to stay focused. His good eye was worse than he let on.

Rudy grabbed the phone from its cradle. The television was still on and still loud, blaring out the voice of Alex Trebek. He turned toward the old man and stopped, the muscles in his face twitching. Keyes watched him, jumpy and jittery. Rudy's eyes never left the barrel of the gun. It wobbled like a toy in the man's hand, pointing left, right, up, and down.

"Here," Rudy said, extending the phone but keeping it just out of the old man's grasp.

"Toss it." Keyes leaned forward, his empty hand stretching out.

"Whatever you say."

Rudy threw the phone over the old man's head and then dropped to one knee and grabbed for the gun. Keyes fired in panic, sending a bullet into the wall above the television. Rudy's hand locked around the brittle wrist that held the gun, shoving the old man's arm sideways and squeezing it in a vise until Keyes loosened his fingers. The revolver dropped to the wooden floor.

He leaned in to the man's terrified face.

"See, *the thing is*, Jimmy Keyes, I really don't like people getting in the way of my plans," Rudy whispered.

He put one gloved hand behind the man's head. The other clenched his neck, choking off any sound. He watched Keyes's eyes widen, his mouth forming an O, knowing what was going to happen. With one quick, vicious snap, Rudy shoved the old man's skull forward until his neck broke with a sickening crack. Keyes's whole body jerked, as if he'd taken a shot from the Taser. Air gurgled from the man's lungs with a long, labored sigh.

Rudy straightened up. He listened to the roar of the game show, then used the remote control to switch off the television. In the background, the building was silent. If anyone had heard the shot, they didn't care. No one came running. No one called the cops.

His head still buzzed from the electric shock. He disentangled himself calmly from the probes and wires of the Taser and then unzipped his backpack and stuffed the Taser and the revolver inside. When he was done, he did a survey of the studio to make sure that there was nothing left behind that might point to his presence there. No fingerprints. No DNA.

The old man wasn't quite gone yet. His lungs gurgled.

Rudy was hungry. He checked the refrigerator and found a recent deli bag of sliced turkey. He sat on the bed, finished the turkey, and watched the traffic crawling on the street outside as he waited for Keyes to die.

16

Frost tried to decide what he felt about Eden Shay.

He didn't particularly like her. She was a desert saguaro, with a prickly wall around herself to keep away intruders. He sensed a degree of cruelty and instability about her; the only person she would ever put first was herself. As a writer, she would collect all his secrets without sharing any of her own. And yet he also admired her cool calculations, her in-your-face aggressiveness, her drive to get exactly what she wanted. She'd made her physical intentions toward him crystal clear, and her candor had an erotic appeal.

Do you want to talk some more? Or do you want to do something else?

It had been a long time since he'd slept with a woman. Not since Jess. And sex with Eden would be risky because nothing was off the record with her. If she wound up in his bed, she'd make it another chapter in her book.

That didn't stop him from thinking about it.

Frost got up from his sofa by the bay window. It was dark, midevening. Shack slept on his back on the floor, exposing his white stomach without a care in the world. The house smelled of cinnamon, but that was only because his dinner had consisted of two brown sugar–cinnamon Pop-Tarts. There had been no care packages left in his refrigerator since his argument with Duane earlier in the month, and his meals had been mostly takeout.

He went upstairs to the walk-in closet where he kept all the boxes that made up his past. He remembered seeing Eden's Iowa memoir in the Katie box, and he dug out the book. He brought it back downstairs to the sofa with him. The first thing he did was study Eden's photo on the back cover. It was an unusual photograph, but very Eden, now that he knew her. She wasn't in close-up; she was far away from the camera, difficult to see in detail. She sat on the second-floor balcony of her San Francisco house, in a precarious pose, with her legs dangling through the railing. The balcony was held in place by what looked like a stone rope emerging from the mouth of a lion attached to the building wall. Below her legs, he could see two horrific gargoyles mounted above the house's front door.

Her face was younger, angrier, and more raw. Her hair was even fuller. This was a woman who had something to prove. She looked in jeopardy, surrounded by sculpted monsters. The scar on her neck was covered by the cotton fabric of a yellow turtleneck that matched the paint of the house.

Frost opened Eden's memoir to a random page. He read a few lines, then closed it again. He almost felt as if he were a voyeur spying on an intimate moment in her life, even though she had put it out there for the world to see.

He stared at her research boxes about the Golden Gate Murders, which he'd left on the floor near the sofa. He went to the kitchen, opened a pale ale, and returned to the living room to sit down again. Shack made a small, annoyed groan at all the activity. Frost apologized to the cat, then propped his feet on the coffee table and lifted the printed manuscript pages from the box.

The Voice Inside.

He turned to the prologue of Eden's book, which started with the first meeting of Nina Flores and Rudy Cutter in the coffee shop at the Ferry Building. He could hear Eden's voice in his head, like the narrator of an audio book, as he read what she'd written. He liked her quirky style and insights. She looked for unusual details, the fragments of a life that told you who a person really was.

With Nina, it was the fluffy brown hair piled on her head like a chocolate ice cream cone and dripping down the sides of her face. That image summed up Nina. Sweet but a little messy.

With Cutter, it was the melted ice in his latte, the way he stayed and stayed at the coffee counter long after his cold drink had turned warm. In Eden's hands, the ice slowly sweating into the coffee became a scene out of a horror movie, as something grotesque and dark took shape inside Cutter's head.

Frost spent an hour reading before he put aside the manuscript pages.

He realized that Eden had a good eye for the things about a crime that were important. Her first chapter cut to the heart of everything. This mystery had begun right there in the Ferry Building. The chain started with Nina Flores, and typically the oldest link in the chain was the easiest to break.

Was Cutter already thinking about murder when he met Nina? No. You don't hand your credit card to a girl you were thinking of killing a few days later. So what happened between them in the coffee shop that electrified Rudy Cutter? Twenty years had already passed since Cutter's wife murdered their daughter, and as far as anyone knew, he had never been a violent man. And then came Nina, a girl he'd never met, a pretty, innocent girl on her twenty-first birthday. Cutter met Nina, and suddenly he pried open his coffin door like a vampire discovering the night.

Why?

Why did Cutter sit there and make his plans to murder Nina as the ice melted in his drink?

Frost didn't see any answers in Eden's book, but she had given him a place to start. He went back to the third page of the manuscript, where he'd underlined a passage:

Days later, weeks later, years later, nobody at the coffee shop remembered Rudy. Nina's best friend, Tabby Blaine, prepared his order, but she didn't notice anything about him other than iced latte, dark roast, extra ice, no straw. How was he dressed? No idea. Was he angry, happy, sad? Not a clue. Rudy didn't make an impression. To Tabby, to everybody he met, Rudy was an invisible man.

Tabby Blaine.

Tabby wasn't just Nina's childhood friend, she was also Nina's coworker.

His brother was dating a woman who had been there at the exact moment when the destinies of Nina Flores and Rudy Cutter collided.

17

By ten o'clock at night, the food trucks of SoMa had closed their windows, and the customers were gone. Even so, Frost knew that Duane typically stayed late into the night, cleaning up from dinner and prepping for the next day's lunch menu. More often than not, his brother slept in his truck.

But he didn't usually sleep alone.

The street food park was located in the shadows of the 101 freeway, in an area of warehouses and parking lots. The guard at the gate knew him and rolled back the barbed-wire fence to let him inside. Every time he came here, the food trucks were different, but Duane's Asian-Mediterranean fusion truck was one of the anchors, always in the same place at the back. The smells of dinner lingered around him, from shawarma to fish tacos.

The truck was locked up tight, but he heard Duane's voice and a woman's musical laughter. When he rapped his knuckles on the door, Duane answered it, smiling, but his smile was quickly replaced by a scowl.

"What do you want, Frost?"

"Hi to you, too. Can I come in?"

"Depends. Do you have a warrant?"

"That's funny, Duane."

Frost climbed inside the truck. He squeezed past his brother, who was wearing shorts and a T-shirt that read "Keep on Truckin'." Duane squirted a thick orange liquid into his mouth from a plastic bottle. His brother had a bizarre fondness for carrot juice.

Tabby sat on the floor at the other side of the truck, with her bare legs and bare feet stretched out. She looked at home wherever she was. She had a beer bottle in her hand, her red hair was mussed, and so were the buttons on her clothes. The zipper on her skirt was partly undone. He'd obviously interrupted something.

"Sorry to barge in on you two," Frost said.

"If you want dinner, you're too late," Duane said. His brother leaned close to his face and smelled his breath. "Pop-Tarts? Really?"

"The care packages have been a little skimpy lately."

"Yeah, well, I've been busy. You could learn to cook, you know."

"Shack has a better chance of learning to cook than me," Frost replied.

Duane took another squirt of carrot juice and didn't say anything more. He was still angry. Frost kept stubbornly silent, too. Tabby stood up with a sigh and rebuttoned her blouse. She shoved her feet back into flats. If she was waiting for the two of them to grow up, Frost could have told her that wasn't going to happen.

"Duane Easton, apologize to your brother right now," Tabby snapped.

"For what?" he protested.

"For being a dick."

Duane opened his mouth to defend himself, but then he shrugged in resignation. It didn't take much to break the ice between the two brothers after an argument, but they typically needed outside help. "Well, that's fair. Sorry, bro."

"Hey, don't worry about it," Frost replied. "I sprang the whole Rudy Cutter thing on you, and I did it badly. Believe me, I don't like it, either."

"Have you talked to Mom and Dad?" Duane asked.

"Not since the hearing. I need to call them."

"They're flying in from Tucson tomorrow."

"What? Why?"

Tabby answered from the back of the truck. "The family support group is getting together on Saturday. With Cutter getting out, we all thought we needed to talk about what was going on."

Frost felt guilty again, as if this were his fault. "Where are Mom and Dad staying?"

"With the Holtzmans," Duane replied. "Near our old house."

"Are they pissed at me like you are?" Frost asked.

"No, they're not. And listen, bro, I'm not mad. It was just a shock."

Tabby walked over and slung an arm around Duane's waist. Her green eyes were flirty. "Okay, Beaston Boys, this is all very sweet, but speaking for myself, I'm still pretty horny, and the only way this is going to work out is for one of you to leave. Now, who's it going to be?"

For the first time in his life, Frost saw Duane at a loss for words. He began to think his brother had genuine feelings for this girl, and he could see why.

"Actually, Tabby, I wanted to talk to you," Frost said. "It won't take long."

"To me?" she answered. "The plot thickens. About what?"

"Nina."

Her face fell. The innuendo disappeared. "Oh. Of course. Sorry, here I am being inappropriate, and you're in the middle of dealing with—" She stopped, and she looked up at Duane with an apology on her face. "I'm going to let Frost steal me away for a couple minutes, okay?"

"Sure. Yeah." Duane clapped Frost on the shoulder. "I'll work on the care packages, bro."

"Thanks."

Frost descended the steps from the food truck, and Tabby followed behind him. The night air was cool, and she shivered. In the pale glow of the streetlights, her red hair looked darker, like mahogany. She still had a beer bottle in her hand. It was empty, but she played with it uncomfortably between her fingers.

"I talked to the police about Nina back then," she said.

"I know."

"What did you want to ask me?"

"You told me that you and Nina grew up together, but I didn't realize the two of you worked together, too. You were there when Rudy Cutter came to the coffee shop, right?"

Tabby's face was dark. "Yes."

"What do you remember?"

"About Cutter? Nothing. They didn't identify him as a suspect until three years after Nina was killed. When I saw his photograph, I didn't recognize him. Why would I? Except for a handful of regulars, I typically didn't remember faces. There were just too many of them."

"I was thinking more about Nina," Frost said.

"What do you mean?"

"On her birthday. What was she like?"

Tabby smiled. "That girl was so excited. Twenty-one years old! To us, that was the big time. I'd hit twenty-one a couple weeks earlier, so watch out, world. A bunch of us went to a Mexican bar in the Castro that night. Three shots of tequila, and Nina was in the bathroom throwing up."

"It's nice that you guys were so close," Frost said.

"Yeah, we were. I was the one who reported her missing the next week. The police jacked me and her family around—no offense—but I knew something was wrong. It wasn't like her to drop out of sight."

"Did she mention anything strange before she disappeared? Somebody watching her? Being followed?"

Tabby shook her head. "No."

"What about any secret boyfriends?"

"Nina? No way. She wasn't involved with anybody." Her expression became troubled. "The police didn't hide something from us back then, did they? There was no sexual assault, was there?"

"No."

"That would have made it worse."

"I know." And he did know. That had always been his darkest worry about Katie, too. Whatever twisted pathology drove Cutter, it wasn't about his sexual fantasies. This was something else.

"I'm sorry, Frost, I can't imagine why he came after Nina. Believe me, I've racked my brain all these years to think of something. Nina never hurt anybody. She was just a sweet, decent soul."

"Tell me more about her birthday," Frost said. "What was the day like at the coffee shop?"

Tabby stroked her fingers through her deep red hair with both hands. "It was fun. I got her balloons, and we tied those up everywhere. She wore a big crown all day, because it was her day, and she was the queen. She was wearing some big buttons on her T-shirt that she'd made from old photos of herself. Her high school grad photo. Me and her in her bedroom getting ready for a party. All of her siblings at Christmas. She kept singing, too. 'Happy birthday to me.'"

"What did the customers think about this?" Frost asked.

"Most of them got into it. Nina got some great tips. The men sure liked it. She was showing off the buttons on her shirt, and let's just say Nina had a lot more to show off under there than me."

"Nobody got upset?"

"Not that I remember."

Frost shook his head. He'd been to that coffee shop in the Ferry Building dozens of times. It was small. If you sat at the counter, the baristas were right in front of you. Cutter would have had plenty of time to study Nina Flores close-up while he drank his latte. The young woman would have had plenty of time to brag to him about her birthday. It was a half hour that had changed both of their lives. He just didn't know why.

"Do Nina's parents still live nearby?" Frost asked. "I want to talk to them."

"Yes, they're in the same little house on Silver Avenue they've owned for years. My parents had a place one block over, but they retired up in Oregon a couple years ago. I haven't seen Mr. and Mrs. Flores for a while now. I don't know if they'll be at the support group this weekend or not."

"Okay."

"I'm sorry, Frost, I wish I could be more help."

"No, I appreciate it, Tabby," he said. "And thanks for the other thing, too."

"For what?"

"Being a mediator between me and Duane. We need it sometimes. Stubborn Easton boys and all."

"Yeah, I picked up on that," Tabby said.

They were silent for a moment in the chilly air. He heard the noise of trucks on 101 behind them. Her cheeks were pink. She crossed her arms over her chest and stared at the ground. He felt oddly awkward around her, but he was rescued by a chime from his phone. It was a text message from Jess.

Need to see you right away.

"I have to go," Frost said.

"Of course. I understand." Tabby turned toward the food truck, but then she looked back at him with a curious smile and a toss of her red hair. "Hey, can I ask you something?"

"Sure."

"I know I'm putting you on the spot, but I was hoping you could tell me if I'm making a horrible mistake. With Duane, I mean."

"Why would you think that?" Frost asked.

Tabby rolled her eyes. "Your brother is a great guy, but he doesn't exactly have a reliable track record when it comes to relationships."

"You're right about that. All I can tell you, Tabby, is that Duane seems different around you than with other girls."

"Yeah, maybe. That's what he says, too. I like him, but I don't want to get serious with someone who's not capable of being serious. Do you know what I mean?"

"Yes, I get it."

"When I fall in love, I fall hard and fast. That's why I'm careful about what I get myself into."

Frost weighed his words and then said, "For what it's worth, I don't think you're making a mistake. Not about how Duane feels."

She stared at him, as if trying to decide whether he was simply telling her what she wanted to hear. Then she closed the distance between them again and kissed him softly on the cheek. When she was done, she wiped away the smudge of her lipstick. Her eyes didn't know where to look.

"Thank you, Frost."

At that moment, he felt a sudden chemistry with her that took him by surprise. He wasn't looking for it, he didn't want it, but there it was.

18

When Frost rang the bell at Jess's apartment, she answered the door with a knife in her hand. He put up his arms in mock surrender. After she saw that he was alone, she opened the door wider and put the knife down on a table by the entry. He nudged past her.

"Taking no chances?" he asked.

"No."

"Well, that's smart."

Jess locked the door behind him. He'd been to her apartment many times before. It wasn't fancy; she didn't waste time or money on frills. She could eat, sleep, watch TV, and work on a computer here, but not much else. The white walls were mostly empty. She'd lived in this apartment since she and Captain Hayden had divorced almost two years earlier, but it wasn't really a home. The only home Jess had was at work. He didn't know how she was going to adjust to the idea of not being a cop.

"Did anyone see you?" she asked.

"No. If Hayden was watching you, he's pulled his surveillance. And the media gets bored easily."

"Guess I'm already old news," Jess said.

Without asking, Jess went to the kitchen to get him a beer. Frost let himself out onto her second-floor balcony. It was small, and she hadn't decorated it with ferns or flowers like the other apartments near her. She had two uncomfortable chairs, and he sat in one of them and put his feet on the railing. The apartment looked out on the alley at the back of the building and the green cliff leading up to Chestnut Street.

Jess joined him, handing him a bottle. She leaned her strong arms on the railing and stared into the darkness.

"Did you talk to your lawyer?" he asked.

"Yeah."

"What did she say?"

"She says perjury is a serious felony," Jess said.

"No kidding."

"Yeah. She's trying to do a plea bargain. A judge could give me four years, but she thinks we can get it down to a year. It depends on whether the DA wants to make an example of me. 'We won't tolerate bad behavior by the cops.' That sort of thing. He probably has to have his political people do a poll first."

"Nobody wants them to come down hard on you, Jess. Inside or outside the department."

"We'll see."

He got out of the chair and stood beside her. He took a drink of his beer and then put the bottle on the concrete next to him.

"I picked up the research materials from Eden Shay," he told her. "I'm starting to review them. She talked to a lot of people. I'm hoping there may be something in her notes."

"You want me to look at them, too? Off the record?"

"No, I can handle it," Frost said.

"Okay. Whatever."

"By the way, Eden knows we slept together."

Jess didn't look surprised. "I don't care if people know. Do you?"

"No. Not anymore."

She dug in the pocket of her jeans and extracted a pack of cigarettes. She lit one and blew smoke off the balcony. Then she stared at him from behind her bangs. "Want to do it again?"

"Me and you? I thought we decided that was a bad idea."

"I'm not your boss anymore."

His body stirred at memories of the two of them together. With Jess, it was never about making love. It was sex, fast and furious. He could spend an hour in bed with her, and there would be no strings, and they would both be satisfied. He was tempted, but it was still a bad idea.

She saw the rejection in his face, and she looked away and continued to suck on her cigarette. "Well, I'm having a hell of a month."

"Your text said you needed to see me."

"Did you hear about the murder on Stockton?" she asked.

"Old guy in the wheelchair? Yeah. I've been seeing reports on it come through all evening."

"What are they saying?"

He hesitated, not sure why she was asking. "There aren't any leads on the perp so far. The apartment was clean. They found the body because the woman in the apartment next door came home from work and noticed a bullet hole in her wall. She called the cops. Vic's name is Jimmy Keyes."

"He was shot?" Jess asked.

"No. The gunshot went high. It looks like Keyes fired at somebody and missed. Whoever he was aiming at broke the old man's neck. The cops found debris from a Taser in the apartment, but no sign of the Taser itself. The gun was missing, too. Why are you asking about this, Jess?"

"Motive?" she went on, ignoring his question. The habits of being the boss died hard.

Frost shrugged. "Robbery, probably. Keyes's wallet was gone."

Jess stared at him through a cloud of smoke. "It was Cutter."

"What makes you think so? This isn't Cutter's MO."

"I called a tech buddy of mine," she told him. "He ran the vic's address through some of the local sites that weapons traders use. This guy Keyes was trying to unload a Taser."

Brian Freeman

"Okay, so the killer's probably a buyer who didn't feel like ponying up cash. That doesn't make it Cutter."

"It's him," Jess insisted. "The sixth victim, Shu Chan, was Tasered before he grabbed her. You think that's a coincidence?"

Frost exhaled long and slow. He wasn't sure if it was suspicious enough to call it more than a coincidence. Maybe Jess really believed it, or maybe she was looking for any excuse to be back in the game.

Then again, he thought, *Tick tock.*

"Look, I can call the detectives on the case. They'll be pulling street cameras from the area around the crime scene. I can make sure they keep an eye out for Cutter."

"They won't get him that way. The guy's a ghost."

"Jess, you know there's nothing I'd like better than to pin a new murder charge on Cutter—"

"That's not what I'm talking about. I don't think we'll ever *prove* it was him behind the Keyes murder. He's too smart. I still think he did it, and that means now he's walking around out there with a Taser and a handgun. We both know what that means."

Frost frowned. "He already has a new target."

"Right. I know you're focused on solving the old murders, but we may not have time. You need to find him, Frost. Fast."

3:42 a.m. In or out of prison, it didn't matter. Rudy was awake.

He slipped out of bed. His clothes were on the floor, but he didn't put them on yet. He stared at the brunette whose naked torso extended from the blankets. He didn't remember her name. Her apartment in the Castro was small. He knew the neighborhood well, which meant he knew the bars you went to when you didn't want to spend the night alone. After a few drinks together, she'd invited him back to her place.

118

The sex hadn't been memorable after four years of prison celibacy, but the woman was too drunk to care.

When he drew a finger down her bare spine, she didn't stir at his touch. Her eyes were closed, and her breath whistled through her nose. He didn't expect her to be conscious for hours.

He was restless, so he did yoga. That was one of the tricks he'd learned to cope with prison time. He could feel his heart rate slow. He could feel his blood pressure go down. He exercised silently for an hour, and it was still dark outside when he finished and got dressed. In the kitchen, he made himself a cup of coffee using the woman's single-cup machine. While he sipped it, he found her laptop computer and booted it up. He navigated to the cloud website he'd used to store his research materials. No one knew about it; no one had found it. It had been four years since he'd been online, but he'd purchased a long-term plan before he was arrested to make sure his account wasn't deactivated.

The documents were all there. The names, the jobs, the home addresses, the phone numbers, the secret photographs, the maps. The information was four years old, and much of it was probably out of date, but it gave him a place to start.

He studied the names on his list:

> ~~Nina Flores~~
> ~~Rae Hart~~
> ~~Natasha Lubin~~
> ~~Hazel Dixon~~
> ~~Shu Chan~~
> ~~Melanie Valou~~

And below them was the first name that was not crossed out:

> Maria Lopes

He'd been part of Maria's life during the last weeks before he was arrested. He could still picture her face. He knew where she worked, where she lived, where she ate, where she shopped. He'd been targeting her before Jess Salceda got in the way of his plans. Now he had to find her again.

Rudy typed her name into the Google search engine:

Maria Lopes San Francisco

Before he could review the search results, his head snapped up as a Fall Out Boy song played loudly from the bedroom. The woman's phone was ringing. Rudy slapped the laptop shut. The song was deafening in the silence of the apartment, but when he got up and went to the bedroom doorway, the woman in bed didn't move. She was still unconscious and showed no sign of waking up. Even so, he didn't want to take the risk that someone would come over to the apartment when they couldn't reach her on the phone.

Rudy decided it was time to go.

He went to the sink in the woman's small kitchen. He put a stopper in the drain and filled the basin, and then he found a large container of salt in one of the cabinets and emptied it into the water. Using his fingers, he swirled the water around. He grabbed the laptop and slid the machine into the salty bath. When a few minutes had passed, he retrieved the laptop and carefully dried it with a dish towel, so there was no evidence of tampering. He pushed the "Power" button. Nothing happened. The laptop was dead. He replaced it carefully in the exact place he'd found it, matching the rectangle of dust on the bookshelf.

Through the apartment window, dawn crept over the city.

He began quietly opening drawers in the bedroom where the woman slept. He found a pair of mini binoculars that he tucked into his backpack. He checked her closet and found a men's wool cap, probably left over from a previous one-night stand. He took it. In a zippered compartment in one of the woman's purses, he found three hundred dollars in cash. He shoved it into his pocket.

Rudy went into the kitchen. He found the drawer where she kept her cutlery, and he selected one of the steak knives inside, with a serrated blade. She wouldn't miss it. He held it in his hand, feeling the handle, running a finger along the dull side of the steel. It brought images into his brain. Memories. He thought about what it would feel like again, after so long.

He wandered back into the bedroom. The woman—What was her name? Wendy?—was still asleep. She was on her side. Long hair spilled over her face. Her neck was exposed, showing off the ridges of her ligaments and the swell of her trachea. Inside, under the skin, arteries pumped blood to her brain. He stood over her, with the knife in his hand. He lay the flat of the blade against her pretty neck as she slept. One flick of the wrist was all he needed. It was tempting, but he had to be patient. He didn't have much longer to wait.

The woman made a noise, almost like a moan in her dreams. He removed the knife from her skin and secured it in his backpack. As he watched, she shifted onto her back, and the sight of her body brought a twinge of arousal. He thought about waking her up and having sex again, but he couldn't indulge himself. Not now.

Instead, silently, he let himself out of the apartment and wandered down the steps to the street.

He counted the hours. Tonight it would begin again.

19

When Frost needed to find someone in San Francisco, he turned to an unofficial network of homeless people and street performers known as Street Twitter. The way into the network was through his best friend, Herb, who was clued into everything that was happening in the city.

Wherever Herb went, he drew a crowd. Typically, Frost found him near one of the city's sightseeing bus stops, painting three-dimensional sidewalk illusions that had made him a tourist attraction in his own right. At seventy years old, he was Mr. San Francisco. He'd spent his youth in the pot-drenched, pill-popping '60s, and he'd reinvented himself in every decade since then. He'd been a microbiologist. A four-term city councilman. And now a famous street artist. For the most recent Bay Area Super Bowl at Levi's Stadium, he'd done a three-dimensional painting of Dwight Clark making "The Catch" in the 1981 NFC Championship Game. Herb had his own gallery on Haight Street and regularly held classes for aspiring artists.

Today, as usual, a crowd gathered around Herb, but he wasn't painting. Instead, he sat on a tall chair in the open courtyard of the Palace of the Legion of Honor, posed in front of Rodin's *The Thinker*. Like the sculpture, he was hunched in meditation, and like the sculpture, he was naked, except for a discreet loincloth draped between his wiry legs. Gold glitter flocked his skin, and a rainbow of beads adorned his long gray hair. A photographer swarmed around him, taking pictures.

"Performance art, Herb?" Frost asked, standing below him.

Without breaking his pose, Herb replied from the chair, "Magazine photo shoot."

"Ah."

Herb's eyes flicked to the dark sky and then to the photographer. "Are we about done here, young lady? If it rains, this glitter is going to become paste, and I'll be scraping it out of some very awkward places. Plus, I need to teach a class at my gallery in about an hour."

"Yes, I have what I need," she replied.

"Thank heavens. Frost, toss me that robe, okay? These tourists all have cameras, and I really don't want my bare backside showing up on Snapchat."

Frost chuckled and threw a black satin robe to Herb, who carefully slipped it over his tall, scrawny body and climbed down to the glistening marble floor of the courtyard. His friend limped as he stretched the kinks out of his muscles. Herb retrieved a canvas bag and slipped old-fashioned black glasses over his face. The bag also yielded an urn of coffee, and he poured himself a cup.

"How do I look?" Herb asked.

"Like a cross between Egyptian pyramid art and Madonna on her last tour."

"Exactly what I was going for."

As the crowd dispersed, the two of them drifted toward the white columns lining the museum courtyard. They had a bubble of privacy around them, but Frost spoke softly.

"Rudy Cutter has gone off the radar," he murmured.

"So I hear."

"It's urgent that we find him as soon as we can. Jess thinks he's already targeting a new victim. Can you help?"

"Of course, I'll do what I can," Herb replied. "Actually, I put out an alert to the network yesterday, because I figured you'd be looking for him. However, Cutter seems to be skilled at not being found."

"No sightings?"

"Nothing at all, which is unusual."

"Well, if anything comes in, let me know right away."

"I will." Herb added after a pause, "I'm sorry about Jess. What she did was egregious, but I don't like seeing a smart, tough cop lose her career like this."

"I wasn't crazy about being the one to turn her in."

"Of course. Have you talked to her?"

"Yes, I saw her last night."

Herb knew all about his history with Jess. "I know you didn't come looking for my advice, Frost, but—"

"Don't worry, nothing happened between us," he said, anticipating the question.

"Good. It's better that way. To paraphrase what a wise young man said to me once, she's not your Jane Doe, Frost."

Frost rolled his eyes because he was that wise young man, and Herb liked to tease him about it. It made him think of his college days at SF State fifteen years earlier, when he and Herb had met for the first time. Back then, Frost had been a loner trying to figure out the world and not doing a very good job of it. His one point of pride had been getting a degree without any debt, so when he wasn't in class, he was out on the streets, driving a taxi.

One September evening, near midnight, he'd received a call for a pickup at city hall. He arrived at the mammoth domed building on Van Ness to find a fifty-something man stretched out on his back on the steps, wearing a '70s-era powder-blue three-piece suit. When the man staggered into the back seat of the cab, he'd brought an aroma of pot so overwhelming that Frost had been forced to open all the windows. Herb wasn't his name, but that was the nickname he'd had for most of his life, and it was richly deserved.

Herb had nowhere to go; he just wanted company. They'd spent the next seven hours, until dawn, driving around the city. Although Frost was a San Francisco native, Herb had given him a tour unlike anything Frost had experienced before. As they left city hall, Herb had told him about seeing Dan White on November 27, 1978, and hearing the shots that had killed Harvey Milk. He took Herb to the Haight and heard stories of flower power and the Summer of Love from someone who'd lived through it. Herb talked about Jonestown. Joe Montana. The 1989 quake. AIDS.

Somewhere during the night, as the pot wore off, Herb had told him about a woman named Silvia. They'd met in July of 1968 and done what all young people had done that summer. Protested. Gotten high. Had sex. It was an era without promises, but back then, Herb had been convinced that he and Silvia had found something that transcended free love. Then she'd disappeared. He'd awakened alone one morning in August and never saw her or heard from her again. Since then, he told Frost, he'd never loved anyone else the same way.

That was when Frost had offered Herb his philosophy of love, which could only come from a twenty-year-old college kid who'd never had a serious relationship in his life. Which was still true today.

Sounds like she was your Jane Doe, Herb. You know, we all have one Jane Doe out there. That one girl who will change our lives. Some people die not knowing who she is. At least you found yours.

Herb, in his powder-blue suit, had taken in that dubious pearl of wisdom and roared with laughter. Eventually, so did Frost. By the next morning, when he dropped Herb back at city hall, they'd become close friends, and they'd been friends ever since.

"Mock me if you will," Frost told him, "but Duane claims to have found *his* Jane Doe."

"Duane? Pigs must be sprouting wings."

"It's true. They've been dating for six months. He only just told me about her. Her name's Tabby Blaine. Redhead, pretty, thirty years old."

"So about ten years older than Duane's usual girlfriends?" Herb asked with a grin.

"Exactly."

"Your mother must be thrilled."

"No doubt. She and my dad are flying in from Arizona tonight, so I'm stopping over to see them this evening. I'm sure I'll hear all about it."

"Have you met this girl Tabby?"

Frost hesitated, which didn't escape Herb's eagle eye. "I have."

"And do you like her?"

"I do. A lot."

Herb tried to decipher the expression on Frost's face, as if he'd already guessed that Frost was hiding something. The old man sometimes seemed to know Frost better than he knew himself. Herb's next question was pointed.

"What about you? Any unidentified Jane Does dropping into your life lately?"

"Sorry. Shack and I are confirmed bachelors."

"No one at all?" Herb challenged him, with the impish smile of someone who had inside information.

"Did you have someone in mind?"

"Oh, I hear that you've made the acquaintance of an attractive journalist. Eden Shay."

"How do you know about her, you old fox?"

"She came to interview me yesterday," Herb told him.

"About the murders?"

"No, about you. She knew we were friends."

"What did you tell her?"

"Nothing. I simply confirmed what she already knew—that you were handsome, unattached, and a notable philosopher on love and romance."

"Ha."

"She seemed interested in you, Frost, and in more than a professional way."

"Don't get carried away. What Eden wants is a good story, and she'll do whatever it takes to be in the middle of it. That's her thing, you know. She likes to get close to the people she's writing about."

"She called you the hero of her new book," Herb said.

"I'm not. Just a guest star at the end."

Herb clapped a hand on his shoulder. "Don't be so sure. You've been a part of this particular book for some time."

"Longer than I want."

"Well, remember what they say," Herb told him slyly. "Sooner or later, all writers fall in love with their heroes."

Frost grinned. "Yeah, or they get them killed."

20

"I'm glad you called me," Eden said.

She sat in the passenger seat of Frost's Suburban. They were parked on Silver Avenue across from the home of Gilda and Anthony Flores. Nina's parents.

"I needed your help," Frost admitted. "Gilda Flores was one of the family members screaming at me in the courtroom. She turned me down when I asked to talk to her. I'm glad you were able to change her mind."

"I relate well to victims. Gilda was the very first interview I did when I started working on the book. She trusts me." Eden played with her black curls as if she wanted to flirt with him, but then she put her hands in her lap. "But *you* don't trust me, do you?"

"I don't know where the writer ends and where Eden Shay begins."

"That's easy. We're the same person."

"And that's why I don't trust you," Frost said.

"Aw. What a shame." She was flirty again.

"I hear you've been talking to my friends."

"That's what writers do."

"What did you learn?"

"I learned that with Frost Easton, what you see is what you get," Eden told him. "You don't play games and pretend to be something you're not."

"Is that all?" he asked.

"You want more? Okay. You're smart, but that's a given. You're an introvert, and you don't fit in with the cop buddy system. Most of your friends are outside the force. You don't seek out relationships with women, because you don't think you're good at them and you don't want to hurt anybody. You know you're good-looking. You probably know that a little too well. The biggest love in your life is San Francisco, but if you had your choice, you'd probably go back to an earlier time in the city's history, not now. The 1860s maybe. Mark Twain days. Just you and Shack out on the frontier."

Frost smiled, but he was a little unsettled by the accuracy of everything she'd said. "We should go."

"Whatever you say, partner."

He climbed out into the afternoon drizzle. The Flores family home was a Spanish-style two-story house with freshly painted white stucco and cherry-red shutters. Flowers grew in a brick-lined bed by the sidewalk. A fuchsia tree had been trimmed into a neat ball by the front door, and the door itself was protected by a locked gate. This was a family that had learned the hard way to take no chances.

Gilda Flores answered the buzzer. Her face was hostile, but she said nothing as she unlocked the outer gate and ushered them into the house. He noticed that Gilda hugged Eden as if they were long-lost friends. Inside, the Flores home was dark on a dark day, but the furniture shined, as if dust had no place here. The air bloomed with a smell of roasting peppers.

"Thank you for seeing me," Frost said.

"Ms. Shay said it was important that I talk to you, so I'm talking to you."

"Is your husband here?"

"No, he didn't think he could be civil."

Frost felt the woman's lingering anger, and he didn't blame her. He looked for a different way to connect with her. "I met one of Nina's closest friends recently. Tabby Blaine. She said to say hello when I saw you."

Gilda's face brightened. She was plump and small, but he could see a resemblance to her daughter, Nina, in her bushy brown hair and wide-open eyes. She wore a yellow one-piece dress with a belt tied around the middle.

"Tabby! I haven't seen her in ages. She is such a ray of light, that girl. She and Nina were inseparable. Much like me and her mother. We were pregnant at the same time, and Nina and Tabby were first babies for both of us, so we went through it all together."

"Tabby's dating my brother," Frost told her before he remembered to stop himself. Immediately, he saw Eden's face awaken with interest. This was a new angle for the book.

"Really?" Gilda said. "I guess grief can bring people together. I know that you and your brother lost a family member, too. Please don't think—based on my behavior in the courtroom—that I forgot that. I really didn't."

"I understand."

"Eden, do you know Tabby?" Gilda asked.

"I talked to her years ago," Eden replied. "I know she was very close to Nina."

"Oh yes, those two were like sisters. I had three more children after Nina, but they were all boys. I don't think it's the same thing for a girl, having brothers."

Frost, who'd been closer to Katie than anyone else in his life, didn't bother correcting her. "I'm sorry to reopen an old wound, Mrs. Flores, but your daughter is an important part of this case. In order to get Rudy Cutter back in prison—and make sure he doesn't harm anyone else—we need to understand what really happened between him and Nina."

Gilda's weary face showed that she'd been down this road many times. "Yes, I know. She was the first."

"That's right."

"I don't know what more I can tell you. Nothing I said back then seemed to help."

"We know a lot more about this case—and about Rudy Cutter—than we did in those days," Frost said.

"I suppose so, but by the time we found out about Cutter, years had gone by. It's been even longer now. What exactly do you want?"

"I'm interested in finding similarities between Nina and the other victims," Frost said. "I know the families have gotten together over the years. Did you discover personal connections to any of them? Was there any overlap in your lives? It doesn't matter how trivial it may have been."

"No, Tony and I never really got to know the other families. We went to a couple of the early support-group meetings, but we chose not to participate after that. It was too painful to be reminded of it."

"Is there anything else about Nina that might help me?" Frost asked.

Gilda glanced over her shoulder at the stairs. "Would you like to see her bedroom?"

"Yes, I would. Thank you."

Nina's mother led Frost and Eden to the second floor. It was obvious that Gilda's hip bothered her; she didn't climb well. At the top of the stairs, she pointed at a bedroom with a closed door at the end of the hallway. A framed photograph of Nina—one of her high school graduation pictures—was hung on the door.

"That's her room," Gilda said. "You're welcome to look inside. I'm sorry, but I don't think I can go in there myself."

Frost nodded. Eden put an arm around the woman's shoulder and squeezed. They waited until Gilda made her way back downstairs, and then Frost walked to the end of the hallway and opened the bedroom door. Nina's sunny smile in the photograph beckoned him inside. He turned on an overhead light, and then he went to the window, which overlooked the street, and parted the curtains. Eden hovered in the doorway.

"Have you been here before?" Frost asked.

"I have."

"Does it look the same?"

"Frozen in time," Eden replied.

It was a teenager's bedroom, more for a girl than a young woman. Nina had been twenty-one when she was killed, but the room still felt as if it belonged to a high schooler. Frost saw a life that had revolved around religion, family, and friends. A crucifix was hung over the twin bed, which was perfectly made with a red flowered comforter. He saw a collage of photographs of Nina and her brothers and cousins on the wall. A pewter star engraved with the word *believe* dangled from a thumb tack. He saw a beautiful pen-and-ink sketch of Gilda in the hospital, holding her newborn baby. Underneath the sketch was a label written in script: *Gilda and Nina.* And below it was the date—April 1—which was Nina's birthday.

Several photographs, handmade into buttons, were spread like polka dots across the bed, along with a plastic crown that had the number "21" glued to the front with rhinestones. He remembered that Nina had been wearing these buttons, and the crown, at the coffee shop on her twenty-first birthday.

Rudy Cutter would have seen the buttons pinned to Nina's shirt. It had to have been a reminder that Wren would have turned twenty-one that year, too. If his daughter had lived.

Frost picked them up one by one. There were five of them. One button was made from the same graduation photograph that was hung on her bedroom door. Another was obviously a wedding photograph of her parents. Two others were vacation photos: Nina in a one-piece swimsuit in a Las Vegas hotel pool, Nina and her brothers posing by the rim of the Grand Canyon.

The last photograph had been taken right here in Nina's bedroom. He could see the wall, the pictures, the pen-and-ink sketch, and the pewter star in the background. There were two girls beaming in the picture, their cheeks together, their smiles like high-wattage lightbulbs. Two best friends. Nina Flores and Tabby Blaine.

Tabby hadn't changed much in nine years. She had a self-awareness that stood out next to Nina's little-girl innocence. *Watch me,* her face said. *Go ahead, I dare you.* Her green eyes teased the camera. Her freckles made a constellation of stars around the button of her nose. He saw streaks of gold hiding in her long red hair.

Frost retrieved his phone and took close-up pictures of each of the buttons so he could review the details later.

"So your brother's dating Tabby Blaine," Eden murmured, coming up behind him.

"How about we leave that detail off the record?"

"Sorry, Frost, I can't do that. Two murders that give birth to a love story? That's a perfect anecdote for a true-crime book."

"Duane and Tabby are dating. I didn't say it was a love story."

"No? Your face says otherwise. Is it serious between them?"

"If you want to know more, talk to them. Not me."

Her eyes narrowed with curiosity. "You sound annoyed. Why, are you jealous? Do you like Tabby, too? I remember her as being pretty cute."

He dodged her innuendo because he didn't want to admit that she'd struck a nerve. "You interviewed Tabby back then?"

"I did."

"What did she tell you?"

"Not much. I don't think she liked me."

"Surprise, surprise."

Eden offered him a look of mock astonishment. "Why do you say that? I'm very likable. Mrs. Flores likes me."

"Mrs. Flores isn't a single woman. How many single women friends do you have?"

"A number approaching zero," she acknowledged.

"And male friends?"

"Countless. Okay, you've made your point."

Frost's lips twitched into a smile. Eden was the one who looked annoyed now. She liked to analyze others, but he didn't think she appreciated being analyzed herself.

He put Nina's buttons down on the bed, trying to position them exactly as they'd been. There was a reverence about them, he thought, which was why Gilda Flores had kept them all these years. Even so, if the buttons held a secret, he couldn't figure out what it was.

"There has to be a clue here, but I'm missing it," Frost said, surveying the bedroom again with frustration. "You've been here before. What do you think?"

"I'm just a writer." Her voice had an impatient note. She was still unhappy with him.

"You're a writer who doesn't miss much," he said.

"Well, all I see is what you see. I'm sorry. If I knew more than that, Frost, I'd tell you."

Eden turned with a swish of her curly hair and stalked out of the bedroom, and his gaze followed her long legs as she left.

It occurred to Frost that spending more time with Eden hadn't changed his mind. He still didn't trust her.

21

"Another drink?" the bartender asked.

Rudy stared into the ice melting at the base of his lowball glass. He swirled it in his hand. "Sure. Why not?"

"Same again?"

"Yeah. G and T. Bombay."

"Coming up."

The young bartender made the empty glass disappear. He was small and Asian, with feminine features and black hair gelled into a bird's nest. Maybe he was transgender, maybe not. Rudy had been away from the San Francisco scene for too long to be sure.

The downstairs lounge and sushi restaurant in Japantown was almost impenetrably dark and half-empty. Sconces over the liquor bottles on the bar made the mirrored glass shine red. Rudy sat at the far end, away from the stairs that led down from the street. He wore a black fedora with two braided yellow bands around the brim. His sunglasses had tiny square lenses, like postage stamps. Wearing sunglasses in a dark bar didn't attract attention here. It was the cool thing to do. He'd shaved for tonight, and he'd found dress clothes at a secondhand shop to fit the look. Gray mock turtleneck. Leather jacket. Black jeans and boots.

"Here you go," the bartender told him, putting another gin and tonic in front of him. "You want some sushi?"

"How about a volcano roll?" Rudy said.

The man—if he was a man—grinned with his pale lips. "Sure thing."

Rudy took a sip and felt the cold of the gin chill his insides. He had a ritual for these nights, and Bombay was part of it. He took each breath slow and long, feeling the air swell his lungs. He put up his right hand and slowly turned it around, front and back, admiring its steadiness like a work of art. He bent and unbent his fingertips, which were loose and limber. He'd wondered after all this time if he would be nervous, but he wasn't. He was a machine.

He checked his watch. It was already midevening, and time was passing more quickly than he liked. He eyed the others in the bar, who were getting drunk and loud. They were mostly twenty years younger, but age didn't matter. Someone always had a yen for an older man who looked like he had money. His gaze moved from face to face, connecting with the women. Some looked back, and some didn't.

The bartender leaned on one elbow in front of him. He was bored without a big crowd to serve. Rudy thought he was wearing lipstick, and his eyebrows were neatly plucked. The bartender's eyes narrowed as he surveyed Rudy's face.

"Do I know you?" he asked.

"I don't know," Rudy said without removing his sunglasses or his hat. "Do you?"

"You look familiar, but you're not a regular."

"I guess I have that look," Rudy said. "Mind if I ask you a question?"

"Shoot."

"Are you a guy or a girl?"

The bartender didn't look offended. "Depends. What are you into?"

"Girls."

"I can pull that off, if you don't mind some surplus parts."

"Pass," Rudy said. "Sorry."

"That's okay, your loss." The bartender grabbed a towel and began wiping down the bar.

Rudy drank more of his gin and tonic. This one was strong. He looked around at the middling crowd in the bar again and decided that his plan needed some help. "Actually, I'm drowning my sorrows," he told the bartender.

"Yeah? How so?"

"My girlfriend dumped me today."

"Sorry about that." His girlish eyes checked out Rudy's face again. "I mean, you're a decent looker and all. A rough type, but a lot of girls like that. You must have a couple bucks, too, if you're ordering Bombay. You ask me, you should just forget about her and move on."

Rudy slid a hand inside the pocket of his leather jacket and put two concert tickets on the bar. "Yeah, I'm not crying about it, but I've got two tickets for the Fillmore tonight. I don't really want to go on my own."

"Who's playing?"

"Japandroids. I could sell the tickets, but I'd like to hear them play."

"No kidding? You ready for decibels like that? You don't look like the 'Evil's Sway' type."

Rudy cocked his head. "What?"

The bartender laughed, as if Rudy were speaking a different language. "Um, duh? That's one of their songs?"

"Oh. Sure." Rudy laughed, too, but he seethed inwardly at his mistake. That was what happened when he didn't have the time to anticipate every detail. "Anyway, I'm looking for a girl who wants to go with me. I figure somebody must want a free show, right? Plus, it'll just *kill* my girlfriend."

"Revenge. Nice."

Rudy reached into his jacket again and found a fifty-dollar bill that he slid across the bar. "I was hoping you might be able to help me hook up. It's always a little easier when you've got somebody to break the ice, know what I mean?"

The cash disappeared into the bartender's pocket. "An icebreaker, sure. I've been known to do that. What kind of companionship are we talking about? If you want the paid kind, I have to make some calls."

"Not paid," Rudy said, "but let's say open-minded about what happens after the concert."

"Alcohol has been known to open many a closed mind," the bartender told him.

Rudy slid another fifty across the bar. "Well, work your magic."

The bartender pursed his lips to blow him a kiss, and he disappeared. Rudy stopped trolling the bar and decided to let his wingman do the talking. He nursed his drink. Somewhere in the bar, he heard the noise of bad karaoke, but he didn't recognize the song. That was the price of four years away from the music scene.

His volcano roll came. It was an artistic blend of spicy tuna, cucumber, avocado, and shrimp tempura. The sauce had kick. He alternated between the fiery sushi and the cold cocktail. He stared straight ahead, ignoring the other people in the bar, but his senses were alert. Conversations drifted in and out of his head. Every few minutes, he examined his hand again, his killing hand, as if it belonged to someone else. His fingers were still steady as a rock.

Half an hour passed.

Then, behind him, he heard the tap of feminine heels. Perfume broke over him like the opening of a candy shop door. Lips brushed his ear, along with a voice that had trouble putting together words. "So what's your name?"

He turned as a thirty-something brunette poured herself onto the stool next to him. She wore a black dress down to her knees. Half a martini was in her hand.

"Rudy. What's yours?"

"Magnolia," she said, drawing out the first syllable with her mouth slightly open.

"That's a pretty name."

"It's the name of a tree. I am a tree. A magnolia tree." She drew it out again as *Maggggggggnolia.*

"Well, magnolia trees have lovely flowers," he said.

"That's a sweet thing to say. You're sweet." Her tongue licked the wet rim of her martini glass, and she took a swallow of her drink, which was pink with a layer of white foam.

"Do you come to this place a lot?" he asked.

"First time."

"Me, too. What brings you here, Magnolia?"

"I never leave my apartment. I work all the time, and I'm sick of it. Tonight, I promised myself I would go out and have fun."

"What do you do?"

"I code. I'm a programmer."

"Really?"

"Yeah. You know, so my fingers are really, really nimble."

Magnolia blinked seductively, but she had some trouble focusing. He suspected the bartender had concocted strong drinks for her. Her big eyes were blue, and she wore matching eyeshadow that was a little too dark and applied a little too thickly. In the scarlet glow of the bar, she was pretty, but her lips kept squeezing into an embarrassed smile. She tossed her long hair nervously out of her face.

"So whatcha eating, Rudy?"

He had two pieces of sushi left. "A volcano roll. Want some?"

"Okay."

He picked up a piece of sushi, dipped it into a bowl of soy sauce mixed with wasabi, and slid it into her open mouth. She smiled and chewed at the same time in a failed attempt at sexiness. When she swallowed, he leaned over with his napkin and wiped away a little drop of soy sauce that had dribbled from her lip.

"Mmm. Spicy."

"Do you like it?" he asked.

"Sure. Spicy is good."

He smiled and watched her stare intently at him as she drained the last of her martini. Her eyes squinted, as if she'd begun to realize he looked like someone she'd seen before. This was the delicate moment, wondering whether she would put two and two together. The face on the news. The face in the bar, hiding behind sunglasses. Sometimes people could recognize a photograph come to life, and sometimes they couldn't.

She didn't make the connection.

"I hear you have tickets to Japandroids at the Fillmore," Magnolia said.

"I do."

"I love them."

"Well, maybe you'd like to go to the concert with me."

"Well, maybe I would." She squirmed on the chair; she wasn't good at this. "You got dumped, huh? That's what the bartender said."

"Yeah."

"Getting dumped sucks. I got dumped last month."

"Sorry."

"That's okay. I didn't really like him. Screw both of them, right? We don't need them."

"No, we don't."

"Do you smoke?" Magnolia asked.

"No."

"Good. I don't like smokers. They stink. Smoking will kill you, you know."

"I've heard that," Rudy said.

"When's the concert?"

"Pretty soon."

"Guess we should go," she said.

"I guess."

He climbed off the bar stool, and he held out an elbow for her. She giggled, stumbled a bit as she disentangled herself from the chair, and held on tightly as he pointed her toward the stairs. She had trouble climbing back to the street, and she grabbed the railing in a death grip for support. Outside, it was a little wet, and he took the fedora he was wearing and dropped it on her head.

She grabbed the brim with both hands and smoothed it. She tilted the hat far forward on her face. "Cool. Bet I look cool with this."

"You do." Rudy patted the pockets of his jacket. "Hey, I forgot something at the bar. Wait right here, okay? I won't be thirty seconds."

Magnolia put her head back against the glass door, which had a greenish glow from the lights on the stairs. She closed her eyes, and she shivered. "Hurry back."

Rudy steadied her shoulders to make sure she didn't fall, and then he jogged back down the steps into the bar. He waved over the bartender, who approached him with a grin on his delicate lips.

"How'd I do?" the man asked. "She what you were looking for? I made sure those martinis packed a punch."

"Perfect." Rudy slid another fifty-dollar bill from his jacket, and then he took out a notepad and wrote a phone number on a piece of paper. He handed both of them across the bar. "Do me a favor, okay? Call this number. Tell the woman who answers that Rudy says hi."

"Sure thing. Is she your ex-girlfriend? You want to rub it in her face?"

"That's exactly right," Rudy said. "And be sure to tell her that I'm leaving with a pretty girl."

22

Frost's old neighborhood hadn't changed.

He parked at the southern end of Forty-Fifth Avenue, where the side-by-side houses looked like rows of multicolored Legos. He was a block from the zoo and two blocks from the ocean. Memories chased him in the darkness as he got out of the Suburban. Most of the memories were about him and Katie, stalking this area like pirates when they were children.

Frost made the mistake of walking up the stairs to his old house. Force of habit. His parents had sold the family house a year earlier, when they moved to Tucson, but their long-time neighbors, the Holtzmans, were still here. The Easton and Holtzman houses had shared a wall for decades. One was brown stucco; one was aquamarine stucco. Both showed their age.

He corrected himself and knocked on the Holtzman door, and his mother, Janice, answered. She smiled at him, but most of her smiles had a sad quality in recent years.

"It's good to see you, Frost," she murmured. "It's been way too long."

Parents had a way of channeling guilt into the most innocent of greetings. He knew he hadn't been down to visit them in Arizona, and he vowed inwardly to schedule a trip soon.

His mother was almost as tall as he was. She had a soft beauty in her face, and her mannerisms were slow and precise. She never hurried. Her brown hair took a lot of work to keep perfect. She wore a blouse and skirt, not expensive, but carefully selected. She had a quietness about her that she'd passed on to her middle child. They were both the introverts of the family.

Janice looked over his shoulder, as if, one of these times, he would bring a girlfriend with him, instead of arriving alone. She gave a tiny sigh of disappointment.

"How are you?" Frost asked.

It wasn't a throw-away question. There were no simple questions between him and his mother. They'd struggled for years about Frost's choices in life. She'd wanted him to be a lawyer, not a cop. She'd wanted him to be married by now, not single. When it came to her own life, however, she didn't usually share her feelings.

"This situation is challenging," Janice acknowledged in her understated way. "That's why the support group decided to get together again."

"Sorry."

"We don't blame you for what's happened, Frost. Duane said you were worried about that. Don't be. Whatever you did, I'm sure you felt you had no choice."

"Many of the families don't see it that way," Frost said.

"Well, they'll get over it. We'll talk to them. I hope you'll join us this weekend."

He hesitated, thinking about the support group. The gathering of families in one place was potentially a valuable source of information to help him identify the missing link among Cutter's victims. On the other hand, he was the last person they would want in the room, asking personal questions. He also had no interest in sharing his own grief with people he didn't know.

"It would mean a lot to us, Frost," his mother added pointedly when he didn't reply. "I'd like you to be there."

Zing. She was like a mafia don, making an offer he couldn't refuse. He wanted to say no, but instead he said, "I'll try to make it."

Janice led them into the living room, where the Holtzmans sat with his father. The house and its dark furniture hadn't changed since Frost was a boy, and seemingly, neither had the Holtzmans. They always looked and acted the same. They'd never had children, and their mission in life was to be parents to the rest of the world. They were good at it. Mr. Holtzman—Frost could never call them by their first names, even now—jumped to his feet to get him a beer. Mrs. Holtzman said she had some things to do upstairs, which was a discreet way to give the Easton family time to reconnect.

His father, Ned, got to his feet and wrapped Frost in a bear hug. He was warm where Janice was cool. His parents were the textbook case of opposites attracting each other.

"Frost, we have missed you so much!" Ned told him.

"You too, Dad."

"How's Shack? Did you bring him along? I love that cat!"

"Sorry, no. He was sleeping in my laundry basket and looking pretty pleased with himself. I didn't want to disturb him."

"Well, I want to see him before we go home," his father said.

"Ned, it's just a cat," his mother said wearily from across the room.

"Ignore her," Ned said, winking.

Mr. Holtzman arrived with two Torpedo ales for Frost and Ned— like father, like son—but then he headed upstairs to be with his wife and left the three of them alone.

As usual, his mother didn't know what to say, and his father didn't know when to stop. Janice hid her pain; Ned used light conversation to pretend his pain wasn't there. Emotionally, Frost was more like his mother, but over the years, he'd always been closer to his father, even if it was only to talk about history and sports. They also shared a love of San Francisco. Ned had been a convention planner at the Moscone Center for most of his career, and even in retirement, he talked up the city as if he'd never left it behind. If it had been up to Ned, they'd still be living in the house next door, but Janice couldn't stay there with Katie's ghost in all the rooms.

His father was like a shorter, squatter version of Frost. In his late sixties, he kept a bushy head of brown-and-gray hair and a trimmed beard, and he had the same laser-like blue eyes he'd given to his children.

"How about that Duane, huh?" Ned asked, swigging his beer. "Have you met Tabby? Isn't she great?"

"She is," Frost agreed.

"I love her. We both do. Cute, smart, way too classy for that boy."

"I thought the same thing," Frost said, smiling.

"As soon as we met her, we thought she'd be perfect for Duane," his father went on. "Janice was on top of that fix-up from minute one. Every time we saw her, she'd be pushing her to call Duane."

"Because she's a chef," his mother pointed out from across the room. There was an apology in her tone, as if she had to explain why they'd chosen to fix up Duane and not Frost.

"I get it," Frost said.

"Of course, it took them forever," Ned said. "And we all know Duane's reputation for going from girl to girl. Your mother told him right from the get-go that he was *not* going to see Tabby unless he was looking for something more. I guess he was finally ready."

"I hope that's true," Frost said.

He waited for his mother to grill him about his own relationship status, but her silence was eloquent. She didn't need to say a word to make him realize that he'd disappointed her again.

His father, on the other hand, had never met a pause he didn't need to fill, and he recognized some of the tension between Frost and his mother. "I want to stretch my legs," Ned said. "I'm all cramped up after the flight. Frost, how about taking a walk around the old neighborhood with me? That okay?"

Frost glanced at his mother. He sensed an ulterior motive. "Sure, Dad."

"Great."

His father grabbed a jacket as they left the house, and he zipped it up as they made their way to the sidewalk. The evening didn't feel cold to Frost, but Arizona life had already thinned Ned's blood. His father walked fast on his short legs, but Frost's long strides kept pace with him. He noticed his father eyeing their old home in the glow of a streetlight.

"Do you miss it?" Frost asked.

"Every damn day," Ned said. "I miss the house, the city, you and your brother. But it is what it is. Janice likes Tucson. She says she's free there."

"How are you two doing?"

"Better. I won't say perfect, but better."

When his parents had taken the first steps toward reconciling after their split, Janice had made it clear that she needed a fresh start somewhere else if they were going to put their relationship back together. That meant leaving San Francisco. So Ned retired. They sold the house and moved.

"You could come back more often," Frost pointed out. "Even if Mom doesn't want to. You could stay with me and Shack. There's a ton of room in the house."

"I'll keep that in mind," Ned said, but Frost knew it was never going to happen. His parents always let him down easy about things they didn't want to do, by telling him they'd keep it in mind. Or they'd run it by the committee. Or they'd put it on the to-do list. Those were the places that ideas went to die.

"Where's the family gathering this weekend?" Frost asked.

"Natasha Lubin's parents are hosting it at their house. They have a place near Stern Grove. I know it would mean a lot to your mother if you could join us at this one, Frost."

"So she said."

"Look, you know Duane. He never has time. Tabby can't get out of her shift at the restaurant. So we'll be on our own, and that's not good for Janice. This will be a big gathering. A lot of family members from out of town are coming in."

"I already told her I'll be there if I can."

"Good. I appreciate it."

They kept walking at the same fast pace, and they reached the end of the avenue at the gates of the zoo. The street was quiet. Down the block to their right, invisible in the darkness, was the Pacific, but he could taste it in the strong wind. Mist was in the breeze, too, dampening their faces. His father sucked in a chestful of air, as if he needed to fill himself up with the city again. Ned looked at home here.

"I remember when you and Katie sneaked into the zoo at night that time," his father reminded him. "You were what? Eleven years old? I still don't know how you guys got the ladder down here from the garage. Then security caught you, and the cops called us. Jeez, the two of you could be trouble."

"The scary thing is, it was Katie's idea," Frost said. "And she was only seven."

"That doesn't surprise me in the least. Nothing ever fazed that girl. She could talk to a stranger for two minutes and know their whole life history."

"Yes, she could."

His father jammed his hands in his pants pockets. The ocean breeze rustled his hair, and his face was full of shadows. "Hey, listen, Frost, I want to talk to you about something. That's why I suggested we take a walk. I didn't want your mother to hear this. She's got enough on her mind right now without me adding anything more."

"What's up?" Frost asked.

"It's about Katie. I don't know if it's important or not, but with everything happening—"

"Tell me," Frost said.

"Okay. Look, you remember, three days after we found her—after you found her—it was our anniversary."

"I remember."

"You know me. Gift giving has never been my thing. And your mother is not exactly the easiest person to shop for. So the week before, I asked Katie for help. I gave her a hundred bucks and told her to find something nice. Naturally, she picked the perfect thing, like always. A beautiful Tibetan Buddha water fountain. It was delivered on our anniversary. At any other time, Janice would have loved it, but of course, getting it then, she went to pieces. So I put the fountain in a box, stored it in the garage, and we never looked at it again."

"I'm not sure I'm following you, Dad," Frost said. "What is this about?"

"Well, the thing is, the box went to Arizona with us. We didn't really take the time to downsize. Janice wanted to get out of the city as fast as we could. It wasn't until earlier this year that I started going through a lot of the boxes that were still sitting in storage that we didn't have room for and had never bothered to unpack. And I found the box with the fountain in it."

Ned slid an envelope out of the inner pocket of his jacket.

"The receipt from the store was inside with the fountain. I had never even opened it. See, I had given Katie the money a week earlier, so I assumed she'd bought the fountain the next day. She was always efficient. But for some reason, she must have waited, because when I looked at the receipt, I realized that she'd gone to the shop to get the fountain on the day she died."

His father extended the envelope to him, and Frost took it. He opened the flap and slid out what was inside, and he used the glow of his phone to light it up. It was a handwritten packing slip describing the Tibetan fountain, and stapled to it was a cash register receipt. He read through the details and saw not just the date printed on the receipt, but the time.

March 10. 7:57 p.m.

"Dad, do you realize when she stopped at this store?" Frost asked. "This was *after* Todd Clary placed his order. She must have stopped there while she was making her last delivery."

"Yeah, that's what it looked like to me, too."

"Why didn't you tell me about this before?"

"Cutter was in prison. I didn't think it mattered anymore."

Frost looked at the receipt again. This time, he noticed the name and address of the Tibetan gift shop where Katie had stopped, and he saw the next piece of the puzzle taking shape in his mind. It was a puzzle piece that didn't fit.

"Do you know this shop?" he asked his father. "Do you know where it is?"

"I know it's on Haight."

"Yes, but the shop is four blocks *east* of the restaurant where Katie worked. It's practically as far as Herb's gallery."

"So what?"

Ned was directionally challenged. Frost got his own sense of direction, which had saved him time after time during his taxi-driving days, from his mother.

"To get to Todd Clary's place near USF, Katie should have gone *west* from the restaurant," Frost told him. "By stopping at the gift shop, she was headed in the opposite direction of where she needed to deliver the pizza. That doesn't make any sense. Where the hell was she going?"

23

"Are you the one who called me?" Jess asked the Asian bartender in the downstairs bar in Japantown. He had plucked eyebrows, and his eyelashes were as full as any model on the cover of *Vogue*. She thought about asking him what shade of lipstick he was wearing, because she wanted it for herself.

"I called you?" he replied. "Who are you?"

"You said a guy named Rudy had a message for me."

He checked her out, and his lips bent into a smile. "Oh, you're the *girlfriend*. Oh, sure. Well, sorry, your ex is long gone, and he's not coming back. He left with a horny little thing."

"When did they leave?"

"I don't know. I lose track of time in here. An hour ago? It got busy, so I didn't call you right away. Hey, as long as you're here, you want to cry into a martini? I make a pretty sweet cosmo."

Jess dug in her back pocket for a piece of paper, which she unfolded on the bar. "Is this the guy?"

The bartender picked up the file photo of Rudy Cutter. His soft eyes narrowed in suspicion. "What's this about? Are you a cop or something?"

Jess reached for her badge by instinct, but her badge wasn't there. The reality hit her for the first time that she wasn't a cop anymore. That part of her life was over. She didn't even know what she was doing here, putting herself in the middle of an investigation that no longer had her name on it.

"Do I look like a cop?" she asked him.

"Yeah, you do," he replied, as if it were finally dawning on him that he'd made a mistake.

"Then answer the question. Is this the guy?"

"Yeah, that's him," the man replied.

"Does he still look like this?" Jess asked, stabbing the photo with a finger.

"Pretty much. He had a clean shave. No stubble. He was wearing a trendy fedora with a double brim in yellow. Sunglasses, too. Little rectangular sunglasses and a leather jacket."

"His full name is Rudy Cutter. Does that mean anything to you?"

The man picked up the photo again and stared at it, and he looked as if his powder makeup were going to dissolve in a soup of sweat. "Oh, shit. That guy? That's him?"

"That's him."

"I thought he looked familiar. Damn it, I knew I'd seen him before."

"What did he tell you?" Jess asked.

"He said his girlfriend dumped him, and he was looking to hook up."

"Did he?"

"Yeah, I told you, he left with a girl."

"You also told me that you were the one who fixed him up," Jess reminded him.

The bartender squirmed. His eyes darted back and forth. "Look, he asked for my help in finding a girl with the right attitude, you know? Someone looking for a party. He gave me fifty bucks to make an introduction."

"And you found someone for him?" Jess asked.

"In here? It wasn't hard."

"You slip her anything?"

"What, like drugs? No! I may have made her drinks a little strong, but nobody complains about that."

"Who was she?" Jess asked.

"I don't know. I've never seen her before. She's not a regular."

"Did she give you a name?"

"Maggie, I think. Or something like that. No last name. She paid cash for her first couple of drinks, and then this guy picked up the rest. No credit card. I'm telling you, I don't know who she was."

"Describe her," Jess said. "How would I pick her out in a crowd?"

"You wouldn't. She looked like a hundred other girls. Long brown hair, too much makeup, little black dress."

"Did you eavesdrop on their conversation?" Jess asked. "Where were they going when they left?"

"A concert at the Fillmore. He had an extra ticket for Japandroids, and he was looking for someone to go with him."

"Japandroids. Is that a real group?"

"Hell yes. Great rockers."

"Did you actually see these tickets?" Jess asked.

"Yeah, he showed them to me. It wasn't a con."

"Do you remember anything else? Anything that would help me find this girl or where she lives?"

The bartender shook his head. "Look, if I'd recognized this guy, if I knew it was this psycho, I wouldn't have helped him."

Jess wanted to believe that, but she knew that money talked. A fifty-dollar bill erased most moral objections. She left the bar and jogged back up the steps to Post Street. Japantown was crowded with traffic and pedestrians hunting for sake and sushi. Across the street in the plaza, the Peace Pagoda was lit in green, looking like a giant laser weapon in some sci-fi movie. The night was cool, and drizzle gave a wet sheen to her trench coat.

She studied the faces around her, but she knew that Cutter was long gone, and he wasn't coming back. Maybe he was at the Fillmore, or maybe the tickets were just a ruse to lead her in the wrong direction.

The only thing she knew for certain was that Cutter had paid the bartender to call *her*. He wanted her to chase him.

Frost found Jess standing next to a stoplight on Geary Street, across from the yellow-brick building that housed the Fillmore. A cigarette leaned out of her mouth, as usual, and her lips tilted downward into a perpetual frown. Her hair and skin glistened with rain. She had eyes that never seemed to blink, and they were focused on the doorway to the theater, where mist blew through the glow of a streetlight.

For up-and-coming bands, the Fillmore was the ultimate high. It meant you were playing the same stage where '60s music royalty had been crowned. Grateful Dead. Jefferson Airplane. Santana. Even hardened rockers felt the awe.

"Did anyone remember seeing Cutter?" Frost asked Jess.

"No, I showed his photo around the box office, but nobody could pick him out. When you've got a few hundred bodies shoving to get close to the stage, you don't see the individual faces."

"You think he's really inside? Or is this all some kind of trick?"

"I don't know. I'm not sure what his game is. But he flashed those concert tickets for a reason. He wanted us here."

"Did you call Hayden?" Frost asked.

Jess exhaled something that might have been a laugh and might have been a snort. "Yeah, because I'm the person he wants to talk to. I'm not supposed to be here at all. If Hayden scrambles cops on my say-so, the new investigation's already poisoned. Maybe that's what Cutter is counting on."

"Even if he's inside, I can't arrest him, you know," Frost said. "He hasn't committed any crime that we know of. We don't have any probable cause to tie him to the murder of Jimmy Keyes."

"Yeah, but you can put the fear of God in him. And you can scare off the girl he's with."

"Okay. I'll check it out."

"Thanks. I hope I didn't pull you away from anything important. Like a date with Eden Shay."

It was a joke, but a joke from Jess always had an edge. He knew what this was about. She'd put herself out there by offering to sleep with him, and he'd turned her down. She wanted to know if he'd done the same with Eden. Jess was as tough a cop as he'd ever known, but she was still a woman, and he'd hurt her feelings. She was also in a dark place and looking for reasons to feel bad about herself.

"I was with my parents," he told her.

"Yeah? How are they?"

"Fragile," he said.

"Well, I'm sorry to take you away from them."

"No, I appreciate the rescue," he said. "I wasn't in much of a mood to talk right now. Why don't you go back home? There's nothing more you can do here."

Jess shook her head. "I'll keep watch while you're inside. I want to be here in case he rabbits."

"And then what? You can't stop him."

He saw the cloud on her face. She kept forgetting. Twenty years as a cop didn't go away easily.

"I can follow him," she said. "I won't let him see me. At least we'll know where he goes and whether he's alone."

It was pointless for him to argue. Jess was stubborn, and she was going to do whatever she wanted.

"Did you find out anything more about the girl at the bar?" Frost asked.

"Brown hair, lots of makeup, black dress."

"That really narrows it down."

"Cutter's wearing a fedora. Double yellow stripes on the brim."

"Just like half the hipsters in the city," Frost said.

"Look who's talking, Justin Timberlake," she muttered sarcastically.

Frost laughed without taking offense, but he knew Jess was trying to be cruel. He was running out of patience with her. She was more upset than she let on about her life being turned upside down, but if she wanted to feel sorry for herself, he couldn't do anything except let her wallow. She'd brought it on herself, and they both knew it.

"I'm going over there," he told her in a clipped voice. "Keep your eyes open."

Jess didn't reply. She smoked, and she shrugged with false bravado, as if she didn't care about anything. Her eyes were as cold as the rain.

Frost put his head down and crossed Fillmore Street toward the theater door. As he got closer, he could already hear the music trying to bust through the walls and the screams of the people inside. There was something animal-like about a concert floor. Pack the crowd together, turn up the volume, turn down the lights, and shatter your eardrums with noise. In a room like that, you couldn't tell the hunter from the hunted.

The thought flitted in and out of his mind that he could shove his gun against Rudy Cutter's heart in there, pull the trigger, and no one would ever know.

It was just a bad fantasy.

He went inside.

24

The music thumped inside Rudy's chest like the beating of a second heart, wild and loud.

Hundreds of people squeezed shoulder to shoulder, screaming and throwing their hands in the air. Spotlights, like bright eyes, streamed through clouds of fog and cast an orange glow over the mass of bodies. The crowd undulated in unison, like a single living thing, dancing up and down. Elegant chandeliers dangled over their heads, strangely out of place here, as if a revolutionary army had stormed the royal palace. The floor shook. The band ruled.

Rudy didn't dance like the others. He stood where he was, as motionless as a wooden mannequin, except to swivel his head to study the faces shining in the moving lights and monitor the exits out of the theater. He hid behind the mask of his sunglasses. His hands were in his pockets. He had nothing with him, other than cash; his backpack was hidden in an alley two blocks away. It would be easy enough to retrieve when he needed what was inside.

Beside him, Magnolia shoved her fingers in her mouth and whistled, but the noise was soundless amid the din. She tossed her head back and forth, and her long hair swirled underneath the brim of the hat he'd dropped on her head. Her forehead was dotted with sweat. Her lips mouthed the lyrics of whatever song the band was playing, but he couldn't make out the words.

As she danced, the spaghetti strap of her little black dress slipped down one shoulder. He admired the exposed bare skin and the creamy curve of her neck. She saw him watching her, and she shouted something, but he couldn't hear it. Then she grabbed his waist, pulled her body next to his own, and kissed him with her tongue snaking inside his mouth. He could see her eyes, which were big and drunk. He wondered if she'd scored some pills from someone in the crowd.

That was fine. That made it easier.

Magnolia's lips found their way to his ear. She shouted at him, but he could barely hear her. "You're cute."

She was definitely drunk. Definitely stoned. He let his hand drift downward on the back of her dress.

"So are you," he mouthed at her. He didn't know if she understood him, but her eyes had a horny fire.

"I'm having a *great* time. The music is *great*." She pressed herself hard against his body and breathed into his ear again. "Wanna get lucky?"

Rudy grinned at her, which was all the encouragement she needed. She kissed him again, and down below, where the hips of strangers bumped around them, her fingers fished inside his loose pocket. Squeezing. Tugging. His breath caught with what she was doing to him. It wasn't going to take long for him to explode that way, but after she'd teased him to the edge, her hand disappeared. He tried to grab her wrist, but she nimbly avoided him and patted his cheek. She gave him a wicked smile and shook her head. With her face an inch away, he read her lips as she said, "Save that for later."

She didn't know there would be no later.

The band's song ended. The split second of silence in the hall was followed by whoops and cries. His ears rang. Everyone was breathless.

"I need a drink," Magnolia said.

"I'll get you one."

"I gotta pee first," she said.

"Okay, we'll drink when you get back. You like champagne?"

"I *love* champagne."

"What kind?"

"The most expensive kind."

He smiled. "Sure."

"What if I lose you in here?" she asked.

"You won't."

Her hand dipped into her purse. She pulled out a business card and nestled against him and slid it into the pocket of his jacket. "Just in case. My address is on the card."

Magnolia twirled away, stumbling against two other men. If the collision had been harder, it would have been like toppling dominoes. She wiggled a finger at Rudy to say good-bye, and then she weaved into the crowd. He followed her progress by watching the bounce of his fedora on her head, but he lost her among the sea of bodies.

Japandroids started playing again, drowning out whistles that were as sharp as knives. The throbbing guitars of the song growled like a monster in his head. He checked his watch and did another slow survey of the hall. The exits. The balconies. The cautious gazes of the security guards. If they were looking for him, if the alert had come down, they didn't show it.

And yet his sixth sense tingled. That was the one that saved you in the prison yard. Someone was watching him.

Rudy was casual about trying to figure out who it was. He pretended to be into the music. He pumped the air with one fist and shouted into the echo chamber. No one could hear him. Fresh fog spilled from machines in the ceiling like a damp cloud, giving him cover. He turned slowly, with his stare sweeping the faces behind him. They went in and out of focus in the haze.

There she was.

A stranger, not even ten feet away. Her eyes drilled into him.

She had blond hair and was probably twenty-five years old. She was dressed to party, in a gold dress bare up to her thighs, with stiletto heels. A threaded chain adorned her neck, and matching earrings dangled from her ears. She had blue eyes, and the only way to describe them now was arctic blue. Cold as ice.

He watched two words form on her lips, as if she were talking to herself. *Rudy Cutter.*

He didn't see any fear in her expression, and he knew why. She had a date with her who loomed head and shoulders above the crowd, at least six foot five, built like a fullback. She tugged on his arm, and the man leaned down. As she spoke, his eyes darted among the people in front of him until they landed on Rudy. Then they stopped dead, and his face hardened.

There was no doubt. The giant recognized him, too.

Rudy turned away from them. He focused on the stage again, as if he were in no hurry. Two couples danced near him, and he sidled between them and used them as a screen. Glancing back, he could see the giant's head. The giant was on the move, coming after him. Rudy pushed faster, swimming against the current in an ocean of bodies. Deliberately, as he passed a cocktail waitress, he used an elbow to nudge her tray, causing drinks to fly. Shouts and shoving ensued, and the disturbance made a wall. The giant was cut off.

He worked his way toward red curtains draping the fringe of the hall. It was darker back here; the hot lights focused on the stage. The fog covered his escape, too; it wafted through the crowd like a ghost. The music roared on; the noise and dancing and drinking went on. No one noticed him. Carefully, he peered over his shoulder to study the seething mass of people around him, but he was invisible now, one face among hundreds, and the giant was nowhere to be seen.

The main doors beckoned him from twenty feet away. He was almost free. It was time to go.

That was when he turned his face upward toward the balconies over his head and saw a man scanning the crowd on the floor below. He recognized the swept-back brown hair and beard.

It was Frost Easton.

Rudy shrank backward among the bodies. The crowd and the smoke weren't enough to hide him. The cop looked down as Rudy looked up, like two flashlight beams connecting and growing brighter.

Their eyes met.

"That's him," Frost said to the security guard next to him. "Three o'clock, gray turtleneck, blond hair."

"I've got him," the guard replied.

"He's heading for the doors. Ask your men to hold him until I get there. Don't let him leave."

Frost fought through the knot of people on the balcony and broke free into the cocktail lounge. A handful of customers stood around lonely tables, amid walls filled with hundreds of rock band posters. The music from the stage made the entire room vibrate. He bolted for the stairs and ran to the concert floor. Downstairs, the ushers waited for him at the theater doors, but there was no sign of Rudy Cutter.

"Did you see him?" he asked.

The two men shook their heads. "He didn't come this way."

Frost waded into the crowd. His head bobbed back and forth, hunting among the faces. He made his way to the red curtains where he'd spotted Cutter, but the killer had already backtracked and disappeared. Cutter was nowhere to be seen. He turned around, saw that the head of security had followed him downstairs, and shouted in the man's ear, "He's heading for one of the other exits. Do you have a man on each door?"

"Always."

"Make sure they're watching for him," Frost said. "Tell them to be polite but firm. Keep him inside."

Frost cast his eyes around the crowded concert floor and saw the nearest exit behind the stage. He texted a quick update to Jess—Cutter's here, he's on the move—and headed toward the rear of the theater. The security guard trailed behind him. The dense crowd, tangled with bodies, slowed his progress. It was like hacking through a rainforest. He heard the wail of the band, the screams of the fans, and then, almost like a whisper, someone nearby called out a name.

"Cutter."

He froze and spun around, but he didn't know where the voice had come from, and he didn't see the killer in the crowd. He looked for someone looking back at him, but there was no one.

Then it happened again. Another voice.

"Rudy Cutter."

And again.

"He's here. Cutter's here."

"The killer?"

"Cutter."

"That guy, the killer."

"Rudy Cutter."

"Cutter."

The voices were everywhere, an odd underground chorus. Cutter's name was on everyone's lips, blowing through the hall like rumors of a fire. A killer was here. A madman was on the floor. One by one, in fragments, the edge of the crowd flaked away. They headed for the main doors; they headed for the rear doors; they snaked along the curtains and shoved toward every exit. Dozens of them. It was fear, rippling from friend to friend and stranger to stranger.

Don't take chances.

Let's get out of here.

Rudy Cutter.

The exodus trapped Frost where he was, winding around him as tightly as a knotted rope. He couldn't move. Beyond the stage, he could see doors opening and closing beneath the red exit sign. Over and over. Again and again. People wanted out. The same was true at every exit in the hall. The guards couldn't do a thing except stand helplessly by as streams of nervous concertgoers flooded onto Geary and into the alley and into the lounge and the lobby. The hall was still packed, but the damage was already done.

Somewhere in the parade of people fleeing the scene, losing himself in the crowd, was Rudy Cutter.

Frost knew he'd lost him. Cutter was gone.

25

Dozens of people milled on the sidewalk outside the Fillmore.

Frost followed the narrow curb to the Geary Boulevard overpass, watching Uber drivers do pickups at the theater. Buses came and went. The coffee shop around the corner was doing a brisk late-night business. He saw men, women, and couples dispersing into the neighborhoods, some holding colorful umbrellas against the rain. The ones who weren't done partying crossed the pedestrian bridge to the Boom Boom Room.

It was midnight. He was wasting his time. Cutter wasn't here.

He tracked down Jess, who was sitting behind the wheel of her Audi a block north of the theater. He was soaking wet as he sat in the passenger seat. The windows were steamed, and she had to wipe them with her elbow.

"Anything?" he asked her.

"No. Sorry. If he was in the crowd that bolted, I couldn't pick him out."

"I counted about fifty brunettes in little black dresses," Frost said. "Any one of them could have been the girl he was with. He was alone when I saw him, so he may have ditched her when he made his escape."

Jess shrugged. "Well, that's one good thing. You got in the way of his plans by spotting him."

"Maybe."

"You don't sound convinced."

"I'm not. Cutter's smart. He led us here for a reason. We've been playing *his* game tonight. I'd feel better if we knew what this was really about."

"Don't overthink Cutter," Jess replied. "After getting out of prison, his ego's only gotten bigger. He thinks he can tell us exactly what he's going to do and still get away with it."

Frost frowned. "I'm not sure he's wrong."

"Well, I'm counting tonight as a win. You spooked him."

"Maybe," Frost said again.

Jess put a hand on his shoulder. "Thanks for doing this off the books, Frost. You know, not calling Hayden and letting me stick around here. Cutter made this personal by having the bartender call me. I hate being on the sidelines."

"No problem, Jess."

Frost felt the warmth of her hand, which she left where it was. She didn't have to say anything; the invitation was in her face again. He could slide across the seat, and they'd kiss, and then they'd drive to her place, and they'd have sex. Herb had told him that Jess wasn't his Jane Doe—his one-of-a-kind mystery girl—but Frost wasn't sure that he had a Jane Doe waiting for him at all. The only thing that mattered was right now.

But he waited too long, the way he usually did. The moment passed. Right now was already gone, and it wasn't coming back. Jess peeled away her hand and dug her keys from her pocket. She switched on the sedan.

"Anyway," she said.

"Yeah, anyway."

"Call me tomorrow, okay?"

"I will. I'll keep you posted."

Frost got out of the car onto the sidewalk on Fillmore and shut the door. The Audi lurched from the curb, sending up spray. Her wheels skidded. Jess always drove fast, but he thought she wanted to put as much distance as she could, as quickly as she could, between the two of them.

His own Suburban was two blocks away. He headed toward Geary past the late walkers leaving the theater. In the rain and darkness, he turned left, and the dirty asphalt glistened. He walked past an old brick post office building to the end of the block, where his SUV was parked next to a fenced soccer field.

He started the truck and did a U-turn. The red light at Geary stopped him, and he waited impatiently for a couple of drunk Japandroids fans to stagger across the street hand in hand. He was tired and wanted to get home. When the intersection was clear, he turned right into an underpass, but as his headlights swung through the cross-walk on the other side of Geary, he spotted a woman coming down the walkway from the street's pedestrian bridge. He only glimpsed her for a second before she disappeared behind the concrete columns, but something about her made him hesitate.

She was one more brunette wearing a little black dress—but she was wearing a hat, too. The hat had a jaunty angle, pushed low on her forehead. It was a man's hat. A fedora.

Frost stopped in the concrete tunnel, waited for a car to pass, and then bumped over the barrier and shot back uphill in the opposite direction. He reached Geary quickly, but the girl was already gone. He drove through the intersection under the pedestrian bridge and parked the SUV near the steps of a neighborhood recreation center. He got out and checked the sidewalk in both directions, but he didn't see her.

She couldn't have gone far.

The recreation center was locked and dark. Ahead of him was a children's playground, leading to a fenced set of tennis courts. He jogged to the end of the building, where a narrow sidewalk led to the other side of Hamilton Square. Not far away, he heard the tap of heels on concrete, and he ran again. The sidewalk took him to Post Street.

He saw her. She passed under the glow of a streetlight in the next block, and he could see her hat clearly, just for a second. It was definitely a man's fedora. She disappeared around the corner, and he followed. His own footsteps were loud. He reached the next block, but when he rounded the corner, he'd lost her again. The street was lined with apartment buildings, but none of the building entrances was near enough for her to have gone inside.

Frost listened and heard nothing except a patter of rain.

He took a few steps down the street. As he neared the gated entrance to a building garage, the woman suddenly stepped out of a recessed doorway directly in front of him. She had a small canister clutched in her fingers, pointed at his face.

"Stop!" she screamed. "This is Mace. Get the hell away from me, or I'll use it."

Frost immediately stepped back, his hands up. "I'm sorry, ma'am—"

"You were *following* me! You better run right now!"

"Ma'am, it's okay, I'm a police officer." Frost nudged the flap of his sport coat aside. He used two fingers to slide his identification out of his pocket and lay it open on the ground. Then he backed away again, giving her space. "Check it out. My name's Frost Easton. I'm a homicide inspector."

"Homicide." The woman hesitated. She took a step toward the badge and knelt down to examine it. She picked it up and studied the ID under the streetlight. Her eyes went to Frost's face. "What do you want with me?"

The fedora was askew on her head. Long brown hair spilled from underneath it. The hat had two yellow braided bands around the brim. Just as Jess had described it.

"That hat you're wearing," he said, "did someone give it to you tonight?"

"Yeah, I got it from a guy I met."

"Did you meet him at an underground bar in Japantown?" Frost asked.

"How do you know that?"

"It doesn't matter. Were you with him at the Fillmore?"

"Yeah, but we got separated. I figured he bailed on me. Guys do that, you know."

"What was this man's name? Did he tell you?"

"Rudy. He said his name was Rudy."

Frost felt his breathing accelerate. He took a look up and down the street, which was empty. He forced a smile onto his face to put her at ease. He needed her calm in the next few minutes. "And what's your name?"

"Magnolia."

"Do you live nearby, Magnolia?"

Her eyes flitted to the badge again to make absolutely sure he was who he'd said he was. She tossed it to him, and he caught it. She slid the Mace into her purse. "Yeah. I have an apartment in the next block. Why? What's this all about?"

"This is very important," Frost told her. "The man you met tonight. Rudy. Did you tell him where you live?"

Rudy put the binoculars to his eyes. He examined each of the apartment balconies, to make sure no one was smoking or drinking in places where they could see him. It was late, and most of the rooms were dark, but he checked those that had lights to see if the curtains were closed. He reviewed each of the parked cars in the alley, too. No one was watching the street.

He secured the binoculars and slid his backpack onto his shoulders. He broke cover and slipped across the alley to the building wall. His hands were gloved. The first-floor apartment was protected by a gate, and he used the steel cross section between the bars to hoist himself silently up to the next floor. He swung one leg over, then the other, and dropped down onto the balcony.

The door was locked. The blinds were closed, but he saw no lights inside. He assumed the apartment was empty. He slid the black-handled revolver he'd taken from Jimmy Keyes out of his backpack and secured it in his jacket pocket. The gun was a last resort, but he wanted it accessible. Just in case.

Rudy checked the street again. It was still quiet.

He dug in the backpack for a spring-loaded window punch, which was compact and designed to fit on a keychain. Bending down, he primed it on the concrete floor of the balcony. Then he pressed the device against the window glass near the metal handle of the door. The hammer fired, punching an eight-inch hole with a quick, sharp crack. Kernels of glass sprayed inside.

He listened.

No one came running. No one shouted. Rudy reached his hand through the hole, undid the lock, and slid the glass door open. He pushed through the vertical blinds into the dark apartment, with one hand on the gun in his pocket. The blinds shuddered, flapping like baseball cards in bicycle spokes.

He was alone.

Quickly, he checked the bedroom. The bed was made, and it was empty. He returned to the living room. It was hard to see in the darkness, but he left the lights off. There was no time to waste; he had to make sure everything was ready. He held his hands in front of his face to make sure his gloves hadn't torn and that the broken glass hadn't cut his skin. He donned a plastic shower cap over his hair. Then he retrieved a chair from the kitchen and brought it to the front door.

He positioned the chair so that the door would block him from view of anyone coming inside. He would be invisible until it was too late.

The kitchen wasn't well stocked, but he found a knife that would suffice in one of the drawers. It had a six-inch blade and a heavy, comfortable feel in his hand, and it was sharp. He had another knife waiting in his backpack, but that was only a spare, in case he didn't find what he needed in the apartment. This knife, the one in his hand, would do fine.

He sat down in the chair behind the door.

He removed the Taser from the backpack. He put the knife on his thigh, where he could grab it as soon as the Taser did its work.

The setup wasn't perfect. Nothing ever was. Where the glass door at the back of the apartment was broken, an occasional burst of city wind whistled like a witch and made the blinds go tap, tap, tap. If she stopped to listen before she came in, she might hear it. The risk couldn't be helped.

In his mind, he rehearsed how it would go. He played out the motions one at a time, again and again. He was ready.

He breathed in and out in the darkness, and he waited for her.

26

"This is my place," Magnolia told Frost. "I'm on the second floor."

He stood in the street, studying the three-story Victorian apartment home on Sutter. The lower level was occupied by storefronts that had been built out to the sidewalk. The shops were locked and dark. A staircase led up from the street to the building entrance.

"Is there anywhere else you can stay tonight?" Frost asked.

"No. I don't just live here, this is my office. I work here, too. Look, I'm cold and tired, and I just want to go to bed."

"I need to make sure you're safe," Frost said.

"I sleep with my Mace on the nightstand."

"Cutter's a lot more dangerous than that. Trust me."

"I know, you keep saying that. He's a killer. Are you sure? I thought a dirty cop framed him or something."

"A police detective did something wrong, but that doesn't change who Cutter is."

Magnolia shrugged, as if she didn't want to face the close call she'd had. "Well, he didn't seem like a bad guy."

"He is. A very bad guy."

"Whatever. If you say so. Look, if you want to come inside and make sure the bogeyman's not in there, knock yourself out."

"I want to check the street first," Frost said. "Wait right here, and don't go into the apartment until I get back."

He walked down Sutter past the lineup of parked cars and examined the porches and doorways of the other buildings. The hiding places were empty. Most of the apartments on the street were dark, with their blinds shut. He continued to the end of the block, seeing no one else around, and then retraced his steps. Magnolia leaned against the shop window at her building with her legs squeezed together, her arms crossed, and the fedora pushed high up on her forehead. Her eyes kept blinking closed, and she shivered.

"You done?" she asked.

"Let me take a quick look in back."

"I'm telling you, Rudy's not here. He probably hooked up with somebody else."

"This won't take long," Frost said.

He walked to the corner and turned right, leaving Magnolia behind him. The cross street was deserted. He followed the sidewalk beyond the streetlight, where the building butted up to a narrow alley, barely wide enough for cars. It was a dead end that didn't go all the way through to the next street. He walked into the alley past the rear walls of the apartments. His shoes splashed in standing water. It was pitch-black here, and he grabbed a penlight from his pocket. It cast a weak glow, enough to surprise a rat foraging at a dumpster. The smell of trash wafted in the damp air. A handful of cars were parked below the balconies and fire escapes, and he peered inside each one.

Nothing.

Maybe he and Jess were wrong.

Frost retreated to the street. He walked quickly back to Sutter and turned the corner. Twenty feet away, the sidewalk outside the Victorian apartment home was empty now.

Magnolia was gone. She'd headed inside alone.

He took the steps of the apartment building two at a time. The heavy front door was ahead of him under an arched portico. He grabbed the doorknob, and the door spilled inward. It wasn't latched. He bolted into a hallway lined with musty carpet and fading yellow paint on the walls. Stairs wound upward to the next level of the building.

There was only one apartment on this floor. One door.

It was open.

Frost reached for the holster inside his jacket and slid his pistol into his hand. Through the crack in the door, he saw lights. He took a step closer, his movements muffled by the carpet. When he reached the door, he nudged it wide with the toe of his shoe. The only thing he saw was the fedora lying in the middle of the floor.

"Magnolia?" he called.

There was silence for a long moment.

Then the woman's face popped around the kitchen doorway. "Hey."

Frost started breathing again, and he holstered his weapon. "I told you to wait outside until I got back."

"I was cold."

He didn't argue with her. "I want to check the place out, okay?"

"Sure, go ahead."

The apartment wasn't large. It didn't take him long to confirm it was empty. He checked the balcony and the alley below, and then he locked the sliding door. When he was done, he returned to the kitchen. Magnolia, still wearing her black dress, sat at a small table. She'd kicked off her heels; her feet were bare. She'd poured a glass of white wine from a half-empty bottle.

"You want a drink?" she asked.

"No, thanks."

She took a large sip of wine. "Rudy was cute, you know."

"He murdered seven women, Magnolia."

"Yeah, I know what they say online, but I still can't believe it. He didn't seem like the type."

"There is no type," Frost said. "You can't tell by looking at someone."

"You really think he'll come back here?"

"I don't know, but it pays to be safe. I wish you'd go somewhere else tonight."

"Sorry, I can't. I'll nap for a couple hours, but then I have to get to work. You sure you don't want a drink?"

"No."

"Okay." Magnolia finished the glass and stood up, wobbling. "Anything else?"

"Be sure to lock the door behind me when I go. And never leave the front door of the building unlatched." Frost slid a card from his wallet and put it on the table. "If Rudy contacts you, call me immediately. Don't meet him anywhere. If he shows up at your door, don't open it. Call nine one one. I'm not kidding."

Frost left Magnolia in her apartment. He checked Sutter one more time and did another survey of the alley in back of the building. Nothing had changed, but he was still troubled. He found a dark doorway on the corner where he could see the front of the building and the entrance to the alley, and he waited there. It was late, but most of Cutter's dirty work was done in the middle of the night. He might still show up.

He texted Jess: Found the girl Cutter was with. She's safe.

And then a minute later, he sent another text: No sign of him, but I'm staking out the neighborhood.

He shoved his phone back into his pocket.

He tried to understand Cutter's plan. Jess said Cutter always had a plan; he knew what he was doing. First, he hooks up with a stranger at a bar, and then he brags about it to Jess and leaves a trail a mile wide. He was practically begging her to chase him. Then Frost hunts him down inside the Fillmore, and Cutter disappears.

He was beginning to suspect that this was all a diversion. A head fake. While Frost cooled his heels outside the girl's apartment, Cutter was somewhere completely different.

Where?

Frost grabbed his phone and texted again: I think he's playing us.

That was when he noticed that his earlier texts to Jess had been delivered, but not read. She hadn't checked messages on her phone, which was normally like an extension of her arm, day or night. He felt a tiny chill of anxiety, like a pinprick on the back of his neck.

He texted: Jess?

And again: Jess? Where are you?

He punched the speed-dial number for her phone. On the other end, the phone rang without being picked up, and it shifted to her voice mail. He heard her message, which was the same as it had been for years. He listened to the impatient voice he knew so well. This was the woman he'd been with less than an hour earlier, the woman whose face he could see in his sleep.

"Jess? Are you there? Call me as soon as you get this."

In the brief silence before he hung up, he added, "Are you back at your apartment? If you're not, don't go home. Go to my place. Meet me there."

Frost stepped out of the darkness of the doorway. He realized that he'd been right all along. Cutter had set up the events at the theater as a ruse. Magnolia was the distraction, and the man's real target was someone else entirely. Something washed over Frost like a wave, but the rain had stopped. This was something else. This was terror. This was every instinct, every intuition, screaming at him to *run*.

He did.

He sprinted for his truck, his chest hammering.

But he knew that his closet of horrors, the closet where he kept the memory of Katie, had a new monster inside. He already knew that he was too late.

◆ ◆ ◆

Two uniformed officers, a man and a woman, met him at Jess's apartment building. He'd called for backup from the Suburban.

"There's no answer at her apartment, Inspector," the policewoman told him.

"Have you searched the area?" Frost asked.

"No, we just got here."

"Circle the building," he told her. "Be careful. This is Rudy Cutter, so expect him to be armed and dangerous."

"Yes, sir."

He gestured to the other officer. "Let's check the back."

The two of them headed for the rear of the building, where the apartments faced a dead-end alley and the densely wooded hillside. A river ran along the curb, where rainwater trickled from the muddy slope. Jess's apartment was on the second floor. He stood below her balcony, and then he walked out to the other side of the alley to get a better view. Even in the darkness, he could see it.

The broken window. The open door.

Frost bolted for the locked gate below her apartment and hauled himself up until he could grab the railing of the second-floor balcony. He shouted at the cop waiting for him. "Get around to the front, I'll let you in. Call more backup out here right now! And an ambulance!"

He swung his leg up, jumped, and landed hard on the other side of the railing. The vertical blinds beyond the open patio door slapped back and forth with the breeze. Glass glittered on the carpet. He had his gun out, and he stormed into the apartment.

"Jess!"

His voice was loud, but no one answered. The apartment smelled like Jess, which meant it smelled like cigarettes. He couldn't see anything in the darkness. He knew where the light switches were, and he turned on the nearest lamp, squinting at the sudden brightness. Then his gaze swept the living room.

His heart stopped.

She was there. Just inside the front door. On her back, limbs sprawled. Blood was everywhere.

"Jess."

He didn't know if he'd said her name out loud or whether it was simply in his heart. He went to her and knelt over her. He checked her pulse, but there was nothing for him to do. Grayness had painted over her face. Her eyes were closed. Her skin was still warm, but she was gone. Fragments from the Taser blast that had stunned her sprayed the carpet. The knife that had opened up her throat, drowned her, bled her out, lay on the floor next to her.

Frost saw a chair tipped over on the carpet. It wasn't in the right place. Cutter had sat in that chair and waited for Jess to come home. He'd lured her out of her apartment and sent them on a false chase at the Fillmore after a girl who meant nothing, while Cutter crossed the city to stalk his real target.

Jess was the eighth victim.

Every "what if" that might have changed this moment played out in Frost's mind in a split second. There were a thousand different things he could have done, and Jess would still be alive.

What if he'd stopped Cutter at the Fillmore.

What if he'd gone home with Jess tonight, instead of leaving her alone.

What if he'd thrown Melanie Valou's watch off the Golden Gate Bridge and let Cutter rot in prison.

But none of it changed the reality that he'd failed her. Cutter had won. Jess was dead.

Frost took her hand. He squeezed, but she didn't squeeze back. That was when he noticed that Jess had a slim gold watch on her wrist. Jess never wore a watch. The crystal on the face was smashed, but he could still make out the time, which was frozen in place and would stay that way forever.

3:42 a.m.

27

The night passed for Frost in a haze of sleeplessness and grief.

He never went home. Instead, he spent hours in a small interview room in the police headquarters building in the Mission Bay District. This was where he typically talked to witnesses and suspects, but this time, he was the witness. The detectives on the case went over the details of the night with him. They asked the same questions again and again, trying to tease out new facts from his memory. In the end, he didn't have much to tell them.

He hadn't been there when the murder happened. He hadn't seen anything.

Everyone knew Rudy Cutter was guilty, but knowing something was true didn't mean they could prove it.

The building was dead quiet. The death of a cop always hung over the force like a cloud, but this was Jess. She was a cop's cop, third-generation SFPD, an angry fighter for all things blue. Except, Frost knew, that was all in the past. She'd lost her badge. She'd gone down in disgrace and had been staring at prison time for her sins. Her murder was a tragedy, but there would be no city funeral, no parade, no speech from the chief and the mayor.

It was still dark when they were done with the interview.

He stopped at his desk and could feel the eyes of everyone watching him, but no one said a thing. He had a reputation for being a lone wolf, and it was mostly deserved. He didn't hang out in the police bars; he didn't party and drink with the other cops. That made him different, still a stranger after five years. His one real ally was Jess, and now she was gone.

Frost felt exhaustion weighing him down, although he knew he wouldn't sleep. He headed for the elevator, but he stopped when a voice cut across the stillness of the room.

"Easton."

He turned around. It was Captain Hayden.

"Let's talk," he said in a voice that always sounded as if he'd just come back from a root canal.

Frost followed Hayden into his office, which had windows looking north toward the Giants stadium. It was a nice office, but Hayden had his sights set on the office upstairs. He'd started out as a street cop thirty years earlier, and he'd climbed the promotions ladder, greasy rung by greasy rung, until the only step left was the one that would make him the chief. Hayden wasn't going to let anything stand in his way. Not even the murder of his ex-wife.

"So you're the one who found her," the captain rumbled.

"Yes, sir."

"Did she suffer?"

"I don't know, sir. I imagine it was brutal but quick."

"Hard to believe anybody getting the drop on Jess," Hayden said.

"Cutter had it well planned. He was waiting for her where she couldn't see him. First the Taser, then the knife. She didn't stand a chance."

Hayden coughed, and then he wiped his eyes. "Cutter," he murmured.

"Yes, sir."

The captain walked around to the back of his desk and squeezed into a high-back leather chair. Pruitt Hayden was one of the largest human beings Frost had ever met. He was six foot four, well over three hundred pounds, and he could bench-press his weight. His black skin was freckled and mottled, and his scalp had a dark shadow of stubble. He always wore his dress blues, with folds impeccably creased.

"Sit, Easton."

Frost took the chair in front of the desk. He noticed that Hayden still kept a framed photo of Jess where he could see it. The photo had been taken ten years earlier, when they were just married and honeymooning on a Hawaiian beach. It was one of the rare photos in which Frost had seen Jess smiling. Divorce didn't change the fact that there had been happier times between them, but they were two volcanic personalities who didn't know how to do anything except work. Sooner or later, Hayden's ambition, and Jess's willingness to break rules, were going to collide.

"You know I'm angry," Hayden said, although any emotions he felt barely moved the mask of his face. "I'd be angry if this happened to any of our people, but this is personal. I loved her. What happened in the past between us doesn't matter."

"I'm angry, too."

"This department will get justice for her. *I* will get justice for her." He emphasized the I, as if to make sure Frost realized that he wasn't part of the mix. This case didn't include him.

"I hope so," Frost said.

"None of this changes the fact that Jess did a stupid, inexcusable thing by planting evidence."

"I know."

"You were right to bring the watch to me and the district attorney. Don't ever doubt that, Easton."

Frost said nothing. He'd been doubting himself all night. "Where do we stand on Cutter, sir?"

"Right now? Nowhere."

"He did it," Frost said.

Hayden's face clouded over. "Of course he did it! You think I don't know that? If it were up to me, I'd beat that prick to death with my own fists. Any cop in this building would do the same. He's throwing it in our faces like there's nothing we can do, and he's going to pay."

Frost waited for the outburst to pass, and then he dealt with the reality in front of them. "But we don't have a case, right?"

Hayden rocked back in his chair, which squealed in submission. "Not yet we don't, no."

"Do we know where he is?"

"No, he's still off the radar. His brother called me. Phil Cutter. Very helpful piece of crap. He said he'd heard about the murder. He thought we might leap to the wrong conclusion, so he wanted me to know that Rudy had been with him all night after midnight."

"He's a liar," Frost said.

"Yes, but the trouble is, we can't prove he's lying without some physical evidence to put Rudy Cutter in Jess's apartment or anywhere near the crime scene. Which, right now, we don't have. The forensic people are still over there, but they don't sound happy. Cutter is pretty careful about not leaving any DNA or fingerprints that we can hang on him."

"He knows what he's doing," Frost said. "It was the same with all of the other murders. What about the old man on Stockton? Jimmy Keyes?"

"The Taser used on Jess belonged to Keyes. The ID tags match. But we're no closer to getting Cutter for the Keyes murder, either."

"So what do we do?" Frost asked.

Hayden didn't answer immediately. He took the photo of Jess from his desk and held it in his big hands. His eyes didn't mist, but they became empty, as if the weight of her death were too much to bear. Behind his anger, behind his ego, was a crushing loss. And he wasn't about to share that loss with Frost.

"*You* don't do anything, Inspector Easton," Hayden told him.

"With respect, sir, I can't live with that answer."

He expected the captain to lose his temper and fire back, but Hayden actually smiled at him. "No bullshit. I appreciate that. I know Jess always liked you, Easton. She liked you enough that it pissed some people off around here. A pretty long list of people, in fact."

Frost suspected that the list included Hayden himself.

"I liked Jess, too," Frost said. "And whatever you or anyone else may think, she never cut me any slack."

"Oh, I know that. If she did, I would have been on her like a ton of bricks. You're good. No one says you're not."

"Thank you, sir."

"I also know about the rumors," Hayden said.

Frost said nothing. He wasn't going to try to explain his relationship with Jess, because he didn't know if he could explain it to himself. He simply waited to see what would happen next. Hayden's eyes were like coal on the other side of the desk, and his breathing was loud through his wide nose. Then the captain waved his hand, as if whatever had happened between Frost and Jess meant nothing at all.

"Mind you, I'm not asking whether the rumors are true. I don't care. It's not like I can complain about anything Jess chose to do, before or after our divorce. I was no saint. We both brought plenty of baggage to the breakup."

"I'm not sure why we're talking about this, sir," Frost said.

"We're talking about this because we both have the same goal. We want Rudy Cutter back in prison. And I'm aware that you have just as much motivation as me to make that happen."

"Yes, I do."

"Then let the rest of us do our jobs. Jess already went rogue on this case. The result was that Cutter went free, and Jess paid for it with her life. I'm not going to let you screw up our next shot at putting him away."

"I have no intention of doing that," Frost said.

"No? You don't think I have spies, Easton? I know exactly what you've been doing on your *vacation*. You've been dredging up old witnesses. Talking to family members of the victims. Asking questions. I hear you've been working with a writer who's doing a book about the case, too. Am I right?"

Frost made no attempt to deny it. "Yes, you're right."

Hayden exhaled, making a whistling noise through a little gap in his front teeth. "We are already on thin ice with Judge Elgin. He threw out the entire investigation, Easton. Five years of work. If he smells so much as a hint of impropriety again, he'll toss the case entirely, and we'll never get our hands on Cutter. None of us want that to happen."

"No," Frost said. "We don't."

"Good. Now here's what I want you to do. Go home. Grieve for Jess. Grieve for your sister. Take another week of vacation, and make it a real vacation this time, got it? Fly to a beach somewhere, or go hiking in the mountains, or just sit at home and clear your head. But whatever you do, *stay the hell out of this case*. Have I made myself absolutely clear?"

"You have," Frost said.

"That'll be all, Easton."

"Yes, sir."

He got out of the chair and headed for the door, but Hayden called after him in a voice not much louder than a sigh. "Frost."

He turned around in surprise. The captain stood up and came around to the other side of the desk again. "I assume that once upon a time, Jess gave you her little speech about the line," Hayden said.

"Several times."

There was a silence between them. Frost expected something more, but Hayden simply whispered, "Good, good."

That was it. The meeting was over.

Frost didn't know what had just happened. He was in the elevator, leaving the building before he understood. *The line*. It was the line you had to cross as a cop sometimes, even if you got fired for doing the right thing, even if no one could protect you.

Hayden had given Frost a direct order to drop the investigation against Rudy Cutter. Then he'd added a postscript off the record.

Keep going.

28

The sun pushed above the East Bay hills, casting a golden glow on the water and making silhouettes of the Bay Bridge towers. Rudy stood with a takeaway cup of black coffee in his hand, steps from the Ferry Building, as he watched the dawn. He was freshly shaved and showered; the shower basin was bleached. His underwear, shirt, and jeans were clean and new. Half a mile away, at the bottom of a street corner trash bin, he'd deposited a tightly sealed plastic bag with last night's bloody clothes.

Now we're even, Jess.

Dealing with her had slowed him down. He'd wanted to cross her off his list on the first night he was free, but she'd been waiting for him, and that had forced him to develop a different plan. He felt satisfaction that the attack had gone as he anticipated, but he also felt oddly empty about the experience. He'd expected adrenaline. He'd expected the high of being back in the game. Instead, the violence itself had done nothing for him. Watching her realize that he'd won, watching the light go out of her eyes, had been a hollow victory.

Maria Lopes would be different.

Hope would be with him for Maria Lopes, as she had been for the others. Screaming for him to stop.

Rudy sipped his coffee. He'd bought it at the same coffee shop in the Ferry Building where he'd met Nina Flores. He hadn't been back there since that first time. He'd been idly curious if anyone would recognize him, but no one did. He'd ordered, got his coffee, and left. There had been no life-changing, heart-stopping moment as there had been with Nina.

In the shadows of the Ferry Building, he watched the woman sitting on the waterfront bench not far away. They had the Embarcadero mostly to themselves. She wasn't aware of him, although he'd been following her for half an hour. She had coffee, as he did, from the same place; he'd been four customers behind her in line. He thought it was interesting that she went there, bypassing other coffee shops on the route that led from her apartment to the water.

He walked along the sidewalk, approaching her. She was too caught up in her thoughts to notice him. She was on the bayside bench, and he sat down on the city-facing bench directly behind her. All the other benches around them were empty. He could feel her stiffen with annoyance that she was sharing her morning with a stranger.

"Hello, Eden," he said.

His voice was like the touch of a live wire, jolting her to her feet. She spun around, and he heard some of her coffee splatter on the sidewalk. He stared at the palm trees of the Embarcadero without looking back at her.

"What are you doing here, Rudy?" she demanded.

"I miss our chats."

"Get the hell away from me!"

"That's no way to talk to an old friend," he replied smoothly. "You're the one who wanted the voice inside, remember? How can you get that if we don't talk?"

"How did you find me?"

"I do my research, just like you. I like your new place, by the way. High-floor condo. Security building. No one's likely to wander in off the street and surprise you, are they?"

He didn't think she would run away. Not from him. He saw her studying the street in both directions to confirm that they were alone.

She came around to the other side of the bench and sat down next to him. Her face was drawn and tired, without makeup.

"Not sleeping well?" he asked. "Still having nightmares?"

"I don't need your concern."

"Well, I know how it is. You close your eyes, and you're right back in the past. That's how trauma works. I'd like to tell you it gets better, but it doesn't. It's with you until you die."

"Shut up, Rudy."

He watched her touch the scar that adorned her skin like a necklace. He'd seen her do that many times. It was a habit, like a way to remind herself who she was. She was layer upon layer of toughness. That was how she'd survived. If it came to a battle between the two of them, he didn't know who would win.

"Have you seen the news?" he asked.

Her fingers tightened around her coffee cup. "Yes. You killed Jess Salceda. Why? She was never part of your plan."

He didn't say anything. Even around Eden, he was cautious.

"Do you think I'm recording you?" she asked.

"No, but you have new friends. Your book has a new hero."

"I hope you don't think you were ever the *hero* in my book."

"Maybe not, but your loyalties are divided now. That worries me. We had an agreement, Eden. If you break the rules, don't be surprised if your opponent does the same. Jess learned that the hard way."

"Don't threaten me, Rudy. It's not smart."

"I could say the same thing," he replied.

Eden shrugged. Her face was a shell that didn't crack. "If you stay here, if you keep doing this, they're going to catch you. Or kill you."

"Well, that should make for an exciting end to your book."

"You're right. It will."

"How's the book coming, by the way? Are you almost done?"

"You tell me," she said.

He couldn't suppress the barest smile at that remark.

"Do you already have a deal with a publisher?" he asked. "I imagine this project will make you a lot of money. Big advance. Book tour. Maybe another movie. I wonder who they'll get to play me."

"It's not about the money," Eden said.

"Right, it's about proving yourself as a writer. It's about getting inside my head. Or is it about getting inside *your* head, Eden? Honestly, I've always wondered about that. Is the book really about me, or are you trying to understand who you are? After all this time, you still can't come to grips with what happened to you in that basement."

"Don't psychoanalyze me, Rudy. Experts have tried and failed." She crushed her empty coffee cup in her hand. "Enough with the games. Why are you here? Why did you find me?"

"I need your help."

"Forget it," Eden snapped. "I'm done with that. It's over."

"That's not how it works. You know that."

Eden jumped to her feet. "No? I'm leaving, and you're going to stay away from me. Got it? The next thing I do is buy a gun, and if you come near me again, I'll put a bullet between your eyes. Do you think anyone would care if I killed you? Do you think they'd put me on trial? I think they'd give me a medal. Now *that* would be quite the ending for my book, Rudy."

"Fine. Walk away. I won't stop you."

She stared at him, breathing fast. Her eyes were fierce. The seconds ticked by, and the day got brighter. A trolley train passed them on its way to the Wharf, its bells chiming.

"And yet here you are, Eden," Rudy went on. "We both know you're not going anywhere. Face it, you need me to keep your secret."

Eden said nothing. He watched her stand there, frozen, as if her feet were glued to the pavement. When she spoke, she practically spat her words back at him. "What the hell do you want, anyway?"

Rudy calmly sipped his coffee. He was in no hurry.

"I want you to tell me everything you know about Frost Easton."

29

Frost had spent all night wanting to get home, but when he got there, the silence of the house felt oppressive. He was too tired to sleep, and when he closed his eyes, the memory of Jess haunted him. He found himself wandering up and down the stairs, through the house's dusty rooms, with Shack keeping pace beside him. He wasn't looking for anything; he was just restless and hurting.

Downstairs, at the mirrored bar, he found the bottle of Trago Reposado he kept for Jess. Only a third of the tequila was gone, but she wouldn't be having any more shots. He unscrewed the bottle and inhaled its aroma, which he remembered on her breath. Then he over-turned it in the sink and watched the alcohol splash and swirl as it disappeared down the drain.

He couldn't stay here.

"Road trip?" he said to Shack.

The cat propped his front paws on Frost's leg to be picked up, and Frost scooped him up and deposited him on his shoulder. Shack hung on with his claws. The two of them left the house and headed for Frost's Suburban.

Like most San Franciscans, Frost avoided the tourist-infested area of Fisherman's Wharf whenever he could, but in the early morning hours, he could usually get in and out ahead of the crowds. He parked at the red curb near Alioto's on the bay and got out. Shack, who knew exactly what it meant to be down here, patrolled the dashboard impatiently. Frost greeted his old friends behind the counter at the seafood stand and ordered a Dungeness crab cocktail. They all knew him here. The cop with the cat. If there was one thing Shack loved, it was crab.

He got back in the Suburban, and Shack was all over him. It made it hard to drive, keeping one hand on the wheel and one hand on Shack's nose to prevent him from eating all the crab before he got where he was going. In the end, he gave up and started feeding Shack pieces of crab to eat on the front seat, and in between, he took some for himself, too.

He drove out of the Wharf area into the Marina District. Duane owned a tiny one-bedroom condominium a block from the yacht harbor. For the price, it was a ridiculous indulgence, because Duane was hardly ever there. But his brother had wanted a waterside apartment his whole life, and when he sold his first restaurant to an investment group, he channeled some of the profit into his Marina dream.

The morning was still early, but the sun was up. He parked across the street from the three-story building and eyed the top-floor window behind the fire escape where Duane lived. The curtains were closed. Half a block away, he saw the masts of the million-dollar boats whose owners could afford a slip on the bay. He rolled down the window and smelled the sea air. He and Shack finished the crab cocktail, and the cat licked the empty container until it fell on the floor of the truck.

When he looked at the building again, he saw a woman hurrying down the plaza steps that led to the sidewalk. Her red hair bounced. She wore big sunglasses and a purple dress, with a matching long-strapped purse slung over her shoulder. She looked as if she always had some place to go and couldn't wait to get there.

It was Tabby.

Frost called to her, and she stopped in surprise next to a red Saab that was parked on the street. She saw him, and a warm smile lit up her face. She crossed the street and took note of Shack, who hopped on the dashboard and pushed his pink nose toward her face.

"Well, look who the cat dragged in," she told Frost as she pulled off her sunglasses and let him drink in her green eyes. "Literally."

"Yeah, I know who people really want to see," Frost replied as Tabby rubbed Shack's head.

He didn't think he was wearing his grief on his face, but with a single knowing glance, Tabby assessed his expression and saw through him. "What's going on, Frost?" she asked. "Are you okay?"

He told her.

Tabby's smile vanished. Her face broke into sad little pieces. She put a hand on the back of his head and leaned closer until their foreheads touched through the car window. The simple intimacy of the gesture made him breathe harder. "Oh, Frost, I am so, so sorry."

"Thanks. It doesn't feel real."

She opened his car door and grabbed his arm. "Come on, let's take a walk."

"No, you're on your way somewhere. It's okay."

"I have to buy today's fish down at the piers. Don't worry, they know I'm coming. They'll put aside the best catch for me even if I'm a couple minutes late."

Frost let her pull him out of the Suburban. She reached in and grabbed Shack, too, despite her allergies. The cat nuzzled against her neck and settled comfortably in the crook of one arm. They walked down the block and crossed Marina Boulevard, with Tabby's other arm slung through Frost's elbow. She led him across an open space of green lawn until they found a bench in front of the bobbing speedboats and sailboats. Across the bay, the hills of Angel Island and Tiburon rose in front of them. Tabby put Shack down, and the cat sat calmly between them on the bench, squinting his eyes against the sea breeze. The sun was warm.

"Tell me about Jess," Tabby said. "If I'm not prying."

"You're not." He hesitated, not because he was reluctant to talk, but because he didn't know how to describe her. "Jess was a deep track," he said finally.

"What do you mean?"

"She wasn't radio friendly. She wasn't the song with the hook you can't get out of your head. You'd have to listen to her a bunch of times to appreciate her, and then you'd be glad you did."

"What a generous way of describing someone," Tabby replied. "I really like it. I'd like to be a deep track for someone, but I'm afraid I'll always be 'Shut Up and Dance,' you know what I mean?"

He thought she was being exceptionally unfair to herself.

"I know Jess was your boss," Tabby went on, "but I get the feeling there was something personal with you two. Or am I wrong?"

"No, you're not wrong. Jess and I were never going to be a great love affair. Even so, we had a connection. I'm not sure either one of us could have explained exactly what it was."

"Sometimes those are the most important people. At least when you're not driving each other crazy."

Frost laughed. "Yes, that was me and Jess."

Tabby smoothed the fur on Shack's back. Her eyes were already pink and watery, but that didn't seem to stop her. "Did you need something over at Duane's place? He's got plenty of leftovers in the freezer, so help yourself."

"No, I just wanted to talk."

"With Duane? Good luck. He's always up and out at four in the morning. I feel like a slacker when I sleep until six."

"Yeah, that's Duane. Early riser."

She gave him a strange look. "Did you want to talk to *me*?"

"Actually, I did," he admitted. He went on quickly, because he felt the need to explain. "You've been there. You know what it's like to lose a friend. Especially that way."

Even as he said it, he knew that he was lying. It was more than that. The fact that he was able to open up to Tabby about losing Jess was a neon warning sign that he felt a connection with her. Except he couldn't afford to feel that way. Tabby had barbed wire around her. She was with Duane.

"Wow, I—I'm glad that you thought of me." She added after a pause, "Hey, Duane and I are having dinner with your parents tonight at Boulevard. You should come with us."

"I don't want to intrude. This is your chance to get to know Ned and Janice. Away from the support group, that is."

Tabby took his hand. It felt way too natural for her to do so. "Really, Frost, I'd like you there."

The safe thing to say was no, but he heard himself tell her, "Sure. Okay."

"Excellent. Seven o'clock." She added, "Speaking of the support group, the families of the victims are meeting on Saturday afternoon. I have to work, but I hope you can make it."

"I'm under orders to be there," Frost said. "I'm sure they'll all be happy to see me."

"It won't be so bad. I promise."

"We'll see about that." Frost slid his phone from his pocket. "I met with Gilda Flores, by the way. I was in Nina's room, and I saw a photo of the two of you. I thought you'd like to see it again."

He showed her the picture he'd taken of Nina's birthday button, showing Tabby and Nina cheek to cheek in her bedroom, with the memorabilia of her life on the wall behind them. They were two friends, inseparable, with the world at their feet and their whole lives ahead of them.

But that would only turn out to be true for one of them.

Tabby enlarged the photo to show their faces. "We look young."

"You were."

"I know, but nine years ago? It's like an eternity. I can't believe she's been gone for so long. Look at us. That was a week before her twenty-first birthday. We had no idea. I mean, imagine if you could spin a wheel and know exactly when you were going to die. What if we'd spun it that day, and Nina saw that two weeks later, she'd be gone?"

"I'm glad there's not a wheel like that," Frost said.

"You wouldn't want to know?"

"No."

"I guess you're right. I guess that's the mystery." She gave him back his phone, as if she didn't want to stare at the past anymore. "I better go buy some fish."

"Of course."

"Unless you want me to stick around longer? I can if you want. Are you going to be okay?"

"I'll be fine," Frost said.

"What's your number?" she asked. When he gave it to her, she worked the keyboard on her phone. "I just texted you my number, too. Call me whenever, okay? I'm serious."

"Thanks."

Tabby stood up. She was about to leave, but then she tucked her phone back in her purse and sat down again. Shack bumped her with his head to get her to pet him. "There's something I've always wondered about."

"What's that?"

"Why do you think Cutter picked her?" Tabby asked. "Why did he pick Nina instead of me? She and I were both there at the coffee shop. He must have talked to both of us. We were so similar that we were almost like sisters. I mean, what if it had gone the other way? She'd be here, and I'd be dead."

"You shouldn't think like that."

"Oh, but I do. I do all the time. I feel guilty about it."

"The only one who should feel guilty is Rudy Cutter," Frost said. "And maybe me."

"You? You didn't do anything wrong. You just did your job."

"Me doing my job got Jess killed."

He watched Tabby's lips part in dismay, as if she wanted to tell him, *No, that's not true.* But she couldn't. Her green eyes reached for him across the short space because she had no comforting words to say. He felt her wanting to get closer to him. Her hand made a gesture in his direction, as if the next motion would be to touch his shoulder or his cheek. He saw her lean in, just a little, just enough to encourage him to lean in to her, too. Her chin tilted in what was unmistakably an invitation to a kiss. At that moment, he knew that she felt the chemistry, too. There was something magnetic and dangerous between them.

Then her whole face changed as she remembered the situation. A tiny flash of horror came and went across her features.

Tabby slid away from him in embarrassment. "Sorry."

He said nothing.

"You know, about Jess," she added.

"Right."

She hugged herself tightly, as if the air had grown cold. She stared out at the water. She bit her lower lip and looked upset with herself. "I still miss Nina."

"I know. I still miss Katie, too."

"Sometimes I need a girlfriend to talk to about things."

"Sure."

Tabby shivered. "Cutter's out there looking for someone new, isn't he?"

"That's what I'm trying to find out."

"It's some girl just like Nina," she went on. "She has no idea. I hate that."

"Me, too."

She shook her head. "I guess you're right, it's better not to know the future. Not if you can't change it. I mean, what if it were me this time instead of some stranger?"

"It's not," Frost said.

Tabby stood up again, and he noticed that she wouldn't look him in the eyes. "Are you sure? If I spun the wheel right now, how many days would I have left?"

◆ ◆ ◆

Rudy climbed down from the top deck of the tour bus at the vista point on the Sausalito side of the Golden Gate Bridge. His cheeks were windburned from the cold. He had his jacket zipped up. He wore sunglasses and a Chicago Cubs baseball cap that he'd picked up on the Wharf.

Outside the bus, white morning fog poured down from the bridge toward the water like overflowing cotton candy. The city on the other side of the bay looked as if it were floating on top of a cloud. Behind him, the green hills were bathed in sunshine. He was part of a crowd of tourists, all of them with phones and cameras snapping pictures of the view.

Rudy made sure he was out of the camera angles. He didn't want any record that he'd been here.

The tour guide, who narrated the city's history as the bus went to each hop-on, hop-off stop, texted on his phone with his thumbs. He was on a break, waiting for the bus to continue its route. The man was in his thirties, with gold studs in both nostrils and a beret over his rainbow-colored hair. He wore a leather jacket decorated with chains.

"What a view," Rudy said.

"To a kill," the guide replied without looking up from his phone.

Rudy recoiled. It took him a moment to realize the guide was simply echoing a James Bond movie, and then he laughed. He stayed in profile, so the guide didn't have a chance to see his face straight on. "I just wanted to tell you that you do a great job with the narration."

"Thanks."

"I take these bus tours in all the cities I visit," Rudy said, "but some of the guides aren't great at telling stories. It's more like, here's this building, here's that building. Here in Frisco, you guys always make the place come to life."

He watched the guide wince at the term *Frisco*, but the man made no effort to correct him. Instead, the man pointed at Rudy's blue hat. "So you're from Chicago?"

"Yeah. Out in the suburbs."

"What do you do?"

Rudy was prepared with a lie. "I sell wholesale furnace replacement parts. Not too exciting."

The guide shrugged. "Hey, we all have to do something."

"Yeah. Have you been giving these tours for a while?"

"Three years," the man said. "It brings in some extra bucks."

"Well, like I say, you guys are all really good. Last time I was out here, we had an amazing tour guide on the bus. This woman was like an actress, acting out stories at all the stops, singing, telling jokes. She was great. Do you know her?"

"Long dark hair?" the guide asked.

"I think so."

"That would be Maria. Maria Lopes. You're right, she really got into it. Got terrific tips. We were all jealous."

"Is Maria still with the bus company? I'd love to take one of her tours again."

"No, she left a couple years ago."

"Oh, too bad," Rudy said. He waited a beat and made sure his voice was casual. "What's she doing now?"

The guide shook his head. "I don't know. Some office job near the Civic Center, I think. I heard she got married, too. Some rich tech guy."

Rudy hid his disappointment. "Well, good for her."

"Yeah, no kidding." The tour guide checked his watch. "I better start herding the cats onto the bus. Time to go."

Rudy didn't say anything else. He got back on the bus ahead of the other tourists and made his way to the upper level, where he took a seat in the front row. The East Bay air was cold, but on the other side of the fog, the city would be warm. He turned up the collar of his jacket.

Maria Lopes didn't work at her old job.

She didn't live in her old apartment; he'd already checked. It was a setback, but that was to be expected after four years. Maria was still somewhere in the city. She could run, but she couldn't hide.

He'd find her.

30

Frost found Phil Cutter's house on the southern fringe of the city in the Crocker-Amazon area, near the border with Daly City. The two-story house was an eyesore on a street where most of the homes around it were small but well maintained. The yellow siding hadn't seen paint in years. The windows were shaded by misaligned horizontal miniblinds. A sad little boulevard tree needed water. The only other thing alive on the postage-stamp front yard were tall weeds that had squeezed out the grass.

The house's garage door was open, and the interior was crowded with so many boxes and so much rusted junk that no one would have been able to fit a car inside. A dirty black Cadillac from the '90s was parked on the street, blocking the driveway. Frost took a quick look inside the car, which was littered with old newspapers and crumpled fast-food bags. An air freshener in the shape of an evergreen tree hung from the mirror.

He climbed the steps and banged a fist on the house's front door. Phil Cutter answered with a bottle of brandy in his hand. His clothes drooped on his tall, skeletal frame, and so did his gray skin. He was in his early fifties and looked seventy.

"Easton, right?" the man said with a raspy voice that ended in a cough. He smoothed down his wispy dark hair.

"You know me?"

"Sure, I figured you'd be here sooner or later. A couple other cops already stopped by a few hours ago. Don't you guys talk to each other?"

"This isn't an official visit," Frost said. "I just want to chat."

"Just a chat, huh? Okay, come on in."

Frost followed the man into the house. It had the smell of someone who hadn't showered recently, with a layer of cigarette smoke on top of the body odor. Phil had an impatient, wiry walk, which was more athletic than his appearance suggested. In the living room, which faced the street, the man dropped into an armchair near the windows, and his knee bounced like a tic. Rows of shadows from the blinds fell across his face. Frost didn't want to sit on any of the musty furniture, so he stood.

"You look tired, Easton," Phil said. "Don't you get enough sleep? Alarm clocks keeping you up or something?"

The man's weathered face bent into a ghost of a smile.

Frost got the joke. He also realized the cigarette smoke in the house had a familiar bitterness. "It was you? You broke into my house. You sent me on a chase to find the watch."

Phil retrieved a smoldering cigarette from a tin ashtray. "I don't know what you're talking about."

"Who really found the watch?" Frost asked him. Phil looked like a man who could follow instructions, but it was hard to imagine him connecting the dots to the street thug who'd mugged Melanie Valou and stolen her watch. Rudy would have needed a private investigator for that.

"Like I said," Phil repeated, blowing out smoke and reaching for his brandy bottle. "I don't know what you're talking about."

Frost studied the small room. The wallpaper was heavy and dark, and it was peeling away at the ceiling. An old Doberman—as skinny as its owner—slept on the floor. It hadn't even barked when Frost arrived. He examined a few photographs hung on the walls and recognized younger versions of Rudy and Phil Cutter among the people in the pictures.

He turned back to Phil.

"Where's your brother?" Frost asked.

"No idea."

"Last night, he murdered a close friend of mine."

"That cop? I heard about that. But you won't pin that on Rudy. He was here with me when that woman got killed. He came here straight from the Fillmore."

"That's your story? We had a police car on your street. The officer didn't see a thing. Nobody came or went."

Phil shrugged. "Rudy came in the back."

"Climbing fences? Sneaking through yards? Why would he do that?"

"He's done it since he was a boy. He was always good at coming and going without our parents knowing about it. So was I. We made a good team."

Frost studied the man in the chair. He had bags under his eyes and a two-day beard on his face. His forehead was high and furrowed with long lines. He looked lost, like one of those men who falls behind early in life and never catches up to the rest of the world.

"Why do you cover for him?" Frost asked. "You know what he does."

Phil was silent. His jaw moved, as if he were trying to dislodge food from his teeth. Then he said, "You got a brother?"

"Yes."

"Then you should understand."

"I wouldn't protect my brother if he killed someone," Frost said. "I wouldn't lie for him over something like that."

"It's easy to say that if you've never faced it."

"All those years, you knew what Rudy was doing, and you never said a word to anyone. I don't know how you live with that, Phil."

"What I know is that Rudy is everything I've got, and he always has been. For thirty years, it's been him and me. Longer than that if you go back to when we were kids."

Frost didn't push him. He wanted to plant a seed of guilt, and that was all. He pointed to a photograph on the wall that showed two young boys with their parents. The background looked like a Giants game, and he figured the picture had been taken at the old Candlestick Park.

"Is this you and Rudy and your folks?" he asked.

"Yeah."

"Are they still alive?"

"You know they're not," Phil replied. "They died when Rudy and I were in our teens. Car accident. Truck driver lost control on 280 and nailed them both. This was their house."

"Do you work?" Frost asked. "Other than breaking and entering, that is. I know about your record."

"I was an electrician for BART. I got injured on the job a decade ago."

"So how do you spend your days?"

"What does it look like?" Phil asked, holding up the bottle.

What it looked like was a man who was committing slow-motion suicide.

Frost stared at the photograph again. He figured that Rudy Cutter must have been twelve years old at the baseball game. He mugged for the camera the way kids do. There was nothing in his face to suggest the man he would become. It would take decades for the evil to emerge.

"Help me understand your brother, Phil," Frost said.

"Why should I?"

"Because deep down, you know he's sick and he has to be stopped."

"You want to stop him? Go find a watch and hide it in the ceiling like your friend did. She did it right here, you know, at the top of the stairs. She slipped it in behind the smoke detector."

"I'm not defending what Jess did," Frost replied, "but what Rudy did to her was a hell of a lot worse."

"I already told you. Rudy was with me."

Frost shook his head. He couldn't shake the man's lies. "If you won't tell me about Rudy, then tell me about Hope. I know what she did to their daughter. I can only imagine how that affected Rudy."

Phil hissed between his teeth. "Hope. What a freak show."

One of the other framed photographs on the wall showed Rudy holding a baby in his arms. Half the picture had been torn away, leaving a white space inside the frame. Frost suspected that Hope had been in the picture and that Phil had excised his sister-in-law from his memory.

"You didn't like her?"

"She was trouble. Like Dr. Jekyll and Ms. Hyde. You never knew what you were going to get with Hope. One minute she'd be juiced, running around with so much energy you just wanted to unplug her. Then she'd go into a dark place, and nothing could pull her out. When she got like that, she was a witch. I mean, she'd scream at Rudy. Ugly, ugly stuff. She'd hit him, too. She slashed him with a knife once, right across the chest. He still has the scar."

"A knife," Frost said. "Knives come up a lot with them."

Phil was cool, not reacting to the verbal jab. His rheumy eyes didn't blink. He kept smoking.

"I don't know why Rudy picked her," he went on after a long silence. "Rudy was a good-looking guy. Still is. He could have done better than Hope. You ask me, she manipulated him. She knew how to pull his strings. If he ever talked about divorce, she'd go crazy, crying about how she couldn't live without him. You talk about husbands abusing wives? This was a wife abusing her husband. She was an awful piece of work. Freaking psycho."

"And Wren?"

Just like that, tears gathered in Phil's eyes. He was an uncle who still missed his niece. "Aw, Wren, she was an angel. I'm telling you, that little girl had sunshine in her face. I don't care what you think of my brother or what you think he's done. He loved that girl. If she needed blood, he would have slit his own wrists to save her."

"So what really happened?" Frost asked.

Phil's face hardened. His eyes had a grim, faraway look. "Docs said Hope had a bad case of PPD. Bipolar, too. They've got lots of buzz-words, but if you ask me, she was just evil. She was *jealous* of Wren. Jealous of this sweet, beautiful girl, not even a year old. The baby got all the attention from Rudy. Hope just wanted to take her away from him. That was all it was. She couldn't stand to see Rudy happy. So she smothered her own daughter and then killed herself like a coward."

The dog on the floor roused from his slumber and growled. Phil snapped his fingers to quiet him.

"At 3:42 a.m.," Frost said.

"Let's just say it was the middle of the night."

"What happened to Rudy after that?" Frost asked.

"Rudy? He stopped."

Frost was puzzled. "What do you mean?"

"Life stopped for Rudy that day. Time stopped. Everything stopped. It was like he was frozen, you know? He quit his job. He was an under-writer, and he was good at it—the guy is wicked smart—but he couldn't stomach it anymore. All the people who knew what had happened, all the sad stares, it was too much. He got some nothing job in data entry at B of A, where no one knew about his background. He moved in here with me. He just—stopped. He never started again. Not for years. Not until—"

Frost stared at him. "Not until?"

Phil didn't say a word, as if he'd already said too much. It didn't matter. Frost knew exactly when Rudy Cutter had come to life again.

"Not until he met Nina Flores," Frost said.

31

Eden Shay was waiting on Frost's front steps when he arrived back at his Russian Hill house. She had her elbows on her knees and her hands clasped tightly together in her lap. She wore no makeup today. Her black curls looked flat. He grabbed Shack, who was sleeping on the front seat of the Suburban, and sat down next to Eden on the steps. She inched away from him.

"You heard about Jess?" Frost asked.

She nodded without looking back. "Sorry. I know she meant a lot to you."

He didn't reply. He noticed the way Eden kept space between them now. She was the opposite of Tabby. She didn't reach out, take his hand, or hug him.

"Do you want to come inside?" he asked her.

"Sure."

Frost led her up the steps. Inside, he put Shack down, and the cat scampered away and disappeared. Normally, Shack stayed close whenever someone was in the house, as if he needed to be part of the conversation, but not today. Frost heard him thunder up the stairs to find his favorite spot in the closet.

Eden wandered to the bay window. She was subdued. She opened the door and went out to the patio, and she stood at the railing, where the hillside fell off below her and the city stretched down toward the waters of the bay.

He came up beside her. "What's wrong?"

"I think you should quit what you're doing. Don't go after Cutter. Let the other detectives do it."

"Why?"

"Because it's *dangerous*," she said. "Doesn't what happened to Jess prove that to you?"

He didn't think this had anything to do with Jess. "What's going on, Eden?"

"Cutter found me."

He reached out for her shoulder, but she drew away. It was as if she were back in the basement in Iowa, recoiling from any touch, suspicious of every man. "Are you okay?"

"No. I'm not."

"Did he threaten you?" Frost asked.

"He didn't need to. He knew how to find me. He knew where I was living. I got the message. If I didn't help him, I'd be next."

"What did he want?"

Eden's head turned, and she stared at him now. "He wanted to know about you."

"Me? What about me?"

"Everything. What I'd found out about you. What you knew about him and this case. He wanted to know if you're getting close."

"It doesn't feel that way," Frost said.

"Well, maybe you're closer than you think. The point is, you're getting in his way, and he doesn't like it. Jess got in his way, and you saw what he did to her. That's why you should stop."

"I'm not going to stop."

She shrugged. "No, I didn't think you would."

"What did you tell Cutter about me?"

"I told him to go to hell," Eden replied.

He wondered if that was the truth. Eden was complicated. She'd built relationships with the men on both sides of this case. Him *and* Rudy Cutter. It was impossible to know where her loyalties lay, other than with herself. Her book came first. He also realized that he needed to keep her close to him so he could watch what she was doing.

"Do you think he'd come after you again?" he asked her.

"I live in a security building. He can't get close to me."

"He already did," Frost said. Then he made a risky decision. "Do you want to stay here with me for a few days?"

There was curiosity in her eyes. "Are you serious?"

"Yes."

"Why would you do that?"

"One, to keep you safe. Two, to get your help. If Cutter thinks we're close to the truth, then maybe we can figure it out together."

He didn't add, *Three, to keep an eye on you.*

"It's sweet of you to offer," she said, although he was sure that she suspected he had ulterior motives.

"So stay. Your notes are already here. You can work when you want. I have plenty of room. I don't use the master bedroom, so you can take it for yourself."

Her eyes were calculating again. "If I do this, I can't stop being a writer. It doesn't work that way."

"I get it."

"Anything that happens is fair game for the book. Including anything between us."

"I'll take my chances."

"Okay then," Eden said. "You and Shack have a roommate. I can pick up some things from my place later."

"Good."

He wondered how quickly he would regret his offer, and he didn't have to wait long. As he turned to go back inside the house, Eden grabbed his arm. This time, she stood very close to him. "Frost, wait. There's something else."

"What is it?"

"I've been keeping a secret from you," she said. "Cutter was trying to hold it over my head. I should have told you before, but I didn't know how you'd react."

"So tell me now."

"It was me," Eden said. "I was the one who found the watch."

Frost's jaw hardened. He understood immediately what she meant. "Of course you did. I should have known right away. I knew it wasn't Phil."

"Cutter told me in prison that he'd been framed. I thought it was crazy, but he laid out this whole scheme of what must have happened. He wouldn't agree to any of my interviews if I didn't help him look for the watch. So I did. I never expected to find anything, but Cutter was telling the truth. I found out about the muggings in the Mission District. Lamar Rhodes. His sister. I *saw* her wearing the watch. It didn't take long to figure out what Jess had done."

Frost shook his head. "And you told Cutter all about it."

"Yeah."

"So I guess you had to listen to the voice inside, too. Not just me."

"You're right, I did," Eden said. "And I made the same call you did, Frost. I couldn't cover it up."

"What about Phil and the games he played with me? Breaking into my house? Leading me on a treasure hunt?"

"That was all Cutter. I didn't know what he was going to do. I figured he'd simply call his attorney, but he can never do things the easy way."

Frost wanted to be mad at her. He wanted to be furious. Eden had been the one who put the entire plan in motion. Because of her, Cutter was free, and Jess was dead. But that was a lie. She was right. They'd both seen the same facts, and they'd both made the same decision. He couldn't blame her for it.

Eden watched the emotions play across his face. "Do you want to rescind your invitation?"

"No."

"I don't have to stay here. I understand if you think I betrayed you."

"This doesn't change anything," he told her, although he couldn't keep the coolness out of his tone. "I made the offer because I think it's safer for you to be here with me. Now let's get started."

She looked relieved. "Started at what?"

"Figuring out what Cutter is going to do next."

Frost went back inside the house, and Eden followed him. He put the watch out of his head. He went to the boxes that he'd stacked in the foyer, and he grabbed one off the top and brought it back to the inlaid coffee table in front of the sofa.

"When I talked to Phil today," Frost said, "he gave me an idea. Jess was originally focused on finding a connection among the victims to Cutter's daughter. Nina turned twenty-one the same year that Wren would have turned twenty-one. That kind of thing."

"Sounds right," Eden said.

"Yes, but if the victims reminded him of Wren, I don't think Cutter would have been able to kill them. I wonder if we have it backward. Maybe, somehow, the victims reminded him of *Hope*. She's the one who took everything from him."

Eden sat down on the sofa. "I don't know, Frost. I didn't find anything that Nina and Hope had in common. They were about as different as two people could be. I still think Jess was right. Nina must have reminded him of Wren. Somehow the others did, too."

"Yes, but Cutter *loved* Wren. Whereas he still hates Hope like this all happened yesterday."

"True. So what do you want?"

207

Frost pointed at the box of notes. "Is there anything in there about Hope?"

"Quite a lot."

"Okay. Tell me about her. Help me get inside her head."

"I wish I could," Eden replied. "She may be even more of a mystery than Rudy is. I mean, how does a mother murder her own child? The docs all talked about PPD, but that's the clinical explanation, not the emotional explanation. Most people I talked to just called her a monster."

"You don't believe that," Frost said.

"No. You're right. When you say someone is bad to the bone, it lets them off the hook. Hope wasn't evil. That's why it's hard to understand her doing something so terrible. And it's not like she didn't do good things in her life, too. She was an ER nurse, which is as tough as it gets. Nobody remembers that now, because it doesn't balance the scale."

"Was Rudy abusive to her?"

Eden shook her head. "The opposite, in fact. He put up with a lot."

"What about her childhood?"

"Pretty normal middle-class stuff. It sounds like Hope was a troubled kid going way back, though. I talked to her mom, Josephine. She feels guilty. You would, too, if you spent all those years raising a girl who grew up to kill her own daughter."

"There has to be more. You said Hope was troubled. In what way?"

"Depression. Mood swings. That was the bipolar part of her. If you're looking for connections to Nina, that's not it. Nina was a happy kid. No sign of mental illness."

Frost frowned. He didn't see any connections, either. Even so, he was beginning to believe that he was on the right track. If you wanted to catch a killer, you had to follow the anger. And Cutter's anger was all about Hope.

"Rudy was dead inside for years," Frost said. "That's the part I don't get. What woke him up?"

"What do you mean?"

"Phil said that everything stopped for Rudy after Wren died. He didn't talk about him being angry. It sounded like he was numb."

Eden nodded. "A few of Rudy's coworkers said the same thing. Losing Wren drained all the emotion out of him."

"But then his anger flooded back when he met Nina," Frost said. "I want to know why. There must have been something about Nina that reminded him of Hope and what she did. You said you interviewed Hope's mother. Is she still local? Where does she live?"

"She's in the same house in Stonestown where Hope grew up."

"Let's go talk to her," Frost said.

32

Rudy leaned against one of the flagpoles in the Civic Center plaza. The wind had kicked up, and the flag snapped to attention over his head. Warm sun from a cloudless sky offset the wind. He had his hands in the pocket of his sweatshirt, the black hood covering his head. Around him, a few homeless people slept on the green grass, and children played on the monkey bars.

On the sidewalk on Larkin, he spotted two uniformed police officers walking side by side toward city hall. Cops never missed a thing. They were always watching even when they weren't watching. Rudy squatted and fumbled with his shoelace with his head down. He waited until the cops had passed him, and when he stood up, he didn't look back over his shoulder. Looking back was a dead giveaway that you didn't want to be seen.

He could hear their boots, walking away. They hadn't spotted him.

He focused his attention on the six-story downtown library building on the other side of the plaza. That was his destination. He strolled along the sidewalk, and behind his sunglasses, his eyes moved from face to face. The sleeping bodies on the grass. The mothers on the benches, watching their children. The parking police, doling out tickets on the cars.

At the intersection, he crossed the street with a cluster of pedestrians. On the opposite side, the library loomed like a prison of gray stone, with rows of small square windows adorned with X's, as if the architect had been playing a game of tic-tac-toe. People came and went through the doors. He followed them, marching into a circular atrium, which rose toward a vast ceiling skylight that looked like a spiderweb. The building hummed with the quiet echo of voices.

Rudy knew where he was going. He'd been here before. He got on the elevator and punched the button for the fifth floor, where the library kept its computer training center. He kept his hoodie up and his sunglasses over his eyes. He stared straight ahead.

The doors began to close, but then they opened again as a small, skinny black man in his thirties slipped inside. The man wore a jean jacket covered in San Francisco patches and an Alcatraz baseball cap. He had the look and smell of a homeless person taking refuge from the streets, and he swayed in the elevator as if he were listening to the beat of a song that only he could hear.

"Beautiful day outside, ain't it?" the man said to Rudy. "You been outside? That is one gorgeous day God made for us."

Rudy nodded but didn't look at him. "Yeah."

"You here for the books? Most folks come for the books. Lots and lots of books in this place. Me, I like the magazines. Motorcycle magazines, mostly. Daddy had a motorcycle when I was a kid, and he let me ride on the back. That's how I got my nickname. People call me Bike."

Rudy said nothing.

"You ever been on a motorcycle?" the man asked.

"No."

"Daddy loved it. Nothing like riding on the open road, he said. Wind in your face and bugs in your teeth." The man broke into a fit of laughter. "Daddy made that joke a lot. Bugs in your teeth."

Rudy forced a smile, but his mind was elsewhere. The arrival of the fifth floor rescued him from further conversation. He got out of the elevator and immediately turned right toward the computer center. The man in the jean jacket sauntered out behind him and headed toward the magazine room on the other side of the library.

The computers were set up on long white tables near a series of cubicles occupied by library staff. A glass wall separated the training center from the corridor. It was a busy day, and most of the computers were already taken. He spotted one open computer halfway down the aisle, and he walked there quickly, avoiding eye contact with the employees inside the cubicle walls.

Sitting down, he glanced in both directions at the people close to him. On his left side, a teenager with a cross shaved into her orange hair tapped the keyboard at lightning speed. She seemed to be writing fantasy fiction; he could see references to otherworldly monsters coming through time portals. On his right, a man in his sixties in a worn business suit worked on his résumé. Nobody paid any attention to Rudy. He silently slipped plastic gloves on his hands before touching the keyboard, and he slid off his sunglasses so he could see better.

He called up a search engine on the Internet and typed the name Maria Lopes on the keyboard. He got millions of results. He was about to narrow the search when someone thumped loudly on the glass wall in front of him. It was the black man from the elevator. He had a motorcycle magazine in his hand, and he pointed at it and gave Rudy a thumbs-up. Rudy responded with a quick smile and looked down again, hoping the man would leave, but the man stayed on the other side of the wall, repeating, "Hey!"

People in the library began to look their way.

"Hey!"

Rudy looked up again, an impatient question in his eyes.

"Bugs in your teeth, huh?" the man called, laughing. "Right?"

Rudy tried to laugh at the joke, and when he did, the man finally took his magazine and walked away. Rudy was alone again. He felt stares directed his way; he needed to work quickly. He tapped in a new search term:

Maria Lopes San Francisco

He still got an unmanageable number of results.

However, he noticed a row of thumbnail photographs included with the search. He clicked on the "Images" tab and found a larger array of hundreds of pictures of different women. Apparently, they were all named Maria Lopes, and they all lived in San Francisco. Some were old; some were young. Some wore cowboy hats; some wore bikinis. They were brunettes and blondes. Interspersed among the photos were religious icons, dolls of Spanish dancers, and pictures of the Golden Gate Bridge.

He scrolled down.

And there she was.

Rudy recognized her immediately. He'd seen that face day after day for weeks; he'd sat two rows away from her on a double-decker tour bus; he'd spied on her bedroom window through binoculars across from her old apartment. Maria Lopes—*his* Maria Lopes—was thirty-two years old. Her birthday was February 19. She had long, straight brunette hair, but he could see that she'd added blond highlights in the last four years. Her eyebrows had a wicked arch. Freckles dotted her forehead. She smiled with only her lips, in a perky, sexy way.

In the online photograph, Maria wore a business outfit, gray skirt and scoop-neck black blouse, with a slim gold chain around her neck. The picture didn't say who she was or where she was, but it was an unusual photograph: Maria stood next to a tall woman dressed in a silk kimono with a styled black wig and a gold butterfly on top of her head like a tiara. The two women posed in front of a backdrop of garish multicolored streamers.

Rudy was puzzled.

Then he thought, *Opera.*

He was about to click on the picture for more information when he realized that someone was standing over him beside the computer.

"Buddy," a male voice said, low and unpleasant.

Rudy looked up. A teenager with a bald head and loose-fitting jeans crowded the chair.

"Buddy, that's my computer. I was sitting here."

"Sorry, it was empty," Rudy murmured, trying not to attract attention. "Nobody was here."

"I was taking a leak, man. I've been here for almost an hour. I *reserved* it, so take a hike." The young man raised his voice and gestured at the nearest employee working in one of the cubicles. "What's the deal here? Somebody can just take my computer when I go to the damn bathroom?"

Rudy slid his sunglasses back on his face and yanked up his hood. He pasted a smile on his face. "No problem, it was just a misunderstanding. I didn't realize the computer was reserved. Go ahead, take it, I'm done here."

He slid the mouse to the top of the screen and clicked out of the browser. He stripped off his gloves and shoved them in his pocket.

One of the librarians called to him. "If you want to reserve one of the other machines, sir—"

"No, that's okay," Rudy replied quickly. "Thanks."

"Out of the chair, man!" the teenager insisted.

Rudy stood up. "All yours."

He bumped hard against the teenager with his shoulder, nearly knocking the kid over, and tucked his head down into his chest as he walked away. He could feel everyone in the computer lab watching him go. He listened for a voice saying his name. A whisper. A warning. They'd all looked right at him.

That's Rudy Cutter.

But no one recognized him. He was safe.

He made his way back to the library elevators, where he waited impatiently, pretending to stare at the paintings on the wall. With a musical ding, one of the elevators arrived, and he studied his feet and wiped a hand over his face to hide himself as the people inside got out. When the car was empty, he stepped inside, but as he did, he threw a last glance at the open interior of the library's fifth floor.

Not far away, the black man with the patch-covered jean jacket and the Alcatraz cap sat in an overstuffed armchair, staring right at Rudy over the top of a motorcycle magazine.

33

"Why are you stopping here?" Eden asked as Frost pulled to the curb on Haight in front of a Tibetan boutique with Asian lanterns and brass-and-turquoise jewelry in the store windows. The bright paint on the trim was the color of sunflowers. Like seemingly every other business on Haight, its neighbor was a tattoo parlor.

"Quick detour," he replied.

They were heading for the house where Hope Cutter's mother lived near the Stonestown mall, but he wanted to stop here first. This was the gift shop where Katie had purchased a ceramic fountain as an anniversary gift for their parents. It was probably the last place anyone would have seen her alive. And the shop was in the opposite direction of where she should have been headed with Todd Clary's pizza.

He explained to Eden what his father had told him. She studied the storefront with a little frown on her face.

"It's not really so strange, is it?" she said. "We're only a block past Masonic, and you can get through the Panhandle there. She could have turned around and headed north after she stopped at the shop."

Frost shook his head. "A U-turn? On Haight? Good luck with that. Come on, you know what the traffic is like around here. Even going around the block would probably have added ten minutes at that time of night. The next cross street that cuts through the Panhandle is Baker, and by then, she would have been half an hour away from Todd Clary's place. Katie was a little scattered, but she was a native, like me. She wouldn't make a mistake like that."

Eden pointed at the boutique window. "The shop closes at eight o'clock. You said the receipt was dated right before eight, right? Maybe she remembered that she needed to get a gift for your folks just as she was heading out to make her delivery. She dashed over here to buy something before the store closed."

"Okay, but why make a special trip? She had two more days before their anniversary. She could have gone to the shop on Friday or Saturday. The only reason to stop was if it was right on her way. And it wasn't."

"So what happened?" Eden asked. "What are you thinking?"

Frost tried to put himself inside his sister's head again. He tried to picture what she was doing on that last night. What she was thinking. Where she was going. He could imagine her in her car, singing along to the radio. The smell of the pizza on the seat next to her would have made her open the windows. He was familiar with all of the evidence from that night, but the evidence didn't help him. Katie hadn't made or received any calls or texts after she left the pizza joint. She was on her own.

"Katie broke the pattern," he said. "It was March, not November. She was the only victim other than Nina Flores who wasn't murdered in November."

"But the police ruled out a copycat, didn't they?"

"Yes, it was definitely Cutter. Katie was wearing Hazel Dixon's watch on her wrist when I found her. And then Katie's watch showed up on Shu Chan in November, so we know he took it from her. This was Cutter, but somehow Katie's murder was different from his other crimes. I want to know why."

He got out of the Suburban and went around to the sidewalk. Eden got out, too. The street was crowded. Tourists window-shopped. A double-decker sightseeing bus passed behind them. Haight was like a museum now, an artifact of what the '60s had been. It looked real, but it wasn't. The hippies had been replaced by technology yuppies, who were the only ones who could afford the city anymore. The customers getting the tattoos made a hundred and fifty thousand dollars a year, plus stock options.

He smiled, seeing one of Herb's three-dimensional sidewalk paintings two stores down from the boutique. Herb's paintings filled the Haight-Ashbury area, pointing tourists to his gallery a few blocks away. This one showed a young Jerry Garcia playing guitar, and it appeared to rise off the pavement so realistically that people detoured around the painting to avoid bumping into him.

"I've been searching the wrong streets for years," Frost said as he looked up and down the block. "I followed every route from the pizza joint to Clary's place a dozen times, but I went the wrong way. I assumed that Katie headed west, which is what she *should* have done. Except she didn't. I never checked the streets going this way."

"What were you looking for?" Eden asked.

"Any place where Katie and Cutter might have intersected. I studied his life. I studied his credit-card receipts. I did the same with Shu Chan, because I figured he might have been targeting her already. There was nothing that would have put them in the same area."

Eden shook her head. "East, west, it doesn't really matter, does it? If you'd found a connection close to here, it would have jumped out at you. A few blocks wouldn't have made a difference."

"You're right about that."

He stared at the boutique door. It was easy to picture Katie rushing inside before they closed, with the hot pizza in her car. She'd spot the Buddha fountain immediately; maybe she'd already seen it in the window. It was the perfect gift for their mother. She would have haggled over the price, but not much. Katie wasn't a bargainer, and she didn't have time to negotiate. She would have scribbled down their parents' address for the delivery, probably had to write it out again so they could read it, and then she would have dashed back to her car to head in the opposite direction to Todd Clary's place.

It still didn't make sense to him.

"I always assumed that Katie stumbled onto Cutter on the delivery route," Frost told her. "She saw something she wasn't supposed to see."

"That makes sense," Eden said. "So maybe Shu Chan was in the Asian boutique that night, and Cutter was watching her. If Katie saw him near Shu, that would explain everything."

Frost nodded. "I thought about that. And you're right, it's probably what happened, but it doesn't explain everything."

"Why not?"

"Because it doesn't explain why Katie was in this store that night to begin with," Frost said. "That's what I don't understand. She shouldn't have been here at all."

The owners of the Tibetan boutique didn't recognize the photographs that Frost showed them. Katie Easton, Rudy Cutter, and Shu Chan were all strangers to them. They didn't remember the purchase or delivery of one ceramic Buddha fountain six years earlier. It was a dead end.

Frost put it out of his mind for now and headed for Stonestown.

Hope's mother, Josephine Stillman, was in her mideighties. She still lived in the same little white house on Eucalyptus Drive that she and her husband had purchased in the '60s. She was one of thousands of elderly house orphans in California who enjoyed low property tax rates because of Prop 13, as long as they never sold their home. So they stayed put year after year, watching their net worth grow on paper. Josephine's three-bedroom matchbox was probably worth two million dollars now.

She was spry for her age. When she opened the door for them, she was dressed for pickleball in a white skirt and cotton top. Her hair was colored to a delicate auburn. Her skin had the artificial tautness of someone who'd had work done. She didn't pretend that she was happy to see them or that she welcomed the idea of talking about her daughter. Her attitude was busy and impatient.

"I really don't have time for this," Josephine complained, waving them into the house with a flutter of her hand. "And I don't see how I can help you. Hope's been gone thirty years. Honestly, I try to put all of that unpleasantness out of my head. I don't think about it anymore."

Frost knew that was a lie.

In reality, Hope stared down at her mother every day. There was a watercolor portrait of her over the fireplace in the living room. For Frost, it had a strange, haunting familiarity. He recognized Hope from photographs he'd seen, although the painting must have been done when she was a teenager. Even knowing what Hope would do a few years later, it was easy to see that she'd been an unhappy child. The face in the painting stared desperately into the distance. The watercolors, which blurred her features, made her look as if she had no identity at all and was in danger of disappearing into the canvas.

"Hope did that painting herself," Josephine murmured when she saw him looking at it. "It's the only self-portrait I have of her."

"She was very talented."

That was true. The craft in the painting was impressive, especially since she'd done it so young. But the girl who'd stared into the mirror as she made the self-portrait was obviously tortured.

"What is it you want?" Josephine asked. Then she rushed ahead, as if to answer their questions before they could ask them. "Back then, you know, people didn't talk about mental illness. There was a stigma. And no one realized what postpartum depression could make a mother do. All they saw in Hope was a freak. A monster. That wasn't her. She was sick, and no one could help her. Not her husband. Not even me."

Frost could hear her voice quivering as she got upset.

"She *wanted* that baby, you know," Josephine went on. "She did. She loved Wren. People didn't believe that after what happened, but it's

219

true. She'd talked about having children for years. She was *ready*. She would visit pediatrics on her breaks at the hospitals and chat with the new mothers. She was over the moon when she got pregnant herself. She couldn't wait to have a child of her own. It's just that she had no way of knowing how it would affect her mentally."

"We understand," Eden reassured her. "We know Hope was sick."

Josephine took a handkerchief and dabbed at her nose. "Well. You don't know what we went through. The awful things people said. Jim couldn't take it. That's what killed him. I spent years living with the guilt myself, and finally, I decided I was going to put it behind me. What's done is done."

She didn't sit down, and she didn't invite them to sit down. She wanted to move this along.

"Did you stay in touch with Rudy Cutter?" Frost asked.

Josephine waved her hand. "No, no, no. Rudy and I never spoke again after the funerals. And mind you, that was his choice. Jim and I reached out, but he wanted nothing to do with us."

"You know he's been released?" Frost said.

"Oh yes."

"Has he tried to contact you?"

"No, of course not. I can't imagine why he would. I literally haven't set eyes on Rudy in years."

Frost glanced at the portrait again. He felt as if Hope were following the conversation. He had the strangest sensation that he'd met Hope before, but he didn't know why. He didn't know her as anything but a face in a picture, and yet he'd felt her presence with him somewhere. He couldn't place it, but the time was recent.

"We think that Rudy's killing spree is somehow an expression of his rage toward Hope," Frost said.

"Don't you blame my daughter for what *he* did!" Josephine snapped. "What Hope did was awful enough, but she was *ill*. She wasn't in control of her mind. Rudy is the real monster. He has no excuse at all for the crimes he committed. None. Besides, I don't know why you think there's any connection. The things he did happened years later."

"Those furies can stay inside a person for a long time," Frost said.

"I won't hear talk like that!"

Eden interrupted to calm her down. "Josephine, please, we're not blaming Hope. This is all on Rudy and no one else."

"That's right," Frost said. "We're just trying to understand why he picked the women he did. If we can establish a connection that links the victims together, it will help us gather the evidence we need to put him back in prison. And we're wondering whether that connection somehow involves Hope."

"I don't know anything about that."

"I'm sure you read about the murders. You must have followed Rudy's original trial. Was there anything about the victims that made *you* think of Hope? Did you know any of them or their families? Was there some physical resemblance? Some behavior? It might have been the smallest thing."

She shook her head firmly, without even thinking about it. "Nothing at all. Now are we done? I have to go."

"Just one more thing," Frost said. "I'd like you to look at some pictures."

Frost slid his phone out of his pocket. He found the photos he'd taken of the buttons that Nina Flores had worn on her birthday. He held out the phone so that Josephine could swipe through the pictures, and she took the device from him with obvious reluctance.

"The girl in these photos is Nina Flores," he told her. "She was Rudy's first victim. There are pictures of her family here, too. Nina was wearing these buttons the day that Rudy met her. He *saw* them. I want to know if something in these photographs could have brought back his anger over Hope."

Josephine studied the pictures one by one, but she didn't say a word. Her face was dismissive. He could see her getting ready to hand back the phone with an impatient sigh, because he'd wasted her time. And then she stopped. Her finger hovered over the screen with the tiniest quiver. Her eyes narrowed. Something about one of the images grabbed her like a magnet.

"Do you see something, Mrs. Stillman?" Frost asked.

The woman's mouth puckered unhappily. She was silent.

"Josephine?" Eden asked.

She pushed the phone back into his hands with a decisive gesture. She was done. "I don't know any of these people."

And yet her face was ashen.

"They may be strangers, but if you can think of anything—" he said.

"I can't. I told you. Now I'm late, and you really have to leave."

The woman busied herself with her purse. Clearly, the interview was over. She wanted them gone. Frost turned his phone over and looked at the photo that had grabbed her attention.

It was the picture of Nina and Tabby.

He saw them in Nina's bedroom. Two young women. Nina with her dark hair and round, smiling face, about to turn twenty-one. Tabby, redheaded and already sure of herself. They were dressed for the night, ready to party and dance.

He didn't see anything in the photograph that could be a motive for murder, but Hope's mother obviously had. He could see a strange horror hiding behind the woman's eyes. In five seconds, she'd spotted something about Nina Flores that he and Jess had missed for years. Something that connected Nina and Hope.

She had no intention of telling him what it was.

34

When they were back at the Suburban, Herb called to report that one of his contacts on Street Twitter had spotted Rudy Cutter. Frost gunned the engine of the Suburban and headed for the 280 freeway, which was the fastest way back uptown. Unfortunately, in late-afternoon San Francisco, there was no way to get anywhere fast. Every route was a parking lot.

"Where are we heading?" Eden asked him.

"The library at the Civic Center. Cutter was there."

He wondered if it was a mistake to tell her everything about the investigation. He'd already decided that it was safer to keep her close than to push her away, but their interests were likely to diverge sooner or later. He'd sacrifice her book and keep things from her if it meant getting Cutter. She'd sacrifice just about anything if it meant a better story.

Her expression, the wary smile on her face, was obvious. She seemed to read his mind and know that he was doubting her.

"We want the same thing, Frost," Eden reassured him.

"Do we? I thought you just wanted a bestseller."

"I want Cutter back behind bars. Or dead, if it comes to that. That's how the book is supposed to end. With justice."

"Then you're right. We want the same thing."

But he wasn't convinced, and she knew it.

"Do you mind if I ask you an uncomfortable question?" she said.

"That seems to be your specialty."

"Why aren't we having sex? I've made it pretty obvious that I'm interested, haven't I?"

"Yes, you have."

"Well? Most men don't play hard to get with me."

"I think you've got the wrong idea about why I suggested you stay with me," Frost said.

"I don't think so. Like I said, we want the same thing."

Frost kept driving with his eyes on the road. "Are you always so direct?"

"Aussie girls aren't shy about what we want. We usually get it, too."

"And then you write about it in your book?" he asked.

"Maybe, but you shouldn't let that scare you. I don't give performance reviews." She smiled at him. "Unless you turn out to be Iron Man, that is."

"You're a public person, Eden. I'm not. I like to keep it that way."

"At least let me make dinner for us tonight," she suggested. "Wine. Candlelight. No book talk. It's my way of saying thanks for letting me stay with you and being my protector. Then we can see what happens."

"Sorry, I have a family dinner tonight," he told her. "It's my parents, plus Duane and his girlfriend."

"You mean Tabby Blaine?" she asked with a penetrating stare.

"That's right."

Eden was silent for a while. Then she said, "Well, maybe I'll wait up for you."

They didn't talk the rest of the way.

Frost finally exited the freeway and wound through the streets to the Civic Center. He parked outside the library building, and he and Eden made their way into the atrium. Herb was waiting near the elevators with a scrawny black man wearing a jean jacket covered in patches. Herb had a suitcase with him, in which he typically carried his painting supplies.

"Thanks for calling," Frost told Herb. "I think you've met Eden Shay before."

Herb's mouth broke into a little smirk. "Indeed I have. Hello, Ms. Shay. And both of you, this is my friend Bike. He's the one who spotted Rudy Cutter in the computer room on the fifth floor."

The man in the jean jacket looked nervous talking to a cop. He twisted an old Alcatraz baseball cap between his fingers. "I rode up in the elevator with him first. I was telling him about my motorcycle magazines, but he didn't say much. Then, yeah, just like Herb says, I saw him again, and he was using one of the computers."

"When was this?" Frost asked.

Bike glanced at the clock in the atrium. "About two hours ago, I guess."

"Can you show us where?"

"Oh yeah. Sure."

Herb leaned in. "I took the liberty of asking the librarians upstairs to take the specific unit offline that Cutter was using. I didn't want someone accidentally deleting any of the cache."

"Good thinking," Frost agreed. He said to Bike, "Did you recognize this man immediately?"

"No, I was thinking he looked familiar, but I didn't put it together until later, when I saw him leaving. There was some kind of argument in the computer room, and Black Hoodie hightailed out of there fast."

Eden smiled. "Black Hoodie?"

"Yeah, that's what he was wearing. Black hoodie, jeans, shades."

"But you got a good look," Frost said. "You're sure it was him."

"Oh yeah, he's the guy you want."

"How long was he at the computer before he left?" Frost asked.

"Not very long. I don't think it was more than five minutes or so. Like I said, there was an argument. Some other guy reserved the computer, so he basically kicked your guy out. Hoodie didn't put up a protest. He just left. He looked squirrelly, like he wanted out of here fast."

"Did he know that you'd recognized him?"

"Hard to say. Like I said, I didn't realize who he was until he was almost gone. Then I remembered that Herb had posted something about this guy out on Street Twitter."

"We need to hurry," Frost said. "Cutter might be coming back, and I don't want him to know we're on to him."

Herb hoisted his suitcase in the air. "I had the same thought. I figured this would be a good time to bring my sidewalk art to the front of the library, don't you think? I've been looking to do a 3-D landscape of Angel Falls in Venezuela. I went BASE jumping there a while back. It's not for the faint of heart."

"Is there anything you haven't done, Herb?" Frost asked.

"I have a fairly long bucket list," his friend replied with a shrug. "Anyway, I'll set up shop outside. If I spot Cutter on his way back, I'll let you know."

"Thanks."

Frost, Eden, and Bike took the elevator to the fifth floor. At the glass wall outside the computer center, Bike pointed to the unit that Cutter had been using. The computer was turned off, and a handwritten sign had been taped to the monitor that read, "Out of Service."

Frost thanked Bike with a twenty-dollar bill, and then he and Eden found the nearest librarian, whose name tag said Wally. Wally could have been an inspiration for his namesake in the *Dilbert* cartoons. He was short, round, bald, and wore glasses. Frost showed him his badge and spoke in a low voice so that the other patrons around them couldn't hear their conversation.

"Thanks for keeping everyone off that machine," Frost said.

"Of course. Herb said it was important."

Frost smiled to himself. Everyone in San Francisco knew Herb.

"Do you remember the man who was sitting there?" Frost asked. He found a photo of Rudy Cutter on his phone. "Is this him?"

"I wish I could tell you, but I can't," the librarian replied. "There was a disagreement about the computer being reserved, but I didn't see the face of the man who left. He wore some kind of hooded sweatshirt."

"Has anyone used the machine since then?" Frost asked.

"Well, the other man didn't stay long. Another ten minutes or so. There may have been one or two other users who sat down before Herb asked us to take the unit offline, but no more than that."

"Okay. Thanks. If this man comes back, don't approach him, and don't give any sign that you've recognized him. But send me a text right away." He handed the librarian his card.

"I will."

Frost and Eden sat down in chairs in front of the computer. He peeled off the sign and booted up the machine. They sat shoulder to shoulder. He was aware of the perfume she wore.

He slid gloves onto his hands. He opened up the browser on the computer and checked the search history, hoping that Cutter hadn't had time to delete it before he was chased out of the library. He was lucky. The history was intact. He saw a long list of Google search terms stretching back throughout the course of the day.

"When did Bike say he saw Cutter?" Frost asked.

"About two hours ago," Eden replied.

Frost checked his watch and scrolled to a point in the history two hours earlier in the afternoon. He reviewed the search terms one by one. Most were innocuous, but then Frost saw a name among the search history:

Maria Lopes

And below it a similar search:

Maria Lopes San Francisco

He froze the screen where it was. Eden stared at it, too.

"You think Cutter did that search?" she asked.

"The timing is right," Frost said. "Does the name mean anything to you? Do you recall Cutter mentioning a woman named Maria Lopes?"

She shook her head. "No."

"The searches before and after seem to be unrelated. It doesn't look like he clicked on any of the results he found. Either he didn't find what he was looking for or he was interrupted before he could do anything more."

"Or he knew what he needed as soon as he saw it," Eden suggested.

Frost nodded. "True."

"So who's Maria Lopes?" she asked.

"If my gut is right, Cutter's in the process of targeting his next victim. He knows *who* she is, or at least what her name is, but apparently, he doesn't know much more than that. That's interesting."

He stood up and returned to the librarian named Wally. "I'm going to be calling for an officer to watch over that machine. And we're going to need to have our forensics people study it in detail. In the meantime, we need to keep it off and unused. I don't want anyone touching it. Okay?"

The librarian nodded. "Yes, of course. Anything you need."

Frost returned to Eden. He switched off the machine. Next to him, another of the computers in the lab was open. "Let's rerun the search on a different unit. I want to see what we get when we start looking for Maria Lopes in San Francisco."

The two of them sat down at the computer, and Frost booted up the same browser and reentered the search term that Cutter had used. He was dismayed but not surprised by the number of results. There appeared to be numerous women with the same name around the city.

Eden reached out and put her hand over his on the computer mouse. "Let's look at the 'Images' tab. If he clicked to enlarge a photograph, it wouldn't show up in the history as a separate search. But maybe something will jump out at us."

He felt the warmth of her fingers. She kept her hand there as she scrolled downward through an array of photographs.

"See anyone you know?" he asked.

"No. Do you?"

Frost shook his head. "I don't."

Eden took away her hand and rolled slightly backward on the chair next to him. "So what do we do? We don't know which woman he was trying to find."

"I need to talk to every Maria Lopes in San Francisco," Frost replied. "At least the younger ones. One of them is in danger."

"Cutter's going to work fast, Frost. He won't wait weeks this time. He knows you're close."

Frost knew that was true. Time was short. Even so, he was hoping that he was finally one step ahead of Rudy Cutter.

"He may suspect that we're close, but he doesn't know we've gotten this far," Frost said. "That's our advantage. We know his next move now. When he goes after Maria Lopes, whoever she is, we'll be waiting."

35

Rudy listened to footsteps echoing on the marble floor of the San Francisco Opera building. The lobby felt like a palace, with rows of Doric columns and brass-and-crystal lanterns hanging from an inlaid gold ceiling. People came and went, mostly in business suits, and their conversations made a constant, hollow murmur that hung in the air. There was a performance of *Rigoletto* scheduled for the evening, and that meant a wave of activity in the hours before the show.

He'd been here once before. That was decades earlier, not long after he and Hope had been married. Someone had given them tickets to Bellini's *Norma*. He didn't even remember who it was. They'd been underdressed because they couldn't afford opera finery. He remembered feeling out of place, and he'd sat through the opera in severe discomfort, feeling assaulted by the screeching voices in Italian. He'd assumed Hope would feel the same way, but when he looked at her at one point, he saw tears running down her face.

He'd never even asked her what it was that affected her so much. They didn't talk about things like that.

It wasn't a good memory.

Rudy found what he wanted near the entrance to the theater hall. A printed program. He stuffed it in his pocket and turned around and exited the building onto the stone steps leading down to Van Ness. Colorful opera banners flapped in the light breeze over his head. The sun was already low, and the temperature was dropping. He headed to the street corner and crossed to the other side, where he sat down on the cold ground with his back propped against a sculpture outside Symphony Hall. From where he was, he could see the main steps of the opera building and the porte cochere for vehicles on the cross street.

The late-afternoon traffic jammed the intersection in every direction. Commuters were heading home.

He took the program out of his pocket and flipped through the pages to the listing of administrative staff. There were more people than he expected. Accountants, system administrators, music librarians, school-program coordinators, communication managers, marketers, and dozens of other people working behind the stage. He went through the list name by name, and he finally found her.

Maria Lopes. She was their assistant director of annual giving. A fund-raiser asking for money.

He was in the right place.

It was Friday. Maria was probably working. And it was almost the end of the day, which meant she should be leaving soon.

Rudy leaned forward with his arms on his knees, looking like a San Francisco street person with nowhere to go. Behind his sunglasses, he studied everyone leaving the opera building. It wasn't easy. Dozens of people left simultaneously, heading in different directions. Trucks and buses blocked his view. He was far enough away to see both sides of the building, but the distance made it hard to distinguish each face. As the minutes passed, it also got darker.

Maria didn't show.

Lights came on around him. Headlights blinded him as the cars passed. His vantage became useless. Most of the people who looked like office staff had been leaving through the side entrance on Grove Street, so he took a chance that Maria would do the same. He got up and crossed the street and staked out a new position near the wall of the opera building. It was after six o'clock now. He only had a moment to study each face emerging through the glass doors before they passed out of the lights and were lost on the dark street.

Six thirty came and went.

Then seven o'clock.

He began to think he was wasting his time. Either he'd missed Maria or she wasn't at work. Then, through the nearest doors ten feet away, he spotted a profile that had a familiar cast. It had been four years, so he wasn't sure, and the hair was much shorter than he remembered. The woman reached the sidewalk and headed away from him; she'd disappear soon. He had to make a choice. Stay or go.

Rudy followed her.

He remained half a block back, tracking her in and out of the crowd of pedestrians. The height was right. The walk was right. It might be Maria, but he couldn't risk getting close enough to confirm it. She wore a leather jacket down to her ankles, and her shoulder-length hair was tucked under a purple beret. She led him directly east toward Market Street, and he guessed that she was heading for the BART station to catch a train. He was right.

He was ten people behind her on the crowded escalator leading underground. The BART station was a dangerous place for him. There were cameras everywhere. He had to buy a ticket, using cash, and by the time he did, the woman had disappeared. He waded back into the mass of people, and he spotted what looked like a purple beret among the bobbing heads. He forced his way through the push-and-shove of the crowd, and he found her again, on the platform for the Millbrae line heading south.

The woman momentarily turned his way, checking the departure monitors for the next train. He hid his face before she could see him, but he recognized her.

It was Maria Lopes.

Four years had changed her. He saw someone who was older, more serious, more mature. The free spirit on the tour bus had responsibilities now. But that was to be expected. Wren would have been the same, all these years later.

It was cool down below near the train tunnels. Rudy waited, watching the crowd gather, keeping an eye on Maria. Five minutes later, with a roar and a gust of wind, a train surged into the station. It was standing-room only. Maria was among the people pushing shoulder to shoulder to find space inside, and Rudy let himself get a little closer behind her. There were only three people between them inside the packed train car. If she'd peered back between the strangers, she would have seen his face, but she didn't. She had headphones in her ears. She read her phone, head down. She was oblivious to the world.

The train left the Civic Center station. He held on to a shoulder strap as the car jostled. Throughout the downtown stops, more people got on than got off, squeezing the crowd closer together. Soon, Maria was so near he could have reached out to touch her. If he'd pursed his lips and exhaled, she would have felt the warmth of his breath on the back of her neck. Even when he'd stalked her four years earlier, he'd never been this close. And yet she was unaware.

They headed out of the city together. Maria didn't live in San Francisco now. Going south, the train stopped in Daly City. Then Colma. Then South San Francisco. As the crowd thinned, he drifted to the far back of the car, putting more people between them. He found a seat; so did Maria. There were only two stops left: San Bruno and Millbrae.

As they neared the San Bruno station, Maria slid her headphones out of her ears and secured them in her purse, along with her phone. The train pulled in, and she got up, not looking behind her, and headed out onto the platform. She walked toward the tall escalators. Rudy followed, letting the distance between them increase. There was nowhere for her to go.

Maria emerged into the night outside the station. The bay was less than a mile away, sending a cold breeze off the water. The dark hills loomed to the west. She walked briskly toward the multilevel parking garage, with the look of someone who did this every day. Her leather jacket swished; her heels tapped. She tugged the beret down on her head.

Rudy noticed a police station immediately adjacent to the garage, but there were no cops outside. He lagged behind her, watching the way in and the way out of the garage. She reached the elevators and got inside, and when the doors closed, he ran, taking the steps and jogging up to the next floor. The elevator got there just as he did, and he hung back. Maria walked down the middle of the garage aisle, and he spied her from a distance as she climbed inside a Chevy sedan. She backed out and headed down the ramp.

She was gone.

Rudy turned around and went back down the steps.

He considered his options as he returned to the station. The garage was a possibility. If he took her there, he'd have her car in which to go somewhere more private. But the garage also had cameras, and BART riders came and went with every ding of the elevator doors. There was also the threat of cops at the nearby police station. It was a risk. And the weekend was already here, so Maria wouldn't be heading back to the garage until Monday. Two days was a lifetime for him now.

He had to find out where Maria lived, and he had to be ready to move fast.

As he waited on the cold platform for the next northbound train, with only a handful of other people heading into the city, Rudy heard his phone ringing in his pocket. The only person who had that number was Phil. He walked to the far end of the station where he was alone, and then he answered the phone.

"What's up?"

"Hey," his brother replied. Phil knew better than to use names; somewhere, the government was always listening. "That person you told me to keep an eye on? I'm on the case."

"Where?"

"A restaurant near the Ferry Building."

"Alone?"

"No. Looks like a family dinner. What do you want me to do?"

"Just keep watching," Rudy said. "And keep me posted."

36

It didn't take long for Frost to regret going to the family dinner.

"A toast!" his father said, raising a bottle of beer in the direction of Duane and Tabby. His voice was loud, but everyone in Boulevard was loud on Friday night. "To my oldest son and the girl who finally managed to get him to spend ten minutes outside that food truck of his. Honestly, Tabby, I didn't think it could be done. Duane, you make sure this one sticks around."

Tabby, who sat between Duane and Frost, poked Frost's brother in the side. "But no pressure or anything, right?"

Duane chuckled. His voice was as loud as Ned's. "Just for the record, it's every bit as hard getting Tabby out of the kitchen in this place as it is getting me out of mine."

"Or getting me into a kitchen at all," Frost added to no one in particular.

They all drank. Frost, Ned, and Tabby had beer, and Duane had his usual carrot juice. His mother had a glass of chardonnay.

Tabby had arranged for a table where they could see the frenzied work of the chefs in the restaurant's open kitchen. That was where Tabby could be found on most evenings. The interior of Boulevard was like stepping into a '20s French bistro, with hanging art-deco lights, bronze sculptures of half-naked women, iron grillwork, and a brick ceiling over their heads. Even the signage made the place look like a station on the Paris Metro line.

Frost's mother eyed him from the opposite side of the table. He was waiting for the quiet verbal stiletto, and he didn't have to wait long.

"And now that Duane finally has a girl in his life," Janice murmured from behind her wineglass, "perhaps the day may actually come when we can say the same thing about Frost."

Tabby covered her mouth, and Frost knew she was laughing hard enough to bring tears to her eyes. She slung an arm around his shoulder and whispered in his ear, "Aren't families great?"

"I wouldn't know," he replied. "I've only had mine."

Duane leaned forward. His brother's long black hair was loose tonight, and he wore a tie for what was probably the first time in a decade. The tie was for his parents, but below the tablecloth, he wore cargo shorts.

"Actually, bro, is there a secret you want to share with us?" Duane asked with a wicked little grin.

Frost was puzzled. "Um, no."

"Then I guess it's up to me to spill the beans. Tabby and I stopped at Frost's place on the way over here so we could drop off a care package for the weekend. Frost was already gone, so I let the two of us inside. And my, my, my, what did we find? There was a girl in residence at Chateau Shack."

"And a very pretty girl, too," Tabby added.

"With a travel bag in hand," Duane went on.

His mother looked cynical. "Frost, is this true?"

"Don't get the wrong idea," he told them, bursting their bubble. "It's professional, not personal. Eden's a writer working on a book. She's helping me, and I'm helping her. I had reason to think she might not be safe at her place, so I suggested she stay with me for a couple days. That's all."

"So are you denying that Eden Shay is pretty?" Tabby cross-examined him.

Frost looked at her in mock exasperation. "How is this helping?"

"It's not," she said with a wink.

"Yes, Eden is pretty. And no, we are not dating."

His mother sighed under her breath, but in a way that Frost couldn't miss it. She had an appetizer of sea scallops in front of her, and she speared one and ate it while staring everywhere in the restaurant except at her son.

Fortunately, he didn't have to wait long for the attention to shift away from himself. After his parents decided that there was nothing new in his life, they turned back to Duane and Tabby. Duane talked about the food truck and the award he'd received in the Best of the Bay rankings in *San Francisco* magazine. The executive chef and owner of Boulevard stopped by to sing Tabby's praises and to spar with Duane about James Beard awards. Ned and Janice talked about Tucson and the hummingbird aviary at the Arizona-Sonora Desert Museum. For the most part, Frost sat silently and listened to the conversation bounce back and forth across the table. The food made it worthwhile, but two hours still passed with agonizing slowness.

Dessert was never optional at Easton family dinners, so he chose the dark-chocolate cream puff, which was Tabby's recommendation. She shared it with him. As they finished, Frost thought the evening was finally over, but then Duane and his mother ordered espressos, and his father ordered a double shot of Dry Sack. They were still going strong.

Frost excused himself from the table. He navigated the long, narrow restaurant and found the restrooms in a corridor beyond the bar. He simply wanted a couple of minutes of quiet to himself, and the men's room was empty. He splashed water on his face at the sink and stared into his reflection. His eyes stared back, hard and blue. His brown-and-gold hair was swept back over his head. He rubbed a hand along his trimmed beard, and his forehead was a furrow of discontent. It was good to see his parents again; it was good to see Duane showing every indication of being in love. And yet a deep, empty cavern surrounded him, like a moat with no bridge.

He left the restroom. Someone stood in the dimly lit hallway, waiting for him.

"Hello there," Tabby said.

Even in the shadows, her red hair was luminous, and she wore a simple white dress that still managed to look like Oscar fashion.

"Hey."

"You were gone a while. I was worried about you."

"There's nothing to worry about."

"I thought maybe you were upset—I mean, because of Jess—"

"It's not that." He came and shared the wall beside her. Their shoulders brushed together. "I can only handle so much family togetherness. Ned and Duane are crazy extroverts. They're more out there than me. And Janice—well, she and I are cut from the same cloth, and that's not always a good thing."

"Is that all it is with you, Frost?"

He wondered what she really wanted to know.

Is there something else on your mind?

Is it me?

"That's all," he said.

No, that was not all. He stared awkwardly at the floor. His dress shoes needed polishing; they didn't shine. Tabby's heels were black pumps that positively glistened. Everything about her glistened.

"So, you and Eden Shay," Tabby said.

"There's no me and Eden Shay."

"I heard what you said, but I know what I saw in her face. She'd like there to be something more between you."

Frost didn't say anything. He didn't want to talk about Eden. Not with Tabby.

"She doesn't have to be your Jane Doe, you know," Tabby added with a teasing smile.

"Duane talks too much."

"Oh, he means well. He wants you to have someone. We all do."

He heard her use the word *we*, as if she were pushing him into Eden's arms and away from her. He wondered if she was thinking about the moment they'd shared at the harbor, or whether she'd already forgotten it.

"I'm fine," Frost said.

"Sure, but does fine mean being alone? Not every girl has to be the one. Maybe Eden is just Miss November. What's your hesitation? Is she a deep track, like Jess?"

"Honestly, I don't know what Eden is," Frost said.

"But she's not 'Shut Up and Dance,' like me?" Tabby asked, smiling again.

"You are way more than that," he told her before he could stop himself.

"Thank you." Her face had a little blush in the shadows, but then she changed the subject. "I met Eden a few years ago, you know."

"I know. She mentioned it."

"I confess, I didn't like her much."

"She mentioned that, too."

"I don't think it was her. It was me. She caught me at a dark time. She was asking about Nina, and I didn't appreciate anyone prying into our lives."

"Sure."

Tabby picked up on his reluctance to talk. "I'm sorry, Frost. Sometimes I get too personal with people too fast. I didn't mean to go where I don't belong."

"You didn't," Frost said.

"Well, I'm making you uncomfortable. That's the last thing I wanted."

She looked unhappy with herself, and she put distance between them and smoothed her dress. They stared at each other in strained silence. Neither one of them knew what to say. When that had gone on for too long, Frost returned to the busy restaurant, and Tabby followed behind him. She took her seat again without looking at him, but he didn't bother sitting down. He was ready to leave. He said his good-byes to his family and tried to pay for his meal, but his father wouldn't let him, as Frost expected. He kissed his mother, and Janice gave him one of those maternal looks that didn't change no matter how old a child got.

"We will see you tomorrow afternoon, right?" she asked. "At the Lubins' for the support group?"

"I'll be there," he said.

He suspected that Janice would only believe it when he actually walked in the door.

Frost picked his way between the restaurant tables and exited onto the sidewalk at the Embarcadero. The Bay Bridge was lit up as it crossed to Yerba Buena Island. Bushy heads of palm trees were silhouetted in the median of the wide avenue. He still felt unsettled and unhappy, but he was liberated by being outside in the cool city air. He turned toward Mission Street to walk to the garage where he'd parked his Suburban.

As he did, he stepped into a faint cross wind of cigarette smoke. It was distinctive and acrid. He'd smelled that smoke before. Inside his own house.

Frost spun around quickly.

Across the Embarcadero, in the streetlights near the bay, he saw an old Cadillac sedan, its lights off but its engine rumbling loudly, like a death rattle. The driver's window was open, but he couldn't see inside, other than to spot the pinpoint ember of a cigarette. He started across the street, but as soon as he did, the window rolled shut, and the Cadillac peeled away into an illegal U-turn across the trolley tracks and disappeared at high speed.

He couldn't read the license plate, but he knew who it was. He'd seen that Cadillac in front of a seedy house in the Crocker-Amazon neighborhood.

Phil Cutter was watching him.

◆ ◆ ◆

The first thing Frost did when he got home was check the locks on the doors and windows. Eden watched him curiously, without asking questions. He went from room to room, but there were no signs of tampering or break-ins. Everything was secure.

When he was done, he returned to the living room. Eden sat in a lotus position on the floor, with a laptop balanced on her calves. Cheater glasses pinched the end of her nose. She had a half-full glass of white wine on the carpet beside her. He didn't recognize the music playing on his Echo, but it had a new-age serenity. The overhead chandelier was dimmed. Eden had lit a fire in the wood fireplace, and the logs crackled and smoked.

He sat down beside her. The fire made it hot.

"Everything okay?" she asked.

"Phil Cutter was following me. I wanted to make sure that Rudy wasn't trying to find you while I was away."

"He doesn't want me. He wants Maria Lopes. Whoever that is."

"I thought the same thing before Jess was killed," Frost said. "I don't want to be wrong again."

"Well, I like being worried about."

She drank her wine, but her gaze didn't leave him. The firelight danced around her face. A few of her corkscrew curls swished her forehead. She lifted the glasses from her nose and put them aside, and she closed the cover of her laptop. There was no misreading her eyes. She'd already admitted that she wanted him. He wanted her, too, but with a hollow, physical need that he hated giving in to. And yet he knew he would. Tonight, with his brain fogged by alcohol and Tabby, he didn't care.

"I didn't even know that fireplace worked," Frost said, stalling.

"You've never lit a fire here?"

"Never."

"There was wood in the garage," she said.

"It must have been there for years."

Eden leaned back on her hands. "I brought some personal things with me. Not for long, just a day or two. I put them in the master bedroom. You said you didn't use it."

"I don't," Frost said.

"Shame. It's a soft bed. Really nice."

"Good."

The dance went on. They both knew where this dance went.

"Shack's hiding in the closet up there," Eden said. "Doesn't he like me?"

"That's one of his spots. He goes there when the world gets too overwhelming."

"Your cat has issues?" Eden asked.

"He's very complex. And protective. When the old woman who owned this place was killed, Shack wouldn't leave her. Practically mauled anyone who got close. But I persuaded him everything was going to be okay."

"That's sweet," Eden said.

They didn't say anything else. They didn't need to. Frost took a long look at her body, from the smoothness of her face to the gray silk blouse with two buttons undone to the shorts that left most of her honey-colored legs bare. She waited for him to start. He slid a hand behind her neck and pulled her to him, and she bent into the kiss. Their lips met, soft, warm, and wet. Her fingers worked gracefully on each button of his shirt.

He laid her back on the carpet, and his body slid on top of hers. He was propped on his forearms. They kissed again; they struggled piece by piece out of their clothes. As her blouse opened, as he parted the silk, he was conscious of the scar just above the hollow of her neck.

She saw his eyes go to it, and she said, "Touch it. Please."

His thumb caressed the smooth gash.

"Kiss it."

He leaned down. His mouth and his tongue found it.

"Oh my God," she murmured.

Then they weren't tender anymore. They were rough with each other, as if they both had something to prove. They didn't go upstairs; they didn't bother with the soft bed. They stayed in front of the hot fire until every inch of their skin was damp with sweat.

37

Sometime in the middle of the night, Frost woke up alone. The fire had died to gray ash, and cold, whistling air blew onto his body through the chimney. He stood up. Their clothes were strewn on the floor, and he grabbed his boxers and stepped into them.

"Eden?" he called softly.

There was no answer in the house.

He surveyed the downstairs, which was lit only by the outside city lights through the patio doors. At some point, Shack had gravitated back to his usual spot on the sofa, where Frost typically slept. The cat didn't bother opening an eye. Nothing around the house was out of place. The boxes of research materials for Eden's book were still stacked against the foyer wall.

Frost went silently upstairs. The door to the master bedroom was open. From the doorway, he could see Eden stretched across the bed. He walked inside and stood over her. She was on top of the comforter, lying on her stomach, with her head sideways on the pillow. Black curls draped over her face. The memories of their lovemaking went through his mind. Expressions on her face. The catch of her breath and the pleasured rumbling in her throat. The warmth of her fingers. Her legs wrapped around him. He stared at her and remembered all of it, and he asked himself what he felt about it.

He didn't like the answer.

Frost turned away to let her sleep, but before he left the room, he heard her voice calling to him. "I'm awake," she murmured.

He came and sat down on the side of the bed. Eden rolled onto her back. Her eyes opened. Her body was an attractive shadow, and she let him watch her, like a sculpture on display. They stared at each other in the darkness, but it was a long time before either of them spoke.

Finally, Eden said, "I guess I got what I wanted."

"Why was that so important?" he asked her.

She sat up in bed. She slid behind him and massaged the muscles of his back with deep, insistent fingers. Her bare legs were on either side of his hips.

"I'm selfish. I can't write about you unless I know you inside and out." She lightly bit his neck. "Which doesn't mean I didn't enjoy it."

"And what did you discover about me?" Frost asked with morbid curiosity.

"That you want things you can't have."

He twisted around to face her. "What the hell do you mean by that?"

"I've been with enough men to know when someone isn't fulfilled by being with me. That's okay. Don't apologize if you were using me simply because I was here. I was using you, too."

"Then I guess we both got what we wanted," Frost said.

He was angry with her, and with himself, because she was right. She was right about everything. He'd used her. He'd met two attractive, desirable women recently, and the one he wanted was the one he couldn't have. And so he'd slept with the other simply because he could.

Looking into his eyes, she smiled at him, as if she could see through him. He found that he was beginning to dislike her smile.

"You want to do it again, don't you?" she said, pulling him closer, kissing his neck.

She was right about that, too.

◆ ◆ ◆

Frost drove south out of the city on Saturday afternoon. He'd already talked to six different women named Maria Lopes. He'd questioned each of them about their backgrounds, hoping to find a detail in their personal lives that would explain which of the women was on Rudy Cutter's list. But none of their stories had brought him any closer to an answer.

Now he was on his way to meet number seven. She was farther away, high in the San Bruno hills. He didn't mind the drive. He usually listened to audiobooks in the car, and he was nearly done with a Barbara Tuchman book about medieval Europe. There was something about times that were dead and gone that appealed to him.

It was a grim day, as unsettled as his mood. The forecast was for rain and wind moving in overnight, and black clouds had already slouched over the coast from the ocean. The inland temperature hovered at a damp, warm sixty-five degrees, but it was always colder closer to the water. As he drove higher, the low hills were a deep shade of emerald.

The next Maria Lopes lived in the shadow of the trails of Sweeney Ridge. He'd hiked there many times, where the peaks gave a 360-degree view of the Pacific and the bay. Her house wasn't new or lavish, but it had one of the best locations in the Bay Area—except when the fog blanketed the hills, which it did most evenings. Up here, he imagined it was hard sometimes to see your hand in front of your face.

Frost got out of his Suburban. He climbed the front steps past a garden dotted with desert succulents. When he rang the doorbell, Maria Lopes answered almost immediately.

"Ms. Lopes? I'm Inspector Easton. I called you earlier." He showed her his identification, and although she had an anxious look on her face, she swept the door wider for him.

"Please, come in," she said.

She'd known he was coming, and she'd dressed for him in the kind of dark business suit she probably wore during the workweek. She was in her early thirties, attractive and freckled, with brown hair that fell to her shoulders. Her expression was serious, but he spotted evidence that she'd been a wild child in her past. Tattoos crept up her neck like snakes. She wore tiny gold loops in both nostrils. Her living room walls had posters from the San Francisco Opera, where she worked, but also from metal bands like Mastodon and Wintersun. He spotted a piano in one corner and an electric guitar propped near it against the wall.

She directed him to a wicker sofa on the back porch. Behind him, through the windows, were the dark clouds and coastal hills. She sat in a rocking chair that was probably a hundred years old.

"I have to tell you, Inspector, your call made me nervous," Maria told him.

"I know. I'm sorry. Are you familiar with who Rudy Cutter is?"

"Of course. Are you saying this monster may be after *me*?"

"I don't know for sure. We know he was researching your name, but there are quite a few women with the name Maria Lopes in San Francisco. We don't know which one he was looking for. It may have nothing to do with you, but we're being cautious."

"I don't even live in San Francisco anymore," Maria pointed out.

"But you work there, don't you?"

"Yes, I take BART back and forth every day. Why, do serial killers commute?" She gave a weak laugh, which covered her tension.

"As I say, we're not taking any chances. We don't know how he picks the women he stalks. According to the DMV records, you used to live in the city, is that right?"

"Yes, I was born at Saint Mary's near the park. I lived my whole life within six blocks of there until two years ago. I never thought I'd become a commuter."

"What happened?" Frost asked. "Why did you leave the city?"

Maria wiggled one of her fingers for him. He spotted a large diamond ring. "Love happened. When Matt and I got married, we both wanted kids right away, and frankly, there aren't a lot of kids left in San

Francisco. So we came down here. We're both fitness freaks, and we like running in the hills."

"You can't get a better location than this," Frost said.

"That's true. I thought I'd miss the city, but I never looked back. And I still get my fill of city life, thanks to the opera."

"Do you have kids now?"

"Yes, a son. Jeremy. He's two. He's with Ranya, our nanny." Maria rolled her eyes. "It feels strange to say that. You can probably tell that I was sort of a flower child growing up. Money was the root of all evil. Now here I am with a corporate husband and a house in the suburbs and a nanny and a nonprofit job raising money from the San Francisco elite. Life comes at you fast."

Frost smiled. He liked her. She didn't take herself too seriously.

"Is your husband home?" he asked.

"No, he's a road warrior for PlayStation. He's overseas a couple times a month. He's somewhere in Southeast Asia right now."

Frost took his phone from his pocket and found the best picture he had of Rudy Cutter. He handed the phone to Maria. "Does Cutter look at all familiar to you? Is it possible you've seen him around you recently?"

"Now you're scaring me."

"I'm sorry, but his pattern is to watch the women he's after."

She studied the face on his phone and then shook her head. "No, I don't think so," she said.

"Are you sure? You're hesitating."

"Well, there is something vaguely familiar about him, but maybe it's just that I've seen him on the news so many times. If I met him before, it wasn't any time recently. I feel like it would have been a few years ago. And I could be wrong. He may just have one of those faces."

That was true. It was easy to think you'd seen a face before. However, she was the first of the women he'd talked to who thought Cutter looked at all familiar. To the others named Maria Lopes, he was a total stranger.

"Would you mind looking at some more photos?" Frost asked. He took back his phone and found the folder where he kept the photos of Cutter's victims. "If you swipe through this album, you'll find several women here. I want to know if you remember any of them."

"Who are they?"

"They're the women Cutter killed," Frost said.

Maria's mouth pinched into a frown, but she went slowly through the pictures. "I remember seeing some of these photos on television back then. I followed the Golden Gate Murders pretty closely. Everybody in the city did. But I didn't know any of these women personally."

"What about their names?" He rattled off their names from his memory, where they were all indelibly filed. Including Katie. "Do you remember any of these names among people you knew or worked with or grew up with?"

"I'm sorry, no." Then she noted Katie's last name. "Easton? Is there a connection?"

"My sister."

"Oh my God, I'm so sorry."

"Thank you." He pushed Katie's shadow from his mind and went on. "I'm not trying to scare you unnecessarily, Ms. Lopes, but I want you to be vigilant. Do you have an alarm system in your home? Is it typically turned on?"

"Always."

He handed her his card. "My contact information is on here if you need to reach me for any reason. If you see Rudy Cutter anywhere near you, don't approach him. Don't talk to him. Don't indicate that you've seen him or recognized him. Just call nine one one."

"Wow." Maria looked shaken.

"I know. This is a lot to take in."

"You really think he picks these women for a reason? It's not random?"

"He was in the library yesterday, and he was looking up someone with your name. That's not random."

Maria stood up from the rocking chair, and she still had his card in her hand. He noticed that her fingers were trembling. "What makes a person do something like this? What kind of diseased soul could take a stranger's life so purposefully? I don't understand it."

Frost stood up, too. "After Katie was killed, my mother said that some mirrors were too dark to look at."

"I think that sounds right."

Maria led him back to the front door. He heard the squeal of a boy playing somewhere in the house, and a smile instinctively sprang to her face. She was a happy woman with an ordinary life. It was unimaginable that she could be put in the path of someone like Rudy Cutter. But that was how it worked.

"Remember, if you see anything that concerns you, call me," Frost told her. "If I find out any more details that you should know about, I'll be in touch."

"Thank you, Inspector."

Frost went back outside, and Maria closed the door behind him. He heard the click of the deadbolt. She was taking no chances, and that was good. He went down the steps, but before he got into the Suburban, he took a short walk to the deserted end of the road, where dirt trails climbed toward Sweeney Ridge. The gray day had kept away most of the hikers. The seam of the valley made a V like the jaws of an open mouth. Dense green brush clung to the hillsides.

He saw a hawk circling overhead. Circling and circling beneath the low clouds. Looking for prey.

It reminded him that Rudy Cutter was out there somewhere, doing the same thing.

38

Rudy studied Frost Easton through binoculars. The detective's head swiveled as he watched the hills and tracked the ridgeline. Rudy was too far away to be seen, no more than a dot on the hillside, and there was no sunlight to catch on the lenses of his binoculars. Even so, he wondered if the detective's intuition told him he was being watched. He'd found that to be true with victims sometimes. Every now and then, one of them would turn for no reason, as if some instinct for self-preservation had alerted them.

Five minutes passed. They stared at each across the distance, invisibly. Eventually, Easton turned around and went back to his truck and drove away.

Rudy frowned. Seeing Easton here meant the police knew about Maria Lopes.

He wondered how that had happened and how far it had gone. Did Easton know *why*? Did he know about Hope and the other victims? If he did, then the game was up, and they would be coming for him. Regardless, Rudy had no intention of going back to San Quentin. Not again. He wouldn't be locked up in a cell with Hope's ghost. He wouldn't wake up every night at 3:42 a.m. That road had come to an end.

The cold ocean air climbed over the peak, settling on top of him. Under his camouflage fleece blanket, he shivered. He'd built a nest for himself off the trail, on the eastern slope of the summit, where he was invisible to anyone hiking above him. He'd borrowed Phil's Cadillac today, and the sedan was parked half a mile away in the parking lot of Skyline College. From there, he'd hiked into the hills that gave him a bird's-eye view of Maria's house.

Her new location had been easy to find. He'd stopped at the San Bruno library that morning and run a couple of Google searches and found a local website with Maria's name, address, and phone number. In this case, it was a community theater group that had posted contact information for all their board members. There Maria was, living on Sneath Lane.

Now, hidden in the hills, Rudy could spy on her yard and her windows. He'd spotted her several times inside the house. She'd had coffee on the back porch and done yoga in her bedroom. Soon enough, she would do what she always did, assuming her daily routine hadn't changed completely in four years. She would run. She ran every day, rain or shine. Seeing her now, he could tell that she still had the lean, wiry build of a runner. And she'd moved here, to the fringe of a park, where the running trails were literally outside her front door.

The cold didn't matter. The fog didn't matter. Not to a real runner. Maria would come, and he would be waiting for her.

I'm going to take another one, Hope. Watch me. There's nothing you can do about it.

It was all a question of how much time he had. Sooner or later, the police would find him. He could measure it in hours, or he could measure it in days. It was a race between him and Frost Easton, and there was only one way to find out if Easton was getting close. Rudy dug in the backpack for his pay-as-you-go phone, and he dialed a number.

It rang once, and then a voice answered.

"Inspector Easton."

Rudy took a breath. "Hello, Inspector."

There was a long stretch of silence on the phone. He could hear the noise of traffic outside the truck. The detective was already back on the freeway. Finally, Easton said, "Cutter. Where are you?"

"I'm watching someone. Do you know who I'm watching?"

Easton didn't answer. Rudy listened for a change in the vehicle's engine. If the detective had figured out the truth, he'd be turning around. He'd go back to find Maria Lopes and scour the ridge. But he didn't. The traffic noise didn't change. Easton kept driving. He knew the name Maria Lopes, but he didn't know more than that. Not yet.

Rudy thought, *The library.*

The guy with the motorcycle magazine had spotted him at the downtown library, and they'd found his search history.

"What do you want?" Easton asked.

"I thought we should talk," Rudy said. "The way these things go, we might not have a chance to talk again. The next time we meet will probably be under more difficult circumstances. It's easier now, when we both have time."

"You have less time than you think," the detective said.

"Really? I think you're bluffing. I don't think you know anything about me at all."

"I know the victims are all connected to Hope," Easton told him. "I know that punishing Hope for what she did to your daughter is pretty much the only thing that keeps you alive."

Rudy waited a long time to reply. If Easton was taking a shot in the dark, the shot had landed perilously close to its mark.

"You can't possibly understand my relationship with Hope, Inspector," Rudy said. "I loved her. I still do, despite everything. You can hate and love at the same time. Hope was very complicated and troubled. I never saw the depth of pain she was in."

"Then I guess you weren't looking," Easton said. "It's right there in the self-portrait she did as a teenager."

"It's always easier to recognize things in hindsight, but you're right. I should have seen it. I used to look at that painting on the wall and not realize that it was a cry for help. I suppose if you've seen the painting, that means you've seen Hope's mother? Josephine?"

"I have. I showed her the photo of Nina Flores. She spotted the connection to Hope right away."

Rudy felt another body blow. *Was it possible? Did he know?* There was only one other person in the world who would understand with a single glance why he'd chosen these women, and that was Hope's mother.

"What did Josephine tell you?" he murmured.

As Rudy spoke, the wind gusted behind him suddenly, like the shriek of a witch. He wondered if the detective could hear it through the phone and whether he would put it together. The wind. The ridge. Maria Lopes and her house in the hills. Instead, Easton said nothing, not answering the question. The detective was baiting him to talk. To say more. Rudy couldn't stop himself.

"Hope was always afraid that she was going to harm Wren," he went on. "I think she was terrified of that even before she got pregnant. She saw something in the faces of *other* mothers. Contentment. Joy. Love. They were so happy holding their children, and she knew she would never feel the same way herself. It took me a long time to realize that. Far too long."

Rudy closed his eyes. In his mind, he saw all their faces. All that terrible, infuriating joy.

"Of course, understanding what Hope did doesn't make it less evil," Rudy went on. The edge was back in his voice now, as sharp as a knife. "She gets no mercy for what she did. None."

"Neither do you," Easton replied immediately.

Rudy heard the rage thrown back at him. "I'm not asking for mercy. I know I won't get any from you. Are you saying you want to kill me, Inspector? Is that your plan? Be honest. If I gave you the chance right now, would you put a bullet in the head of the person who cut your sister's throat?"

He listened to the detective breathe. Slowly. In and out. Trying to wrest control of his emotions.

"I want to stop you, Cutter," Easton said. "I don't want you dead. I'd rather see you back in a box to torment yourself for the next thirty years."

"Oh, you don't need a box for torment, Inspector. Free men suffer, too. Sometimes the only thing you need for madness is a memory burned into your eyes. I have that."

"I have that, too," Easton reminded him. His voice was a low, bitter growl.

"You think you've seen it all, but you haven't. There are plenty of other demons out there for you. Horror can always get worse. Don't make this personal between us, Inspector."

"Too late."

The noise of the phone became dead air. Easton had hung up abruptly; the call was over. Rudy powered down his phone and took out the battery. He picked up the binoculars again and settled in to wait.

Evening would be coming soon. Maria would be running.

He'd wavered about his plans for Frost Easton, but now he knew what to do. No mercy. If Easton wanted to make it personal, then Rudy would oblige. The detective had no idea just how personal it was going to get.

39

Frost threw down the phone on the seat beside him. He swore loudly in the silence of the truck, and his hands squeezed into fists. He'd lied to himself and to Rudy Cutter about the violence gripping his heart. If he had the chance right now, he would do just what Cutter had suggested. He'd put a bullet in the man's head.

He tried to calm himself as he drove the last few blocks. He was late, and he was somewhere he didn't particularly want to be. Parked cars crowded the street beside the eucalyptus trees of Stern Grove as he turned off Nineteenth Avenue. Natasha Lubin's parents had a full house for the gathering of families of Cutter's victims. Their bay window fronted the park, and he could see people inside.

Frost got out of the truck. Stern Grove was like a dense forest inside the city, and the trees loomed over his head like giants, with their bony branches knotted together. He shoved his hands in his pockets as he crossed the oil-smudged street. He climbed the steps, and he could hear voices through the front door. He steeled himself to face down the cold stares of the families.

What could he tell them?

Rudy Cutter was still free. He was still killing. And he was going to kill again.

A slim woman in a dark-green dress answered the door. He'd met her once before. Dominika Lubin was Natasha's mother. It was obvious from her tight-lipped expression that she recognized him, too.

"Mr. Easton," she said. "Janice and Ned told me you would be here. Come in."

He crossed the threshold into the lion's den. The space in the living and dining rooms was small and crowded. Family members clustered together, talking in hushed tones with no smiles. The conversations came to a sudden end as people noticed him, and he felt a wave of silent hostility. No one said anything, but they didn't need to say a word to convey their message.

His parents spotted him. Ned broke away from the people he was with to welcome Frost with his usual smothering hug.

"Thanks for coming," his father murmured in his ear. "It means a lot to your mother."

"That's why I did it," Frost replied.

"What a great dinner last night, huh? Your mother and I are so thrilled about Duane and Tabby. Isn't she great?"

"She is."

"Next time, bring this Eden woman with you," Ned said.

"We're not a couple, Dad. Really."

"Well, bring her anyway. It will make Janice happy to see you with someone."

Ned steered Frost into the gathering with an arm around his shoulder. Polite, lukewarm smiles greeted him. His mother was in a circle with three others, including Gilda Flores and a thirty-something Chinese couple, whom Frost assumed were related to the sixth victim, Shu Chan. Janice took hold of Frost's shoulders and kissed him on the cheek.

"This may be uncomfortable for you, but I'm glad you're here," his mother whispered.

He saw that furniture had been pulled into a rough circle of sofas and chairs, with an open area of gold carpet in the middle. There wasn't enough seating for everyone in the room. Frost estimated the crowd at nearly thirty people. He saw members of different families holding hands and clinging to each other. Hugging. Crying. There was some laughter, too. Around the room, he saw a handful of framed photographs of an attractive young woman he knew to be Natasha Lubin. Some of the other family members shared photographs on their phones.

It was probably cathartic for many of them, but for Frost, it was suffocating. As a rule, he didn't do well in crowds.

"Shall we do the reflections?" Dominika Lubin announced after twenty minutes that felt like an hour.

Frost eyed his mother with a question.

"It's a chance for people to share memories," Janice murmured.

The parents and the older people in the gathering gravitated to the chairs, and Frost stayed in the back with the rest, which included siblings and children. He spotted Camille Valou, looking wealthy and pained in one of the armchairs. Their eyes met, and her mouth opened slightly in unhappy surprise. He remembered their confrontation and her grieved reaction as she studied the inscription on the back of Melanie's real watch. *La rêveuse.*

Camille half stood from the chair, as if she were possessed by a desire to cross the room and slap him. Then she sat back down and looked away, biting her lip.

The stories began.

Dominika Lubin started. Her husband, who was very tall and several years older, sat next to her. She recalled the empty house after Natasha had gone away to college and how long the four years had felt while their daughter was away. Eventually, Natasha had moved home and taken a job with the parks department, which meant she could walk across the street to work in Stern Grove. Mother, father, and daughter had been able to have breakfast every day.

Until Rudy Cutter came.

After that, the house had felt empty again, as if Natasha had gone back to school; only this time, Dominika knew her daughter was never coming home.

Rae Hart's father spoke next.

Then Gilda Flores. Then Camille Valou. Then Hazel Dixon's husband, with their young son in his lap. Everyone was crying. Frost himself felt dizzy, hearing all the names again, victim after victim. He knew their faces, but he didn't *know* them, not really, not until now. They were like the ghosts in the room, haunting the ones they'd left behind. He listened to the voices, but all he could hear in his head was the voice of Rudy Cutter over the phone, and he'd never felt angrier or more helpless in his life.

While he was consumed with his own thoughts, his mother spoke to him from across the room.

"Frost? Would you like to share something about Katie?"

They all looked at him. Every face turned to him expectantly. The silence was like the ticking of a clock. *Tick tock.* He thought about what he could say, but he had nothing. Heat gathered on his neck. His mouth felt dry. He ran his hand back through his brown hair and said, "I need some air."

Just like that, he turned and bolted from the house. He slammed the door behind him. He crossed the street to the trees, where he steadied himself against one of the thick eucalyptus trunks. It was difficult to breathe. In the dense gloom of the woods, day felt like night.

Close by, someone spoke to him. "You part of the group?"

Frost glanced sideways and saw a man about his own age sitting on a fieldstone bench with his legs jutting out into the dirt. He held a cigar in his hand, leaching peppery smoke into the air. He wore a rust-colored sweater and jeans, and he had black hair and red glasses on his face.

"Excuse me?" Frost said.

"I saw you come out of the house. I figured you must be a member of the families."

"I am. My name's Frost Easton."

The man pushed himself off the bench. He extended a hand, which Frost shook. "Robbie Lubin. Tash—Natasha—was my sister."

"Katie was mine," Frost replied.

Robbie dug in the pocket of his jeans, and his hand emerged with another cigar. "Want one?"

"No, thanks."

"Tash always gave me a hard time about cigars. She said they stank. So naturally, I smoked them around her whenever I could."

Frost smiled. "That sounds about right."

Robbie gestured at the house. "The whole group-hug thing has never been my style. I prefer to grieve in my own way."

"Me, too." Frost tried to remember what he'd heard about Natasha's brother. "Someone told me you were from Minnesota. Is that right? Or am I thinking of someone else?"

"That's me," Robbie told him. "I live in a suburb of Minneapolis called Maple Grove. I work for Medtronic. My parents can't understand what I'm doing out there. They think of Minnesota as the frozen tundra."

"I have some Minnesota roots of my own," Frost said.

"Oh?"

"Well, if you believe my mother, they were taking a cross-country driving trip while she was pregnant with me, and they were debating baby names. Apparently, they were passing through Southern Minnesota, and they saw a highway sign pointing to the town of Easton in one direction and the town of Frost in the other. 'Frost Easton.' My mother took it as a sign from the universe."

"I like it." Robbie sucked on the cigar and blew out a cloud of smoke.

"So was Natasha older or younger?" Frost asked.

"Tash was four years younger than me."

"Same with me and Katie."

"Were the two of you close?" Robbie asked.

"Best friends since we were kids. We hung out together all the time. How about you?"

"As kids, not so much," he replied. "I was a science geek. Tash was into athletics. A basketball player. She was freaky tall, like our dad. We did our own thing in those days, but that changed when she went to college. I was doing an internship at Medtronic, and as luck would have it, Tash got recruited to the U of M basketball team. So she moved in with me. We lived together all four years she was in school. At that point, we became super close."

"But then she moved back to California?" Frost asked.

"Right. The winters out there weren't for her. She hated them. And I think she felt bad having both of us so far away from our parents. I'm glad Mom and Dad had those couple of years with her living at home again. You know, as things worked out."

"Yeah."

Robbie studied him from behind his bright-red glasses. "You're the cop, right? The one who found the watch?"

Frost nodded.

"My parents aren't fans of yours," Robbie told him. "They thought you should have kept your mouth shut. For what it's worth, I told them they were wrong. I'm in a business where you can't take shortcuts, and I don't approve of anyone who does, even when they do it for the right reasons."

"I appreciate that."

"I can only imagine what an agonizing choice it was for you. You're not a disinterested observer."

"No."

"Do you have a picture of Katie?" Robbie asked.

"Sure."

Frost pulled his phone out of his pocket and called up the screen-saver photo he used. It showed him and Katie on a beautiful summer day at Alcatraz, the year before she was killed. Her head leaned against his shoulder; she had a big smile; and her hair was sunny blond. That was how he liked to remember her.

Robbie took a long look before handing the phone back to him. "You two look a lot alike."

"Everyone says that," Frost agreed. He added, "Do you have a picture of Natasha?"

"Of course."

Frost had seen many pictures of Natasha Lubin over the years—including horrible ones from the crime scene—but he knew that Robbie was looking for an opportunity to show off his sister. That was what siblings did. Robbie pulled out his own phone and scrolled through a long series of pictures to find the one he wanted.

"This is us in my apartment in Minneapolis," he told Frost, "when Tash was a senior."

Frost turned the camera sideways to make the landscape image bigger. It was a sweet shot. Natasha was in her yellow basketball uniform, with long dark hair tied into a ponytail. She towered six inches over her older brother. Robbie looked younger and skinnier, with longer black hair but the same glasses. The two of them mugged for the camera, fighting playfully over the basketball that Natasha held in her big hands. They were obviously in Natasha's bedroom; Frost could see basketball trophies lined up on a bookshelf behind them.

"You're right, she was really tall," he said.

"Six four," Robbie replied. "And you can bet she reminded me about that every time I saw her."

"Of course she did," Frost said, smiling.

He was about to hand the phone back to Robbie Lubin.

And that was when he saw it.

He stared at the picture and squinted to make out the details. At first, he didn't realize what he was looking at, but when he did, chills ran up and down his body. With his thumb and forefinger, he enlarged the photograph, not to look at Natasha and Robbie, but to zoom in on the bookshelf behind them. There, on the shelf, beside the basketball trophies, he could see a small picture frame no larger than five-by-seven inches.

Enlarged, the image was blurry, but that didn't matter. He wasn't wrong about it. Inside the picture frame was the puzzle piece that had eluded Jess for years. Inside the picture frame was the answer. The connection. The motive. The reason why all those women had to die. Behind that sliver of glass was the evidence that would put Rudy Cutter back in prison for the rest of his life.

"What is that?" Frost murmured, pointing at the screen with his finger. "Where did it come from?"

Robbie leaned in to see what Frost was looking at. "Oh, the sketch? Mom gave that to Tash when she turned eighteen. It's just a little portrait of Mom holding Tash as a baby when she was at the hospital. Tash thought it was pretty cool. I still have it on the wall in my place in Minnesota. It's a little reminder of her."

Frost kept staring at the sketch in the frame.

It was a drawing of a mother with a baby in her arms. The sketch was roughly done, but by a talented hand. He could recognize Dominika Lubin, younger, glowing with triumph and exhaustion. Her eyes beamed at her child, at the new life she was holding. And the baby had her own eyes closed, asleep and at peace in a new world. The sketch must have been done within hours of Natasha's birth.

He saw the label inscribed underneath the portrait: *Dominika and Natasha*. Below it was Natasha's birthdate.

"Do you know who made this sketch?" he asked.

Robbie shrugged. "Sorry, no. Honestly, I don't even know where Mom got it. Why?"

Frost didn't answer. He already knew who the artist had to be. He knew, because he'd seen an almost identical sketch in the bedroom of Nina Flores, and it was obviously done by the same hand. He'd seen that same sketch of Nina Flores somewhere else, too. It was clearly visible in the background of the photograph of Nina and Tabby that Nina had worn as a button on her twenty-first birthday.

Anyone looking at the photograph, anyone who knew what that sketch was, would have recognized it, even in miniature. Seeing it, seeing the technique, Frost realized that he'd seen the same artist's work in the self-portrait over the fireplace in Josephine Stillman's house. That was partly why the painting had seemed so oddly familiar to him. It wasn't just the face. It was the style.

Rudy Cutter would have recognized it, too.

He would have spotted it instantly when Nina Flores showed off the buttons she was wearing in the coffee shop.

He would have seen that sketch and known that his wife, Hope, had drawn it.

40

When Frost went back inside the Lubin house, he shared what he'd discovered with the families, and the parents began to remember. They'd all owned similar sketches of mother and daughter.

Camille Valou had given a sketch like that, of herself and Melanie in the hospital, to her in-laws during a family visit to Switzerland. She assumed they still had it at their chalet in Wengen.

Rae Hart's parents had kept a similar sketch in a box of memorabilia in their attic. They hadn't looked at it in years.

Shu Chan's mother had sent her sketch to Shu's grandmother in China.

Hazel Dixon's father remembered the sketch, but they'd lost it and most of the other keepsakes from Hazel's childhood in a fire several years earlier.

No one except Gilda Flores had ever hung the sketch on a wall, and that was only because she'd left Nina's bedroom exactly as it had been years earlier. The sketch of Natasha was still on display in Robbie Lubin's house, but he was two thousand miles away in Maple Grove, Minnesota. None of the other families had known that similar sketches existed. And neither had Jess.

He couldn't blame her for missing it.

Even if Jess had researched *where* the victims were born, she wouldn't have seen a pattern. The mothers had used three different hospitals in different parts of the city, and Frost assumed that Hope

Cutter hadn't stayed in any given job at a particular hospital for a long period of time. Hope was also an ER nurse, not an obstetrics nurse. There was no reason for her to be in the maternity ward. However, he remembered what Hope's mother, Josephine, had told him. *Hope would visit pediatrics on her breaks at the hospitals and chat with the new mothers.*

And then there was Katie.

Just like every other part of her murder, Katie didn't fit the pattern. She hadn't been born in San Francisco at all, but had been an unexpected surprise while Janice was visiting Frost's aunt in San Luis Obispo. His parents had no similar sketch of her. It all reinforced his belief that Katie had stumbled onto Rudy Cutter and not the other way around. She'd seen him somewhere, doing something that no one was supposed to see.

There was only one problem with the new evidence.

The parents all remembered the sketches of their babies, but none of the parents in the room remembered Hope Cutter at all. The sketches weren't signed. There was nothing to tie her to any of them.

"The only thing I remember about the sketch," Camille Valou told him, "was that it was a sweet little mystery. I never knew where it came from. When they release you from the hospital with a child, they send you home with all this material. It's overwhelming, and of course, you're already tired and anxious. It was several days before I opened this plain manila envelope that was in the packet. The sketch was inside. No explanation. No note. No signature. Just the picture. I thought it was lovely, of course, but I had no idea who had made it."

Gilda Flores said the same thing.

So did the other mothers.

"I actually called the hospital about it," Rae Hart's mother recalled. "I wanted to know who had made the sketch, because I wanted to send a thank-you note. I thought maybe this was a little gift that the hospital did for all the mothers. But they didn't know anything about it."

"My wife called, too," Steven Dixon told him. "No one at the hospital knew where it had come from. I remember them telling her that she wasn't the only one who had found a sketch tucked in with their materials. Several other mothers had called about the same thing. But apparently the artist had kept it a secret, because they hadn't found out who was doing it."

No one knew Hope.

No one remembered Hope.

And yet Frost *knew* Hope Cutter had made those sketches. It was her. That was what had triggered Rudy's rage all those years later. A sketch. A link between Nina Flores and Rudy's wife.

A link that one of the women named Maria Lopes shared, too.

All he had to do was prove it. And find out who was next.

He knew someone who could help him.

Frost parked outside Josephine Stillman's house near Stonestown.

Hope's mother answered the door, and she didn't look surprised to see him. Her face had a defiant cast. She patted her auburn hair, and then she folded her arms across her chest. "I assumed you'd be coming back here," she said.

"And you know why, don't you?" Frost asked.

Josephine simply opened the door and let him walk into the house. He went into the small living room, where Hope's self-portrait stared down at him, full of quiet despair. Hope had been keeping her secret in plain sight all this time.

He showed Josephine the same photo he'd shown her the previous day.

"This sketch in the background of the picture," Frost said. "That's what you saw when you studied it. That's why you reacted the way you did. Hope drew that sketch, didn't she?"

Josephine didn't need to look at it again. "Yes, she did."

"You should have told me immediately."

"After so much time, why does it matter?"

"It matters because all the victims had sketches like this done when they were babies. That's the connection that ties them together. Did you know that Hope was doing sketches of new mothers at the hospitals where she was working? Did you ever see them?"

The old woman stared up at the portrait of her daughter. "Of course."

"Tell me about them."

Josephine walked over to an old-fashioned mahogany martini table. She opened the drawer and dug through a stack of letters and photographs inside. She found what she was looking for—a yellowed sheet of paper torn from a spiral notebook—and handed it to him. It was a sketch done in ballpoint pen of a mother and child, almost identical in structure to the sketches Frost had seen. This one had the artist's signature written in script below the sketch: *Hope Stillman.* Even the handwriting matched the names written on the other sketches.

"I had a photograph of myself in the hospital holding Hope on the day she was born," Josephine said. "I showed the picture to Hope when she was ten years old. A day later, she came back to me with this sketch. She did it from memory. You can see she had a gift for art even then. I was proud and sad at the same time."

"Sad?" Frost asked.

"Look at Hope's face in the sketch," Josephine said.

Frost did. The face of the baby was like the face in the self-portrait over the fireplace. Unhappy. Tortured. Even at ten years old, Hope was already wrestling with demons.

"That's the one thing she changed from the photograph," Hope's mother went on. "She's smiling in the original picture. The way any innocent baby would be. But not in the sketch."

"And what about the drawings at the hospitals?" Frost asked.

"I told you, Hope liked to visit the new mothers. I think she was looking for something that had always eluded her. She wanted to believe that a baby would complete her. She saw joy in the faces of the mothers, and it was a joy she'd never been able to find herself. After she talked to them, she would make these little sketches at home. All from memory. She made sure the original went to the mothers, but she kept copies for herself. And she made copies for me, too. She only sketched the girls, though. Hope never wanted anything for herself except a daughter. She made dozens of these portraits."

Dozens.

Hope had visited each of the mothers. She'd probably held each child in her arms. They were all on Rudy Cutter's list. Unless Frost could stop him, Cutter was far from done. But now, finally, they had hard evidence to tie him to every murder. They could rearrest him. If they could find him.

"Do you still have copies of those sketches?" Frost asked.

Josephine nodded. "Yes, I kept them in an album."

"I really need to take that album with me," he said.

A wistfulness came over Josephine's face. "I know. I already went and retrieved it from the attic. It's in the other room. I'll get it for you. I was going to call you today to tell you about it. I couldn't live with the secret. Back then, you have to believe me, I had no idea that those sketches had any importance. It never occurred to me. If I'd realized what Rudy was doing, I would have told someone."

Frost wondered if that was true, but it didn't matter.

What mattered was seeing the faces, names, and birthdates in those sketches.

Josephine left the room. He waited near the fireplace with Hope. He could feel her watching him. The portrait had an odd way of making her come to life. Her madness hadn't left; it had somehow found its way from those sketches into Rudy Cutter's mind.

Hope's mother returned, carrying a small photo album with both hands. She handed it to Frost, who treated it delicately. The album had a musty smell, and dust was on the spine. When he opened it carefully, he saw that the album had nothing but black paper pages with rough, unfinished edges. No hooks, no plastic. On every page, Josephine had carefully taped one of Hope's sketches. They were all the same, but they were all different. The paper and tape had become brittle; the ink was fading.

Frost turned one page after another. He saw the faces and names. Mothers and children. Many were strangers, but he also saw those he recognized. Daughters who had become victims.

Camille and Melanie.

Gilda and Nina.

Kelly and Hazel.

Weng and Shu.

This album, gathering dust in an attic, could have changed everything. Cutter would still be in prison. Some of the victims might still be alive. Katie might be alive. And Jess.

He turned another page, and he saw two names under the next sketch.

Sonja and Maria.

Maybe there were others—Maria was a common name—but he knew he'd found Maria Lopes, simply by looking at the mother's face. The woman he'd met earlier that day in the hills of San Bruno looked just like her mother. He called up on his phone the DMV records he'd pulled for the various women named Maria Lopes in the Bay Area, and when he checked the birthday for Maria Lopes in San Bruno, he saw that it matched the birthdate written on the faded sketch.

She was the woman he was looking for.

He thought about Maria's house, near the hills and trails of Sweeney Ridge.

He remembered the phone call from Rudy Cutter and the fierce, intermittent noise of the wind blowing in the background.

Frost knew where Cutter was. He grabbed his phone to send the police to hunt him down.

41

The late afternoon became dusk.

Fog massed like an army on the ridge, and the temperature fell. Lights began to come on in the houses that dotted the valley. Rudy waited, motionless and half-frozen, in the nest on the hillside where he'd spied on Maria Lopes for hours.

He didn't feel alone. Hope was with him. She was always with him, like a bad angel. Every time he wielded the knife, he killed her, but time after time, she came back to life, and he had to do it all over again. One by one by one by one, he erased each glimmer of who she was. Each trace of what she'd left on earth.

And still she sat beside him.

It had been a long, terrible journey from April 1 nine years ago until now. He had never sought it out; instead, fate had found him that day, like an April Fool's joke. It was supposed to be the last day of his life. He'd finally been ready to kill himself, to shut the door on his empty world. He'd tried several times before and failed. With pills. With a rope. With the tailpipe of Phil's Cadillac. In the end, he'd backed out every time before death took him away.

But not again.

He'd had it all planned. April 1. He was going to go to one last Giants game with Phil. He was going to have a burger and a beer. And then, as it neared midnight, he was going to drive to the Golden Gate

Bridge and follow the example of the jumpers who'd come before him. Once he cleared the rail, second thoughts didn't matter. You couldn't change your mind on the way down.

Instead, his life and destiny had changed completely before he got to the bridge. He thought of all the improbable things that had happened that day to set him on a different path.

If Phil hadn't been late to pick him up for the game, Rudy would be dead at the bottom of the bay.

If he'd chosen another coffee shop in the Ferry Building, he'd be dead at the bottom of the bay.

If he'd picked a different day, not April 1, he'd be dead at the bottom of the bay.

Instead, he'd gone to that coffee shop to wait for Phil and met Nina Flores on her twenty-first birthday.

He remembered sitting on the stool at the coffee bar, with an iced latte in front of him getting watery and warm because he could barely summon any interest in taking a sip. That had been Rudy's life at that moment, sucked clean of purpose. The stool next to him had been vacant, but Hope was there in his mind, as she always was, immortal and inextinguishable. He'd felt numb. He'd wanted nothing more than to die, if it meant it would finally drive her away.

Meanwhile, Nina Flores talked.

He'd never met anyone who could talk so much. He didn't know how she found the time to breathe, because she filled every second with chatter. She talked. She sang. She laughed. She danced. She called out to people passing in the Ferry Building: "Hey, come wish me a happy birthday!"

Rudy had done his best to ignore her. When you are getting ready to throw yourself off a bridge, the last thing you need is a chirpy barista telling you how wonderful her life is. And it was impossible not to do the math. This girl was twenty-one years old. Wren, if she'd lived, would have been turning twenty-one in November.

Until Hope snuffed out her life. Until 3:42 a.m. came.

He'd found himself staring at Nina and thinking what Wren would have looked like at this point in her life. He'd tried to imagine her face, all grown up. He'd thought about the things they would have done together, father and daughter. The things he'd missed. The Giants game tonight? He'd be going with Wren.

The longer he'd stayed at the coffee shop, the more oppressive it had felt to be there. He'd wanted to get up and leave, but something had kept him glued to the seat, listening to this young girl babble about her life. Again, fate had conspired. If he'd left, if he'd walked away, nothing would have changed. He would have gone to the bridge. He would have gone through with his plan.

Instead, he stayed.

The less attention he'd paid to Nina Flores, the more she'd made it her mission to draw him out. After half an hour, that meant shoving her body halfway over the counter to point out the buttons she wore on her T-shirt.

"And this is my high school grad photo. Can you believe that hair? Look at all of it! I was heavier then, too. That was twenty pounds ago. These days, no carbs! Or at least, not very many. Of course, everybody has to have cake on their birthday, so I'll make an exception tonight. Plus, I have to have a drink. What do you think? Beer? I was thinking of something stronger. Maybe tequila shots.

"This photo here, these are all of my brothers! Three brothers, no sisters. Tabby here is as close to a sister as I'll ever have. Do you have sisters? It can be a struggle, brothers and sisters, but I'm the oldest, so they know they can't get away with much around me. I love them, but don't tell them I said that.

"And this is me and Tabby! Aren't we cute? This was just like a week ago. We were heading out to a party, pretty hot stuff, huh? Look at those smiles. See—like sisters! People talk about BFFs and don't really mean it, but that's me and her, for sure. Right, Tabby?"

Rudy didn't listen to what the other barista said.

He'd found himself staring at the oversized button pinned below the collar of Nina's T-shirt. Leaning closer to get a better look. At first, he'd thought he was imagining things. It was a vision, brought on by what he planned to do, a last little joke played on his brain by Hope's ghost.

But it wasn't. It was real.

Right there on the bedroom wall behind the photograph of these two girls was a sketch of a mother and child. He knew those sketches. He had dozens of them in a box in the garage at home. Hope had made them of new mothers and new babies ever since she'd started her work as an ER nurse.

The awful reality of it had gathered like a storm in Rudy's brain. Hope had been in a hospital room with *this girl* on the day she'd been born. Hope had talked to her mother. Laughed with her. She'd probably held this child in her arms. She'd sketched her face and captured her forever. Hope had seen the beauty in this girl and the love her mother had for her. This girl had grown up in a family and lived with her parents and her siblings.

This girl was alive. Wren was dead.

It couldn't be an accident that Rudy had found her. On that day of all days.

Something about the intersection of Nina and Hope had stirred a fury in Rudy where there had previously been nothing but hollow grief. This girl was a direct connection to Hope. It was like Hope lived on in Nina Flores. She was a perennial coming back year after year—a flower that needed to be yanked out of the ground and destroyed once and for all. Maybe, if he could do that, he could be free.

Rudy had walked out of that coffee shop a different man.

He'd still gone to the Giants game with Phil. He'd had his burger and his beer. But afterward, he hadn't gone to the Golden Gate Bridge to throw himself to the hard surface of the water. Instead, he'd spent the night in the garage with a box from his past that he hadn't opened in twenty-one years. The box was filled with the memories of his life with

Hope. He'd tried for two decades to crush those memories, but now he realized that was a mistake. He wanted to remember. He wanted to strike back. He wanted Hope to feel what he felt, to have her know that he could kill, too. He could strip away someone else's future, someone else's dreams, just the way she'd done to him.

He'd found the copies of the sketches. All of them. Dozens of them.

Going through them, he'd found the one he was looking for. *Gilda and Nina*. Staring at it, he'd finally had a plan. For years, he'd had no way of taking revenge on Hope for what she'd done. Until that moment.

Gilda and Nina.

Two weeks later, when it was done, he'd come home and taken a match and burned the sketch into ash. That night, he'd slept all the way through from dark to dawn, not waking up at 3:42 a.m.

And he'd known that he wasn't done.

The next year, he'd taken Rae Hart away from Hope. The year after that, he'd done the same with Natasha Lubin. He'd burned more sketches and watched the flames. It was as if Hope could feel the pain of what he'd done. As if she were on the other side of a window, silently screaming at him. It was the battle that never ended. Not while he was alive.

Rudy shivered.

Behind him, a wet finger of fog caressed his neck and passed in front of his eyes like a cataract. He didn't have much time. Night was coming soon. There was barely an hour of daytime left, and the fog was already stealing it away. He lifted the binoculars and studied the house at the base of the hill. Lights shined behind the windows, and he could see clearly into Maria's bedroom. She read a book as she lay on the bed, but her face was grim with tension. She showed no indication of getting ready to leave the house before dark.

Why wasn't she running?

She always ran. She ran every day. And then he knew: Frost Easton had warned her. Scared her. She was staying home, changing her routine, because of him.

Rudy didn't think he'd get a second chance with Maria. Everything would be different tomorrow. It was now or never, and he had to do something. He reached into his backpack and booted up his phone, and he dialed her number. Through the lenses of his binoculars, he could see her get up to answer the call. In his ear, he heard the mellow sound of Maria's voice.

"Hello?"

"Ms. Lopes? This is Inspector Wolff with the San Francisco Police. I work with Inspector Easton." Rudy's tone was official but friendly.

"Oh, is there news?" Maria asked.

"Yes, there is. We were able to identify the woman that Rudy Cutter has been targeting, and the good news is, it's *not* you. We're calling everyone we talked to, in order to let them know they're safe and don't need to worry."

"Oh my God, what a relief."

"I'm sure it is. Inspector Easton sends his apologies for alarming you, but of course, we had to take every precaution."

"Of course."

"Have a good day," he told her.

Rudy hung up.

He watched Maria, and he waited. She paced back and forth in her bedroom. She went to the window and stared out at the dark hills, and her face broke into a nervous smile, drained of fear. She looked almost giddy now. Then, just as he'd hoped, she began to change her clothes. She put on a tight-fitting, long-sleeved athletic shirt that had bold stripes. She found a pair of black shorts. She bent over and tied the laces of red high-top sneakers.

Maria was going for a run.

Rudy reached into his backpack to retrieve his knife. *Watch this, Hope.*

42

Maria knew the hills as intimately as a lover. She ran them every single day of her life. As she stepped out of her front door, the cool air from the ocean hit her with a bracing blow to the face. She felt dampness; rain would be coming overnight. She jogged down the steps to the street, where she did an elaborate series of stretches to loosen up for the trails.

The warning about Rudy Cutter from Inspector Easton hadn't seemed real, but until the call came from his partner telling her she was safe, she hadn't admitted to herself how much the threat had unnerved her. Now, she was keyed up and flooded with restless energy. It was almost too late to run—darkness was coming soon—but if she didn't run, she knew she'd never sleep. She needed to do something normal after a day filled with crazy fear.

When she was done stretching, she studied the hills. They were lush green and bathed in gloom, with only a handful of trees looming over the densely matted vegetation like solitary soldiers. The cloud of fog had reached the summit of the ridge and was starting to spill into the valley. She wanted a demanding run tonight, on a trail that climbed sharply uphill toward the slope that overlooked Pacifica and the ocean. A hard, strenuous workout was the way to burn off her anxiety. She slid earbuds into her ears and kicked off the playlist on her Nano. Right now, she was obsessed with Ellie Goulding, so she listened to "My Blood" as she took off toward the park. With the music pounding, she couldn't hear anything else around her.

Running was therapy to Maria. Some runners cleared their minds as they ran, thinking about nothing except their pace and their breathing, but Maria brought her whole life with her onto the trails. Right now, she thought about Jeremy. She was a wife, singer, actress, and fund-raiser, but more than anything, she was Maria Lopes, mother to Jeremy. He was her everything. The thought of being on Rudy Cutter's list hadn't scared her because of what might happen to herself. The heaviness in her chest was the unspeakable fear of missing her son's life. Not seeing Jeremy grow up before her eyes. Not being there for school, sports, dances, and girls. Not seeing what he would do and where he would go in this world. His future was far more important than her own.

Maria pushed herself higher and faster, sprinting away from the dread she'd felt all day, almost crying with relief that it was over. Tendrils of fog wrapped around her arms and legs like fast-growing rainforest vines. She felt a vibration on the phone that was lodged in the back pocket of her shorts, but she didn't let it break her stride. If you stopped halfway up the hillside, you lost your momentum. Above her, the ocean-side ridge was invisible, just a milky cloud. She ran upward into nothingness, and the only way she knew she'd reached the peak was that the ground finally leveled off under her pounding strides.

Up here, the fog swirled, like a living thing, silver and impenetrable, constantly changing. She headed west toward the ocean. The land was mostly flat but no longer paved, and she slowed her pace, because it was easy to turn an ankle on loose rock. Thick scrub brush pushed up to the trail on both sides, and the fog, as it always did, gave her a strange, disorienting loneliness. She lost track of time, and she lost track of where she was, but it didn't scare her. She'd done this many times before.

Maria thought about the evening ahead of her. Once the nanny left, and it was just her and Jeremy in the house, she would take out her guitar and sing for her son, the way she always did. It was partly for him and partly for herself, a little piece of her past that she hadn't given up. Years from now, she wondered if Jeremy would hear an Ellie Goulding song on an oldies station and feel a little tug in his heart and try to remember where he'd heard it before and why it reminded him of his mother.

In her pocket, her phone buzzed again and went to voice mail. It was probably Matt, calling from Malaysia or Singapore or wherever he was today, but he would understand. Running was sacred, and you didn't interrupt the run.

She finally stopped where the trail began to turn downward. If she kept going, the path would take her all the way to Highway 1 near the Pacifica beach. It was time to head home. Maria retraced her steps, absorbed in a world that didn't stretch more than a few feet around her in any direction. When the trail widened into an X, she knew she was back at the cross trail leading along Sweeney Ridge. Jeremy was a mile away from her at the base of the hill.

The land opened up here into a broad stretch of dirt and rock. Somewhere close by, there was a stone monument to the discovery site of San Francisco Bay. She decided to walk a while. She took the earphones out of her ears. The fog continued to play tricks with her eyes. She'd seen the oddest things up here and not known what was real and what wasn't. One time, she'd been certain that she was surrounded by a kaleidoscope of thousands of orange monarch butterflies. Another time, she'd convinced herself that she was standing on the brink of a chasm that didn't exist at all. She'd stood there, frozen, for several minutes before persuading herself that the cliff was nothing but an illusion.

This time, squinting into the fog, she saw a face.

A man stood on the ridge, not ten feet away from her, dressed in jeans and a black hoodie, his hands hidden. He stared at her with fixed, dead eyes. And just as quickly, he disappeared. The face vanished, obscured by the moving cloud of fog. In that split second, she recognized him.

The face, coming and going, belonged to Rudy Cutter.

He was *right there*.

Maria felt a chill, not from cold, but from fear. Instinctively, she took a step backward, and the trail gave way to the crackle of branches under her sneakers. She told herself that this was another fantasy conjured by the fog. Cutter wasn't targeting her; he was going after someone else. The police had said so.

She listened and heard no footsteps anywhere around her. She was alone.

Or was she?

Something was behind her, and she spun around. Except there was nothing. And then, just as quickly, she felt someone coming near her from the other direction. She turned again.

Nothing. No one.

She wanted to call out, but she clamped her mouth shut. She didn't move. She didn't make a sound. She realized she was holding her breath. *If I can't see him, then he can't see me.*

But was any of it real?

Maria remembered the buzzing of her phone. She reached into her pocket and grabbed the phone and stared at the glow of the screen. Two missed calls. Both of them from Frost Easton. She had voice mail waiting for her, and she held the phone tightly against her ear to listen to the message. She wanted him to reassure her that everything was fine. Instead, his voice brought all the terror back.

"Maria, stay home. I'm sending the police. Rudy Cutter may be nearby."

She tried to hang up the phone. Instead, her fingers trembling, she accidentally punched the speakerphone button, and the message started over and boomed into the fog. It took forever to shut it off. The silence, when the noise was over, felt ominous, as if she'd told the world exactly where she was. She stood there, waiting, panicking.

The fog got thicker and thicker.

Maria was certain now. Cutter was here. She could feel him. Blindly, not even looking down, she ran.

The San Bruno police beat Frost to Maria's door. They were waiting for him when he arrived. Three uniformed officers stood around two squad cars, and he could see that Maria's front door was open, with another officer just inside the doorway. He introduced himself to the cops on the street.

"What's the status?" Frost asked.

"The homeowner isn't here," one of the officers replied. He was a burly Filipino kid in his early twenties. "The nanny answered the door. She said Ms. Lopes left on a run about forty-five minutes ago."

Frost shook his head. "She went for a run? Now? I can't believe she would take a risk like that after I talked to her."

"Well, the nanny said she got a call from the SFPD giving her the all clear," the cop told him.

"*What?*"

"Yeah, some detective called and said not to worry, she wasn't the target."

Frost knew who had made that call. Rudy Cutter. The spider had lured her into the web. They were running out of time.

"Where did she go?" he asked.

"The park trails. Beyond that, the nanny doesn't know. She says Ms. Lopes likes to vary her route."

Frost was too far away to hear noise from the ridge. A scream wouldn't even be a whisper. All he knew was that Cutter was after

Maria. And Maria wasn't answering her phone. She thought she was safe, when in fact, she'd been lured to the hills by Cutter himself.

He stared up at Sweeney Ridge. The fog descended toward him, heavy and thick. It had crossed the summit and was stealing like a prowler into the valley. From where he was, he couldn't see the slope of the hills now. Daylight was already fading to night, adding a black shroud to the haze of the fog.

Maria was up there. They had to go get her.

"Leave one officer inside the house, in case she gets home," Frost said. "The rest of you, let's go."

43

Frost led them into the valley. The only noise was the clap of their boots on the trail. There was almost no wind. After a hundred yards, they reached the first fork, where one path descended toward the lake and the other climbed sharply to the top of the ridge. He sent one of the uniformed officers straight ahead, and the two others stayed with him on the route up the hill.

He locked his knees as he pushed higher with each step. The fog thickened. The handful of trees clinging to the slope became silhouettes against a gray wall. It was a mile from the valley to the summit, and as they reached each lower peak, the trail descended into the next seam and then rose again. The tight switchbacks were like horseshoes. He stopped regularly, hoping to hear the thump of Maria's footsteps descending toward them, but they were three solitary ghosts on the hillside.

Far below, the wail of sirens rose from the city. Reinforcements were on their way. He called Captain Hayden from the slope and asked him to coordinate with the police in San Bruno and Pacifica to place men at the obvious trail outlets. Even so, he knew their best chance of catching Cutter was here on the ridge. The reach of the hills was vast, spilling down into neighborhoods in the west and east. In the fog and the growing darkness, Cutter could easily slip away.

Frost dialed Maria's phone again. As before, she didn't answer.

He shouted for her: *"Maria!"*

His voice sounded loud, but he didn't know how well it carried. A crow, disturbed by the noise, ascended with a mocking cry from the brush nearby. They waited for Maria to call back, but stillness hung over the trail. There was nothing for them to do but keep climbing.

As they neared the high peak of the ridge, the wind revived and slapped their faces like a wet hand. Pockets of clear air wormed into the fog. With one step, the path would be invisible; with the next, they'd momentarily see a snapshot of the low foliage around them. Telephone poles crowned the hillside. Where the paved trail curved northward, he spotted a smaller, unpaved cross trail leading south. At the intersection of paths, he saw a small stone restroom with an angled tin roof.

Frost crossed the stretch of dirt and took out a small flashlight from his pocket. He yanked open the restroom door and examined the tiny interior with the light. The sewage smell was strong. No one was inside.

"What now?" one of the cops asked.

The trails followed the up-and-down peaks of the ridge. Frost shined a light along the path in both directions, but the fog threw the light back in his eyes. There were no footprints on the dry ground. He cupped his hands around his mouth and called for Maria again. She didn't answer.

"The two of you head south," he told the other cops. "The trail splits past the discovery monument, so you can each take one. I'll go north. If you find anything, shout."

They split up. Frost watched the fog envelop the officers as they headed down the path. He turned around and made his way back to the paved trail, which continued higher at a shallow climb. He marched, completely alone, through a milky bubble. The damp air got into his bones.

His flashlight swept the ground at his feet as he walked. Near the next peak, amid the sea of gray, he spotted a tiny flash of color. When he reached it, he found a red sneaker tipped over forlornly on the trail. It was an expensive shoe, a Nike Flyknit, and it looked almost new. No one would have voluntarily left it behind. He crouched down and slid a finger inside, and the interior of the shoe felt warm and wet.

Frost cast his flashlight around the dense brush. Not far away, a dead-end spur off the main trail led to an old weather station. He jogged that way, keeping an eye on the gravel for other clues that Maria may have left behind. The hilltop was cold. The wind roared, making music on the steel instruments tower. He felt as if he were on the summit of the world up here.

A squat white storage tank dominated the open ground. The dirt was lined with rutted tire tracks, but they weren't recent. He made a circuit around the building, finding nothing. This was the highest spot on the ridge, and from where he was, the land flattened. The fog thinned slightly, but the light of the day was mostly gone. He shouted Maria's name again. He could barely hear himself.

Frost tramped through the brush back to the main trail. He continued north. Two hundred feet along the ridge line, he squinted as he saw another flash of color in the light of his flashlight. It was a second shoe, a matching red Nike. The shoes were like breadcrumbs left by Maria. She'd been taken up here; she'd been dragged this way. She couldn't be far.

Less than a quarter mile away were the ruins of an old missile complex that had been built in the '50s to protect the Bay Area from a Soviet air assault that never came. The remote buildings had long since been abandoned to decay, but every Sweeney Ridge hiker knew about them. Frost ran. Through the fog, he saw the first of the lonely missile buildings take shape ahead of him, with its commanding view over the Pacific, where soldiers could monitor the skies. The cinder-block walls were painted over with wild graffiti. The doors and windows were long gone, leaving empty shells for birds to nest and animals to take shelter. It was a Cold War ghost town.

"Maria!"

This time, he heard something. Muffled. Not far away. A woman screamed. The voice rose in a shrill wail and then cut off sharply.

The eddies of the wind made it impossible to tell where it had come from.

Frost drew his gun into his hand. He crept forward into the missile complex. Weeds sprouted through the cracks in the stone and trembled in the breeze. The cement platforms, like the buildings, were covered in graffiti. He saw drawings of alien heads. Peace signs. A beatnik with black, empty eyes. Long ago, someone had painted a warning on the ground in bold capital letters:

WE ALL MUST MEET OUR MOMENT OF TRUTH.

That was exactly how Frost felt.

He climbed the cracked steps into the first building. Most of the roof was gone. The interior was dark, and when he cast his light around the space, he saw fallen rubble and the remnants of people who had come here to party in the ruins. Broken bottles. Needles. Moldy food picked apart by birds.

But no one was here.

He returned into the growing darkness. There wasn't much time.

"Cutter!" he shouted into the wind. "Give it up! I know you're here. I know about Hope and the sketches. I know *everything*. You're done. It's over. Don't make it worse."

He made a slow circle, trying to peer through the fog. Nothing moved, other than the fragile weeds. He felt mist on his face. Leading the way with his gun, he crossed the trail onto a circular cement platform in the middle of a spiderweb of dirt trails. Whatever had been housed here was gone. There was more graffiti. More loose stone. The bushes grew taller here, partially blocking his view of the next building in the missile complex, which was fifty feet away. Behind the waving branches, as the fog blew in and out, he saw rusted vent grills on top of the cinder-block wall and wild red-and-orange graffiti letters spelling out the word *RIOT*.

He could see the shell of a doorway, too.

And there was Rudy Cutter. Alone.

Frost saw no sign of Maria Lopes. For a long, frozen moment, he stared at Cutter, and Cutter stared back at him. The man's face was a mask, a mystery, without any happiness or sadness. As Frost's gaze followed the line of the man's body, he saw something else, too, secured in the man's hand.

A knife.

Red blood dripped from the blade to the dirt.

Frost leaped forward through the tangle of vines rooted in the ground. The brush trapped him, making it almost impossible to move. As he ran, he couldn't see. The weeds were as tall as he was. He dragged himself through a sharp, tight web that scratched his face, and then he finally burst out onto the cracked pavement in front of the building. Cutter was already gone. The darkness had swallowed him up. Frost lit up the walls and the hillside behind the missile complex, but there was no sign of him.

He sprinted for the building and threw himself inside. His flashlight reflected a shiny spattered blood trail across the debris on the stone floor. It led him under the rotting wooden timbers in the ceiling and toward a huge open window frame that was bordered with peeling green paint. In the next abandoned room, he saw a plastic mannequin, its body crusted with dirt, its head cut off, its arm pointed straight ahead, as if it were beckoning him.

He ran to the window frame and climbed through to the other side.

At the feet of the mannequin was Maria Lopes.

Seeing her, Frost felt his heart seize. Her blood was everywhere. Her blood made a lake. Rudy Cutter had slashed her throat deeply and ruthlessly. Frost ran to her and held her, but her eyes were closed, and each breath she drew was labored and long. He called 911; he alerted the paramedics and police; but he knew he was already too late. The hillside was too remote. There wasn't enough time. He ripped the sleeve off his coat and wrapped her neck and applied pressure, but he was holding back a heart pumping its life into the cold air with each beat.

This woman, this lovely woman, had been alive when he met her hours earlier. A mother. A wife. And then, like the others, she'd crossed paths with Cutter, and he'd stolen all of it away from her.

It made Frost want to scream. It made him want to cry. He'd been too late for Katie. Too late for Jess. And now too late for Maria, too. Cutter had won again. He always won.

Frost murmured lies into Maria's ears as the two of them waited in the dark ruins. *It's okay, hang on, help is coming, you're going to be fine.* But she wasn't going to be fine. Her eyes never opened. All the while, her ragged breaths came further and further apart, until only a few minutes later, they stopped altogether. A breath went out; nothing came back in. The silence was awful as she died in his arms.

44

One of the other detectives at police headquarters gave Frost a new shirt to wear. He changed in the bathroom. His own shirt was soaked in Maria's blood, and when he took it off, he saw that blood had seeped through onto his arms and chest. He cleaned himself at the sink as best as he could, but when he was done, he still saw remnants in the seams of his skin and under his fingernails. When he looked in the mirror, he saw gruesome red highlights in his hair.

It was already past midnight. The hunt was on. The police had converged on the missile complex at Sweeney Ridge, but Cutter was nowhere to be found. He'd disappeared into the sprawling hills. There were police helicopters overhead, shining spotlights on the trails, but he was either hidden in the forest or he'd escaped back to the city. Every cop in the Bay Area was looking for him.

Frost waited for Pruitt Hayden in the captain's office. He'd already been waiting a long time. He hadn't realized how tired he was until he sat down. The room was warm, and his head swam. He found his eyes blinking shut, and without realizing it, he drifted to sleep. In his dreams, he saw ten long, jewel-encrusted daggers dangling from his living room ceiling at home, tethered by silver threads, all of them dripping blood. He saw identical gleaming platinum watches on both of his arms, five on the left, five on the right, all of them set to 3:42 a.m.

A woman stood directly below each knife. All the victims. Nina, Rae, Natasha, Hazel, Shu, and Melanie. And now Maria, too—and Jess—and Katie. They seemed unaware of the lethal danger just over their heads. Slowly, one by one, as he shouted to warn them, the knives fell, burrowing into their skulls and vanishing. One by one, the women calmly lay down on his living room floor. With each victim, a watch disappeared from his wrist and appeared on the wrist of the woman at his feet. There was no rush. It was leisurely and horrible and silent. A knife fell. A victim died. His watch became her watch.

One, two, three, four, on and on. He couldn't stop it.

Soon it was Maria's turn. Maria in her red sneakers. He called out, but his voice didn't make a sound. The knife fell, and she was gone. Then Jess. His deep track. She stared at him in the moody and intense way she always did, but she didn't say anything. The knife penetrated her skull, like all the others. She sank to her knees, and she toppled sideways, and she lay still.

He had two watches left on his wrist, but there was only one victim left in the room. Katie.

His sister grinned at him. She held a pizza box and stared around with wide blue eyes at the Russian Hill house. She called out to him, in the familiar Katie voice he hadn't heard in years.

"Hey, did you order this pizza? Because I think I'm in the wrong place."

Frost tried to answer. He tried to scream at her: *Go, go, go, go, go.* But he was too late. He was always too late. He was too late for every one of them; they were all gone; they were all dead. The thread broke, and the knife fell. His pretty, sunny sister put down the pizza box carefully on the floor and then stretched out beside it, as if she were no more than a child taking a nap.

There was one watch left on his wrist. One knife dangling from the ceiling. But no victim. There was no one else in the room. It was supposed to be over, but he knew it wasn't over yet. A voice whispered in his ear. He was alone in the room with the victims, but Rudy Cutter's voice was in his head: *You think you've seen it all, but horror can always get worse.*

Frost started awake as he heard the rattle of the handle on the door behind him. He checked the clock on the wall. Nearly two hours had passed. Pruitt Hayden rumbled inside, as huge and threatening as a grizzly bear. The captain dropped heavily into his office chair and leaned forward.

"Sorry to keep you stuck in here for so long. I just got back to the office. How are you, Easton?"

"Fine, sir," Frost replied, which wasn't true. The bad dream clung to him and refused to go away. "Have we found Cutter?"

"No, but the man can only hide for so long. Someone will spot him."

Frost didn't share Hayden's optimism. Cutter was smart, and he'd already proven that he could stay below the radar for days at a time. If he wanted to disappear, he could. If he wanted to strike again, he could.

Hayden read the skepticism in Frost's face. "Cutter may not be back in prison yet, but he will be soon. That's thanks to you."

"It's too late for Maria Lopes," Frost said.

"I know that. I know you're going to take that hard for a long time, but it's not your fault. It wasn't your fault with Jess, either."

"It doesn't matter whether it was my fault. If I can't stop things like this, what the hell am I doing here?"

The captain sighed. He hauled his bulk out of the chair and went over to the window. Reflections of the city lights glowed on his mottled skin.

"You don't think Jess said the same thing to me with every one of Cutter's victims?" the captain said. "He was always one step ahead of her, and he finally broke her. She was a good cop who became a bad cop to get him behind bars. You played by the rules. That's what we have to do, even when we lose people because of it."

"I'll feel better when we have Cutter in custody," Frost said.

"Well, then let the rest of us do our jobs and find him. Go home."

"Yes, sir."

Frost left the office and headed straight to the elevators. There was nothing more to do here. He emerged outside the Mission Bay headquarters building into a cold, driving rain. He made no attempt to cover himself, and the rain soaked down over his hair and clothes. He shoved his hands in his pockets and walked two blocks to his Suburban. There were almost no other cars on the street. When he opened the driver's door, he saw that the seat was covered in Maria's blood. He stood there, staring at it, as the rain poured inside.

Finally, he got in and closed the door. The gusts of wind made the truck shiver. He listened to the hammering on the roof. The nightmare was still vivid in his brain, and he actually checked his wrist to see if the last platinum watch was still there. But it wasn't. This was the real world. In the real world, victims didn't simply lie down and go to sleep the way they did in his dream. They died slowly, choking, gasping, as you whispered to them and held them in your arms.

Now he knew how Jess died.

Now he knew how Katie died.

It was almost as if Rudy Cutter was teaching him a lesson. You already saw death up close. You need to see the dying, too.

Frost reached into the back seat and grabbed the photo album of Hope's sketches. In the aftermath of Maria's murder, he'd neglected to bag it and bring it inside to be logged as evidence. He thought about going back to the building now, but he couldn't drag himself out of the truck in the rain. It could wait until morning.

He flipped through the early pages. He knew what he was looking for. The sketch of Maria Lopes as a baby, held by her mother, was a third of the way into the album. He stared into Maria's innocent eyes. She was a baby on her first day of life. Welcome to the world. Thirty-two years later, she would bleed out in the abandoned shell of a missile station. It was a good thing she didn't know her fate back then, because fate was a jerk. Fate was a son of a bitch.

Go home.

He was still tired, but he wasn't ready to go home yet. He wondered if Eden was in the house. Waiting for him. Sleeping in his bed. She was a lover, but she was also a writer, and he wasn't ready to talk to a writer yet. He didn't want to have his thoughts taken down so that he could read about them in a book someday. He'd avoided reading the part of Eden's manuscript that dealt with Katie, because he didn't want to see the reality of her murder in black and white. He didn't want to know how Eden dealt with it, how she described it, and what she'd said about him. The brother who found the body. The brother who became a cop. The brother who let the killer go and then hunted him down. He was no hero.

Frost drove aimlessly through the city. He didn't have a destination in mind. It was as if he had to search every street corner for Rudy Cutter, as if he could cover every inch of San Francisco on his own. Eventually, he realized how pointless it was. His hands turned the wheel block by block and chose a new destination for him without engaging his brain. He found himself on 280 heading south through the pouring rain, at a time of night when the freeway was mostly empty. He got off near Balboa Park and wound through the jumble of city streets to the neighborhood where Phil Cutter lived.

The house was dark, but he didn't think Phil was asleep.

There was a squad car on the street, just in case Rudy showed up here. Frost showed his badge to the cop in the car, and he knew that he looked like a sight. The borrowed shirt didn't really fit. The back of it was soaked with blood because of the blood in his car. He was wet to the bone. Even so, the cop didn't ask any questions. He probably figured Frost was planning to beat the hell out of Phil to get answers about his brother.

Phil obviously thought so, too. When Frost rang the bell, Rudy's brother kept the chain on the door and didn't invite Frost inside.

"It's the middle of the night!" Phil barked. "What the hell do you want? I already told the other cops I don't know where Rudy is. I haven't seen him. You think he's stupid enough to come here? This is the last place he'd go."

"Do you know what happened tonight, Phil?" Frost asked quietly.

"I don't care what happened. It doesn't have anything to do with me."

"Your brother killed another woman," Frost snapped. "Can you live with that?"

Frost couldn't help remembering how this had all started. Phil had left him an anonymous note. *Can you live with a lie?*

"Quit hassling me, man. What Rudy does has nothing to do with me."

"If you helped him, we'll put you in jail, too."

"I didn't do a damn thing," Phil replied.

"Then why were you following me?"

"I wasn't following you," the man replied.

"I saw your Cadillac, Phil. You were outside the restaurant on the Embarcadero last night. You took off when I started across the street."

"So what?" Phil asked. "Is that a crime? You going to arrest me for making an illegal U-turn?"

"What did Rudy want to know about me? What did you tell him?"

"Nothing."

Frost shook his head. "Where were you this evening?"

"Home. Alone."

"Did Rudy call you? Did you help him get away?"

"I was here," Phil rasped, his voice cracking. "I told you. I didn't go nowhere."

A rattling cough bubbled out of Phil's throat. His eyes looked sunken and gray. He was a skeleton, dressed in black shorts and a black tank top. Alcohol breathed like fire from his mouth, along with the same bitter cigarette smoke that Frost had smelled whenever he crossed paths with Phil. Frost realized that the man was telling the truth. He hadn't gone anywhere tonight. He'd been home. Smoking. Drinking himself into a stupor.

Frost looked at the empty street, then at the garage. Last time he'd been here, the garage door had been open, and the inside was a dumping ground for years of broken equipment and debris. There was no room for a car.

"Where's your Cadillac, Phil?"

The man shrugged. "In the shop."

"Yeah? Which one?"

"Somewhere over on Mission."

Frost leaned into the crack of the door. He was inches from Phil's face. "Rudy's got it, right? You met him somewhere, and you let him take the car. That's how he got to San Bruno."

Phil didn't say a word, but the squint of fear in the man's eyes was enough to convince Frost that he was right. Rudy was in the Cadillac. He grabbed his phone to call in an update on the search, and he started down the steps. He was done here. He was done with Phil turning a blind eye to what his brother had done.

But as he turned away from the front door, he heard Phil mutter something behind him, in a burst of shock and surprise.

"Holy hell."

Frost turned back. "What is it?"

"Nothing," Phil replied quickly, but the man swallowed hard and stared down at the cracked concrete on the porch.

Frost realized that the back of the white shirt he'd borrowed was covered in Maria's blood. Phil couldn't handle seeing it. It was one thing to know that your brother was a murderer. It was another thing to see the victim's blood, only hours after she'd died.

"Yeah, that's what he does," Frost said softly. "He cuts their throats. You can't believe how much blood there is."

Phil's left eye twitched. He breathed loudly through his nose.

"Is there anything you want to tell me?" Frost asked him.

Phil opened his mouth, but then he clamped it shut. Frost waited, wondering if the man would break, but Phil stayed stubbornly silent. Eventually, Frost hissed in frustration and went back down the steps. He had the door of the Suburban open when Phil finally shouted at him through the sheets of rain.

"Hey."

Frost looked up. Phil had come out of the house onto the porch. His hands were on his hips. Wind buffeted his tall, skinny frame.

"Hey, I wasn't lying, man," Phil called. "I wasn't following *you*."

Before Frost could ask any questions, Phil turned around and stormed back inside and slammed the door shut. Frost got into the Suburban and sat in the darkness of the truck, with the rain pounding on the windshield. He replayed what Phil had said in his head, and he heard the emphasis on that last word.

I wasn't following you.

Frost felt a sickness in his soul that he hadn't felt since that day at Ocean Beach. A crushing fear. A wild despair.

He knew. He knew.

He heard another voice in his memory. This one was the voice of Gilda Flores, Nina's mother.

Tabby and Nina were inseparable. Much like me and her mother. We were pregnant at the same time, and Nina and Tabby were first babies for both of us, so we went through it all together.

Frost snatched up the album of Hope's sketches again. He wanted to be wrong. There was no way that Rudy Cutter could know the truth, no way he could realize that Frost had a vulnerability so deep that he could barely even acknowledge it to himself. He wanted to believe it wasn't possible, but he was reminded again that fate was a jerk. Fate was a son of a bitch.

Don't make this personal between us, Inspector.

Too late.

He flipped the fragile pages of the album. He saw the names inscribed at the bottom of each sketch. Dozens of names, spread out over several years. Mothers and babies. Mothers and daughters. Mothers and victims.

And there they were.

Catherine and Tabitha.

Cutter was going after Tabby.

45

Rudy sat in the old Cadillac, two blocks from the marina. He'd been here for hours, hypnotized by the rain, staring through the darkness and haze at the apartment building across the street. It was almost dawn on Sunday, but there wouldn't be any sunrise today, just the gloom of black clouds. The only thing that helped him see was the streetlight overhead. The yachts in the harbor were invisible.

His clothes hadn't dried. They were still a mess of rain, mud, and blood. He'd had a narrow escape from Sweeney Ridge. The cops had descended on the hills like locusts, and even in the fog, he'd barely eluded them on his way back to the parking lot at Skyline College. A helicopter searchlight had passed over the Cadillac only seconds after he'd ducked inside.

He wasn't a fool. He knew he didn't have much time left. Everyone was looking for him.

The street around him was empty in the rain. Above the boulevard trees, a light came on in the third-floor apartment, and a silhouette moved behind the curtains. He lifted his binoculars, but there was nothing to see. He'd already spotted Easton's brother leaving two hours earlier in the dead of night, and after that, the windows had been dark. But not now. She was up. Weekends didn't matter in the restaurant world. She'd be leaving soon.

Rudy reached behind him and grabbed a trench coat from the back seat. He took what he needed from his backpack. The Taser. The knife. The duct tape. And Maria's watch, already smashed, its time stopped at 3:42 a.m. He secured them all in the right-side pocket of the coat. He was ready. He kept his eyes trained on the steps that led down from the apartment building plaza, and he waited.

It was strange. He no longer felt alive. The numbness that had dominated his life for so many years was back. When he'd slid the knife across the neck of Nina Flores, he'd felt a rush that must have been like shooting up with pure heroin. Hope was Nina; Nina was Hope. He'd finally been able to get revenge on his wife for what she'd done to their daughter. With each murder after that, the anticipation had built toward a perfect moment of violence. It became an addiction.

But now he felt empty. The rush was gone.

He'd thought, with Jess Salceda, that it was simply because she wasn't part of the game. She was an outsider who'd trespassed where she didn't belong. He'd assumed that it would be different with Maria, but it wasn't. There was no high, no adrenaline, no vaulting sense of purpose. Killing her gave him nothing.

And yet he couldn't stop himself. He needed the rush even more badly now that he couldn't find it. He would do anything to feel that way again, even if it was only one last time for one last moment.

Up on the third floor, the lights went off again. The apartment was dark.

Rudy tensed, his eyes on the plaza steps. The rain kept coming in waves. The wind roared. He checked the mirrors and saw that he was alone on the street. It would take less than a minute for her to lock the apartment, go down three flights of stairs, cross the courtyard, and emerge onto the sidewalk.

As he waited for her, his backup phone rang.

Rudy thought about ignoring it, but he knew it was Phil. And Phil calling now meant trouble.

"This is a bad time," he said, answering the phone.

"Where are you?" Phil asked.

"You know where I am."

"You should split, man," his brother said. "Now."

Rudy briefly closed his eyes. Phil had always been the weak link, the one who would crack sooner or later. "What did you tell them?"

"Enough that they'll be coming for you," Phil replied. "You better get away from there while you can. Sorry."

Phil hung up.

At that same moment, across the street, Rudy saw Tabby Blaine dash down the steps in the rain. Her red hair was a flame on the dark morning. She wore a belted purple raincoat down to her ankles. She turned away from the bay toward her car, walking easily in heels. It was now or never.

Rudy grabbed his coat. He got out of the Cadillac and shrugged the coat onto his body. He crossed the street and made his way to the sidewalk and settled in behind her. Leaves blew off the trees in the wind and scattered between them. The rain covered the noise of his footsteps. If she looked back, she would see him, but she didn't look back.

Slowly, he increased his pace and closed the gap.

At the end of the block, she crossed the street, and he was off the curb before she reached the other side. He knew which car was hers. A red Saab. He could see it halfway up the block, squeezed onto a short patch of curb between two driveways. Inside the pocket of his coat, his hand closed around the grip of the Taser.

The rain blew into their faces. Rudy had to squint and rub his eyes to see. He was close behind her now, almost close enough to grab. She was at the bumper of the Saab, and she put a hand into her pocket. He heard the beep of the car doors unlocking as she yanked out her key fob.

Then everything happened at once.

Tabby's phone rang. He could hear the ringtone playing a song. "Shut Up and Dance." He was right behind her now, but she stopped as she answered the phone. He stopped, too. They were both on the street, immediately next to the Saab, but she didn't know he was there.

"Hey, Frost," Tabby said into the phone. "You're up early."

Simultaneously, another noise filled the street. The noise of sirens. Instinctively, Rudy looked back over his shoulder, and where the street intersected Marina Boulevard at the harbor, he saw a police car veer around the corner. And then another. And another. They converged at the apartment building, and as the police officers flooded from the vehicles, they already had their guns drawn in their hands.

In an instant, they spotted the Cadillac parked across the street. In the next instant, they surrounded it.

Rudy turned back. The police couldn't see him two blocks away. Tabby was still on the phone, but she heard the sirens, too, and as she turned around, she saw him directly behind her. Her green eyes were smart and alert. She knew exactly who he was and why he was here. She opened her mouth to say something into the phone—a scream, a cry for help—but before she could say a word, he fired the Taser into her neck.

Her body lurched as the electricity jolted her. She crumpled, knees bending, and he grabbed her. Her phone spilled to the sidewalk, and he kicked it away. He scooped up her keys. It took him only a few quick seconds to yank open the front door of the Saab and stuff her inside, facedown. He bent over her body as rain poured in and clumsily pulled her wrists together and wound gray tape around to bind her hands behind her. She twitched, already beginning to recover from the electrical jolt. He slammed the passenger door shut and ran around to the driver's side.

He got in and locked the doors, and he started the car and put it in gear. He eyed the mirror. The police had already filled the street two blocks away, but they hadn't spotted him. They were streaming into the plaza of the apartment building. He heard more sirens, more vehicles getting closer.

Tabby squirmed violently in an attempt to get up, but he shoved her face down hard. As she screamed, he covered her mouth and pushed the sticky blade of the knife below her ear.

"Don't move, and don't say a word," he barked. "If you talk, if you scream, this all ends right now."

The warning made her lie still.

He thought, *One way or another, this all ends right now.*

Rudy spun the wheel, and the Saab squealed away.

◆ ◆ ◆

"Tabby!" Frost shouted into the phone.

Her voice cut off as she began to speak, and all he heard was the pound of the rain, a car door slamming, and the overlapping wail of distant sirens. He shouted her name again, but when she didn't answer, he threw his phone against the passenger door and drove even faster. He had never driven faster in his life.

The Suburban rocketed north down the long hill toward the marina. The street was narrow, crowded with parked cars. His siren carried him through the intersections, which were mostly deserted in the early hours of Sunday morning. Rain poured across the truck. His windshield wipers jerked back and forth in a futile attempt to keep the glass clear, and he had to lean forward to see the road. Even as morning broke, the bay was invisible. Duane's condo was half a mile away.

Ahead of him, he saw headlights coming the opposite way, racing up the hill. The two vehicles were only two blocks apart when the southbound car made a sharp left turn, ignoring the stoplight. In the flash of his headlights, Frost saw a shine of red, and he had a quick mental image of Tabby outside Duane's apartment building, about to get into a red Saab. He hit the brakes hard and turned right. He followed a parallel course one block south, flooring the accelerator, trying to get a jump on the car on the other street. He made a wide, screeching left and reached the intersection at Lombard at almost the same moment as the car he was chasing. It was a red Saab. And he glimpsed the face of the driver through the rain.

Rudy Cutter.

Just for a moment, he also saw a woman rear up in the passenger seat before Cutter pushed her down. The woman had a swirl of red hair. It was Tabby, and she was alive.

The Saab spun away, its right-side wheels jerking off the ground before dropping heavily back down. The car jolted north toward the bay, kicking up spray like a fountain. Frost followed on his bumper. The street was wider here, and they had to swerve to avoid the early morning buses. Apartment buildings lined both sides of the street. Block by block, the bay got closer.

He radioed in a call for backup.

Seconds later, both vehicles screamed through the last intersection at Marina Boulevard, where the road ended at the water. They were on a flat, open stretch of road bordered by the marina's green park, with the Golden Gate Bridge and the East Bay hills coming into view under the low clouds. Cutter sped right, and Frost brought up the Suburban immediately next to him. They raced side by side as the street curved eastward, and he could see bouncing white and red lights as cars ahead and behind them spilled to the curb to get out of their way.

The red-roofed piers of Fort Mason loomed on their left. As they neared the intersection at Buchanan, two more squad cars converged from the south and east, and together, they forced Cutter off the boulevard into an empty parking lot leading to the old fort. Frost lost a few seconds as the Suburban lurched into a clumsy turn. The water was on his left. Dozens of boats bobbed like toys in the fierce wind.

Cutter had a hundred-yard lead as he steered the Saab past the gatehouse at the fort's entrance, but he was running out of pavement. Beyond the barracks and piers, the road dead-ended at the bay. As Frost wheeled past the gatehouse himself, with the two police cars close behind him, he spotted the Saab disappearing between the fort's last dormitory building and a steep hillside lined with cypress trees. He pointed the Suburban across the empty parking lot and headed the same way.

As he passed the last of the fort's white brick buildings, he reached the final stretch of road at the water. Old railroad tracks ran across the pavement. A high retaining wall rose immediately to his right. Ahead of him, a long pier jutted into the bay. Where concrete pylons marked the end of the road, he saw the red Saab, its engine still running, its two front doors wide open.

The car was empty. Cutter was gone. So was Tabby.

46

The rain swept like gunfire over the bay.

The wind made it hard to stand as Frost got out of the Suburban with his pistol in his hand. Two police cars pulled up behind him. The long, painted wall of a renovated pavilion, lined with dumpsters, stretched out over the water. On his right, the fort's old firehouse building blocked his view of the path beside the bay.

Frost gestured for one of the cops to follow the pier. He led the way with the other cop to the trail overlooking the green water. He could see the island and the prison buildings of Alcatraz a mile and a half away across the white-capped surface of the bay. Gulls lined the rusted fence along the water and hunkered down against the storm. The paved trail led behind the firehouse and then ended at the steep, forested parkland that hugged the shore.

He didn't see Cutter or Tabby, but he heard a woman's voice from somewhere inside the trees.

One word. His name.

"Frost!"

He bolted along the waterfront. The other cop was at least ten years older than he was, and Frost easily outdistanced him. He pushed through a gap in the fence where the trail ended and found himself among dense trees. The damp ground fell away to the rocks at the water and climbed the hillside on a slippery bed of mud and pine needles.

There was nowhere to go but up, and he could hear them above him, already near the top of the slope. He shoved his gun back in his holster and assaulted the hill. The wet earth fought him, and he struggled upward for nearly thirty feet until the cliff finally leveled off at a wide, paved bicycle path. From up here, the bay spread out like a postcard, with the Golden Gate Bridge in the background.

Two sets of muddy footprints showed him the way. They headed downhill where the path cut like a terrace along the hillside. He ran, and the trees gave way, opening up the vista below him.

There they were, nearly at the base of the trail. A long pier curved like a crescent moon into the bay, creating a circular cove and beach just beyond Fisherman's Wharf. Tabby looked over her shoulder and saw him. She screamed for him again, but Cutter grabbed her by the neck and dragged her forward as she squirmed in his grasp. He had a knife in his hand.

Frost charged downhill after them. He could hear sirens wailing from the city, getting closer, roaring in from Van Ness and from the Wharf. Cutter was trapped, with nowhere to go, but trapped men had nothing to lose. Cutter looked back at Frost through the rain, and then he pulled Tabby down the crescent pier over the bay.

It was a one-way trip, ending at the water. There was no coming back. They both knew it.

Frost reached the pier seconds later. Cutter and Tabby struggled down the middle of the wide concrete platform fifty yards ahead of him. Behind him, the lights of squad cars flashed in the gray morning. He ran after Cutter, with the wind shoving him forward and rain falling across his face in waves. The pier stretched for a quarter mile, but Cutter couldn't go fast with Tabby in his grasp, and Frost closed the gap.

They were nearly to the end of the crescent when Cutter suddenly stopped and turned to face him. Waves on the bayside hit the pier and cast up clouds of spray. They were surrounded by the water, the hills, and the skyline of the city behind them. On one side was the Golden

Gate Bridge, on the other side the Bay Bridge. It was just the three of them out here. No one else. Frost held up his hand, stopping the cops who were following on the pier behind him. He didn't want Cutter spooked.

"Let her go, Rudy."

He had to shout to be heard. He took another step closer and then another. His gun was pointed straight ahead, but he had nothing to shoot at. Tabby was in front of Cutter. Frost couldn't see more than an inch or two of Cutter's face. And even if he wanted to fire, he could barely hold his arms level because of the onslaught of cold wind that buffeted his body. He was like a boat thrown around by the waves.

"That's far enough, Easton," Cutter said. "Stop."

Frost stopped, but he didn't lower his gun. "This is over, Rudy. You know that. There's no way out of this."

Tabby struggled like a honeybee inside a glass jar, but she was locked in Cutter's grasp and couldn't break free. His left arm trapped her waist. His right forearm kept her neck in a headlock, with the blade of the knife pressed tightly against the bulge of the carotid artery on her neck. Any tighter and he would cut her open. The more she squirmed, the less of a shot that Frost had on the man behind her.

"What are you going to do, Easton?" Cutter called to him. "Are you willing to shoot? It's windy. You might miss. What if you kill her yourself? Can you live with that?"

Frost felt a roaring in his head. It was more than the wind. It was anger and despair creeping up on him. "Let her go. You don't need to do this. It won't change a thing."

"Not for me, but it will change everything for you, won't it?"

He knew that Cutter wanted him to see it happen. Frost had found the bodies of Katie and Jess; he'd felt the life go out of Maria Lopes in his arms. But he hadn't seen the blade go across the throat, seen the spray of blood, heard the cry of pain. Cutter was going to kill Tabby right in front of him. He didn't have a single doubt about that. Nothing he said, nothing he did, was going to change it.

"What do you want, Rudy?"

He kept using Cutter's first name, trying to make a connection with him. But there was no connection to be made.

"I don't want anything at all," Cutter told him. "You know that."

Frost needed a clear shot to drill through Cutter's eyes, but Tabby blocked the way. If he pulled the trigger, he'd hit her. If he fired into Cutter's arm, the bullet would go through him and into Tabby's chest. The only way to fire without hitting Tabby was to get a clean angle on Cutter's head, and he didn't have it.

Meanwhile, Tabby flailed, hot and angry. Cutter held her. Frost stared down the barrel of his gun and tried to hold it steady as the gusts pushed around his arms. He kept blinking as the rain flooded his eyes. The bay went wild around them.

"Drop the knife!" Frost shouted, as if through sheer force of will, he could get inside Cutter's brain and turn him around. As if he could change the future. As if he could rewrite the past.

But he couldn't.

Instead, something came over Cutter's face. It was as terrifying as the whiteness of a shark's eyes as it rolls them back before an attack. Cutter wasn't on the pier anymore. He was in a tiny bedroom, standing over the body of his child in the pool of blood where his wife had killed herself. It was 3:42 a.m. The muscles of his hand tightened. Fury and bottomless grief brought a steely line to his mouth. This was the moment; this was the horror.

Frost could see the next ten seconds of his life. The slash. The scream. Another woman lying at his feet; another woman he'd failed. Katie. Jess. Maria. And now Tabby. Dying in his arms.

It was going to happen. Right. Now.

"Frost."

The voice startled both of them. Frost froze. So did Cutter. It was Tabby, calling to him. She wasn't moving anymore. She was absolutely calm, absolutely still, her knees locked against the wind, her body unmoving. Her green eyes weren't afraid in the least. Only her wet red hair blew like a wildfire. Cutter was still behind her, his head impossible to reach, impossible to kill. The only thing visible, the only target Frost had, was Cutter's arm draped across Tabby's torso, with the knife at the end of his hand.

Tabby said four words to him. That was all she needed to do.

"Shut up and dance," she said.

Frost didn't hesitate for a millisecond. He fired. He fired *perfectly*. The bullet traveled across the short space of air, faster than Cutter could shove in the blade, faster than the sound of the gun. The bullet burrowed into the exact square inch Frost had targeted, carving through the bone, muscles, and nerves of Cutter's forearm, paralyzing his wrist and causing the knife to clatter harmlessly to the concrete pier.

Tabby screamed. The bullet hit her, too. It went through Cutter's arm and into the flesh of her chest below her right shoulder. Despite the pain, despite the blood, she escaped from Cutter's grasp and ran to Frost. Her hands were tied at her back; she stumbled, trying to stay upright. Behind her, Cutter looked dazed. He backed away, his right arm hanging uselessly at his side.

Frost shouted over his shoulder at the police officers storming down the pier behind him. "Get a medical kit and an ambulance out here *now, now, now!*"

He gathered up Tabby tightly with his left arm, and she leaned her weight into him. Her head bowed into his shoulder, her forehead against his cheek. He could feel her trembling with cold and shock. His gun was still in his other hand, pointed across the pier at Rudy Cutter.

"Get on your knees, Cutter," he told him.

Cutter blinked rapidly. Blood ran down his arm and dripped to the pier, where it was washed away in the rain. He looked over his shoulder, but there was nowhere to run. All that was behind him was the bay. The rain sheeted across him; the wind looked as if it would blow him over. He took an unsteady step forward, toward Frost and Tabby. They were no more than ten feet apart.

"On your knees!" Frost repeated.

Cutter sank slowly and awkwardly to his knees. The knife was still on the concrete directly in front of him. He bent and reached out with his uninjured left hand, and his fingers curled around the handle. He raised it slowly in the air. His eyes and Frost's eyes were locked on each other through the rain.

"*Stop.*" Frost aimed the gun at Cutter's chest. "Drop it."

The clatter of the boots from the other cops on the pier was close behind them, but not close enough.

"*Drop it,*" Frost repeated.

Cutter staggered back to his feet. First one leg. Then the other. He swayed.

"Take one more step, and I shoot," Frost said.

Cutter stayed where he was. He brought the blade close to his face and rotated it forward and backward, as if he were studying a strange, foreign object in his hand. Then he turned the sharp edge sideways and laid it against the skin of his own neck. He knew exactly where to place it.

Frost shook his head. His voice was a low warning. "You don't need to do this, Rudy."

Cutter didn't listen. He looked up at the sky and at the rain streaking from the clouds. He licked some of the water on his lips and swallowed. His mouth opened slightly, and he inhaled long and slow. With a curious smile, he shut his eyes and closed out the world.

"I wonder what it really feels like," he said.

Then he slashed his throat.

47

It was late evening before Frost made it across the city to Tabby's hospital room near Golden Gate Park. His entire family was there. Duane sat by her bedside, holding her hand. His parents hovered near the door. Tabby lay propped in bed, her shoulder bandaged and her arm in a sling, and she was hooked to a morphine drip. Even so, she looked alert, not groggy.

Seeing him, Duane leaped to his feet.

"There he is! There's the hero!"

His brother, who was several inches shorter than Frost, grabbed him and practically lifted him off the ground. Frost reacted a little stiffly. He'd been getting a lot of attention all day from his colleagues in the police and from the San Francisco media, and he didn't like it.

Duane whispered in his ear. His brother was the emotional one of the pair, and Frost could hear a catch in Duane's voice. "You don't know what this means to me, bro. You saved her. I can't even tell you what I would have done if something had happened to that girl."

Frost responded with a half smile. "I know."

Duane steered him to Tabby's bedside and shook his shoulders so hard that Frost felt dizzy. "Is this guy amazing?" Duane bellowed in what was definitely not a hospital voice. "Amazing!"

Tabby stared at him from behind those green eyes of hers. "Yes, he is."

Her face had a postsurgery paleness. Her red hair was limp. When she shifted in bed, he could see a grimace of pain. It distressed him to see her that way and to know he'd put her there. Even if he'd had no choice.

"Cutter?" Tabby asked him softly.

"He died in the ambulance," Frost said.

She blinked. She didn't seem to know how to take the news. There was no happiness in her expression and not even any satisfaction that the horror was finally over. He knew how she felt, because he'd felt the same way all day. He took no joy in watching anyone else die. Too many others had already been lost, and they weren't coming back. Cutter's death didn't repair what he'd done.

Frost's mother didn't share their reluctance to pass judgment. "Good riddance. I hope he's in hell."

"Janice, you're still talking about another human being," Ned Easton murmured. It was his father's humanist streak, his willingness to allow mercy for evil, that had been a partial cause of his parents' breakup. They had never seen eye to eye about that.

"Barely," his mother snapped. "I'm not going to apologize. That piece of filth killed my daughter. If it hadn't been for Frost, he would have killed Tabby, too. I'm glad he's gone."

Frost let his parents argue through their emotions. He stared down at Tabby, and Tabby stared uncomfortably back at him. Her attitude puzzled him, although he knew he'd put a bullet in her body. If he'd missed by even a little, she'd be dead. There was a lot he needed to say to her about the last few days, but this wasn't the time or place.

Duane pulled a chair from the wall. His long black hair was loose. "Come on, bro, sit, stay with us a while."

"Oh, no, thanks, I can't. I should get home. I don't want Shack freaking out because I've been gone so much. I just wanted to make sure Tabby was okay."

"I'm going to be fine, Frost," Tabby murmured. "Don't worry about me."

"Good."

Duane winked at her. "Should I tell him the news? Or do you want to?"

Frost looked back and forth between them. "News?"

"Let's not do this now, Duane," Tabby suggested. "Please. Frost said he needs to go. It's been a stressful day for everyone."

"No, no, it's the perfect time!" Duane replied. "Mom and Dad are here. It's the whole family! We should be talking about good news for a change after everything that's happened."

"Don't keep me in suspense," Frost said.

Duane grabbed Tabby's hand again. He looked as giddy as Frost had ever seen him. "We're getting married!"

Frost felt speechless. It was a terrible time to be speechless. A flush rose in Tabby's cheeks, and Duane bent over and kissed her forehead. Frost tried to come up with something to say and finally said, "Oh, wow."

An exceptional comeback.

"When I thought about how close I came to losing her," Duane went on, "it made everything so damn clear. I love this girl. So when Mom and Dad got here, I got down on one knee. I wanted them to see it, too. I know they never thought they'd see the day, but they brought us together. The whole thing is fate. I never much believed in fate, but I do now."

Fate.

Yes, Frost knew exactly what he thought about fate.

"Isn't it wonderful, Frost?" his mother asked from across the room.

"Wonderful," he told both of them. "It's great. Really."

"Get a tux, best man," his brother told him. "And get one for Shack, too."

"Shack's tux comes prefitted," Frost reminded him.

Duane thought about it and laughed. "You're right! Now, that's funny. See? Fate."

Frost tried to read Tabby's face, but she made it difficult by looking out the window instead of at him.

"I hate to celebrate and run," Frost said, "but I really do need to get home."

"Sure, sure, will we see you tomorrow?" Duane asked.

"Of course."

Duane grabbed him for another hug. "Thanks again, bro. You're the best."

Frost squeezed his brother's shoulder without saying anything more. He wanted to get out of there as fast as he could. He hugged his mother, who responded awkwardly in her usual way, and then he headed for the door. His father went with him. Ned put an arm around his shoulder as they walked to the elevator.

"Janice and I are heading back to Arizona tomorrow," Ned said.

"It was good seeing you, Dad. Despite the circumstances."

"I know it's torture for you to leave San Francisco, but it would be nice to have you come visit us."

"I will."

"Come for Christmas," Ned suggested. "We already talked to Duane and Tabby about coming down for the holidays. We've got the room. It would be nice to have the family together."

"I'll keep that in mind," Frost replied, which was the Easton family way of making no promises.

The elevator door opened, but his father stopped him before he could get on. The door slid closed again with the two of them standing outside. It took Ned a minute to get out the words.

"I was wondering, did you find out anything more about Katie?" Ned asked. "I mean, before Cutter died?"

Frost had been expecting the question. He wished he had an answer for him. If there was one thing he'd wanted from Cutter, it was the truth about Katie, but Cutter had never regained consciousness. The secret died with him. Frost felt robbed of the opportunity to stare into the man's eyes and ask him *why*.

"I'm sorry. No, I didn't. He wasn't able to tell me a thing."

"She doesn't really fit like the others, does she?" his father asked.

"No, she doesn't."

Ned shook his head in confusion. "I guess all we can do is live with it, but it still feels like a mystery. I hate that."

"I know it does, Dad," Frost replied, "and I hate it, too. But not every mystery gets solved."

Frost went from the hospital back to Ocean Beach, and he stayed there for two more hours in silence, watching the waves. His phone was off. He didn't want to talk to anyone. The rain had ended, but the winds remained strong, keeping the surf angry and high. It didn't matter that Cutter was dead. It didn't matter that the case was over. He had a sense of unfinished business, but the ocean had no answers for him.

Eventually, there was nothing else to do but go home.

It was past midnight when he let himself inside the house on Russian Hill. In the foyer, he saw that Eden's boxes, with her research notes and manuscript, were still there. He knew she'd be waiting for him when he returned, because she wasn't done with him yet. She needed a last interview. She needed an ending for her story.

Shack bounded to the foyer to greet him and immediately began his typical King Kong climb up Frost's leg.

"Watch those claws, buddy," Frost said, but the cat paid no attention. Shack staked out his spot on Frost's shoulder and stayed there as Frost wandered into the living room with the lights off and then out onto the patio to watch the city and the stars. The storm had vanished; the night was clear and cool.

He turned on his phone, and he had several messages waiting for him. Some were from the media, which he skipped. The first personal message was from Herb.

"Frost, my friend. You're all over the news. I'm grateful that things ended well, although I'm sure that doesn't make what you went through any easier. I've got to teach a class at my gallery in the morning, but we obviously need to have a Sierra Nevada together very soon. If you need to talk in the interim, call me anytime."

The next message was from Eden in her usual smoky voice.

"It's late. I'm not sure when you'll be back, but I hope you're okay. I'm going to bed upstairs. Wake me up when you get home."

And the last message was from Tabby. It had come in only five minutes earlier.

"Hey. It's me. Everybody just left. I took a hit of the pain meds, so I'm probably going to be loopy. I wanted to say . . . actually, I have no idea what I want to say to you. Thanks? I'm sorry? This is hard. I feel like we should . . . I don't know . . . I feel like there are some things . . ."

There was a pause so long that he thought she'd drifted off to sleep. But then she went on.

"I'm not making any sense, am I . . . I guess this is the morphine talking. I better hang up before I say something really stupid. Stop by tomorrow, okay? I'd like to see you. Night, Frost."

He played the message again. And again. Then he went back inside the house. He thought about having a drink but concluded it wasn't a good idea. Shack hopped off his shoulder onto the sofa, and Frost went upstairs to one of the spare bedrooms, where he took a shower. The hot water revived him. Afterward, instead of going downstairs to the sofa where he usually slept, he went into the master bedroom.

Eden was there. She slept on her stomach on the king-sized bed. He sat down in the overstuffed armchair on the other side of the room and watched her. In his memory, he could feel the touch of her skin and the smoothness and curves of her body. It would have been easy to climb into bed next to her. Wake her up. Have sex with her. That was what she wanted, and a part of him wanted it, too.

Instead, he sat in the chair until his eyes felt heavy, and he finally fell asleep right where he was.

When he woke up, he saw the clock on the nightstand, and he was instantly alert. It was 3:42 a.m. That shouldn't have mattered to him now, because Rudy Cutter was dead, but he realized that a disturbance in the house had awakened him. Again. It was the same as it had been weeks earlier.

He'd heard something in the house below him. And unmistakably, he smelled the dark burn of Phil Cutter's cigarette smoke.

Frost went into the master closet and found a lockbox on the upper shelf. His department weapon had been taken from him because of the shooting, but he kept a backup firearm for himself. He retrieved the gun and padded downstairs in his bare feet. The smell of smoke was stronger down here. Shack, his back fur arched, had taken refuge on top of the mahogany bookshelf, but the intruder was already gone.

He saw nothing amiss in the house this time. No Halloween surprises. No alarm clocks. All that had been left for him was a slim manila envelope in the middle of the floor.

Frost picked it up by the edges. He took the envelope into the dining room, where he put his gun on the table and switched on the lights. He turned over the envelope in his hands and saw a message scrawled on the outside:

Rudy wanted you to have this.

The envelope was light, as if almost nothing were inside. Frost undid the clasp and opened the flap. He saw a small piece of paper tucked near the bottom of the envelope, and he overturned it and let the paper flutter onto the dining room table. It was no more than four inches by six inches, with what looked like grease stains on the surface.

Using the cap of a pen, Frost turned the paper over and saw that it was a green, lined receipt, the kind used for taking orders at diners.

And at pizza restaurants.

Frost recognized the handwriting on the slip. Katie had written it. He saw the name above the delivery address, too. Todd Clary. Clary had ordered an olive-and-arugula pizza with garlic cream sauce to 415 Parker. It was the last order Katie had ever taken. This receipt was what had sent her on a delivery run that would end in her murder. It still made no sense to him.

He checked the envelope again. There was nothing else inside. Rudy Cutter had obviously believed that this piece of paper would offer up the answer to Katie's death, but Frost didn't understand its significance. He studied the receipt for a hidden clue, but all he saw was what Katie had scribbled down from Clary's phone call:

Todd Clary
Delivery to 415 Parker
Large olive/arugula cream sauce
$24.35

The note made him heartsick because seeing it brought Katie to life again. He could see her writing it; he could hear her voice. Twenty minutes later, she'd carried the pizza out the door on Haight and climbed into her Chevy Malibu.

And headed the wrong way.

Why?

Frost stared at the receipt. He knew Katie better than anyone; he should have been able to figure out what she was telling him. But finally, he realized that his closeness to Katie was the problem. He had to stop looking at the receipt like a brother who'd grown up with her.

He stared at it again, like a stranger.

And he knew. Just like that, he saw what Katie had written, and he knew what she'd done. The answer was staring him in the face. He knew why Katie had gone east from the restaurant, not west toward Todd Clary's house. He knew where she was going with that pizza.

It didn't take him long to figure out the rest. He had everything he needed to solve the mystery. The pieces came together, one after another, like gears meshing in an elaborate machine. Half an hour later, he knew why Katie had been killed that night and whose secret she would have exposed if she'd stayed alive.

When the truth finally settled into his brain, he realized that Cutter had been right all along. *Horror can always get worse.*

48

Frost was sitting on the sofa in the shadows when Eden Shay came down from the bedroom at the first light of dawn. She'd put on satin pajama bottoms and a spaghetti-strap top. Her black curls were a wild mess. She saw him and cocked her head in surprise.

"Well, there you are. The hero returns. What time did you get in?"

"Late."

"I was hoping you'd join me in bed."

"I watched you sleep," Frost said.

"Really? There's something sensual about that. I like it."

Frost didn't answer. He was done with the flirting. He was done being played.

"So Cutter's dead," Eden said. "It was all over the news."

"Yes, he is. You must be relieved."

She looked at him strangely. "Relieved?"

"You can finish your book now."

"Oh. Sure." She eyed the kitchen behind her. "Can I make you breakfast?"

"I'm not hungry."

"You say that now, but you haven't tried my hot-and-spicy scrambled eggs."

She wandered in her bare feet into the kitchen. He watched her, unable to move. She retrieved eggs from the refrigerator and frowned at the expiration date, but began to crack them into a bowl anyway. She opened his cabinets and found whatever chili spices he had—which probably dated back to Shack's original owner—and opened the jars. She dug up a pan and swirled some oil in the bottom.

"Do you want to talk about yesterday?" she called to him. "I understand if you're not ready. You need time."

When he didn't answer, she glanced over her shoulder.

"Everything okay?" she asked.

Frost got up from the sofa. He walked over and stood at the entrance to the kitchen. "Do you remember Robbie Lubin?"

Eden's eyebrows arched curiously. "Sure. He's Natasha's brother."

"I seem to recall you telling me that you visited him in Minnesota when you first started researching the case for your book."

"You recall correctly," Eden replied. Her voice was light but wary. "I told you, I always do my homework. Why?"

"When you visited Gilda Flores back then, she showed you Nina's bedroom, right?"

"Of course. You know that. What's this about?"

Frost tried to ignore the roaring in his head. He wanted to be dead inside; he wanted to feel nothing. But that was impossible. This woman had come to him, and he'd let her into his life. He'd given her everything she wanted. He was attracted to her. He'd *slept* with her. And all along, she'd been manipulating him. All along, she'd hidden the truth.

His instincts had told him from the beginning not to trust her. He should have listened to the voice inside.

"This is about the fact that *you* solved the Golden Gate Murders seven years ago," Frost said. "You knew that Rudy Cutter was the killer before anyone else did."

The curiosity, the playfulness, the innocence all vanished from her face, which became a mask of icy calm. He read her expression. In an instant, she realized that he'd figured it all out. She was already wondering how far he'd gone and what he could prove.

"What are you talking about, Frost?" Eden asked, giving nothing away.

"Hope's sketches. The mothers and daughters. That's the connection that ties all the victims together. Well, except Katie, but you already know that, don't you? Jess never figured out Cutter's pattern, because she never saw more than one of Hope's sketches. I assumed that no one did, but that's not true. *You* saw the sketches. You saw one on the wall in Nina's bedroom, and you saw another one when you visited Robbie in Minnesota."

Eden shrugged. "If I did, then obviously, I missed it. Or I didn't appreciate the significance."

"You? No, you wouldn't have missed a detail like that. No way. I can only imagine the adrenaline you must have felt. How hard was it to keep the truth to yourself? To keep the excitement off your face so Robbie didn't suspect? You saw that sketch, and you knew you had the clue that would break the whole case open."

Eden turned off the heat on the stovetop. She rinsed her hands, and then she turned around and leaned back against the kitchen counter. Her face showed nothing at all. No secrets. No guilt.

"Frost, are you out of your mind?"

"I get it. You don't think I can prove it. Maybe I can't. But as smart as you are, I still think you left a trail. At first, I couldn't understand why you wouldn't have taken this straight to Jess. That would have been the right thing to do, but it wouldn't have been much of a story, would it? No, the real story for a writer like you would be to find the killer *yourself.* And that's what you did. I imagine you talked to people at the hospitals to track down Hope. Did you lie and say that you had a sketch of your own? Maybe your mother died recently and it would mean so much to you to find out who did that little portrait? It probably wasn't too hard to make the connection. Did you talk to a few retired nurses? Did you bribe someone in HR to run some personnel searches for you? Someone's going to remember you asking all those questions, Eden.

Count on it. We'll get your e-mail and phone records, too. I don't know exactly how you made the breakthrough, but sooner or later, you found Hope's name. And of course, once you did a little research on Hope, you found your way to Rudy Cutter. He would already have been stalking Hazel Dixon by then. And meanwhile, you started stalking him."

Eden couldn't hide her hostility now. He was backing her into a corner, and she didn't like it there.

"If I'd learned Rudy Cutter's name, I would have given it to the police," she said.

Frost shook his head. "No. Not you. This was the ultimate opportunity for a writer like you. You could be *embedded* with a serial killer. You could get inside a murderer's head while he was still committing his crimes. Even your brother had never done anything like that."

"You should be a writer yourself," Eden snapped. "You're quite the storyteller."

"I'm curious, how exactly did it work?" Frost went on, ignoring her denials. "Did you approach Rudy and tell him what you knew? Did you make a deal with him? You'd keep his secret if he let you follow along with everything he did? After all, that was the same deal you made with me. How far did it go, Eden? How far did you take it? Were you with him as he stalked Hazel Dixon? Were you actually there when he slashed her throat? Did he let you *watch*?"

He looked into her eyes, and he knew he was right. She'd been there. She'd been part of the crime. And from that moment forward, she could never go back. She'd become an accessory to murder.

"I think I should go," Eden said.

"You're not going anywhere. Not until you tell me about Katie."

"I'm sorry, Frost. I know you've been under a lot of pressure lately, but you're delusional."

"Did I ever tell you about Katie's handwriting?" Frost asked.

"Excuse me?"

"Her handwriting was awful. Terrible. She'd write things down, and she couldn't even read them herself."

"So what?"

Frost walked over to the dining room table on the other side of the kitchen. He came back with the receipt from Haight Pizza, which he'd secured in an evidence bag. "Recognize this?"

Eden did. Her eyes widened in shock but only for a split second before she regained her control.

"What is that? Where did you get it?"

"Phil Cutter paid us a little visit overnight. Apparently, Rudy decided a while ago that if he was going down, he was going to take you with him. So Phil dropped off this receipt for me. It's the receipt Katie wrote to take a pizza to Todd Clary at 415 Parker. The trouble is, by the time the pizza was ready, she didn't remember the address, and she misread her own handwriting. See what the address actually looks like? She didn't go west from the restaurant to 415 *Parker*. She headed east on her way to 415 *Baker*."

Eden said nothing. Nothing at all.

"And guess who was living at that address back then?" Frost went on. *"You."*

He reached over to the counter behind her and picked up the copy of Eden's memoir he'd retrieved earlier. He held it up and showed her the author photo on the back cover, which she knew only too well.

"This is your house on Baker, Eden. This is where you lived. If you look closely, you can even see the house number. 415. So why don't you tell me how it happened? Was Rudy in the house with you when Katie came to deliver the pizza? Did she see both of you together? She would have *recognized* you. You were practically a household name at that point. You were on all the talk shows. Katie had read your book. She would have gone on and on about how excited she was to meet you. Did she ask what you were working on? Did she want to be introduced to Rudy Cutter? You must have been panicking. You couldn't let her leave, could you? She would have told *everybody* about seeing you."

Eden summoned up a fake smile. "Is this the part where I'm supposed to weep and confess?"

"You can do whatever you want. I already know the truth. I only want to know one thing. Who actually killed Katie? Who actually used the knife? Was it Rudy? Or was it *you*?"

Eden took a deep breath. He could see her weighing her options. Trying to figure out how to get out of the maze.

"Here's what I want to know, Frost," she said. "Do you think I'm stupid? I know a bluff when I hear it. A pizza receipt? A coincidence about a delivery address? Good luck with that. You don't have any proof."

"Actually, you already proved it yourself, Eden."

"And just how did I do that?"

"In your new book."

He saw her hesitate. "What do you mean?"

"I know what kind of writer you are. And I know the kind of odd little detail you can't resist."

"Like what?"

"Like a girl in San Francisco wearing flowers in her hair," Frost said.

Eden couldn't hide the concern on her face. She realized that she'd made a mistake. She just didn't know why.

"I read the chapter you wrote about Katie to see if you mentioned the flower tiara she was wearing when she was killed," Frost went on. "And sure enough, you did."

"What difference does that make?" Eden asked. "I saw the crime scene photos."

"You should have looked more closely at them. The tiara isn't *in* the photos. I took Katie's tiara with me when I found the body. I've had it ever since. That's my secret. Nobody knew Katie was wearing it.

Nobody except me and the two people who killed her. Rudy Cutter and you."

Eden laughed.

It was a cruel, bitter laugh. A laugh of self-disgust. A laugh of giving up. He should have been ready for what she did next, but his emotions had overrun him. He was too consumed with his own rage and grief to stop her. She was fast, and he wasn't fast enough. Her hand grabbed a plastic jar of chili spice on the counter, which she'd been planning to use in the eggs, and she threw the contents at him. He didn't even have time to blink. The powder struck his open eyes like a thousand knives. He was instantly blind and in agony, and his hands flew to his face. All he felt was a searing burn as he squinted and tried to see. He staggered backward, and Eden grabbed the frying pan from the stovetop and swung it toward his head. It connected violently, causing a hot explosion that ricocheted inside his skull. She stepped forward and shoved hard on his chest with both hands, and he tumbled backward onto the floor.

He tried to get up, but his brain was a carnival ride, dizzying him, making him sick. Through his scorched eyes, Eden was a blur. She stood over him, but he couldn't stop her body from whirling in and out of focus. She knelt on top of him, pressing her knees heavily into his chest. He swung a fist at her, but he missed. Eden bent forward. She had a kitchen knife in her hand now, and she lay the edge against his neck. She pressed it in so far that he could feel his skin tearing and the liquid warmth of blood.

"Since you're so curious, Frost," she told him, "*it was me.*"

He struggled to right his mind and clear his eyes. All he needed was a few seconds.

"Rudy said I'd never understand what it was like to kill someone until I used the knife myself, and he was right. If I was going to write about it, I couldn't just watch. I had to do it. And you know what? It was exhilarating. Life and death was right there in the palm of my hand. The feeling was so strong it scared me. That's why I ran back to Australia. I had to get away from what I'd done."

Frost kept blinking, and the fire in his eyes eased as tears worked their way down his face. The spinning world began to drift to a stop. He could feel pain popping like fireworks inside his head, but he could see Eden clearly now, leaning over him. Her curls draped forward. The scar on her neck wriggled as she talked. She had one hand propped on the floor and one holding the blade to his throat.

"It's a shame I can't write about this part," Eden went on. "Because this is a hell of an ending."

He saw the muscles in her hand squeezing tightly around the handle of the knife. Their eyes met, lover to lover, killer to victim. This woman was about to cut his throat and watch him die.

And then something happened.

Frost heard a noise unlike anything he'd heard in his life. An animal noise, primal and savage, enough to run gooseflesh up a human's skin, the noise you would hear from a leopard preying in the nighttime jungle. Eden heard it, too, and she froze in confusion. Frost heard thunder on the floor. He saw a lightning flash of motion in black and white.

It was Shack.

The cat flew across the room. He leaped, landing squarely on Eden's head, his front paws on her cheekbones. With claws fully extended almost an inch deep, he ripped eight deep gashes up her face and sliced through her eyeballs. Eden reared back with a guttural wail of anguish. Blood sprayed. The knife vanished from Frost's neck as her arms flailed. With a wild lunge of her torso, Eden dislodged Shack like a rodeo rider, but simultaneously, Frost slammed a fist into her head and knocked her sideways. He was free.

He tried to stand, but the room spun, and his knees buckled beneath him. He crashed down again. Eden slashed at him with the knife, and the blade cut a deep, red laceration across the bare skin of his calf. His foot shot out; his heel booted her chin and kicked her backward. She toppled against a pedestal lamp, which fell, and the knife spilled from her hand.

Frost half crawled, half dragged himself across the room. The dining room table was a few feet away. His gun was on the table.

Behind him, Eden was on her feet again.

She had the knife.

He groped around the smooth wooden surface of the table. Papers flew. His laptop skidded off and dropped. Then he felt it. The metal barrel. His fingers spun the gun around until the grip nestled in his palm. He scooped it up and cocked it; then he collapsed onto his back and pointed the gun across the room.

"Stop!"

Eden charged with the knife high over her head. Her face was streaked with ribbons of skin; her eyes dripped blood like the ruby eyes of a devil. Frost aimed straight up at the ceiling and fired once, cascading plaster dust over the room.

"Eden, stop!" he shouted again.

But she came and came.

He heard the voice of Rudy Cutter.

If I gave you the chance right now, would you put a bullet in the head of the person who cut your sister's throat?

Eden jumped. Her arm swung down; the knife hurtled toward his chest. He rolled away from the blade, but as he did, he fired twice more at point-blank range at the body cascading toward him.

One shot passed through her neck. The other shot drilled into her forehead.

She was dead as she hit the ground.

49

It was two weeks before Frost had any semblance of his life back. He was in the hospital. He was on television. He was in the interview room at headquarters, grilled by the review board that dealt with officer-involved shootings. By the end, he didn't even know if he wanted his old life back, but finally, Captain Hayden gave him the all clear and told him he was a free man.

That was on a Friday night.

He arrived back on Russian Hill to find Herb waiting for him on the bottom step of the stairs that led up to his front door. His friend wore a white painter's smock, which was smudged with a variety of colors of fresh paint, and overalls beneath it. His long gray hair had a shiny new set of beads tied into the braids. Frost hadn't seen him since the shootings.

Herb got up, putting a hand on his aging hip to steady himself, as Frost pulled up to the garage. He slipped off the painter's smock and embraced Frost with a smile and a look of relief.

"You're a sight for sore eyes," Herb said.

"So are you."

"How are you doing?" he asked.

"Fine," Frost said. "I'm fine."

"Everyone's inside. Act surprised."

Frost smiled. "I will."

"I made you a little gift," Herb told him. The smell of paint was the only thing that outweighed the smell of pot on Herb's clothes. "It's not completely original, but I think you'll like it."

Frost followed his friend up the stairs. Herb had fashioned a makeshift curtain at the topmost step, and he swept it aside to reveal his latest creation. On the landing, Herb had painted one of his three-dimensional illusions that seemed to rise out of the stonework to guard the door. It was a scene stolen from *The Lion King*, with Simba as the new king standing atop Pride Rock, ruling over the animals gathered in the savannah below.

But Simba wasn't the king of Frost's front step.

It was Shack.

Frost laughed out loud. "Now, that just may be the best work you've ever done, Herb."

Inside the house, the king greeted him. Shack didn't understand all the attention he was getting—and he hadn't appreciated the bath he'd had to have to wash off the blood in his fur—but he was happy to climb up to Frost's shoulder and stay there as Frost acted surprised by the people waiting to greet him.

His parents had come back from Arizona again.

Several of his police colleagues were there.

So were a dozen family members of the victims.

Duane was there.

Tabby was there.

Frost didn't like parties, but he put up with it throughout the evening. Everyone else needed this more than he did. They needed a chance to commune and grieve. They needed closure. Duane had made the food, which was amazing; Herb acted as bartender and poured the drinks. Robbie Lubin was an amateur guitarist and singer, and he played a version of "Hallelujah" that had everyone in tears. Frost had a few too many ales and felt the buzz.

It was dark and nearly midnight before people finally started to leave. They poured out to the street, mostly emptying the house. He said good-bye to Herb. He walked his parents to their rental car, and Ned clapped him in a hug and whispered, "Thank you." Janice put both hands on Frost's cheeks and said simply, "I love you."

He didn't think she'd ever said that out loud to him before. He'd always known his mother loved him, but they weren't the kind of family who actually said it to each other. It was simply understood.

He liked hearing it.

When they left, he stood on Green Street by himself for a while. It was December. The trees shook their branches at him in the wind. Holiday lights adorned the windows. It made him think about Christmas as a kid and about coming downstairs before sunrise to find Katie sitting cross-legged in the living room in front of the tree, with her chin propped on her hands, staring at the blinking lights.

God, he missed her.

Frost went back inside. Duane and Tabby were still in the kitchen, doing the dishes, although Tabby couldn't do much; her one arm was in a sling. He took another beer from the cooler and went out to the patio, where the city sparkled below him. Shack hopped up on the table and enjoyed the breeze. He leaned on the railing with his beer, and then he heard the glass door open and close behind him.

It was Tabby.

She came up beside him. Their skin brushed together. They were silent for a long time, in the cool darkness, letting San Francisco charm them. Eventually, he extended his beer bottle to her. He felt pleasantly high on the night.

"Want some?"

"Can't," Tabby said. "You know, shot. I'm still on drugs."

"Oh yeah. I shot you."

"Just a little," she replied with a grin.

"Sorry."

"Well, there's the whole saving-my-life thing, too. You get points for that."

"Thanks."

Silence lingered easily between them again. Then he said, "Will you be back at work soon?"

"Not for a while. One-armed chefs aren't too useful in the kitchen."

"Right."

Tabby turned around and leaned the other way. So did he. She closed her green eyes; her lips made a peaceful smile. Her chin tilted into the starlight. There was something magical about her in the daylight, but at night, she was perfection.

He was thinking things he couldn't afford to think.

"So you and Duane," Frost said.

"Yes, me and Duane."

"You wanted to know if he was serious. I guess he answered that question for you."

"I guess he did. He surprised me."

"Was it a good surprise?" Frost asked.

"Sure. Of course. I guess." Tabby blinked and looked away. "I don't want to talk about that right now. This night is about you, so let's talk about you. I hide behind jokes, but I never thanked you like I should, Frost. For everything you did."

"You don't need to do that."

"Well, good, because there are things that can never be repaid. They're just there. They just are."

"I like that," Frost said.

"So how are you?" Tabby asked.

Everyone had been asking him that. The same question, over and over. He'd given them all the same answer. *Fine.*

"I'm not good at all," he told Tabby.

She took his hand in the warmth of hers. "I didn't think you were."

"I still wake up thinking about killing her," he said.

"She didn't give you a choice."

Frost turned and stared at her and confessed the truth. "I haven't said this to anyone, but I didn't *want* a choice. I wanted to kill her. I'm glad I did."

"Maybe that's true, Frost. I don't think it is, but it doesn't matter. She still didn't give you a choice."

He didn't say anything. All he had to do was close his eyes, and he could see the gun firing and Eden's body falling. It was the first time he'd killed another human being. It wasn't something you ever forgot or ever got over.

"Did you have feelings for her?" Tabby asked.

"No."

"But you slept with her, didn't you?"

Frost would have given anything to say no, but he nodded. "I did."

"I'm sure that makes it worse. I mean, sharing something so intimate with someone who turns out to be evil."

"I don't even know why I did it. I didn't really like her."

"Maybe it was a full moon. I hear that brings out the beast in you."

That got him to smile. "Maybe."

"You're not exactly the first guy to listen to his body, not his heart."

"That doesn't mean I'm proud of it."

"I know." She added after a long pause, "The fact is, we can't control where our hearts take us, either, can we?"

"No, we can't."

She was still holding his hand. Their eyes didn't let go of each other, until her lips broke into a faraway smile and she stared at the ground.

"What about you?" he asked. "How are you?"

"I'm not so good, either," she confessed.

"Because of Cutter?"

"Yes. And other things."

"Like what?"

"It doesn't matter," she said. "Just things."

"Have you talked to anyone about what you went through on the pier?"

"No."

"Why not?"

"Because the only one who can understand is you."

He didn't know what to say to that. He only knew all the things he wanted to say to her. Those were the things he couldn't say.

In front of them, the patio door opened.

"Well, your kitchen is as good as new," Duane called out. "You have enough leftovers to last you through Christmas, bro. I also took the liberty of throwing out some things that should not be consumed by people or cats."

Frost smiled at him. "Thanks."

"Come on, Tabs, we need to rock and roll," Duane said. "You may be on sick leave, but the food truck and me, we have work to do."

Tabby squeezed Frost's hand and then let go. She walked away without looking at him. Frost and Duane went back inside the house, and Tabby was already gone, leaving the front door open, by the time they reached the foyer. Duane, who was just like their father, grabbed Frost by both shoulders. His effervescence radiated from him every hour of the day. That was just one of the things he loved about his brother.

"You know, somewhere Katie is pretty effing proud of you right now," Duane said.

"Yeah?"

"Yeah. And so am I."

"Thanks, Duane," Frost told him.

His brother saluted. He gave Shack a salute, too. The cat was on the white tile of the foyer beside Frost. Duane looked down and chuckled as he walked across Herb's *Lion King* painting, and he gave them a backward wave. "Hakuna matata, bro!"

Frost waited until Duane disappeared, and then he closed the door. He was tired. The house felt lonely and silent. He stood in the darkness for a moment before he turned away. Shack scooted to the kitchen to see if Duane had left anything on a plate for him, which he probably had. Frost was almost back outside to the patio when he heard a soft rapping on the front door behind him.

Surprised, he returned to the foyer and pulled the door open. Tabby stood on the porch, in the pool of the brass light.

"Duane's in the car," she said.

"Okay."

"I said I forgot something."

He stared at her. "Okay."

"I need to ask you something," she said, "and I need you to be honest with me."

Somewhere in his chest, his heart began to beat again. It had been stopped for years. "What is it?"

She had the look of someone standing at a rope bridge, trying to decide if it was safe to cross. He could have told her that those bridges were always dangerous.

"Do you and I have a big problem, Frost?" Tabby asked.

He realized that he was conscious of every detail about her as she stood in front of him. He could have told her how many strands of red hair had fallen across her face. He could have told her that he hadn't stopped seeing her green eyes since he met her. He could have told her that her lips, still slightly parted with the question they'd asked, made him think of nothing but kissing her.

He didn't want to lie. She'd told him to be honest. But lying was the only choice.

"No," he said. "No problem at all."

Tabby didn't ask if he was sure. She didn't say whether she believed him. She bit her lip, then simply turned away and practically ran down the steps away from him. He tried to guess what she was feeling now. Part of him hoped it was disappointment, but it was probably relief. Nothing else was safe.

Frost closed the door again. He closed his eyes, too, as the weight of irony landed on his head.

For the first time in his life, he knew who his Jane Doe was.

Damn.

FROM THE AUTHOR

Thanks for reading the latest Frost Easton novel. If you like this novel, be sure to check out all my other thrillers, too.

You can write to me with your feedback at brian@bfreemanbooks. com. I love to get e-mails from readers around the world, and yes, I reply personally. Visit my website at www.bfreemanbooks.com to join my mailing list, get book-club discussion questions, and find out more about me and my books.

You can "like" my official fan page on Facebook at www.facebook. com/bfreemanfans or follow me on Twitter or Instagram using the handle bfreemanbooks.

For a look at the fun side of the author's life, you can also "like" the Facebook page of my wife, Marcia, at www.facebook.com/ theauthorswife.

Finally, if you enjoy my books, please post your reviews online at Goodreads, Amazon, Barnes & Noble, and other sites for book lovers—and spread the word to your reader friends. Thanks!

ACKNOWLEDGMENTS

The first draft of a new novel may be a solitary endeavor for a writer, but after that, the process is a team effort involving many talented people. This book wouldn't be in your hands without some amazing editors, designers, marketers, and publicists.

I am fortunate to work with one of the best teams in publishing, namely, the people at Thomas & Mercer. Jessica Tribble worked with me on this book from the initial concept all the way through the editorial work and the entire production effort. Charlotte Herscher was invaluable in offering editorial guidance, just as she did on the first Frost Easton book, *The Night Bird*. Laura Petrella did another awesome job as copyeditor; she never misses a thing. I'm grateful to them and to everyone at T&M for their hard work and expertise—and for making me feel like a part of their publishing family.

Before a book even goes to the publisher, I get intensive feedback from my wife, Marcia, and my writing and editorial colleague Ann Sullivan. And by "intensive feedback," I mean they tell me in loving, generous detail everything I've done wrong. For which I'm thankful. Really. This book would not be what it is today without their superb insights.

My agent in New York, Deborah Schneider, makes all of this possible. She and I have been working together for fourteen years now, through all the many changes in this business. She is an extraordinary ally and advocate.

One last note. Many readers know from meeting us and interacting with us online that Marcia and I have a unique partnership in approaching the writer's life. She's part of everything I do, and I truly couldn't do any of it without her. That's why every book begins with the same two words: For Marcia.

ABOUT THE AUTHOR

Photo by Martin Hoffsten © 2009

Brian Freeman is a bestselling author of psychological thrillers, including the Jonathan Stride and Cab Bolton series. His works have been sold in forty-six countries and translated into twenty-two languages. His book *Spilled Blood* was named Best Hardcover Novel in the International Thriller Writers Awards, and *The Burying Place* was a finalist for the same honor. His debut thriller, *Immoral*, won the Macavity Award and was a finalist for the Edgar, Dagger, Anthony, and Barry awards for Best First Novel. His novels *Season of Fear* and *The Bone House* were both finalists for the Audie Award for best audiobook in the thriller/suspense category. He is also the author of *The Night Bird*, the first book in the Frost Easton series.

Brian lives in Minnesota with his wife, Marcia. For more information on the author and his work, visit www.bfreemanbooks.com.